A FAMILY AFFAIR

ALSO BY JULIE HOUSTON

Goodness Grace and Me
The One Saving Grace
An Off-Piste Christmas
Looking for Lucy
Coming Home to Holly Close Farm
A Village Affair
Sing Me a Secret
A Village Vacancy

A FAMILY AFFAIR

Julie Houston

HEAD
of ZEUS

An Aria Book

First published in the UK in 2021 by Head of Zeus Ltd
This paperback edition first published in the UK in 2022 by Head of Zeus Ltd,
part of Bloomsbury Publishing Plc

This is a work of fiction. All characters, organizations,
and events portrayed in this novel are either products of
the author's imagination or are used fictitiously.

A CIP catalogue record for this book is available
from the British Library.

ISBN (PB): 9781800246140
ISBN (E): 9781789546668

Cover design © Cherie Chapman

Cover illustration © Lucia Segura Art (woman);
all other images Shutterstock

Typeset by Siliconchips Services Ltd UK

Printed and bound in Great Britain by
CPI Group (UK) Ltd, Croydon CR0 4YY

MIX
Paper from
responsible sources
FSC® C171272

Head of Zeus
5–8 Hardwick Street
London EC1R 4RG

www.headofzeus.com

'you are enough; a thousand times enough...'

Prologue

Two years previously

'Frankie, you're not *thinking* straight. You've had a shock, I know that. But running off, leaving your nursing career that you love…'

'Career?' I snarled back, shaking off Aunty Pam's outstretched hand and, in doing so, rendering it redundant, hanging useless in mid-air. 'What sodding career? I've been training for all of three months. Florence Nightingale, I can assure you, Pam, I most certainly am not.'

'But you love this new career of yours,' Pam protested, trying to take my hand once more. 'You know you do. Don't throw it away because of what's happened. Stay and make the best of it. We're all here for you. How about you come and live with me for a while? I'd feed you up a bit and be there for you. I can help you get through this. You can have your old bedroom back; you know, how you used to come and stay with me when you didn't want to be with your mum…?'

'Aunty Pam, much as I love you – *and* my old bedroom

– I'm a big girl now.' I tried to smile but, as I'd done nothing but cry throughout the previous week, I was a bit out of practice.

'Yes,' she said gently, 'and hurting as much now as when you were a *little* girl.' She broke off, her own eyes welling up, and I stared. Aunty Pam, strong Aunty Pam who'd always been there for me when my own mother hadn't, never cried. 'Look, Frankie,' she sniffed, 'I've sort of got used to you being around again; you know, settling down in Westenbury, with your new career and with…'

'Yes well, that's the whole point isn't it? I'm no longer with…' I trailed off, unable to say his name.

'Frankie, I don't want you to leave.'

'I'm not leaving *you*, Aunty Pam; this isn't personal. I just, you know, can't stay round here now.'

'Frankie, I have two daughters: Carla, who I hardly ever see because she went and fell in love with a Canadian – and you…'

'Aunty Pam, you're *not* my mother…'

'Thanks for that, Frankie.'

'Don't sulk, Pam. You know as well as I do, I love you as though you *were* my real mum instead of just my aunt, but I'd be off even if you *were* my real mum. I can't stay here any longer.' I turned, car keys in hand, going home to the granny flat where I lived with my dad, desperate to set the ball rolling now that I'd made up my mind. 'I just can't stay here…'

'Running away from your problems never solved anything,' Pam said gently. She hesitated before adding, '*I* stood my ground when things got tough round here; stayed and fought my corner.'

'Sorry, Pam, but I've already told my course tutor at university and at the hospital.'

'Oh, Frankie, you haven't?'

I nodded. 'I just need a couple of days to sort a few things out.' I rubbed at my eyes once more. 'And then I'm off... I'm going...'

PART ONE

1

Frankie

Now

I felt sure there would have been some changes – Luca would have seen to that – but the offices, and particularly the entrance to the boardroom, on the top floor of Piccione's, didn't actually appear to have altered one little bit in the two years I'd been away. I hesitated, touching the raised lettering – PICCIONE'S PICKLES & PRESERVES – on the glazed double door that led to Angelo's inner sanctum, in the same way I always had ever since I was four years old and beginning not only to reach up on tiptoes to trace the black lettering, but also to understand that we were important. The Picciones were important and Nonno Angelo the most important of all.

'Francesca?' Margaret Holroyd – Angelo's secretary, PA and, if rumour were to be believed, also his bedfellow these past forty-five years or so – peered over both her spectacles and computer.

'Hello, Margaret. Yes, it's me. How are you?'

7

'I'm fine, dear. I'm fine. Angelo will be so pleased you're back. Does he know? I mean, he didn't say anything to me.'

Goodness, she must be in her late sixties now, I calculated. Margaret Holroyd was as much a feature of Piccione's as the heavy oak furniture and fittings which, despite Luca's attempts to dispense with the former and update with glass, chrome and blonde Amtico, remained mulishly in situ, along with the steadfast Margaret herself.

I nodded. 'Nonno knows I'm back. I had dinner with him and Nonna last night.'

'And how *is* your grandmother, dear?' This wasn't Margaret simply making polite conversation re Nonna. As Angelo's mistress, as well as his PA, Margaret Holroyd had been poised and on the starter's block to step into Nonna's shoes for as long as I could remember, and she really was interested in the state of my grandmother's health. Despite having had everything removed – her gall bladder, part of her bowel, her womb and, apparently while I was away, her bunions to which she'd long been a martyr – Nonna was still determined, at the age of eighty-eight, not to let 'that bloody Yorkshire interloper' (said with some glee and triumph in her broken Yorkshire and native Sicilian accent every time she came round from dispensing with yet another part of her anatomy) make Angelo entirely her own.

Margaret was patient, biding her time like a croc in the shallows: she had almost twenty years on Nonna, went to Pilates on Mondays, Hatha Yoga on Wednesdays (rumour had it she could sit for ten minutes with one leg wrapped round her neck) and *Cook Italian for Your Man* every Thursday. If she could get her legs around her *own* neck, God knows what sexual gymnastics she got up to with Angelo. Whatever it was, it was keeping Angelo, now eighty-six, on his feet (or maybe his back?) and he was as sprightly and upright, with every one of his marbles still in place, as he'd ever been. While Nonna Consettia was short, grey-haired and – despite the rapidly disappearing internal organs – plump, with her matronly bosom a quite outstanding feature of her physique; her rival, Margaret, was tall, bottle-blonde and *The Fast Diet*-slim with inner thighs that could – allegedly – crack a Brazil nut cleanly from its shell.

Nonna, despite her lack of physical attributes, had one major advantage over her rival: she was *The Wife*, joined to Angelo for the duration on this earth, (and the next if Father O'Leary from St Augustine's who was a regular visitor to High Royd, my grandparents' monstrosity of a house, was to be believed). She was bound by her Catholic beliefs in the sanctity of marriage as well as in the constant battle of seeing off her rival, while Margaret remained *The Mistress*.

For some reason I felt ridiculously nervous about being summoned to join this family meeting. If only Aunty Pam was in there with the others: pulling one of her daft faces behind Luca's back in order to intimate just how pompous my brother was being; putting Nonno Angelo in his place as only she could...

'Oh, Francesca, you're here?' My brother Luca, our mother's inherent Viking genes expressed through his blond hair and blue eyes rather than the Picciones' Sicilian ones, opened the boardroom door and motioned me in. 'What are you hanging about out here for?' he asked irritably. 'Come on, we're all waiting for you.' He brushed at a minuscule thread of lint on the lapel of his immaculate grey suit, ran a hand through his hair and frowned. 'You're wearing jeans.'

'Is that a question or a statement of fact?'

'This is a board meeting, Francesca.' Luca frowned once more as he looked me up and down, taking in the faded Levi's and scuffed Timberlands that had accompanied me home from Sicily. I'd disposed of most of my clothes in a skip near the Da Nang International airport in Vietnam, and certainly had bought very few new ones while living in rural Sicily during the past eighteen months or so, but my beloved jeans had been washed in Mum's all-singing, all-dancing Bosch machine and were – almost – as good as new.

'Oh, for heaven's sake, get over yourself, Luca. It's a family get-together.'

'Bit more than that, actually. Come on.'

My dad, Joe, as Angelo's only son in the family business and, as such, company director to Angelo's presidency, was already in his place on Angelo's left-hand side and Luca passed me a grey buff folder before retaking his place on Angelo's right. I bent to kiss my grandfather and then my dad, and went to sit on the brown leather chair that had been pulled out and was very obviously waiting for me.

'God, I feel like I'm being interviewed.' I smiled as I looked up and across at the three men in my family sitting like the three wise monkeys opposite me. Dad winked at me and Angelo smiled.

Luca didn't. 'You are,' he said, raising an eyebrow.

'Hang on.' I frowned. 'Nonno said just to come in for coffee and see what was going on down here these days.' I turned to Angelo. 'You did, didn't you? I don't see any coffee. And I could do with one.'

'Look, love,' Dad said, cutting to the quick, 'we'll get round to coffee in a couple of minutes. The thing is, we want you in, Frankie. With your Aunty Pam retiring, there's an opening for you here and, more importantly, your grandfather wants you in Piccione's.'

'*In?*' I glanced over at Luca whose face was impassive. He and I had never really got on. Despite my fantasy of having a big brother who would always be there for me and let me be a big part of his life, Luca had remained steadfastly uninterested in me either as a sister, a playmate or, as he grew older and into girls (lots of girls) his confidante.

'Francesca, *cara*,' Angelo purred, 'enough of the travelling now. You have a duty to the name of Piccione…'

Oh Jesus, had the old man been reading Barbara Taylor Bradford again?

'…and we need you here. You big girl now. You grown woman and you need take on responsibility for the family firm.'

Or, was it Mario Puzo?

'You don't appear, Francesca, to be wanting to settle down, to find good man like your Nonna Consettia did with me, and have the babies?' he went on.

'I'd actually love to find good man and have *the babies*, Nonno, but unfortunately good men seem to be very well hidden from me, and those who aren't are either taken, gay or ugly.'

'Don't you worry, Francesca, about the ugly ones.' Angelo sniffed, pointing a finger in my direction. 'You've tried the taken ones – we all know that; I don't advise gay ones, and if all that is left is ugly ones then beggars cannot be borrowers.'

'Choosers,' I murmured.

'Exactly.'

'I told you she wouldn't want to be back here,' Luca said dismissively, reaching for the grey folder. 'Why on earth would she want to be back in Yorkshire when she's been bumming round the Far East and then sloping off to live in Sicily for almost two years instead of coming home?'

I snatched the folder back from Luca. 'Hang on a minute. You've all been talking at me, but not given me any idea what this is all about.' I opened the folder and tried to make some sense of Luca's facts and figures, the line graphs in red and black and the pie charts that I could have turned upside down and they would have made as much sense.

Luca turned his chair, addressing Dad and Nonno in an attempt to shut me out. 'Francesca was given the opportunity to start at the bottom like I did.' Luca reached for the folder once again. 'You know when she'd finished at university? She wasn't interested then and she's plainly not interested now. We'll confirm the American chap we've been looking at. With Pam retiring, there's a big hole to fill here, and I need to get him on our side with a decent package before he gets taken on elsewhere.' Luca glanced at his watch. 'He came up from London last night and I'm meeting him for lunch at one.'

'Will you stop talking about me as if I wasn't here, Luca?' I said crossly. 'And *you* never started on the shop floor with the pickles and beetroot. Oh no, it was suit on and sitting round the boardroom table from day one for you, wasn't it?' Worry about what my darling Aunty Pam would think about me coming into Piccione's was making me sound more irritable than I'd intended. Was I being invited in to take over from her? If so, how on earth could I even contemplate stepping into her shoes? The shoes she'd worn to help steer Piccione's ever onwards and upwards during the last forty years?

'Francesca, enough,' Angelo snapped. 'If you don't want to be part of Piccione family then that fine. I'm very disappointed in your decision, but if you want to waste life playing football and drinking fishbowl of dodgy cocktails under full moon in Thailand, then so be it.'

'What did you have in mind, Nonno?' I folded my arms, noticing the frayed cuffs of my shirt and the – non-trendy – hole in the knee of my Levi's, and made a conscious effort to ignore Luca and appear grown up. I was almost twenty-nine, with very little to show for those years. Making the England Schoolgirls' football team had been my greatest achievement, but it had all gone downhill from then on. I had a (rather poor) Business Studies degree from Northumbria that Dad and Nonno had insisted I take rather than the sports science degree at Loughborough I'd craved. I'd always understood that the master plan for me would be that these business skills accrued would be utilised within the family firm. I'd gone along with their plan up to a point, but after three wonderful years at university, when I did far more drinking and socialising than studying, the last thing I wanted was to come home and bury myself in small-town pickles and preserves. Instead, university was followed by a couple of years working the bars in Australia and New Zealand with my mate Daisy Maddison before we'd both joined Flying High, based in Liverpool, for a stint as air stewardesses. I shuddered at the memory. Then, two and a half years ago, full of zeal and convinced I'd make a brilliant nurse, I'd started my nursing degree at Midhope General.

I actually loved the nursing. I was a whizz at hospital corners when bed making, and absolutely brilliant at finding veins in which to stick needles and cannulas ('send for Frankie' – the call would go up if one of the other student nurses was in danger of turning an increasingly alarmed patient into a pincushion as she struggled to draw blood) and the kids on the children's ward loved shouting '*Goal, Frankie*' every time I kicked a rolled-up bandage into a bed pan.

The senior ward sister didn't share their enthusiasm.

I'd have been just about qualified by now, I mused as Angelo sat back in his chair, waiting impatiently to go into detail as to what he had in mind for me while one of the office juniors brought in a tray of coffee and *cantucci*, the hard Italian almond biscuit that Angelo had first imported from Italy before shelling out on the machinery to develop, make and sell his own brand ten years or so previously. It had been a major diversification for Piccione's at the time and, as far as I knew, so stressful for Angelo being persuaded out of his comfort zone by Luca that it was the last time any real new product development had been attempted.

Angelo waited until Dad had finished pouring coffee from the huge cafetière. 'OK, Francesca, here's the deal.'

'The deal?' I blinked nervously. 'What do you mean, the deal?'

'Francesca, *cara*, you know you've been given a little allowance from the company every birthday?'

'Yes of course and I'm very grateful.' It wasn't a huge amount, I wanted to add. Just enough to allow me some airfares and prop up my meagre savings whenever I'd felt the need to set off once again.

'I'm very glad to hear that,' Angelo went on smoothly, his brown eyes watching, alert to any messages my body language might be giving off. 'We think it time you pay back those allowances now.'

'It wasn't that much,' I protested, sounding, I knew, somewhat callous if not downright greedy.

'You come and work properly for Piccione's now,' Angelo said determinedly pointing a finger once more. 'Or there no more allowances.' He pulled a hand dramatically across his throat and, not for the first time, I wondered as to his Sicilian ancestry.

Definitely Mario Puzo then.

'No more airfares to beach bummer places,' Angelo went on. 'You come into my company, Francesca, before I die or… or I cut you off without a penny.'

Dad started to laugh. 'Oh, for God's sake, Dad, stop sounding like some third-rate TV box set.'

I crossed my legs, covering the hole in the knee of my jeans, and attempted to pull my jersey down around the frayed shirt cuff while Luca sat back obviously bored with the whole interview and Dad continued to smile sympathetically.

'Give it a try, Frankie,' Dad said. 'I know it's not the most exciting place on earth, a village in Yorkshire; I know it's not London or Liverpool, but give it six months, yes? Come home and live in the granny flat again with Tammy and me. You know she loves having you around the place.'

'She doesn't want to be involved, Dad,' Luca said in some triumph. 'Leave her alone to do what she wants with her life; she might grow up one day.' He drained his cup of coffee and made to stand up, obviously impatient to get on with the day's work.

'What would I be doing?' The thought of working shifts on the production lines: filling jars with baby beets, piccalilli and the silver-skinned pickled onions as well as the world-famous *Piccione's Caponata*, as I'd done most school and some university holidays since the age of fifteen, filled me with despair.

Angelo leaned forward, steepling his hands together as he did so. 'Listen, *cara*, despite all the issues with Brexit, *Piccione's Caponata* had its best half-yearly production and profits ever. We've expanded into India and we're almost in China.'

'Really?' I was impressed.

'But the jam and marmalade...' Angelo shook his head somewhat morosely '...that not as good. Not bad, I grant you – it still giving the old Golly jam a run for his money, but I want Piccione preserves to be as famous as the pickles.'

'Nonno,' Luca sighed somewhat patronisingly, 'Pamela and I have been telling you this for the last ten years or so. I may not have always seen eye to eye with Aunty Pam on how this place is run, but on the need to expand and update the Preserves department, we were absolutely agreed: we need a lot more R and D.'

'R and D? Sounds like something you catch when you go with the *puttana*,' Angelo snapped throwing up his hands as only a good Sicilian can. 'Our jams and marmalades are on every breakfast table here in UK as well as in Italy. Piccione's Raspberry Jam was voted nation's favourite again last month but we've never succeeded in getting anywhere with Piccione's Honey.'

'It's the honey we thought *you* could perhaps help take on, Francesca.' Luca leaned back in his chair, his arms folded, his tone mocking. I knew immediately what he was up to: by giving the prodigal daughter something at which she was very unlikely to succeed, he was confirming that I was a waste of space, a hanger-on who shouldn't be given a job in the family firm.

'Take on?' I almost laughed. 'Sounds like a fight.'

'It will be fight,' Angelo said gloomily, dunking *cantucci* into his coffee. 'I'm not convinced people eat honey these days.'

I had a sudden recollection of sitting outside at a table in the warmth of a Sicilian spring almost eighteen months previously, finding my appetite again after several months of heartache that had me leaving my nursing course and my life here in Westenbury and running away, first to the Far East and then to Sicily. With a none too gentle hand on my shoulder, Great Aunt Rosina, Angelo's sister, had placed coffee, soft white bread and a bowl of yellow sunshine in front of me with the accompanying '*mangiare!*' – eat!

'*Crema al limone.*' I smiled across at the three of them. Luca frowned, but Dad and Angelo understood.

'Ah, you tasted Rosina's lemon curd?' Angelo grinned showing still very white teeth. 'It was our mama's recipe.'

'Have you never thought of putting that into full production here?' I asked.

'Aha, she's interested.' Dad nudged Angelo's arm. 'Come on, Frankie, what else are you going to do if you don't do this? Move back into the flat with me and Tam, come and work for Luca and this American chap in the Preserves department. Be a *real* Piccione; you might even enjoy it.'

I looked up and across at the three faces awaiting my decision: at Angelo's and Dad's hopeful expressions and at Luca's patronisingly scornful one. There was no way on this planet my big brother would want me under his feet when he was trying to update the range of preserves. That did it. 'OK, thank you. I will.' I saw Luca lift his eyes to the ceiling and exhale. 'When do I start?'

2

Frankie

Now

I walked out into the huge loading bay, dodging forklift trucks intent on shifting pallet-loads of pickles and jams, before heading for the transport depot. Dad had rung down fifteen minutes earlier instructing Bill Clarkson, its manager, to allow me use of one of the fleet of company cars. 'Won't be a Lamborghini.' Dad had smiled at me, aware of Luca's displeasure. It wasn't. I passed Angelo's ridiculously oversized black Bentley with its registration AP 5; Dad's silver BMW and Luca's gleaming red Porsche and found Bill waiting for me, keys in hand.

'This do you, love?' Bill indicated a lime green mongrel of a car skulking at the very end of a row of company vehicles. 'Best we can do at the moment, I'm afraid, Francesca. It's taxed and tested, insured and full of fuel.' I had a sudden longing for the lovely little racing green Mini I'd owned and then sold (quickly and far too cheaply) over two years previously in order to fund my airfare and travel to Thailand and then on to Sicily.

'Thanks, Bill, it'll do me fine.' I had wheels. I was mobile. I just needed to decide where to live now. My options weren't huge: carry on staying with Mum and my stepfather in their ultra-modern brand-new house on the outskirts of the village at Heath Green where I'd lain my head since arriving back in the country three days ago. Or ask Aunty Pam, who I adored and who was more of a mother to me than my own, if I could stay with her for a while. Or move back into the granny flat at Dad and Tammy's where I'd lived during the months I'd been doing my nursing course. With all the memories that that entailed.

I took a deep breath, opened the car door and, after finding the gears in the funny little car, attempted to move forward.

'What's up, love? Can't you get it going?' I jumped as a face outlined in a black hood knocked on the window, motioning me with a windmill hand signal to wind it down. Since when did anyone wind down windows anymore? I found the electric button and the window on the passenger side lurched down slowly, stopping halfway and sulkily refusing to go any further. The forklift truck I'd seen earlier was now blocking my exit, its driver peering in at me through the car's window.

'Frankie?'

'Oh, Ian?' Daisy, Ian and I had been at primary school together but, while Ian and Daisy had gone on to Westenbury Comp, I'd been shipped off to a boarding prep school at the age of eleven in order to work towards Common Entrance, and then, at thirteen, to Millfield School down in Somerset.

'Last thing I heard you were madly in love and you'd started nursing?' Ian probed gently and then, when I didn't reply, didn't know if I could actually utter the words without crying, he added, 'Sorry, Frankie.'

'I loved him.'

'I heard…' Ian broke off as one of the distribution guys started yelling at him to get back on the forklift and do some effing work. 'Look, Daisy's back as well. She's thinking of going down a very different route. Did you know?'

I shook my head, not quite taking anything in that Ian was saying. 'I knew she was back again, but didn't know what her plans were.'

'Are you staying, Frankie?'

'Staying?'

Ian frowned and stood back from the car as the distribution manager started walking towards him. 'Come on, McKinley, we've got stuff here needs shifting…' He broke off as he drew level and realised who Ian was chatting with. 'Oh, Francesca? Sorry, love, didn't realise it was you.'

'I'm just off, Geoff.' I smiled, attempting to manoeuvre the car's very strange gearbox.

'That's reverse,' Geoff and Ian yelled in unison as I shot back several yards and stalled.

'Give us a ring, Frankie,' Ian said through the still-open window as I kangarooed towards the huge black iron gates at the entrance to Piccione's.

'Doubt she will,' I heard Geoff shout loudly over the jarring strains of Ian's forklift. 'She's joining the directors, apparently.'

News travelled fast.

★

Daler. As I drove back to Mum's place, I tried to think of anything but him: my two years working in Sicily; getting to know my distant cousins, great-aunts and uncles; improving my already pretty good Italian; the couple of gorgeous women-loving Sicilian men I'd had affairs with in the hope of snuffing out memories of Daler. I shook my head now in an attempt to eradicate the memories. They always came back to Daler.

I really wanted to be heading off to Aunty Pam's place rather than back to Mum and my stepfather's soulless modern box, but Pam was still away in a five-star-all-inclusive-dancing-every-night hotel in Lanzarote with her mate, Bev. I had missed her so much while I was away and was desperate to see her. To feel her arms around me once more.

I slowed down at temporary roadworks ahead of me and came to a halt as a young kid in luminous orange overalls held up a peremptory warning hand in my direction, revolving and changing his green GO sign to red. Well, I conceded, at least my new job was – hopefully – going to be slightly higher in the pecking order than his. I finally managed to get the car into gear once more and gathered speed before turning right at the crossroads and heading towards Mum's village.

3

Pam

Then
August 1974

'You're not going, Pamela. I've heard about these places from your Aunty Vera and you're not going. Dad said so.'

'Where is he?'

'Who?'

'Dad.' Pamela tutted but didn't expand further. It didn't do to wind her mother up when she was in the middle of sewing, especially when she was trying to tack a sleeve to the front of Janet's school uniform summer dress she was making and which, by the look of it, she'd cut out totally wrongly. Mary Brown pressed her lips together crossly and, ignoring her middle daughter, tried once again to marry the two pieces of sky-blue and white spotted fabric, only confirming Pam's first assessment of the problem.

'In bed. Where do you think he is? And you'll wake him if you don't stop going up and down the stairs in those ridiculous shoes and playing that awful music of yours. He has trouble enough trying to sleep when he's on nights.

Damn it...' Mary threw the half-made dress onto the chair beside the ancient Singer sewing machine and sucked at her finger. 'Now look what you've made me do.'

'Me?'

'Yes, you, going on and on about Wigan. Wigan for heaven's sake? What is there in Wigan? You're not sixteen yet, Pamela. And I know with all that black stuff on your eyes and your dresses halfway up your backside you think you're all grown up, but you're not. So, forget it, you're not going.'

Pam shook her head. 'For heaven's sake, Mum. I'm sixteen next week. I've done my O levels and CSEs. I've left school and I'm working at Piccione's just like you and Dad wanted me to. I'd actually be old enough to get married next week, so I think I'm old enough to go to a nightclub in Wigan, don't you?'

'Tell you what, Pamela—' Mary Brown moved to the sink to fill the kettle '—you get yourself a decent boyfriend, start saving for your bottom drawer like our Lynne did and then get yourself wed and you can do what you want. You'll be off me and your dad's hands and I won't have to sit here and listen to you going on about some rough nightclub full of drugs and darkies.'

'You can't say darkies, Mum.'

'I can say what I damned well want.'

Hell, Pam thought, Mary must be in a mood if she'd used *damn* twice in thirty seconds. The only time her mother uttered this watered-down profanity was when she was sewing or when her dad was back late from the Liberal Club for his dinner on a Sunday. 'I don't know why you insist on making Janet's school dresses anyway, especially when she'll be back in winter uniform pretty soon. Why don't you just go down to Silvertons in town and buy them like everybody else?'

'Buy them?' Mary looked askance at her. 'What, and pay five times as much as they're worth? The problem with our Janet passing her eleven-plus and going to the grammar school is the uniform has to be just so. That headmistress of hers notices if a buckle or a belt isn't standard issue.'

'Well in that case I think the old harridan will notice that sleeve you've put in the wrong way.' Pam started to laugh, but one furious look from her mother and she turned it into a cough. 'Come on, Mum, let me go to Wigan Casino. There's a load of people going from work.' That was a bit of a fib: after three weeks working in the offices of Piccione's Pickles and Preserves she was still only just finding her feet and, as an office junior, certainly didn't rank highly enough amongst the secretaries and PAs to the directors to merit socialising with those wonderful creatures who rarely deigned to look her way.

'I don't see how you can know a *load* of people when you've only been at Piccione's a couple of weeks. And a casino? A *casino*?' This was enough to have her mother actually look up from the sewing she'd picked up once again and peer at Pam over her glasses. 'You're not allowed into a casino at your age; it's gambling. Your dad'll have a fit.'

'No, no, it's not a casino.'

'You just said it was.'

'It's a club. A nightclub. Over in Wigan.'

'Wigan's over fifty miles away.'

'Yes, and it's straight down the new M62. Not a problem, Mum.'

'Pamela, you might have left school and be working, but there's no way you're going off in some lad's car to some casino that seems to think it's a nightclub. Anyhow, your Aunty Vera says these places don't get going until everyone else is in bed. You're not staying out all night even if you are sixteen next week.'

'And how does Aunty Vera know all this? She's been there, has she?'

'She hears about such things. Same way as I do. *And* there was something about these...' Mary sought to remember the name '...these *Northern soul* clubs in the *News of the World* a couple of weeks back. There's fighting and purple hearts and all kinds of carry-on.'

'Purple hearts? What the hell are purple hearts?'

'Don't swear, Pamela. When you're eighteen you can do as you like, but when you're not yet sixteen, and still under my roof, it's my house, my rules. Look, you've woken your dad up now—' Mary glanced up at the ceiling where a series of creaks from the main bedroom directly above the kitchen were drifting downwards '—and he's not had much more than four hours' sleep. Make yourself useful and peel some potatoes, would you? Mind you,' she added, frowning as she folded the half-completed dress, 'it must be strange having your dinner for your breakfast.'

'Come on, Pam, you've got to come – Edwin Starr's supposed to be on.'

'No! Edwin Starr? Honest?' Pam sighed heavily in exaggerated empathy as, in reality, she tried to remember just who Edwin Starr actually was. She really needed to keep up with who was who now that she was officially going out with Rob Mansell. Rob stroked her hand persuasively. She'd only been seeing him a month or so, but she fancied him like mad. She and Jane Pritchard, best friends since junior school, had been watching him for ages at Moonlight, the nightclub in Midhope town centre where he and his mates always gathered a crowd round them as they executed flashy spins, twists, kicks and backflips on the wooden dance floor. While those aspiring to be as competent as Rob Mansell wore the uniform Ben Sherman shirts and Sta-Prest trousers, Rob always looked that little bit different in bleach-stained Levi's topped with a maroon-coloured suit jacket in a smooth barathea fabric.

He was over three years older than her – Pam knew he had no idea she wasn't actually yet sixteen – and was confident of both his looks and his dancing ability without being arrogant or big-headed. He just took it for granted that all eyes were on him as he backdropped onto the dance floor to Junior Walker, the combination of sweat and soul music enough to transport him to another plane without the help of either booze or uppers.

'I'm driving over there, Pam,' Rob was saying as he ran one hand through his blond hair and dabbed at his forehead with the back of his other. He was sporting a glorious tan, having spent two weeks down in Newquay earlier in the summer although, from what she'd gathered, most of the days had been spent sleeping in his friend Gary's VW Dormobile, recovering from all-night sessions in the resort's nightclubs. 'The music they play here is just so tame,' Rob shouted over The Temptations. 'It's just commercial Motown. We need to dance to the real stuff. I know The

Casino doesn't open until eleven, but there'll be a hell of a queue if Edwin Starr is actually on tonight.' Rob bent his head to Pam's own. The waves of envy coming her way from the gaggle of girls watching his every move from the edge of the dance floor almost palpable. He kissed her long and hard and, still unused to professional snogging such as this, she pulled back, embarrassed, but he just laughed and took hold of her face in his hands. 'Come on, ring your mum and tell her you'll be back late. Tell her you're staying at your mate's if she's funny about you staying out all night.'

'Honestly, Rob, she'd know I was lying. I'd never hear the end of it when I got in tomorrow.'

'But Pam, you're eighteen next week.' Rob bent to kiss her mouth once again. 'You're an adult, a grown-up. You'll be able to have a drink, legally.' He pulled away from her, smiling down at her. 'I hope you're going to let me take you out to celebrate?'

Sixteen next week, actually. Pam didn't say the words out loud: sophisticated gods like nineteen-year-old Rob Mansell didn't look at kids just out of school. With no experience of men. Or sex. At least she was working now and not still *at* school. Pam glanced across at a bevy of fabulously dressed and made-up girls who'd been at school at least two years above her. Red-headed Rosalind – Ros – McCarthy, who'd stalked the corridors of Westenbury Secondary Modern with her foot soldiers, terrorising both pupils and staff alike, was hovering at the edge of the dance floor, just waiting for the right moment. Ros had been Rob's steady girlfriend until a couple of months back, and Pam and her gang from school had stood on the sidelines, watching in awe and envy as

Ros had executed her own dance steps to Otis Redding and Jackie Wilson alongside Rob and his mates.

'If you don't go with him over to The Casino, you do know Ros will be back in there,' Jane said once the pair of them, together with Maureen Cooper, who sat next to Jane in the typing pool at Piccione's, were adding more mascara and Rimmel lipstick to their already made-up faces in the cloakroom. 'You can't miss an opportunity to go over there with him. Ring your mum and tell her you're going down to Piccione's Summer Ball with me and Maureen and that you're going to stay the night at our house.'

'Say you're going to be at *our* house,' Maureen advised. 'Your mum doesn't know mine from Adam. She'll never know.'

'What if she asks for your phone number, Mo?' Pam felt beads of sweat break on her upper lip – a response to the close heat and heavily scented atmosphere of the cloakroom as well as the thought of actually picking up the phone and telling her mum she wouldn't be back until the next day. It wouldn't be too bad if her dad answered the phone but that was highly unlikely, Dennis Brown having an almost pathological lack of interest in the machine sitting out in the hall. It was her mother's pride and joy since having it installed the previous year and she guarded it jealously, keeping it well polished with a daily squirt of Pledge and sitting for hours on the telephone table with its cushioned leatherette seat Uncle Brian – a joiner – had made for her while gossiping with Aunty Vera.

'Tell her we haven't got one.' Maureen frowned. 'Because, actually, we haven't. God, if I had the chance to go to Wigan

Casino with Rob Mansell – with anyone – I'd be off like a shot.'

'Where are you two going to?' Pam emphasised the black eyeliner on both lids and stood back slightly in order to gauge the effect in the huge wall-length mirror.

Jane laughed. 'Maureen told you. We're off to the summer ball at the RAFA club across from Greenstreet Park.'

'Are you? Why?' Pam retied her red and white spotted halter-necked top and pulled at the beautiful white midi skirt she'd bought from Boodlam in the Victoria Quarter in Leeds with her first wage. 'Have you got tickets?'

'You don't need one. Martin said he was going...'

'You're not still after Martin Barker, are you? God he's so, so *hairy*.' Pam had come across Martin, who worked in Pickles, divesting himself of his Piccione green overalls at the end of the production workers' day, the black T-shirt underneath riding up to reveal a quite startling mat of hair on his white back.

'Might be.' Jane reddened slightly. 'Anyway, it'll be good. It's the Miss Piccione 1974 contest as well. We're going to enter for a laugh.'

Maureen looked at her watch. 'Come on, Jane, it's nearly nine o'clock. If we don't go, we'll miss it. So, what are you going to do, Pam?'

'OK, I'm going to go with Rob.' Pam felt her heart pound at her daring. Her mum was so strict she'd absolutely kill her if she found out she was going to get in a car with a crowd of much older lads, and that she'd lied to her into the bargain. But she couldn't let him go off with Ros and her gang. She'd never get him back.

'Good for you,' Maureen said, slipping her arm through

Jane's possessively. Pam was beginning to get the feeling that three was a crowd: whenever she went to find Jane at break times and in the office canteen during the fifty-minute allotted dinner hour at Piccione's, Maureen, she suddenly realised, was always there. Well sod it, there was no way she was going to some daft summer ball organised by work.

Maureen led the way back downstairs and Jane followed, both pulling on identical faded denim jackets against the chill of the late-August evening before hauling almost identical bags onto shoulders as they headed for the door.

From her vantage point on the stairs leading back down to the dance floor, Pam shaded her eyes against the refractive luminescence from the glitter ball spinning hypnotically above her head, trying to locate Rob's gorgeous blond head from where she'd left him five minutes earlier. George McCrae was soulfully extolling those bobbing up and down to 'Rock Your Baby', and it was pretty obvious Ros McCarthy was intent on doing just that with Rob Mansell. RM with RM, Pam thought dully as she plastered a smile on her face and made a determined move towards the pair.

Ros gave Pam a look of triumph as she whispered something in Rob's ear and then said loudly, 'We'll be outside, Rob. Don't be long getting rid of the Kindergarten Kid; we need to get off if we're going to get in.'

Rob took Pam's arm, leading her away from the music to the bar area where a single barman was desultorily mopping at the beer pumps. 'Pint?' he asked Rob, already reaching for a glass tankard with its distinctive dimples.

'No, nothing thanks.' Rob turned to Pam, frowning. 'Look, how old *are* you, Pamela?'

'Hey, if you're not eighteen, you shouldn't be in the bar

area.' The barman frowned. 'Licensed premises. You'll get me done.'

Pam stood in front of Rob as he looked down at her, his hands on her arms. 'Come on, Pam, straight up? Ros says she was *two years* above you at school. Are you only sixteen?'

'Next week,' Pam mumbled, mortified.

'What about next week? You're *seventeen* next week?'

'Sixteen.'

You're still *fifteen*? Jesus, I can't take a fifteen-year-old to Wigan. I'll be done for cradle-snatching. You're illegal. And, you know, Pam, I really fancied you. I thought it was the start of something, you know...' He trailed off, slightly embarrassed. 'Look, I'll give you a ring next week. Honest, I promise. I'm going to have to go... the others, you know...'

She managed to catch up with the other two who, arm in arm and laughing uproariously (had they been drinking or were they on something? Maureen Cooper, she'd been warned by the newly married Margaret Holroyd, one of the girls on Reception, had a bit of a reputation for being a *bit of a one*, if Pam got her drift) were making their way up through the town centre towards the top of Westgate, which led to the RAFA club and then ultimately onto the town's municipal park.

'Hang on,' Pam shouted, breathless and almost beside herself with the exertion. 'Hang on,' she shouted again and, as Jane turned, bent herself double in order to alleviate the stitch in her side.

'What's up?' Maureen asked. '*You're* not coming with us now, are you?'

'What's the matter, Pam?' Jane asked in a much kindlier tone. 'Did you change your mind?'

'Has he gone without you?' Maureen almost sneered. 'Well, *I* wouldn't have let him out of my clutches.'

'Was it Ros McCarthy?' Jane asked.

'Hmm.' *I'm not going to cry*, Pam told herself. 'She told him how old I was. But it's OK. He's going off to Wigan...'

'You're mad letting him go,' Maureen interrupted. 'That redhead will get her claws into him and you'll never see him again.'

She did wish Maureen would butt out. 'It's fine,' Pam said airily, with a confidence she didn't feel, as she eventually caught her breath and addressed Jane. 'He's taking me out for my birthday next week.'

'As if.' Maureen snorted with derision. 'Taking you out for your sixteenth birthday? Rob Mansell? Right, yes, course he is. Come on, we're here. Aw, *you're* not putting yourself in for the Miss Piccione contest now, are you, Pam?'

'Why shouldn't she?' Jane was indignant.

'Not likely!' Pam interrupted.

'Well, if *she* goes in for it, she's going to win, isn't she?' Maureen sniffed. 'We're not going to stand a bloody chance.'

'Speak for yourself,' Jane said crossly and then relented. 'No, you're right, Mo, if Pam goes in for it, we might as well not bother.'

'Oh, for heaven's sake,' Pam said equally crossly, as the suited bouncer on the door took their names and let them through. 'You're not getting *me* in any cattle market.' She'd recently taken up this clarion call after sitting down in the front room with her mum and Aunty Vera to watch the Miss UK contest a couple of months earlier and, while she'd loudly professed disdain at the whole circus (she had, after all, a copy of *The Female Eunuch* proudly displayed on her bedroom shelf between Jean Plaidy and Catherine Cookson) she'd really been as engrossed as her mum and aunt in the swimsuit-attired bevy of beautiful women.

'You cheeky bitch.' Maureen stopped in her tracks and turned to glare at Pam. 'Who the hell are you calling a cow?'

'Oh, for heaven's sake,' Pam snapped once more. 'I'm not calling *anyone* a cow. I'm just going to have one Coke and then I'm catching the last bus home. I've already had enough of tonight.' Why the hell hadn't she turned right at the bus station and made her way home instead of turning left and getting involved in this ridiculous pantomime?

'Girls, girls, come on, or you'll be too late to enter,' Bob Parkinson from Pickles, and chair of Piccione Workers' Social Committee, barked at them importantly. 'Go and sign in and get your number; put your lipstick on, brush your hair...' he leered in their direction, his eyes almost popping out at Maureen's over-inflated chest '...and show us what you've got.'

'No, no, not for me,' Pam said crossly, trying to wrench off the large, numbered card that had been thrust over her head by two sherry-drinking matrons from sales. 'I'm not doing this...'

'Oh, get on with you.' One of them laughed loudly, draining her schooner. 'It's only a bit of fun. I'd be in there like a shot if I was your age again and with your looks...'

And before Pam could reply, or resist further, she was pushed none too gently between the red velvet curtains and was out on stage in front of a clapping and whistling Piccione workforce. Mr Angelo himself was compere for the evening, looking dapper and handsome in black tie, addressing the girls in his broken English as they made their way, one by one, across the stage in front of the panel of four judges who, also in evening dress, obviously fancied themselves hugely important.

There was Miss Bryan from Personnel, who'd interviewed and consequently written to Pam offering her the job as office junior (four days in the office and one day and one evening on day release at Midhope technical college to acquire the shorthand and typing skills needed to be at the beck and call of the managers), Mr Sowerby in charge of Pickles and Mr Atkinson from Preserves. Sitting at the end, to Miss Bryan's left, the fourth judge of the evening was a dark-haired, dark-eyed, much younger man who didn't appear overly engrossed in the evening's proceedings despite Mr Piccione constantly referring to him with, at times, somewhat risqué comments and questions. Of course. This must be Marco Piccione, Pam realised, as she was beckoned forward by Mr Piccione. He must be Angelo Piccione's son.

Oh, sod it, Pam thought to herself, if she was here, she might as well get on with it and enjoy herself. Anything to annoy Maureen Cooper. With a silent apology to Germaine Greer, Pam threw a look of disdain in Mo's direction, tossed back her blonde hair, licked her lips in what she hoped was a sultry copy of the haughty models in *Cosmo* and walked with a confidence she didn't really feel across the expanse of wooden stage to Mr Piccione.

*

'I knew you'd bloody win,' Maureen Cooper sneered once again. The older girl really had practised the art to perfection, Pam thought idly as she sipped at her glass of champagne, feeling the bubbles go up her nose, before looking down at the pink Miss Piccione 1974 sash that was clashing quite horribly with her red and white spotted top. 'Oh, for God's sake, stop sipping at that stuff and get it down your neck,' Maureen said, in an apparent effort to be friendly. 'Or at least give us some. You've got a whole bottle to get through.'

'I'm quite capable of drinking this all by myself,' Pam sniffed. She wanted to share it with Jane, but Jane appeared to have already singled out Martin Barker and was openly necking with him near the entrance to the club, leaning against the wall as the hirsute Martin's hand burrowed like some furry woodland creature up the back of her jumper.

'I bet that's your first champagne ever, isn't it?' Maureen, reverting to the former taunting when she saw Pamela wasn't about to share her prize, folded her arms and glared.

'This?' Pam raised her glass and downed it in one, wondering what Rob was up to at this moment. Ros McCarthy presumably. 'Goodness me, *no*.' Pam heard herself ape her mother's posh put-on voice when she was talking to the Man from the Pru who called round for his money every Thursday evening. 'We drink *bottles* of the good stuff every Sunday dinner time. More at Christmas...' She pictured her dad's home-brewed beer merrily bubbling away by the warmth of the Baxi, its yeasty smell pervading the whole of the kitchen at the start of its brewing, and wanted to laugh. Instead, she raised an eyebrow in Mo's direction, poured herself another glass from the bottle of cheap champagne and raised that towards the older girl as well, before deliberately setting both the bottle and the full glass down on the table in front of Mo and setting off to find Jane, to tell her they'd miss the last bus home if they didn't leave right that minute.

Jane didn't seem to care they were going to miss the bus. Pam had to give her a good poke in the ribs in order to get her to surface from Martin's ministrations. 'It's fine, it's fine, Pam.' Jane giggled, smiling beatifically as she eventually drew breath and immediately went in for more.

'Yeuch,' Pam tutted under her breath and headed back to her table and her drink, where she was immediately accosted by Mr Piccione. 'Pamela, *cara*, well done.' Mr Piccione kissed both her cheeks, breathing alcohol and what she would later come to recognise as garlic in her face. 'You were the obvious choice. *Byoo-ti-ful* girl. Now, you got the cheque, yes?' (Yes, but she didn't have a bank account, Pam thought.) 'And the other prize is a meal out with my boy. Marco, over here, over here,' he snapped as Marco appeared to be drifting off in the opposite direction. 'He love the ladies, just like me, does Marco. You will have a good time, *cara*.' And with that he took Marco's arm, manhandling him towards a somewhat tipsy Pamela.

4

Pamela

Then

'Hello, Pamela. Congratulations. No one else came close.' Marco Piccione kissed Pam on both cheeks as his father had done minutes earlier and, smiling across at her, stroked her arm. Not smiling *down* at her, Pam thought tipsily, like the gorgeous men did in all the romantic fiction she'd been hoovering up lately. Marco was smaller than she was, and so he was looking *across* at her. *Up* at her, even, she conceded, and, for some reason she couldn't quite work out, wanted to laugh at that.

Pam swayed slightly and realised the glass of champagne had gone straight to her head. The only alcohol she'd ever really had was the occasional sweet sherry when she biked round to her Granny Brown's on a Sunday morning and the older woman insisted on sharing a glass with her to *see her on her way back home*. Just a small glass was enough to make her feel giggly, and the ride back home, down the hill, was exhilarating if somewhat fraught with danger, as her second-hand boneshaker manoeuvred dry ruts in the road and the occasional wandering sheep. Alcohol must do this to her, she thought. It was so lovely, was giving her such a floaty feeling and making her forget that Rob had gone off to Wigan without her, but she'd better not have any more or her mother would be after her once she got home.

She was going to have to share a taxi with Jane because the last bus home must surely have gone by now. She needed to ring her mum or she'd be worried when she wasn't in by eleven-thirty.

'I'll leave you two to get to know each other,' Angelo was saying cheerfully. 'Decide when and where you going out for dinner date. Bennani's in town centre just opened. Brilliant place for lovely food... and bit of *romance*.' Angelo dug Pamela suggestively in the ribs. 'I book table, *best* table for pair of you.' He grinned wolfishly, patted Marco determinedly on his black-sleeved arm and kissed Pam once again on each cheek.

'I need to ring my mum,' Pam said, feeling slightly dizzy. 'She'll wonder where I am if I don't get off the last bus.' She squinted at her watch. 'And I've certainly missed it now.'

'I'll give you a lift home,' Marco said.

'My mum's always telling me not to get into cars with strange men.' She heard herself giggle girlishly and that made her want to laugh more. What on earth was the matter with her? 'Just let me go and phone home and then *Miss Piccione 1974* is *all yours*.'

'Have you been drinking, Pamela?' Mary Brown's voice was accusing.

'Just a little belasratory champagne, Mum.'

'Belasratory?'

'Clebatrasory.' Pamela giggled. Why wouldn't her mouth work properly?

'I assume you're trying to say celebratory?' Mary snapped crossly. 'You're fifteen; you shouldn't be drinking at your age. Where are you, Pamela? Do you need your dad to come and pick you up? Mind you, he's in the middle of *Match of The Day.*'

'I'm at the erm, the erm, the RAFA club in town,' Pam said, after racking her brain as to where she was. She *actually* felt as though she were floating up to heaven on a golden cloud. 'I think I'm on my way to the angels...' She giggled down the phone.

'The Angel? The Angel down on High Street? Pamela, get yourself home. You are *not* to go into another pub at this time of night. Just wait, Lady, until you come through that front door. Get a taxi. Is Jane with you?'

The payphone booth, smelling of stale cigs and booze, looked out over the mean little tarmacked garden at the back of the building and, as Pam squinted through the window into the dark, she could just make out Jane wrapped round Martin Barker in an even more compromising stance than half an hour earlier. 'Ugh, I bet that hairy hand tickles,' she hiccupped, giggling to herself.

'What hairy hand?' Mary barked down the phone. 'Who's that with you? Do not let *any* hairy hands anywhere near you in the state you're in, Pamela.'

That made Pam laugh uncontrollably. 'Really, Mum, listen, I'm...' she took a deep breath in order to concentrate '...Jane and me... Jane and I? Is it me or I? And Maureen

– although *she's* not very nice – are at Piccione's summer ball at the RAFA club. And I'm...' Pam paused again in order to get her words right '...*celebrating* because I've just been crowned Miss Piccione 1974.'

'What do you mean?'

'I've won the annual contest and been crowned. You know, like Miss World.'

'Really?' There was a protracted pause from the other end as Mary Brown obviously digested this nugget of information. It could go either way, Pam thought, crossing her fingers on the hand not holding the phone: pride that Mary's daughter had won a beauty contest battling with the fact that Pam was seemingly intoxicated in town and had missed her last bus home. 'I'm getting your dad to drive down to pick you up, Pamela,' Mary eventually snapped.

'No, I'm fine. Really. The dancing's just about to start.'

'At this time of night?'

Pam peered at her watch. 'It's only eleven-thirty, it's fine,' Pam repeated. 'Marco Piccione is giving me a lift home.'

That appeared to stop Mary in her tracks like nothing had previously. 'Mr Piccione's son? There was a photo of him in the *Midhope Examiner* the other day, Pamela. At some charity do. He's *very* handsome, isn't he? And he's going to give you a lift home?'

Pamela felt someone watching her and she turned to find Marco standing quietly to one side. 'Here,' Pam hiccupped, thrusting the phone in his direction. 'Have a word with my mum, would you?'

Pam could hear Mary twittering non-stop from her end of the phone as Marco, smoothly, and in his cultured private-school-educated voice, reassured her mother that yes,

Pamela had been crowned Miss Piccione 1974 and yes, huge congratulations were due: she'd seen off all other contestants; no, *he* hadn't been drinking, Mrs Brown – he didn't actually drink – and no, Pamela certainly wasn't going on to any other pub, he'd make sure of that. They were just going to have a dance to celebrate and then he'd drive her safely home. She wasn't to worry, Pamela was a lovely sensible girl; she'd had a couple of glasses of champagne but no, he'd make sure she didn't have any more…

Marco might have been necessarily verbose on the phone to her mother but, as he led Pam on to the dance floor, her crown listing dangerously to one side and her pink sash looking the worse for wear (and Mr Piccione smiling encouragingly from his table), he said very little.

'*Who's that lady?*' Pam sang as the Isley Brothers belted their melodic words out across the dance floor. 'I just loooove this, don't you?'

'My absolute favourite,' Marco said without smiling and, seeing his father watching his every move, reached a cool hand out to Pam, spinning her around until she was breathless. 'Do you have a boyfriend, Pamela?' he asked as he led her off the floor.

'I'm not sure,' she replied sadly. 'I sort of did have. Until this evening anyway. He's gone off to Wigan Casino with his ex-girlfriend. That's why I ended up here with Jane and Mo.' Pam glanced towards a table where Maureen was sat with several others from the typing pool, but giving occasional surreptitious looks in her direction from under her heavily mascaraed lashes. 'I think I ought to be going home,' Pam said, suddenly feeling totally bereft that Rob had actually left without her. And with Ros McCarthy.

'*Cara*, you go now?' Mr Piccione was at her side, taking her hands in his own. 'Good, good, your mamma be worried otherwise. Marco, you look after this girl. She very special.'

They had to walk quite a way to where Marco said he'd left his car earlier that evening under some huge oak tree at the other side of the park. He took her hand in his, and she liked the feel of its warmth as she floated by his side along the side streets lined with cars, none of which appeared to be his. The evening was perfectly still, just the occasional rustle from the abundant foliage of the late summer trees lightly caressing their clothes as they walked.

Lightly *caressing*? Pam began to titter slightly at her own poetic rhetoric. She'd always really enjoyed poetry at school (especially when Mr Jenkinson, the gorgeous student teacher who all the fifth-year girls were in love with, had read aloud to them) but apart from that one about standing still and staring like a sheep – or was it a cow – she couldn't recall any other. She felt so relaxed and floaty, she could have stood under any number of boughs in order to just stand and stare and take in all this wonderful life that was just waiting around the corner for her now that she was almost sixteen. And a beauty queen to boot.

'What's so funny?' Marco finally spoke. He stopped walking and, without any further preamble, took her face in his hands and bent to kiss her.

Something was going on in the pit of her stomach. No, it wasn't her stomach, it was much lower. Pam had felt a bit like this the first time Rob had kissed her, but this feeling now, as Marco kissed her forehead, her face and now her mouth was so intense she thought she might actually fall over. Right here, on the street. Was this what *swooning* was all about? She mightn't be totally up on her poetry, but she'd read enough romance novels – as well as D H Lawrence's *Sons and Lovers* (which she'd had to hide from her mother who had sniffed and declared anything written by *him* must be smutty) – to understand this was what she must be experiencing herself as Marco moved his hands to her bare back.

'I think you're having me on,' Pam finally breathed as they began to walk – float – up the road once more. 'I don't think you have a car at all.'

Marco smiled but didn't speak as he took a sudden turn and they left the street they'd been on behind and she realised they were floating through the park itself, the scents and sounds of the summer night pervading every one of her heightened senses.

'Whoa.' Pam exhaled in awe as they exited the park through the huge black gates at the other side and Marco immediately stopped next to a shiny red sports car and, taking his keys from his trouser pocket, bent to unlock its door. 'This is *so* lovely,' Pam breathed, 'a really lovely car.' She'd absolutely no idea what it was, but it was *very* lovely. 'You have a *very* lovely car.' Pam sighed once more, as Marco crossed to open the passenger door for her before helping her in. Her long bare legs, still showing off their summer tan from the family's annual week's caravan holiday in Tenby, didn't appear to know where to put themselves once she was actually in and, seeing her problem, Marco hit a button and the seat shot backwards. Finding herself almost horizontal, Pam experienced that delicious floaty feeling making a return visit. Glancing across at her, Marco placed the key in the car's ignition but didn't actually start the engine.

Pam closed her eyes, the heady smell of car leather flooding her senses, and she knew all she wanted was for Marco to kiss her again so she could experience that wonderful feeling, almost of euphoria, once more. He smiled, almost apologetically it seemed to Pam, but didn't make any move towards her and instead turned the ignition. The throaty throb of the car engine, together with the intoxicating smell of the car's new leather interior and the faint tang of Marco's aftershave, was enough to make that wonderful feeling *down below* begin to bubble once more and she wriggled in her seat, her new white skirt rising up slightly as she put out a tentative hand to Marco's arm.

And then there was no going back. Everything her mother had constantly drilled into Pam: *men are only after one thing* and *don't let yourself become used goods* as well as *save yourself for the man who will respect you on your wedding night* shot merrily unheeded into the ether of the warm car and out of the rapidly steamed-up window as the mantra, *good girls don't*, was caught out as a big fat fib. Pam exhaled in ecstasy when Marco shifted his body towards her, warm hands searching out forbidden places and she realised, with a little 'oh' of surprise, not only what this was all about, but also that *good girls certainly did*.

Pamela woke the next morning not only with a cracking head and a mouth that had been slept in by a flock of pigeons, but with Mary Brown standing over her with a large mug of tea and a couple of paracetamol.

This was not normal behaviour: not once could Pam remember her mother bringing her tea in bed apart from the time she'd contracted yellow jaundice from somewhere (allegedly from sharing a hymn book with Katherine Goodbody at Sunday school whose whole family had apparently gone down with it) when she was nine, and frightened both herself and Mary (as well as creating much envy in her younger sister, Janet) by peeing urine the colour of concentrated orange juice.

'Thought you'd probably be needing these.' Mary smiled with unusual benevolence, placing the mug on the bedside table and handing over the two tablets.

Pam screwed her eyes closed in an attempt to rid herself of the unwelcome images and strands of conversation that were jostling for attention in her splitting head: Rob leaving her and going off with Ros McCarthy; being pushed, none too ceremoniously, onto the stage at the RAFA club; the champagne... Marco Piccione... his car... Pam felt her face suffuse with total mortification – and fear – as what she'd done came back to her. With Marco Piccione. In his car...

'You might well look embarrassed, Lady,' Mary was saying, 'coming home in that state.' But there was an amiable indulgence, pride almost, in her mother's tone that Pam's befuddled brain couldn't quite take in or work out. She sat up, burying her nose in the steaming mug of liquid, drinking thirstily in an effort to slake the seemingly unquenchable thirst as well as avoid her mother's questioning eye.

'And these have just come for you.' Mary stood up and left the bedroom for two seconds, returning with a ridiculously over-the-top bunch of some highly scented – and obviously expensive – pink and white flowers Pam couldn't put a name to.

'On a Sunday morning?' Pam asked, stealing a quick glance at her mother's face. 'Flower shops aren't open on a Sunday morning, are they?'

'*Florists*,' Mary corrected. 'And they must be *somewhere*. You know, for Mother's Day and people's birthdays…?'

'It's not Mother's Day, is it?' Pam asked in a sudden panic. Mary Brown would sulk all day if Pam had forgotten Mother's Day, especially as Lynne and Janet could both be relied on *never* to forget.

'No, you daft thing. These've just arrived. For you. Open the card. What does it say?' Mary handed over the card excitedly. 'Are they from Marco Piccione? Oh, Pamela, what a handsome young man. A bit old for you, I know. But, fancy, Marco Piccione bringing you home… Mrs Blackshaw at number 27 and Doreen both happened to be putting the bins out – ha, at midnight—?' Mary almost crowed '—when he said goodbye. He was so polite last night. Apologised that you'd probably celebrated becoming Miss Piccione with too much champagne when you shouldn't have even been drinking, but there you go. He asked if he had our permission to take you out to dinner next week. Your dad couldn't quite work it all out – you know what he's like when he's trying to catch up with his football and do his Pools for next week… What does it say? Read it out…'

Very much looking forward to having dinner with you
next week,

Marco xx

'Fancy.' Mary Brown was obviously bursting with pride and excitement. Pamela felt her head tighten and throb in the vicious vice of her hangover. She knew, as certain as night follows day, her mother wouldn't be offering tea and sympathy if she knew exactly *what* she'd been up to with that *nice, handsome Marco Piccione* in the shiny red car hidden from sight round the back of Greenstreet Park.

'Mum, Mum, there's more of 'em just come.' Twelve-year-old Janet's high-pitched voice shot up the stairs, followed by the girl herself, making Pam wince as it hit its mark, boom, into her pounding head. The excitement between her younger sister and her mother was palpable as Janet bounded into the bedroom with more flowers.

'Another bunch, Mum...'

'*Bouquet*, Janet... Oh my goodness, look at this little lot. Are these from Marco as well?' Her mother, Pam noted, was obviously now on first-name terms with her lover – her *lover*? Mary took the flowers from Janet – a mass of creamy, funereal lilies this time – in an exaggerated pretence of being unable to put her arms round them, while simultaneously and almost greedily searching for a card.

'Here, Mum, it's here,' Janet squeaked in triumph and, reaching into the blooms, like a modern-day Little Jack Horner, pulled out the cream chameleon envelope, attempting to open it before her mother could.

'Give it here, Janet.' Mary laughed almost girlishly, pinching it from the younger girl's hand.

The pair of them appeared to be having their own little drama without her, Pam thought dully, as more and more slides of the previous evening played and replayed in her pounding head in full technicolour, like some sort of distorted and out of sync cine-camera show.

'Oh. Oh?' Mary, it appeared, didn't quite know whether to be pleased or disappointed. 'Not *Marco* this time, Pamela; they're from Mr Piccione himself. Look…'

Congratulations on becoming Miss Piccione 1974

Angelo Piccione and all at Piccione's Pickles
and Preserves

A final slide of herself, her lovely new white skirt rucked up above her backside, her best Debenhams' white broderie anglaise pants lying, an abandoned flag of surrender, in the well of Marco's car as she moaned – she actually moaned – with pleasure, had Pam rushing to the bathroom and throwing up all the guilt, embarrassment and total remorse of the previous evening.

5

Pamela

Then

Mother and youngest Brown daughter were still twittering excitedly like a pair of sparrows at the breakfast table and had been joined by Lynne, Pam's big sister, who had popped in, as she often did on a Sunday morning on her way to pick up the *Sunday Express* (and a bottle of the metal-capped sterilised milk for the compulsory Sunday dinner rice pudding, if she'd run out of the stuff the milkman left every other day) from the corner shop.

Lynne had received a much-longed-for engagement ring on her seventeenth birthday, had saved meticulously for a down-payment on the tiny two-bedroomed terraced house three streets away (as well as for her bottom drawer) for two years before marrying Stuart Hall who she'd met over a game of ping-pong at the local youth club when she was fifteen. Now, at almost twenty-one, she was large and cumbersome with her first pregnancy. She sat with the other two over a cup of tea poured from the huge blue and white tea-cosy-covered pot that had been a feature of this kitchen for ever, and Mary exhorted her to put her feet up for two minutes and 'listen to our Pamela's news'.

'It's like a bloody funeral parlour in here,' Dennis Brown complained, indicating the flowers with a yolk-encrusted fork. 'I can't taste this bacon properly with the smell of those white things up my nose. Who is this chap anyway, Pam?'

'You know exactly who he is, Dennis. You met him last night when he brought Pamela home.' Mary Brown tutted across the table.

'Ruined my concentration doing the Pools.' Dennis winked at Pam who was pouring out the last drops of stewed Tetley's, waving away her mother's proffered slice of toast and wishing there was orange juice from a carton on offer like Rob had once told her his mum always gave *him* for breakfast. 'If I don't win next week, I'll know who to blame.'

'He's a bit *small*, isn't he?' Lynne put in, rubbing at her swollen abdomen under the voluminous smock in an attempt to remind her family of her status as mother-to-be, obviously put out that the usual attention she received on her weekly visit was, for once, concentrated on Pamela. 'He's under Mr Lewis at the surgery.'

'Not literally, I hope.' Pam yawned, absentmindedly peeling at the Piccione strawberry jam jar label. 'Your boss is huge. Fat really.'

'Mr Lewis is not *fat*.' Lynne was in protective mode. 'He's just cuddly; he often cuddles *me*.'

Erlack. Pam wouldn't let *her* boss, Mr Pickersgill, anywhere near herself.

Lynne had been a trainee assistant-dental-nurse at a practice towards the other side of town since leaving school at sixteen. She was now, after several years of day release, a fully qualified dental nurse and right-hand woman to Mr Lewis (with his coffee and digestive-biscuit breath – Pam and all the family had transferred over there once Lynne began to rise up the career ladder of dental hygiene). How Mr Lewis was going to manage without her once she left to have the baby in a couple of months' time was *anyone's* guess.

'He didn't look *that* small, Lynne.' Mary frowned doubtfully. 'He's about our Pam's height. Wasn't he, Dennis?' She turned for confirmation to Pam's dad.

'Hey, don't ask me, love. I never got a look-in with you fawning all over him and offering him coffee and tea and anything to eat in your posh put-on voice; I thought at one point you were going to have him scoffing my corned-beef sandwiches for work.' Dennis began to laugh at the very thought, before picking up the paper and turning to the sports section at the back.

'Can I be bridesmaid?' Janet asked through a mouthful of toast and jam (Piccione's raspberry). 'I'd like to choose my *own* dress this time,' she added as she swallowed and glanced across at Lynne. The teal-coloured satin had been a big bone of contention between both Janet and – particularly – Pam, and their big sister who had insisted on the mallard-coloured monstrosities two years previously.

'Oh, for heaven's sake,' Pam snapped, pain shooting through her head as she spoke. Bad enough what had happened last night without all this damned carry-on.

She wanted to see Rob so badly, wondered if perhaps she could ring him. Mind you, after an all-nighter at Wigan, she doubted he was even home yet and, if he were, he was surely still asleep.

Sunday dinner was underway: slices of cold, white-fat-ringed pressed brisket carved from its pudding basin-shaped mould (which she loathed); huge slabs of Yorkshire pudding cooked in, and cut from, Mary Brown's one and only roasting tin; cabbage and new potatoes under a sea of too-thin, fat-globuled gravy. Pam was beginning to feel as though she were drowning in the tsunami of interest and speculation brought about by the events of the previous evening. Her mother had already been on the red phone hotline for half the morning (giving it a pre-call squirt of Pledge in readiness for imparting the portentous news to Aunty Vera of Pam's success) leaving Pam to wash the dirt and a couple of slugs from Mr Blackshaw's allotment-cabbage freebie. She wouldn't be so happy to boast if she knew her not-yet-sixteen-year-old daughter had given away her most precious bargaining tool in the marriage stakes, Pam had thought, slicing viciously through the dark green leaves – and narrowly missing an AWOL slug – as her mother had instructed.

By the time the custard and rhubarb had been eaten (more stuff left on the doorstep by Ron Blackshaw. Was her mother giving anything in return? Pam thought idly. Oh God, since being introduced to sex herself, she was visualising everyone at it) and the pots washed (Pam washing and Janet drying – despite her younger sister trying to get out of it by announcing she'd not yet done her summer holiday French project and if she got an order mark it would be their fault) Pam knew she had to get out of the house.

'Just off down to Jane's,' she shouted to her mother who, once the table was cleared, had pulled out her sewing machine and was already muttering under her breath as she unpicked the previous day's mistakes with one of those sharp implement thingies no one ever knew the name of.

An *unpicker*, Pam thought crossly as she left their street on her bike, pedalled across the main road of the village and set off up the hill towards the open countryside where Jane lived, several miles away.

If only she could bloody well *unpick* what she'd done last night. What if she got pregnant? What if she was pregnant now? The sweat trickling down the front of her T-shirt increased at the very thought as she changed down into the lowest gear (there were only three on it to begin with) and determinedly kept as fast a pace as possible. You couldn't get pregnant the first time you did it; the ones who'd already gone all the way always said that at school. So, how many times must Sharon Butterworth, Linda Jones and Debs Coleman have done it to be up the duff, have left school and all married off after a quick registry office ceremony before they'd even sat their CSEs?

She'd only had her period a week ago, Pam comforted herself as she freewheeled down Jane's street and pulled up in her drive. Jane's dad was there washing his car and he turned, giving a friendly jiggle of his hosepipe in her direction. *Hosepipe.* She giggled slightly hysterically to herself. More sex. *Stop thinking about it*, she admonished herself.

'Don't know what you two were up to last night,' Jane's mum shouted through the open kitchen window as she washed up their Sunday dinner plates. 'Jane's not at all well. Were you both drinking when you shouldn't have?'

'Drinking? Oh no, they don't serve drink to under eighteens,' Pam lied.

'Hmm, I believe you. Thousands wouldn't. She's still in bed.' Audrey Pritchard, tea towel in hand, indicated with an upward nod of her head. 'Get her up, will you, Pam? Her dinner's all plated up and spoiling in the oven. Tell her I'm giving it to next-door's dog if she doesn't claim it soon.' Mrs Pritchard paused. 'Oh, and congratulations, love. Miss Piccione 1974, eh?'

Pam opened Jane's bedroom door and was immediately hit with the overpowering fug of overslept teenager, perfume, sweat and stale air. 'God, open a window, would you?' Pam breathed.

'Oh, don't let the light in.' Jane peered out from the bedclothes and opened one eye. 'My head won't take it.'

'Were you drinking?' Pam frowned. 'I tried to find you to give you some of my champagne but you were too wrapped round Martin Barker to realise.'

'Honestly, Pam, I just had the one vodka and lime Martin bought me.' Jane closed both eyes once more before sighing heavily and attempting to sit up. 'Close the door,' she whispered conspiratorially, nodding towards it. 'Listen, it wasn't the drink...'

'Are you ill? Have you got a bug? Oh God, you're not pregnant, are you?'

'Certainly not.' Jane was most indignant. 'What do take me for? I intend on being a... you know... a *virgin*... until

my wedding night. I'm not like Linda or Debs at school....'
She lowered her voice once more. 'It was the Mandy...'

'Mandy who? Mandy from Preserves?'

'No, you idiot, Maureen gave me a *Mandy*...'

'A Mandy?'

'Oh. For heaven's sake, Pam, how old are you? A Mandy... Mandrax... a Quaalude...'

Pam's eyes widened. 'Drugs?'

'Hmm. I didn't really want to take it, but Maureen said it would be OK. It would make me feel wonderful.'

'And did it?'

'Well, kissing Martin Barker was just like kissing David Essex. Honestly...' Jane started giggling '...at one point I thought Martin was going to start singing *Gonna Make you a Star*.' Jane sang the words croakily and then held her head. 'God, that hurts. Never again. I don't like that Maureen Cooper. She mixes with some right weirdos. I'm not going anywhere with her again. Just you and me from now on, Pam.' Jane frowned, pointing an accusing bright-red nail-varnished finger in Pam's direction. 'Mind you, you weren't much of a mate, leaving me there like that. My dad had to come and pick me up once you'd gone because I didn't have enough money for a taxi home. I can't believe you left without telling me. I suppose you got a lift home with Marco Piccione?'

Pam nodded.

'Are you seeing him again?'

'I've got to have the dinner date with him next week.'

'He's a bit old, isn't he? And a bit *little*. And a bit, you know, Italian...'

'You know this Mandy...?'

'Hmmm?'

'How did it make you feel?'

'I told you. Like Martin Barker was David Essex. I felt like I was floating. I could have taken my clothes off and… you know… done it with him, there and then in the garden of that club. But I didn't. Honestly, I didn't, Pam.'

'The thing is, Jane, I felt like I was floating above myself too. I thought it must have been the champagne, but I didn't drink that much of it.'

Jane stared. 'You don't think Marco Piccione slipped you something in your drink, do you?'

Pam shook her head. 'No, I don't, I really don't. He's not like that. But I think *someone* did.'

'I bet it was Maureen. She kept going on about how uptight you were, how uncool for not going off with Rob to Wigan. She was really mad when you came with us, and even madder when you won the Miss Piccione contest.' Jane swung her legs out of bed. 'I'm actually starving now. Has my mum left me a bit of dinner?'

It was almost teatime when Pam arrived home. She'd left Jane at the kitchen table tucking into roast lamb, and decided to take her bike a few miles further up the road to the fields beyond. She didn't want to go back home to more questioning about *Marco* from her mother, and was actually dreading going into work the next day. What if Marco Piccione had told everyone what she'd done? *Screweasy*: wasn't that what the lads at school called any girl who went any further than letting them have an exploratory fumble under their jumper? Why the hell weren't the boys called the same? Why was it fine for them – lauded almost (she loved that word: Mr Jenkinson the English teacher had taught it to them) – and yet not alright for the girls who did it with them? And she certainly wouldn't have done it if she hadn't been slipped something in her drink. She supposed Maureen would deny it all, but she'd be saying something to her in the morning. She could have killed her for heaven's sake. Made her have a drug overdose. She could report Maureen Cooper to the police.

Pam dismounted her bike and went to sit on the broken drystone wall at the edge of a huge meadow. Oh, but it was glorious up here. She watched as a lark, singing ecstatically, began its elaborate melodious ascent into the blue sky, until her eyes could no longer make out the black dot that was the bird, even while she could still hear its song tumbling down. She closed her eyes against the bright light, allowing herself to remember the actual act with Marco the night before.

The act? It sounded like she'd taken part in a play. And she'd enjoyed every minute. There, she'd admitted it now. She'd loved the whole thing. She felt that now-familiar bubble of sensation down below and guiltily placed her hand where it had felt so good. She opened her eyes, almost in shock at what she was doing. Oh God, suppose she was a sex maniac? Girls weren't supposed to enjoy it the first few times. It was supposed to hurt, wasn't it? She'd felt only pure pleasure as waves of feeling lapped at her and then sort of did an explosion she hadn't been expecting. Did her mum have these explosions with her dad? Ron Blackshaw with Mrs Blackshaw across at number 27? Pam actually laughed out loud at that, imagining Ron Blackshaw, leek in hand and lascivious smile on his face, taking Mrs Blackshaw behind his greenhouse.

Heavens, she really must stop thinking like this.

As Pam wheeled her bike into the garden shed, wiping sweaty palms down the back of her shorts, Janet shot down the path to meet her.

'More flowers,' she hissed in excitement, catching hold of Pam's hand and dragging her into the house. 'Come on...'

Pam inwardly groaned. This was getting ridiculous. 'Where?' she demanded impatiently as Janet led her past the kitchen. She needed a shower, needed to get out of her shorts that had caught a load of oil from her bike chain. Her bare legs were covered in the stuff too.

'Oh?' Pam stopped in mortified embarrassment as Janet pushed her into the front room where Rob Mansell was sitting on the edge of the sofa awkwardly holding a bunch of gladioli.

'Where's Mum and Dad?' Pam turned to Janet who was beside herself with gleeful anticipation. This was the first boy Pam had ever had round.

'It's OK, they're out. They've just gone for a walk before tea. I told Rob to wait, that you'd be back soon from your bike ride.'

'Right.' Pam didn't know where to put herself or what to say. Janet sat on the arm of her dad's favoured armchair, folding her arms as she grinned across at the other two. 'Thanks, Janet, why don't you go and put the kettle on?'

'It's on.'

'OK, go and start making tea for Mum then. Go and cut

some bread and make some sandwiches.' Sunday tea was always sandwiches, tinned fruit and Carnation milk and one of Mary's brand-new sponge cakes eaten in front of the TV, the only day of the week they were allowed to marry the two.

'I'm not staying long.' Rob smiled up at her as, crimson with embarrassment, Pam tried to make her mouth say something. 'I just wanted to give you these.' He stood up, attempting to hand over the tall orange and yellow stems. 'They're from my mum's allotment.'

'Look, come into the garden… and Janet, go and *do* something for heaven's sake.' Pam led the way, Rob still clutching the flowers, down the steps and to the bottom of the garden towards a wooden bench.

'I'm sorry about last night,' Rob finally said. 'I shouldn't have gone off without you. It wasn't fair.'

'No, no really, it's fine.' Pam didn't know what else to say.

'It was the shock of knowing you're not even sixteen yet. But, you know, there were kids there who looked younger than you. I mean, you easily pass for eighteen, Pam, and there was no one on the door asking for ID. No alcohol, so I suppose you could have got in no problem.' Rob laughed, his hands still clutching the bunch of flowers. 'I guess if you said to most people who're not into that scene, that you're traipsing miles to a club that doesn't open until late and where there's no alcohol and everybody dances totally by themselves, they'd think you were mad.'

'And was it good?'

'I can't tell you how totally wonderful it was. Martha was there and she did "One Way Out" with no backing. Can you imagine…?'

Pam sort of could, but she was also imagining a lot more. 'But you went off with Ros.'

'Phil and I gave her and her friend a lift over there because I had my mum's car. Honest, that's all. It's been over with Ros and me for months. She'd like it all to be back on, but... you know... I met you...'

Pam was amazed that the oh so confident Rob Mansell didn't seem to be able to get his words out. On her home territory, sitting in her front garden, he'd descended slightly from his pedestal as Rob Mansell, demigod, to being just gorgeous Rob, a boy she really, really liked. And wanted to be with. Hope flared.

Neither spoke for a while until Rob said, 'Look, I came over today because I wanted it to be alright between us.' Rob finally handed over the flowers. 'And it's your birthday, next week. I'd really like to take you out somewhere. I thought if your mum and dad met me, they'd see I was OK, you know, not someone who spends all his time clubbing.'

Pam laughed at that. 'I thought you did.'

'I'm doing A levels at tech at night. I want to go to university.'

'Right, I didn't know that.'

He smiled, slightly embarrassed. 'Well, it's not something that I shout about; not good for this image I seem to have acquired as King of the Clubbers.' He grinned down at her, running one hand through his thick blond hair while his long, tanned fingers on the other found the bleached holes in his Levi's.

He was nervous, Pam realised. She suddenly felt so happy, so incredibly *over the moon* that Rob was actually here, in her garden, had come to find her – with flowers

– that she took his hand from its resting place on his jeans and, making the first move – something she'd never dared do before – brought them up to her mouth, kissing them tentatively.

'You know, Pam…' Rob broke off as Mary Brown appeared in front of them. Rob jumped up, holding out his hand.

'Mum, this is Rob.' Pam jumped up as well, the gladioli falling onto the bench as she did so.

'Hello, Rob,' Mary said, ignoring his hand. 'Your tea's ready, Pamela.'

6

Frankie

Now

Irarely allowed myself the luxury, these days, of reliving that very first time at the hospital where I'd met Daler. It was something I'd done repeatedly, like a film on a permanent loop in my brain, at the very beginning, when I'd left both my nursing course and England. I'd run away with my huge pack on my back, first to Thailand, Cambodia and Vietnam and then on to Sicily, initially to stay with Great-Aunt Rosina – Nonno Angelo's much younger sister – before living and working on the dry, often water-starved acres my extended Piccione family owned and worked in Corleone, and finally on down to the coast around Agrigento.

And then, as the months went by and Daler didn't arrive in Sicily looking for me, as portrayed in all good fairy stories and romantic films, I'd packed away all my memories of the man I adored deep in my psyche and allowed the Sicilian sunshine and slow way of life to take over. On my cousins' land, in return for a bed and board, I helped with farming the grapes, almonds, durum wheat and, of course, the huge, sharp, sunshine-filled Sicilian lemons, which were the basis for Aunt Rosina's *crema al limone*.

My already pretty good Italian became fluent as I spoke nothing but the local Sicilian lingo, and I realised it was actually true: after a while one really does begin to dream in one's adopted language. Occasionally my dreams would have me shouting out loud, '*Come hai potuto farmi questo?*' How could you do this to me?

When Aunt Rosina suggested it, I was more than happy to extend my stay in Sicily. The thought of going back home to a cold, wet Yorkshire, and no Daler, filled me with despair and Aunt Rosina, widowed two years earlier, was more than happy to have me stay with her on a more permanent footing. And so it was my flight from Daler, which I'd anticipated being six months or so, became a year and then eighteen months and almost before I knew it I'd been away over two years.

I didn't arrive back in the UK until three days previously, a cold chilly Monday morning in the middle of March, landing at Manchester airport where I then took the TransPennine Express back to Midhope and a taxi to Mum's place.

Because with Aunty Pam apparently away on holiday in Lanzarote, I really didn't know where else to go.

I'd driven the five miles or so from my meeting with Angelo, Dad and Luca back to Mum and my stepfather Paul's place in what I considered to be the quite ugly gated community of seven houses in Heath Green, several miles from Dad and Tammy's much lovelier old house in Westenbury village.

After the sun-baked stone and pantile roof of Aunt Rosina's place overlooking Lake Arancio, with its acres of private woodland in which roamed deer and wild boar – my seventy-year-old great-aunt had a ten-bore shotgun permanently in place by the kitchen door – I found the enclosed area to the huge three-storey houses to which I was unable to gain access without a key fob, dispiriting.

'What on earth's that thing you're driving?' Mum frowned as she let me in through the cream-carpeted, blonde wood and glass hallway. 'The neighbours will think we're turning the place into a scrapyard.' The almost overpowering, certainly overwhelming, cream and magnolia hues weren't disturbed by so much as a potted plant, never mind the huge jug of wild flowers I'd have had as a welcome display were the house mine. Thank goodness it wasn't, I reminded myself. Already, after three days of living here, I thought I might go slowly mad within its cheerless, expressionless and very beige walls.

'One of the Piccione cars Dad and Angelo have lent me to drive.'

'Typical,' Mum sniffed. 'Couldn't they have given you anything better?'

'It's fine, Mum, really.'

'So, have they got you working for them?' I followed Mum through the hall and into the cavernous kitchen where she immediately rubbed and buffed at an area of the beige granite she'd obviously missed on her once an hour, on the hour, mission to eradicate any smear or dust mote on the central island and kitchen work surfaces.

'You knew they were going to ask me?' I said, surprised. Communication between my parents was rare unless it was my mother demanding yet more of the company profits to which, even though she'd abandoned Dad eighteen years previously, she still felt she was due.

'Luca was here yesterday with Verity.'

'Verity?'

'Oh, of course, you won't have met her yet. Lovely girl, very career-minded, immaculate sense of dress. Drives some smart little car.' Mum gave my holey jeans and frayed shirt a disparaging once-over before glancing out of the seemingly never-ending bank of bifold doors to Kermit on the drive.

'So?' Mum asked, pulling hard on her e-cigarette.

'So?'

'Luca wasn't happy about it, but he reckons the old man wants you in. Are you finally going to grow up and stop travelling the world like some ageing hippy and do a decent day's work?' This from Mum who'd never had any sort of job that I could remember since marrying Dad and living off the fat of Piccione Pickles and Preserves.

'Ageing hippy? Mum, I'm twenty-eight. And yes, I'm going to give it a go.'

'Really? Well, I give it three months before you've had enough and you're off once again.'

'Thanks for the vote of confidence.'

'As I say, Luca wasn't overly impressed at the thought of you just swanning back in and into management.'

'Swanning back in?'

'He thinks you should be doing six months or so on the production lines. You know, working your way up as it were. Mind you, I have to say, *I* couldn't stand spending my days in that godforsaken hole. Pickles and jam, for heaven's sake? Does anyone *eat* pickles and jam these days?' She vaped once more, accentuating the deep lines around her nasolabial folds caused by years of smoking actual cigarettes as well as discontentment with her lot. Closing one eye slightly against the exhaled cloud of fruity chemicals, she continued to look me up and down. 'So, where are you going to live? I mean, you can stay here if you really want. You know, until you find something more permanent.'

'It's OK, Mum, I'm going to move back into Dad's granny flat.'

The relief on Mum's face was palpable. 'Yes, Francesca, I think that would be wise. If you can stand living with that trollop of course.' Why Mum, who'd broken Dad's heart when she left him for Paul Stockwell, should feel aggrieved at Dad's second wife, fourteen-year-old son and six-year-old daughter, I could never understand, but she continued to carp on about Tammy whenever she could, berating her too-blonde hair, her too-long nails and her too-big bust as well as 'that miserable little adolescent – he looks just like old man Angelo – and that little princess of a daughter your father and his schoolkid wife have spawned' whenever she got the chance. 'Actually, Francesca,' Mum went on, putting down her vaping machine and folding her arms, 'if you're going to be at a loose end, you know in the evenings and at the weekends, I think it would be a nice thing to do to help Paul.'

'Help him? In what way?'

'There's going to be a by-election at the end of May. Barry Truelove, who stole Paul's seat at the last election, died last week.'

'Stole his seat?' I almost scoffed. OK, I did scoff – I wasn't a great fan of my stepfather's politics. 'Surely the best man won at the time?'

'The best man? Oh, don't be ridiculous, Francesca. You know as well as I do that Paul had held that seat for the past ten years. To be voted out, thrown out like a dog on the street after all he's done for this area, was beyond the pale.'

'People were fed up of him, Mum.'

'Yes, well, *I'm* fed up of him hanging around the house with nothing to do. He gave up his partnership at Brown, Brown and Stockwell to serve the people in this area.'

'Won't they have him back?'

'You're being flippant, Francesca. Of course he can't go back to being a solicitor. Being an MP is what he *does*. It's his *thing*. He likes being in London most of the week. *I* like him being in London most of the week.' Mum sighed. 'He's been like a bear with a sore head since he lost his seat to Barry Truelove. Anyway, very obligingly, Barry had a massive heart attack and died last week – in the middle of Aldi of all places; I mean, if one *will* go to Aldi when there's a decent Waitrose just twenty miles up the motorway from here – and so we're in need of a new MP. *I* need Paul out from under my feet and back in Westminster.'

'And you want me to help?'

'You know, the usual thing: knocking on doors, posting fliers, out in the car…'

'I don't *think* so, Mum.' I've always felt somewhat guilty about my lack of knowledge about, or interest in, the UK political system, but I did know my stepfather and I had clashed on many occasions over the views he held with regards both the economy and, particularly, social issues.

'Well, I can't see you're going to have much of a social

life now you're back,' Mum sniffed. 'Mind you, I'd have thought even a small town like Midhope more exciting than rural Sicily. God, I remember the first time your father took me back there to meet all those dreadful Piccione cousins and relatives. Not much more than *peasants*, and so *many* of them, and all desperate to show off their damned lemons and olives. And the dry heat played *havoc* with my complexion. Couldn't find anywhere to have a decent facial or manicure.'

'Right, OK.' Ten minutes with my mum was enough to have me heading for the hills. Or at least for Dad's place.

'Paul will be back in half an hour,' Mum said. 'He's just having a round of golf; you could have a chat with him about how you could help him...'

'I think I'll get off, Mum. I'm going to move my things over to Dad's flat.'

'What *things*? You've not even opened that old rucksack of yours since you got back. What are you going to do for clothes? I'm assuming you're not going to be on the production line at the works? I hope they're going to find you a place on the board now? I know Luca was dead against it, and to be honest, Francesca, I can see his point; I mean you can't just expect to waltz into a top job. But you are a Piccione, I suppose. Don't let them stick you back in the pickles. Get Angelo and your dad to shell out for some decent clothes...'

Mum continued to talk at me, following me as I went up the stairs to the chilly and somewhat sparse spare room she'd allocated me on my return three days ago. Typical Mum: one minute she was telling me I didn't deserve to be given a job; I couldn't just troll off for two years because some man had broken my heart and then come back out of the blue expecting everyone to put themselves out to accommodate me, while the next she was exhorting me to take what I could get from the Picciones: it was both my right and my inheritance.

Well, if it was my inheritance, which it seemed I'd decided it was, I was jolly well going to make the most of it. I'd give it everything I'd got.

7

Frankie

Now

Tammy, Dad's wife, opened the front door with a welcome grin and huge motherly hug. Bit daft really when she was only eight years or so older than me, but no less welcome for that, and I hugged her back, genuinely pleased to see her. The faint, lingering trace of *Ermenegildo Zegna*, the Italian aftershave Dad had always favoured ever since I'd been old enough to clamber up on to his knee and press my nose into the dark stubble that, by late afternoon, was in danger of becoming an actual beard, hung in the air. He'd always used too much of the stuff, liberally dousing himself in its scent, so that at the start of the working day one was literally overwhelmed by the fumes but, by its end, after a long day down at the works, the scent had settled into his olive skin, allowing the lemony bergamot tones their intended airing.

'I'm so glad you've decided to come back and stay in the flat.' Tammy grinned, hugging me once again to her inflated chest. 'Your dad's really missed you the two years you've been away. He'll be so pleased to have both his daughters at home with him.'

Once Dad, two years after Mum had left him for Paul Stockwell, had noted the new girl Tammy Sykes's concentrated efforts on the production line of Piccione's Premier Piccalilli, it wasn't long before she was promoted to section manager, then into Dad's bed and, a year later, pregnant with Matteo, their now fourteen-year-old, to his wife. While my mum and Tammy were hugely different in both looks, personality and of course age, they did share a love of housework but, while Mum had always depended on a whole army of cleaners to do her dirty work, Tammy, a true Yorkshire lass, would don her extra-thick Marigolds to protect her scarlet gels for a daily 'damned good bottoming' of the house. She did, allegedly, what her own West Yorkshire mother and grandmother had done before her, tackling the washing and ironing on a Monday, downstairs on a Tuesday, upstairs on Wednesdays and supermarket shopping on Thursdays and, although I'd never seen any evidence of this, according to Luca and Mum who didn't hesitate to mock Tammy whenever they could, donkey-stoned the large number of stone steps that led from the immaculate garden up to the highly polished knocker on their heavy oak front door on a Friday.

While M&S and Waitrose food halls had always featured heavily in Mum's repertoire of cooking, Tammy had sought the advice and skill of Nonna Consettia and daily cooked up huge vats of *caponata*, *pasta alla Norma*, and *arancini* – the Sicilian fried rice balls that had won over Dad's heart – and even once attempted *stigghiola*: grilled goat's intestines served with salt, pepper and lemon, that even Dad had drawn the line at eating.

'Where are the kids?' I asked. 'Still at school?'

Tammy nodded, glancing at the kitchen clock. 'I set off to walk down to the village to pick Angel up from Little Acorns in half an hour or so and Matteo gets in from the school bus around five.' Tammy laughed as she added, 'Now, don't be upset if Matty just grunts at you when he sees you. He's an 'orrible adolescent – I don't think he's said one word to your dad and me in the last six months. In fact, I'd say he's very probably just one step up from the vegetable rack at the moment. I mean, your dad said to him last Sunday: "Matteo, I'm not convinced that sitting in the dog basket in your pyjamas all day, plugged into your phone, is making the very best use of your time when you've got exams next week."' Tammy laughed at the memory and went on, 'Walk down with me to pick up Angel if you want. When your dad rang me earlier to say they'd finally persuaded you to join Piccione's, I reckoned a slap-up dinner was due. I've been cooking and baking all day to celebrate your coming home.' She laughed again. 'You know, like for that bloke in the Bible?'

'The Bible?' I might have been christened a Catholic, but religion had never played a big part of my life. My mum, in deliberate tactical opposition to Angelo who had wanted us over at St Augustine's with him in the family pew every Sunday, had made sure of that.

'You *know*.' Tammy frowned, thinking. 'The Prodigious Son? Came back with his tail between his legs and his brother wasn't at all happy.'

'The *Prodigal* Son.' I laughed. 'And yes, Dad and Angelo

might be pleased to finally have me on board, but Luca isn't too happy about it. Apparently, he's got big plans to rev up the preserves side of Piccione's – bringing in some American they've headhunted – and doesn't really see any opening for me in there as well.'

'Hmm, well, stand your ground with him. I've had to over the years.' Tammy paused, fixing me intently with her large baby-blue eyes fringed with the usual false lashes. 'You OK now, Frankie?'

'OK?'

'Well, you ran off so suddenly, leaving your nursing course and Daler…' Tammy hesitated. 'It's been two years, Frankie. Are you, you know, over it all?'

I shrugged, not wanting to discuss Daler.

'Anyway,' Tammy continued, 'the factory is ready for some new input, especially now that Pam's finally decided to retire.' Tammy smiled. 'Which is where you come in. Don't let Luca and this new bloke he's bringing in bully you…'

'Sorry, Tammy…' I grabbed my phone, vibrating in my pocket. 'Daisy? Where are you? How did you know I was back?' I walked out into the hall to talk.

'Ian's just texted me to say he'd seen you. Why haven't you been in touch? I've not heard from you since you were first in Agrigento. I've been really worried about you. You wouldn't answer my texts or phone calls.'

'I'm sorry. I sort of cut myself off from everyone. I found it easier not to know what was happening back here…' I broke off. 'I'm sorry. No excuse really… although, to be honest, the Wi-Fi at Aunt Rosina's place wasn't wonderful. We could suddenly find ourselves without it for days.'

'Sorry, Frankie,' Daisy snapped crossly, 'that's rubbish

and you know it. Both Tammy and your Aunty Pam always rang me whenever they heard anything from you, kept me in the loop as it were.'

'I'm really ashamed.'

'So you should be. You don't just ignore your mates, Frankie.'

'I wasn't in a good place. I'm sorry. So, where are you? At your mum and dad's?'

'Hmm. Are you home for a while?' Daisy sounded excited despite her earlier crankiness.

'For the foreseeable future anyhow.'

'Brilliant. Will you come and live with me?'

'*Come live with me and be my love?*'

There was a heartbeat of a pause before Daisy replied, 'No. Come live with me and be my *lodger*? Look, I'm going to have to go. Dad's calling me and I've loads to tell you – and ask you. Can you meet me later on? The Jolly Sailor?'

Putting every bit of effort into not asking if Daisy had seen Daler (was she still in touch with him? Did she know where he was?) I exhaled, concentrating on breathing normally and said, 'We're having a bit of a homecoming dinner here tonight – Tammy's been cooking her pinny off all afternoon – but I could meet you later? About nine?'

I was really pleased to see the clothes I'd left behind after running away still hanging up in the wardrobe in my bedroom in the granny flat.

'Of course they're still there, Frankie,' Tammy said almost indignantly. 'This is your home; these are your things. Do you think I was going to collect them all up and take them down to the charity shop as if you'd died, you daft thing?'

'I felt as if a part of me *had* died, Tam.'

'I know, I know you did.' She broke off as I pulled out the first couple of dresses, almost excited to see proper, grown-up clothes instead of the ubiquitous jeans, shorts, T-shirts and fleeces that had been the total sum of my clothes collection the previous two years.

'Ooh, I'd forgotten about this skirt.' I smiled, sniffing at the soft black leather before reaching into the depths of the cupboard once again. 'Oh.' I brought out one of the three pairs of mauve scrubs that had been the mainstay of my student nurse uniform at Midhope General. 'Won't be needing these anymore,' I said, trying to smile while gathering them up and bundling them into a pile at the bottom of the bed.

'I'm sorry, Frankie. You loved being a nurse, didn't you?'

'I was a rubbish nurse, Tam,' I lied. 'If I hadn't given up, they'd have probably sacked me. I wasn't very good at taking orders: spent too long holding hands and chatting to the lonely old men when I should have been scrubbing bedpans and writing up notes.'

As well as snogging Dr Daler Dosanjh – for which I'd once received a verbal warning – if we ever bumped into each other in the lift or sluice room.

'Well, that's all behind you now, Frankie. You're going to use your business degree for what it was intended – being a businesswoman. Now,' she went on, 'you're going to need some nice little black and navy pinstriped business suits.'

'Am I?'

'Well, you can't wear those, can you?' Tammy raised an

eyebrow at the state of my jeans and scuffed boots. 'And you with your Italian heritage? All Italians wear little business suits, don't they?'

'Not the ones serving in the pizza restaurants.' I smiled.

Tammy tutted. 'You need to show Luca you mean business. Now, your dad says you're not starting until Monday. If I were you, I'd get over to Manchester or Leeds in the next few days; buy yourself some proper clothes – I'll have a word with your dad – and some heels.'

'I've still got my air stewardess courts somewhere,' I said, beginning to feel excited at the thought of dressing up again. Even though being an air stewardess had been exceptionally hard work, I'd really enjoyed cultivating the groomed look we were expected to present at the beginning of each flight. Well, to start with anyhow. After two years, the thought of yet another five or six hours on my feet, pulling my hair into a tight bun and checking my eyebrows were brushed and pencilled into a prominent arch and my lips perfectly outlined, had begun to pall.

Apart from when I'd been persuaded out on dates with some really handsome, really lovely Sicilian men (who, at the end of the day and through no fault of their own, couldn't live up to not being Daler) I'd gone makeup-less for the almost two years I'd been away. It was going to be a challenge going back to being the girl I'd once been, when I'd revelled in buying new clothes and a new lipstick and spent two hours at least in getting ready to go out.

'Whoa, you've grown,' I whooped, rushing forward to meet Angel the minute she appeared in the playground of Little

Acorns village school and started running towards Tammy, book bag and some artwork in hand.

For a second she looked startled, unsure whether it was me, her big half-sister. Two years is a long time in a kid's life and she'd been only four when I left, but when she realised it was me for sure she took a flying leap and jumped into my arms, wrapping her little legs round my waist, her book bag banging uncomfortably down my spine as she squeezed me hard.

'Gosh, I'll have to go away again if I get such a welcome on my return.' I grinned as I let Angel down and she started boasting to all her little mates that I was her big sister all the way from Italy where her dad and her Nonno Angelo were born.

'Your dad was born in Yorkshire, love.' Tammy smiled as she took Angel's hand. 'Come on, we're going to have a real Yorkshire dinner for Frankie,' she added.

'No *stigghiola*?' I teased as, together, we swung Angel out of the village and up the hill towards home.

'No. Beef and Yorkshires and roast spuds with all the trimmings tonight. And no tiramisu either; it's apple crumble and custard,' Tammy added firmly. 'Your dad's getting a bit porky on all that pasta and those cream-filled puddings; we'll have a fruity dessert instead.'

'Over here, Frankie,' Daisy shouted, standing up and waving at me from a corner of The Jolly Sailor, the main pub in Westenbury village. 'Gosh, look at you.' Daisy stood back, examining me at arm's length. 'You look different.'

'Older, but probably no wiser.' I smiled.

'Hmm, you definitely look older,' Daisy mused. 'You know, sort of grown up.'

'Well, we are nearly twenty-nine.'

'I *am* twenty-nine.' Daisy sighed. 'It was my birthday last month.'

'Oh gosh, sorry, Daisy, I totally forgot.'

'I noticed,' she said. 'Anyway,' Daisy went on, once I'd ordered a glass of wine from the bar and we were facing each other, 'that's why I've made some major decisions about my life.'

'What's why?'

'Being twenty-nine. Another year and we'll be thirty and then, you know, it's all downhill from then on.' She looked gloomy for a second, took a big gulp from her glass of wine, and announced, 'I'm going to be a vet like my dad.'

'Are you? Aren't you too old to be starting out on something like that? It must be five years' training at least? And how are you going to afford it?'

'I know, I know, I've been through all this with my dad and he's tried – and totally succeeded over the years – to warn me off it. Anyway, after much persuasion on my part, he's finally going to help me. He's as fed up as me of my constantly setting off again because I don't really know what to do with my life, while Charlie is doing so well now that she's set up her own architecture practice in London. Anyway, there's a shortened course at Edinburgh university for those already with a science degree – my biology degree is hopefully going to get me a place on the vet degree course in September.'

'What is it? Four years?'

Daisy nodded. 'I know, I know, but it's what I want to do. You know how much I love animals…'

'There's a bit of a difference between enjoying taking the dog out for a walk – how is Malvolio by the way? – and sticking your arm up a cow's bits and pieces.'

'I'm actually working for Dad now,' Daisy said patiently. 'I did tell you this in a couple of texts, Frankie.'

'Yes, I know, I know. I just assumed you were mopping floors in the practice and helping out in Reception.'

'I'm doing all of that. Dad says I have to start at the bottom – quite often the *dog's* bottom as well as the dog's *bollocks*…' Daisy laughed at her own words and then went on '…you know, to show him I'm serious; that I'm not going to be pushing off to Australia or South America or wherever, again. So…' she paused as she reached for the bag of crisps I'd bought with the drinks, tearing it open with her teeth before placing it between us on the table, '…that's what I'm doing. I'm starting off as a vet nurse's assistant, but Dad's being great. He lets me go out to the farms with him – a lot of his work is on call-out to the cattle, sheep and horses round here, and I've *already* had my arm – several arms actually – up both cows' and ewes' fanjoes. And I love it. I should have done it years ago.'

'But how are you going to afford it? It'll cost an absolute fortune, another four years at university, won't it?'

'Well, we were lucky the first time round, weren't we, really? We managed to get our degrees before the horrendous fees came in. Dad's going to help me out with the fees – he likes the idea of being able to pass the practice on to me once he retires – and of course, while I've been travelling again, I've been renting out my cottage over at

Holly Close Farm and saving up every possible penny of what that brings in.'

Daisy and her big sister, Charlie, had been given the most fabulous old cottage down at Holly Close Farm, about five miles out of Westenbury, by their great-grandmother, Madge. Charlie, an architect, had project-managed the whole site, developing and renovating the farm itself, as well as extending the old cottage on the land into two semi-detached cottages, one each for herself and Daisy. Daisy, who'd also qualified as a landscape gardener after gaining her biology degree (I had to hand it to Daisy: she'd never been afraid of hard work and going after what she was really interested in) had sorted the ten or so acres of land belonging to the farm as well as the two cottage gardens, building drystone walls, clearing the area of years of brambles and weeds before planting new trees and bushes and laying many square metres of lawn. With Charlie headed back to London after the renovation and Daisy off once again travelling the world, neither of them had, as far as I knew, actually ever lived in the cottages themselves but, with them being situated in such a wonderful paradise of a spot, they'd been able to demand and secure very high rents and there'd never been a time when the cottages hadn't been occupied.

Until now apparently.

'This is where you come in, Frankie.' Daisy beamed. 'The last people moved out of my cottage just a week ago. I'm dying to live there myself until I go up to Edinburgh at the end of summer – it is mine after all – but I can't really afford to live there by myself.'

'But it's yours, isn't it? I mean, you've no mortgage to pay on it?'

'No, no it's all mine, every bit of it, and the other cottage is all Charlie's. But really, I *should* be renting it out again to put towards the university fees. I just thought, now you're back, *you* could share it with me and pay me rent and help with the bills? I'd love to be able to live in my own house for the seven months or so before I – hopefully – leave for Scotland. Go on, Frankie. Ian said you were going to be working for your dad? You don't want to be *living* with your dad as well. I've had enough of living with *my* dad and I know Mum and Dad have had enough of me living with them. What do you think?'

'I honestly don't know what Dad and Angelo are going to be paying me.' I frowned. Bit daft that, I censured myself – accepting the job without knowing what I was going to earn. 'And I know Dad's really pleased that I'm supposed to be living back at home in his flat...' I broke off, thinking about Daisy's suggestion and suddenly feeling some of the depression I knew was still hanging over me beginning to lift. 'Oh, but Daisy, that would be wonderful, wouldn't it? It would be like being back in Loverpool?'

'*Loverpool?*' Daisy started to laugh. 'Bit of a Freudian slip that, wasn't it? I need to remind you, Miss Piccione, as your prospective landlady, that those days of debauchery are, now that we're pushing thirty, over. It will be cups of tea, a bit of knitting and a jigsaw or two before Ovaltine and bed at ten.'

'So, erm, not to be crass but how much, you know, how much rent would you be charging me?'

'You find out what your dad's paying you, decide how much you think is fair and then we'll see if it's financially feasible. My Granny Nancy's just moved into a new place with her – much younger, allegedly – new man and has dumped a whole load of her unwanted furniture into Dad's shed, which he's not happy about. So we can have that to get us started. We might not have much but we'll get by.' Daisy paused and looked me in the eye. 'So, how are you doing? Really? Has running away got Daler out of your system?'

I shrugged. 'Maybe. Have you seen him?'

'Seen him?' Daisy frowned. 'Why would I? He's living in London, isn't he?'

I nodded. 'You know, I just wondered if he'd been up to visit his parents? Whether he'd called in here…?' I trailed off.

'Oh, Frankie. Two years on and he's still there, isn't he? You still can't get him out of your head.' She knew me so well.

'Every day,' I said miserably. 'Every hour, every minute. I just think constantly about how we met him in A and E when you had food poisoning… And how much he loved me…'

8

Frankie

Then

Almost three years previously during an August heatwave that had left us tired, sweaty and longing for a break, Daisy and I'd both had a few days' leave owing to us and were heading back down the M62 from Liverpool airport where we'd just landed, her from Malaga and myself from Palma, in my lovely Racing Green Mini – my twenty-first birthday present from Nonno Angelo four years earlier. Daisy had had to wait a couple of hours for my flight to land and was, in only the way Daisy can enunciate it: 'bloody starving – I could eat a dead dog.' The burger she was demolishing as we immediately found ourselves bumper to bumper in the usual teatime rush hour was giving every indication of being just that and I lowered all the windows in the car, as much to get the noxious meaty odour out of my precious Mini as to try and let in some cooling air.

We were heading for Daisy's parents' place in Westenbury village. Graham and Kate Maddison were apparently

84

treating themselves to a city break of a couple of days in Paris and Daisy had volunteered to have her four-day leave at home looking after the dog. As the child of a broken home, I didn't particularly feel able to call anywhere 'home'. My parents had divorced when I was ten and I'd spent most of the intervening years away at boarding school and then at university in Newcastle, often remaining up there during the breaks because I usually had a job of some sort in the many pubs, clubs and shot bars in the city. This was what I told Dad and Nonno Angelo anyway.

And Mum never asked.

So, when Daisy suggested I go with her as she was a bit nervous staying alone in the old Victorian pile in which the Maddisons lived – Malvolio, their black Lab being as much use as a guard dog as Daisy herself against the ghost she was convinced lived in the attic, or the burglars who were just waiting to run off with any family silver – I jumped at the chance rather than going back to spend my break either at Dad's or Mum's place.

We'd sit in the garden, Daisy enthused, and even *garden* the garden: Daisy had done a short course in landscape gardening after her initial biology degree and was dying to get in a bit of practical digging and weeding. We'd try for a bit of sun on our white limbs (the only actual sunshine we ever saw on our travels was through the windows of the many air-conditioned airports we were trapped in waiting for our return flight to yet another crowded European destination), we'd notch up some decent nights' sleep (we'd both spent a month on either overnight flights or 4.30am departures) and, when we were tired of that, we could wander down to The Jolly Sailor, Westenbury's village pub.

With Graham Maddison – the village vet as well as Daisy's dad – reminding us that the dog had separation anxiety and was not to be left alone or he'd eat the kitchen bit by bit (they were particularly anxious not to have their new kitchen table and chairs go down Malvolio's gullet) Daisy and I waved her parents off and headed straight for the garden with a bottle of red and two glasses.

The peace and tranquillity of an English country garden in the height of summer was heady to say the least. The nights were drawing in and, as dusk fell, a huge Sturgeon full moon hung almost motionless in the still, balmy warmth. Although never having taken an interest in plants or any aspect of gardening, I could appreciate Daisy's almost palpable enthusiasm as she pointed out the silvery mauves and warm apricot hues of woodbine and Saponaria attracting myriad moths, as well as several hardworking bumble and honey bees out long past their bedtimes.

I was, I realised, as I sat there sipping my wine and pulling Malvolio's velvet ears, ready for a change. I'd had enough – two years – of flying short haul and I needed to think about a new career, but what, I couldn't imagine. I didn't want to become part of Piccione's back then, although I knew both Dad and Angelo were hoping I would. I was envious of Daisy: she adored gardens and plants and I knew it wouldn't be long before she threw in the towel with flying, which at least at the moment paid the rent, in order to set up her own business as a landscape gardener.

Daisy was just exhorting me to sniff at the rhubarb and custard hues of the honeysuckle climbing the green-painted wooden bower to her left, when she stopped, exhaled and came back to sit down with me and the dog.

'You OK?' I asked, surprised.

'Do you know, I suddenly feel absolutely bushed.' Daisy glanced at her wristwatch. 'It's not ten o'clock yet, but I think I'm going to go to bed. You stay up a bit longer if you want.'

'It's fine. You go up. I'm just going to ring my dad and tell him where I am. He won't be happy if he knows I'm back home for a few days and haven't told them.'

I was awakened a couple of hours later by something, and for a few seconds I lay in the single bed in the Maddisons' spare bedroom trying to work out what it was. There it came again: low moans that were making the hairs on my arms stand on end. Was this the alleged ghost in the attic? I knew Kate Maddison had recently had the attics refitted as a studio for her work as a potter and Daisy had reported her mother saying she'd occasionally felt a presence up there, as if something wasn't happy she'd invaded its space. I sat up, reaching for the duvet I'd thrown off in the stifling heat, straining to listen for the sound that had obviously woken me.

There it was again: the low, amateurish *woooh woooh* a child might elicit when pretending to *be* a ghost. I glanced out of the open window at the breaking dawn. An owl, perhaps? A fox?

This was no sodding owl. When the sound came once again, nearer and, I estimated, right outside the Maddisons' spare bedroom door, I was seriously on the point of hiding under the bed like some cartoon character.

Woooh, woooh, woooh. Of course, it must be the dog, frightened at being left alone and missing Daisy's parents. I opened the bedroom door and there he was, pawing at the bathroom door across the landing but not making any other sound.

'Malvolio? Here, boy.' He ignored me, continuing to scrabble excitedly at the closed bathroom door. Did ghosts use bathrooms? Attics and cellars, of which this house had several, surely, but bathrooms?

'*Wooooh, wooooh, wooooh*. Effing hell...'

Ghosts, as far as I know, don't eff and blind or use the loo. I knocked on the bathroom door, the dog whining at my back. 'Daisy? You OK?'

The same ghostly moan rent the air once again before I heard Daisy say, 'No, I'm dying. I really am dying.'

Hell, was the fairly basic first aid course I'd had to pass before being allowed up above the clouds going to cover this? I pushed the door to find Daisy doubled up on the loo, her face white.

'I've been here most of the night...' she whispered, breaking off as another spasm of pain had her moaning and clutching at her side. 'I think it's my appendix. You know, it's all down my left side.'

'That's your *right*.' I frowned, as Daisy continued to hold on to one side of her abdomen, and I reminded myself never to fly with her if she didn't know her left emergency exit from the right.

'I know, I know, it's where my appendix is. I googled symptoms last night and it starts in your stomach and moves to the right of your abdomen. I think I need to go to A and E. I've been sitting here—' she looked at her watch '—three hours.'

'Have you been sick?'

Daisy nodded her head pathetically. 'Loads of times. I tell

you, if being pregnant and then childbirth is anything like this, I'm *never* having kids.'

'You couldn't *be* pregnant, could you?' Daisy had been in an on/off relationship with Raphael, a rather gorgeous French baggage handler, for the past year or so.

Daisy's head shot up at that. 'I thought being pregnant was painful at the end, not a few months in?'

'So, you *could* be pregnant, Daisy? And losing it?'

Daisy shook her head irritably. 'No, I'm not pregnant. I know I'm not. I'm telling you, this is my *appendix*. It used to grumble years ago – don't you remember I had a lot of time off school when we were doing SATS in Year 6…?'

'Daisy, that was nearly seventeen years ago.'

'…and they warned my mum then, if it stopped being dormant and became active again…'

'Dormant?' Despite seeing Daisy writhing around in pain I wanted to laugh. 'You got a volcano in there?'

'A and E,' Daisy breathed through another bout of pain. 'I need to get to the hospital before it bursts and I have peritonitis or… what's the other one? That sepsis thing that someone at work's granny died of last week? I need an ambulance.'

'Daisy, I don't think an ambulance will come out for just a bit of stomach ache,' I said doubtfully. 'You know, with the cuts and everything. They always ask if you're actually conscious. I don't think they'll come out if you're still *conscious*.'

'Tell them I'm *not* then. That I've passed out with the pain. I *am* just about passing out with the pain. Tell them I have an underlying appendix problem.'

I looked at my Fitbit: 5.30am. 'Come on, put a jumper on.'

'A jumper? Why? We're in the middle of a heatwave.' Daisy wiped at her brow before clutching at her abdomen once more. 'I wish my mum was here.'

'So do I,' I retorted. 'Right, put on a top or something over your nightie and I'll drive you to A and E.'

Ten minutes later, with Daisy looking tiny and vulnerable in her hastily grabbed Dad's fleece and Mum's flip-flops – she hadn't bothered to unpack her small valise the previous evening – we were on the drive and heading for my car.

'Stop.' Daisy came to a sudden standstill. 'The dog. I can't leave the dog.'

'You'll have to.'

'He'll eat the house.'

'Well, preferably that than my lovely Mini.'

'He'll have to come with us, Frankie. He'll be fine on the back seat. I'll get his bed; he'll be fine then.'

Through my rear-view mirror I could see Daisy visibly wincing and then bending over before unlocking the front door and almost losing her balance as Malvolio immediately shot out and down the path, flinging himself through the car door I'd left open for Daisy and onto the front passenger seat. I swear the look he gave me was one of triumphant checkmate: *Beat that, Buster*, he gloated.

Unable to budge forty kilos of tenaciously determined, slobbering black Lab, I got out of the car to let Daisy ease herself and a bright red plastic bucket onto the back seat of the Mini and we set off. She was looking incredibly pale and sweaty and intermittently emitting the ghostly moans that had woken me in the first place. The roads were pretty deserted at that time in the morning and we were at Midhope General within fifteen minutes.

Thank God it wasn't pub and club chucking-out time on a Friday evening. Once we'd followed the red arrows to A and E and explained the problem to a brightly efficient and smiley receptionist who was obviously at the very start of her long shift, we sat and waited. The triage nurse saw us within ten minutes and then Daisy and I were back in the waiting room, her with plastic bucket still to hand, while I waxed lyrical about how wonderful and dedicated the nurses on duty were.

'I'm going to be a nurse,' I suddenly said to Daisy. This was it; this was what was missing from my life: a sense of selfless dedication to others.

'Why?' Daisy looked aghast. 'Cleaning up vomit and dealing with aggressive drunks from Malaga will be a piece of cake compared to the bodily fluids you'd have to deal with as a nurse. And,' she went on, 'my friend Ellen from school was training to be a nurse and found herself in theatre where they were *cutting a leg off*. Just like that! Sawing it off with a bloody saw and hammer and chisel like it was a branch on a tree. How do you spend a day like that and then go home for your tea?'

'More easily than the guy who's had his leg off, I guess,' I said, wincing slightly at the thought, but not deterred from the idea of my new career. 'I mean it, Daisy, I might even have a wander and see if there are leaflets somewhere about taking up nursing.'

'Taking up nursing isn't the same as Giving up Smoking

or Volunteering for Visiting the Elderly,' Daisy scoffed, glancing at the leaflets pinned to the noticeboard opposite. 'Or having an STD,' she continued, narrowing her eyes to read the small print. 'I think I need glasses,' she added thoughtfully.

'Daisy Maddison?' a student nurse in the rather lovely mauve scrubs that pointed out her lowly status, but which I was already coveting, shouted Daisy's name down the sludge-green-coloured corridor.

'Do you want me to come with you?'

'No,' Daisy said, looking a bit frightened. 'I can do this. You're not my mum. You'd better stay here in case I'm whisked off to theatre for surgery. If I don't survive, tell Charlie she might sometimes have been a right pain in the backside as a sister, but I love her really. Oh, and her navy T-shirt I borrowed and lost was actually never lost at all, but is in the second drawer down in my bedroom in Liverpool. And...'

'Daisy? Maddison?' The call, more impatient now, had Daisy on her feet with her red plastic bucket into which, as though to prove she really wasn't well, she suddenly vomited loudly and profusely once more.

The waiting room was beginning to fill up but there was nothing exciting or entertaining to write home about: no kid's head stuck in a gate or a goldfish bowl; no early morning drunks with cuts to their heads singing 'On Ilkley Moor B'aht'at' and falling over their own feet; no alarms suddenly sounding and staff running from every direction as an emergency erupted like on *Casualty*.

I could do with a coffee. I wandered out into the corridor looking for a vending machine and finally found an antiquated specimen wobbling on three legs and standing under the stone stairs leading to the floor above. No purveyor of fancy cappuccinos and espressos this one, then. The choice was coffee, tea, or tomato soup. I searched where to insert my coins but, hard as I tried, there just wasn't anything resembling a money slot. Card only? I doubted a machine like this had any notion of card facilities. I almost laughed; this was ridiculous.

'Have you done?' an impatient voice behind me asked.

'Not even started, I'm afraid.'

'Round the side. The coins I mean: the slot's round the side.'

I glanced round. He was tall, dark-haired and dark-eyed. Of Indian or Pakistani heritage, I guessed. Scruffy in jeans, old trainers and a beanie hat from which was escaping a mass of black curls, and obviously in need of caffeine.

He could have been Dev Patel's double. Ever since I'd watched, and wept over, Dev Patel in the film *Lion*, I'd had a bit of a thing about the actor.

He reached forward for my coins, slotted them in. 'Coffee?'

'Hmm, please.'

He handed me a polystyrene cup of something obnoxious – from the orangey-brown concoction, quite possibly all three of the machine's options in one – before repeating the process for himself.

'You obviously know your way round the machine.' I smiled, wincing at both the heat of the contents and the taste.

'I'm here quite often,' he answered, not smiling.

I nodded sympathetically searching his face for clues.

Drugs? Fights? An elderly relative with epilepsy? 'I've brought my friend in with emergency appendicitis,' I offered, hoping he might stay and talk; there was something about him I just couldn't get enough of. I wanted to get to know him.

He nodded back in my direction, slightly alarmed, I think by my close perusal of his features. He gave a long stare of his own in my direction and then, without another word, made his way back through the double doors and into the A and E waiting room. I mopped at my hand with a tissue where some of the liquid had slopped over and then headed back myself, hoping a decision about Daisy wouldn't take too long, as well as for a vacant seat next to the beanie man into which I could just nonchalantly slip and continue our chat.

Both my hopes came to nothing. The beanie man had obviously been called for treatment and, half an hour later, I was still waiting for Daisy and starting to worry that she'd been taken in for an emergency appendectomy and that I should be making enquiries as to any prognosis.

If there was air con in the waiting room, it plainly wasn't working and by around 9am, after what seemed like hours sitting on the slippery, faux-leather banquette seating, I felt my eyes begin to droop and then with a lurch of my heart suddenly remembered.

God, Malvolio, the poor dog. He'd either have eaten my car piecemeal or be dead from dehydration and heatstroke. And Graham Maddison a vet too.

9

Frankie

I ran for the main door and the car park, belting across the tarmac, avoiding ambulances and cars as well as patients in dressing gowns trailing mobile respirators, intent on the smoking shelter towards the top end of the hospital grounds.

I had left the window open slightly for the dog, but hadn't envisaged we'd be the three hours or so we'd already spent in A and E. Luckily for Malvolio, the car was still in the shade but, looking up at the immaculate blue sky, I realised very soon he'd have been in the full glare and heat of the August sunshine. Feeling horribly guilty, and expecting an RSPCA inspector to be awaiting my return, I let the poor dog out of the car. He'd entirely demolished his own bed as well as a rather special cushion of mine, spreading foam like a snowstorm throughout the Mini and depositing a bucketful of slaver on the window I'd left open, but at least he hadn't eaten the gear stick. I found an almost full bottle of water in the boot of the car and poured it into my hands while Malvolio drank long and messily and then, when he'd had his fill, poured the rest over his velvety black head and nose. He now seemed pretty perky and, once he'd lifted his leg on the wheels of the brand-new neighbouring white Evoque, looked at me as if to say, *What now?*

What now, indeed? I decided he'd probably benefit from a quick trot round the car park before I was forced to lock him back in the Mini while I attempted to convey a message to Daisy that I needed her door key in order to take him home, so I unbuckled my shorts' belt to fashion a makeshift leash and we were off.

There was no way that dog was going back in the car. It was like a trailer from *The Great Escape*: despite my gift of water, Malvolio had obviously made up his mind I was the prison warder to be evaded at all costs and, with a mighty pull on the belt that sent me sprawling onto the warm tarmac, he put his nose to the ground and was off. After being wrongly imprisoned by a stranger he was manifestly in need of his dad – Graham – or at least Daisy, and he'd got a Maddison scent in his dog nose and wasn't about to take no for an answer.

While I yelled like a banshee, Malvolio wove himself in and out of incoming and departing vehicles, cannoned into a family ushering an elderly man towards the entrance and then shot through the automatic double doors, nose still to the ground, tail revolving like a robotic windmill. I caught a glimpse of his disappearing back end as he headed for the A and E corridor, scattering patients who obviously thought me, in hot pursuit, either hugely funny or totally irresponsible.

'You can't bring that creature in here,' said the smiley receptionist, who was now not smiling one little bit. She was on her feet and glaring as I shot past her little cubicle.

'He's brought himself,' I puffed. 'Sorry.'

Malvolio had skidded to a standstill, obviously unsure of his next step, when he gave a howl of utter joy and flung himself down the corridor to his right where Daisy was now walking back towards us, chatting to the doctor accompanying her. Well, I assumed he was a doctor because he had a stethoscope round his neck as well as the red scrubs notifying this status. Even in the midst of the confusion at trying to grab hold of Malvolio's collar and makeshift leash, while simultaneously working out that Daisy now appeared remarkably recovered, I recognised the beautiful brown eyes of the Dev Patel guy who'd helped me at the coffee vending machine an hour earlier. He looked totally different now that he'd abandoned his beanie hat, but a quick glimpse downwards to his trainers told me that this was indeed he. I stood and just stared while he appeared to do likewise until the spell was broken by Malvolio launching himself onto Daisy.

'You OK?' I asked Daisy who was now looking faintly embarrassed. 'Was it your appendix?'

'Wind,' Dr Beanie Man said cheerfully, actually laughing.

'Severe food poisoning, you told me,' Daisy protested, gathering up as much of her dignity as possible, as well as Malvolio's lead.

'Well, that'll teach you to eat dodgy burgers in a heatwave.' He smiled. 'I thought I'd better deliver your friend back to you,' he said, looking directly at me until I felt myself go pink and had to look away.

'Top-notch service,' Daisy said, patting his arm. '*And*, he's one of us.'

'One of us?'

'This is Dr Dosanjh, Frankie. Daler lives just outside Westenbury, you know over near Norman's Meadow. Well his parents do, anyhow. I think we should buy him a pint, don't you? You know, for saving me from the maws of death?'

'All in a morning's work.' The doctor grinned. 'You were lucky we weren't busy or I'd have had to leave you to simply fart yourself better.' He looked at his watch and then at the receptionist who was giving Daisy and me distinctly chilly looks. 'Right, must get back…'

'We're having a barbecue, aren't we, Frankie?' Daisy raised her eyes in my direction.

'Are we?'

'Yes, we were planning it last night. Gosh, your memory… now, give this wonderful doctor one of your business cards – I don't appear to have mine on me – and then he can get in touch with you… with us… once he knows he's off duty.'

'So, when is this barbecue?' Daler held my eyes as I fished out one of the cards the airline issued to all new recruits – along with the red uniform, support tights and navy court shoes – from my phone case in my shorts' pocket, before I looked over at Daisy for help.

'Whenever you're off duty over the next couple of days.' She grinned. 'Just let us know. But we're back in Liverpool on…' she broke off to count on her fingers '…on Tuesday… so just get in touch… Right, dog; right, Frankie, I need to go home to sleep.'

Daisy set off at a bit of a trot and I followed, but turned

at the entrance to A and E. Daler, still standing where we'd left him, raised a hand and grinned in farewell before turning back down the corridor from where he and Daisy had just come.

And that was how I met Daler Dosanjh. If Daisy hadn't eaten that disgusting burger on the way home from the airport, we'd have spent the four days' break back home in Westenbury as we'd intended: sitting in the garden, sleeping, reading, maybe a stroll down to The Jolly Sailor, just recuperating from the mad summer we'd both had working non-stop across the skies of Europe.

But it didn't quite work out that way.

10

Frankie

Then

'What the hell was all that about?' I asked, once Daisy had pushed a whining and indignant Malvolio back on to the rear seat of my Mini. He was obviously terrified he was going to be left by himself for another three hours and was making sure we knew he wasn't going to stand for it.

'I had *food poisoning*,' Daisy said indignantly. 'You heard the man.' She attempted to push Malvolio's black head away from where he'd determinedly placed it over the front passenger seat, crying pitifully into her neck and hair.

'Wind, I think the good doctor said.' I grinned, shooting out of the hospital car park while the dog hung on tenaciously to his position over Daisy's shoulder.

'Wind? A bloody great gale – a tsunami even,' she protested. 'I've never felt or been so ill: even worse than when we drank those lethal cocktails of whiskey, cherry brandy and crème de menthe at Leeds Festival when we'd finished A levels.'

'Worse than *that*?' I looked across at Daisy. 'Blimey, really?' I exhaled, remembering.

She nodded, aggrieved, but ready to forgive my former apparent lack of empathy at her food poisoning now that I appeared, after the comparison she'd made and knew I'd understand, fully aware of just how near to death's door she'd once again been.

'Actually, I wasn't referring to your state of health.' I laughed. 'I mean, what *was* that all about back there? Since when did you decide you were having a barbecue and inviting the staff from A and E?'

'Only the very able and rather lovely Dr Dosanjh.' Daisy managed to peer over Malvolio's head in order to gauge my reaction. 'Gorgeous, wasn't he? A bit Dev Patel, I thought.' Daisy rolled her eyes before yawning and closing them. 'I'm absolutely knackered,' she added, laying her head on Malvolio who was still hanging over the front seat for grim death. 'Anyway, Dr Dosanjh? Rather lovely?'

'Was he? I hadn't noticed,' I lied.

'Oh, you mean I needn't have bothered with all that conniving to get you two to meet again?' Daisy was most indignant. 'I could have just given in to my poor wretched body's one desire to give up the ghost and die, without putting on a performance from *Fiddler on the Roof*.'

'*Fiddler on the Roof*?' I glanced across at Daisy.

'You know? The Matchmaker?'

I didn't.

Daisy tutted, bursting into song, with Malvolio, not to be left out, adding several – admittedly quite tuneful – howls to the refrain. I'd forgotten – and I don't know how in God's name I had – the Maddison family were all big – and I mean huge – into singing old musicals. I'd once had to endure a whole evening with Vivienne Maddison – Daisy's bonkers granny – Graham and Daisy, being made to join in with every sodding song of a never-ending repertoire from *South Pacific* to *Oklahoma*. Just when even Malvolio had had enough, slinking off in despair to his basket in the kitchen, and I tried, yet again, to suggest we head off to The Jolly Sailor, one or other of them would shout, 'Ooh, *I* know. How about *Edelweiss/ Rhythm of Life/ Hello Dolly?*' and we'd be off once again, a pint down at the pub at the end of the torture becoming a fading hope.

'Frankie,' Daisy now said, in the patient tones of a mother talking to a five-year-old, 'the only reason Dr Dosanjh came to find me was because you'd told him I was your mate.'

'Did I?'

'Did you *what?*' More patient condescension from Mother Daisy.

'Tell him you were my mate?'

'Apparently. Got a free coffee out of him, I heard. Anyway, he put himself forward as the A and E doctor to assess my burst appendix...'

'It was wind...'

'...but all he was interested in was *you*. My poor appendix didn't get a look-in.' Daisy sat up and yawned once again as I pulled my Mini into the Maddisons' drive. She glanced across at me and grinned. 'You obviously made one hell of an impression, despite your having no make -up on and wearing your old shorts and sweatshirt. Just wait until he sees you in your little white cut-offs at the barbecue on Sunday… Now, who else shall we invite?'

'You have to have Pimm's at a summer barbecue,' Daisy had said the next day as she placed several bottles of the pink liquid, as well as gin and wine, on top of the trolley already laden high with chicken, sausages, salad and ice cream.

'No burgers?' I'd asked.

'Not the "B" word.' She'd shuddered, making very loud and very authentic retching noises over the meat-stocked freezer, much to the admiration of a little kid who was almost falling head-first into its chilly depths as he struggled to reach a packet of family-sized burgers.

'I wouldn't eat those, kid,' Daisy advised, as his legs actually left the supermarket floor and he rocked precariously, like one of those balancing-bird toys, on the rim of the freezer. 'They can make you very ill…' She broke off as I grabbed my phone from my shorts' pocket as a text came through and my pulse simultaneously soared. 'Daler,' I breathed, 'is coming to the barbecue.'

Up until meeting Daler Dosanjh, I'd probably have scoffed at the very notion of meeting 'The One'. There are over seven billion people on this planet of ours, and to say just one of them is 'The One' is probably statistical nonsense. (When I did statistics on my business degree course in Newcastle, I found it all to be pretty nonsensical to be honest, so I couldn't really stand up in court and defend my own hypothesis.)

Anyway, when Daler walked into the Maddisons' garden that Sunday afternoon – the barbecue well under way, with the fifteen or so others we'd invited already stuck into the charred chicken and too-strong Pimm's – I knew I'd found my one and only.

'Sorry I'm late,' Daler said, handing over a bottle of wine and an extremely large and very expensive-looking box of Fortnum and Mason chocolates. 'The chocolates are from my mother.'

'Your mother?'

'Hmm.' Daler looked slightly embarrassed. 'I'm back staying with my parents at the moment: I've spent the last three years in Coventry...'

'What, your parents wouldn't speak to you? What had you done to upset them?'

Daler laughed out loud at that and I let him think I'd been joking when, for a split second, I honestly was about to leap to his defence. 'I was living and working in the city centre there and I'd had enough; I longed for fields and cows and countryside. This job came up at Midhope six months ago and I decided to apply. I got it and I've been living at my parents' place until I find somewhere I like. There's no rush. The village is all a bit new to me – my parents only moved here from Mirfield a year ago. Mum's a stickler for taking chocolate wherever she's invited anywhere, and insisted I bring these.'

'She sounds like my kind of mother.' I laughed, thinking not of my own mother, but of both Tammy, my stepmother, and my Aunty Pam, Dad's older brother's divorced wife, who I adored and who had been more of a mother to me than my real one.

'How's the Sirocco?'

'The Sirocco?' I stared at Daler. I had a Mini, not a Sirocco.

'The Windy One?' Daler went on, grinning.

'Ah.' I laughed. 'See for yourself.' I smiled back up at him, unable to tear my eyes away from his own beautiful brown ones in order to indicate Daisy at the bottom of the garden where she was beating Ian in the limbo competition she'd organised and set up earlier. Daler's eyes were fringed with eyelashes longer than any man should ever be allowed to possess and I found myself mesmerised by them as well as his smile.

'Have you been working?' I asked Daler, finding him a bottle of Pilsner in the green bin of melted ice.

'Yes, I should be on duty now. This afternoon.'

'And you've gone AWOL?' I felt slightly concerned. Was 'The One' actually somewhat cavalier? More than up for playing hooky from his emergencies in A and E in return for a sausage on a stick and a bottle of warm beer?

'No, I managed to do a swap. I don't think there's anyone who wouldn't prefer to work the gentler Sunday day shift than the mad Saturday night – all through the night – shift.'

'Oh, you've been working all night? You must be exhausted.'

'I wanted to see you again, Frankie.' Daler smiled down at me over his bottle of beer, and I was lost.

'So,' I said, going slightly pink at the intensity of his stare, 'you don't really know the village then?'

'I'm getting to know it.' He smiled again. 'And you?'

'Me?'

'Daisy said you're both based in Liverpool?'

I nodded, suddenly having no desire to go back there once our dog-sitting stint was over.

'Are you continuing with that?'

'Do you know, when I was in A and E with Daisy the other day, I suddenly had a bit of an epiphany.'

'I've not come across one of those before.' Daler laughed. 'Not too painful, I hope?'

'I'm going to be a nurse.' I said the words with some pride, and now that it was out in the open, now that I'd actually said it aloud, I was determined to follow it through.

'Good for you.' Daler smiled. 'I think they're actually recruiting at the moment for nurses at Midhope General. The hospital works very much together with Midhope university and, as far as I know, you'd spend about forty per cent of the time in full-time study and the rest of the time on placement...' He suddenly trailed off. 'That's if you were actually intending to stay round here? I mean, there's probably loads of hospitals around the country just crying out for new recruits.'

'I hadn't really thought where I might apply,' I said. And I hadn't. I was so full of enthusiasm and zeal at the idea of becoming a nurse, I'd been prepared to go wherever I might be accepted. I'd loved being in both Somerset and Newcastle and now knew and liked Liverpool as well, and so I suppose those places were high up on my list. It suddenly occurred to me, as I stood in this lovely garden in Yorkshire, that maybe it was time to settle, to stop being such a nomad and put down some roots in my home town. Especially as this equally lovely man was now part of my home town too.

Daler and I totally monopolised each other that afternoon

and even Daisy, who, being a sociable, gregarious type of girl, usually insisted everyone at her dos join in with her drinking and party games (she was now organising a game of rounders in the paddock at the bottom of the garden) left us alone to get to know each other.

Dr Daler Dosanjh was gorgeous. That was the only word for him. He was much taller than me – as I'm only five foot one *everyone* is much taller than me – but not that tall I was going to be left concerned for the welfare of his back when he kissed me. *If* he kissed me. I've not been averse in the past – particularly if I've had rather too much to drink – to making the first, albeit subtle, move when the object of my desire is sitting across from me – you know on a bar stool, or across a dinner table. But there was no way, as we stood talking on the lawn, that I'd be able to reach up almost a foot to kiss this heavenly man without my intention being overtly obvious. Luckily for me Daler made the first move, bending his head and reaching out a hand to my hair. At the ridiculously instant heat suffusing my body at his touch, I felt my eyes close with expectation and then my face flush with embarrassment as he whispered, 'There, got it,' and removed a heat-drunk fly from my hair. But, obviously encouraged by my eyes closing, Daler then did the decent thing and reached forwards in my direction once more. That first kiss – a subtle brush of his lips against my own – had me almost reeling with wanting more. This was it then: what all the poets – Marvell, Shakespeare, Marlowe et al. – had been writing about in their bedrooms, cells and attics as, drunk with lust and desire, they penned words of love. I could see I'd be getting out a biro and writing pad once I was alone.

'You OK?' Daler looked slightly worried, obviously concerned at my seeming inability to speak or react.

'Fine. I'm fine,' I managed to get out. 'I just wondered if maybe…?'

'Maybe…?' Daler still looked concerned.

'Maybe you'd consider doing that again.'

'This?' Daler bent his dark head once more, taking my face in both hands and kissing the corner of my mouth, then my top and bottom lips until I was a bit of a squirming mess.

'There's still plenty of *food* left to eat.' Daisy was at our side, sweating slightly from her exertion at the game of rounders. She grinned. 'I hate to interrupt, but I've just been run out – for heaven's sake, have people forgotten the unforgivable *crime* of running someone out? – and my mum always insisted it good manners to look after guests at my parties. You know, offer round the egg and cress sandwiches and butterfly buns.'

'You have butterfly buns?' Daler smiled.

'No. But there *is* some slightly burnt chicken and salad that needs eating. No burgers.'

Daler actually laughed at that and then looked at his watch. 'That's really kind, but I'm actually going to have to go.'

'Go?' Daisy and I spoke as one, she obviously concerned that Daler was leaving without being fed and that her matchmaking was about to come to nothing, and me because I couldn't bear to let this lovely man, who I'd just decided was my 'one' leave, just like that.

'I've a commitment I can't get out of.' Daler smiled, seemingly slightly embarrassed.

Oh God, he was married. With kids. And he'd promised to be home to read them a story. I could already see the beautiful dark-eyed little girl as well as an older boy who, a mini version of Daler, and determined to be a doctor just like his dad, wore Daler's filched stethoscope around his neck examining his beautiful, patient and loving mother, indulgent granny and long-suffering row of bandaged teddies.

'Oh, right.' There wasn't much else I could say.

Daisy had no such qualms. 'You can't *leave*,' she said bossily, glancing at my face. 'You've only just got here.'

Daler looked at his watch. 'Two hours ago actually, Daisy.'

Goodness, had we been stood talking for two hours?

'And,' Daisy went on, 'you probably don't know this yet, Dr Dosanjh, but Francesca here is one of England's top women footballers. Amateur, of course, but she *could* have been professional. If you leave the party, she'll end up organising a damned football match once the rounders match is over. And to be honest with you, it's far too hot for football.'

'Cricket?'

'Sorry?'

'I'm a pretty good bowler if I say so myself.' Daler directed his lovely smile at Daisy and I could see she was as much taken with him as I was. 'I've been playing for the Westenbury team since I moved here.'

'Oh, my dad's played with them for years.' Daisy was delighted to be finding a connection between the man who'd solved her little wind problem and her family.

Never mind your dad and the damned cricket team,

Daisy. What about the dark-haired kids, the beautiful wife and the indulgent granny waiting for Daler back at home? What about the bandaged teddies, for feck's sake?

'Oh. Right, Daisy.' Daler smiled. You're Graham Maddison's daughter? The vet? I don't know why I didn't make the connection before.'

I frowned, glaring at Daisy who was still monopolising both Daler and the conversation. Could we just stop talking about cricket and Daisy's dad and get back on to why Daler was suddenly making his exit? What sort of a commitment does a thirty-year-old man have on a late Sunday afternoon if it doesn't involve a wife and kids, waiting expectantly at home?

Daler glanced at his watch once more and made motions to leave, placing the one empty bottle of Pilsner on a nearby table and tying a yellow sweater around his waist. 'I'm sorry, I really must go, or I'll be late.' He gave his thanks, kissed Daisy on the cheek and then turned to me. 'Come with me if you want, Francesca?' he suddenly said, jiggling his car keys in his hand and looking at me with some expectation in those beautiful eyes of his.

11

Frankie

Then

'I'm sorry.' Daler frowned as he put his car into gear – a rather sporty little number that was helping to quash any notion he might, at some other point in his life, be squeezing in kids and teddies – before roaring me off in the direction of Midhope town centre.

'What are you sorry for?' I glanced across at him, and he did appear slightly anxious.

'You know, dragging you from your party.' He smiled. 'Especially if you were about to organise a football match. You kept that quiet. The footballing expertise, I mean.'

'I wasn't about to organise *any* football match,' I tutted. 'That's just Daisy showing off about me. For some reason she is inordinately proud that I was in the England Schoolgirls' team years ago.'

'I'm not surprised,' he said seriously and then paused. 'This. I'm not sure *this* is a good idea; I should have left you to enjoy the barbecue with your friends...' Daler broke off, stepping on the brake as a large black cat shot out from the pavement. It stopped and stared in some disdain at the pair of us before walking nonchalantly to the other side of the road. 'I just couldn't bear to leave you this afternoon, once I was getting to know you.'

'Well—' I laughed, cheered by his words '—tell me where we're going and then I'll tell *you* whether it's a good idea or not.'

'We're here, now,' he said, pulling into one of the town's large car parks adjacent to the bus station.

'Are we taking a bus?' I joked, trying to put him at his ease.

'No, we're going to serve some food.'

'At the bus station?' I began to laugh.

Daler shook his head, turning slightly so I could see past him to his right as he indicated the huge golden dome of the town's main Sikh Gurdwara. 'It's my turn for helping serve the Langar meal – the food will already have been prepared and be getting cooked at the moment. Just waiting for me and a few others to serve it up.'

'Langar meal?'

'It's what we do.'

'What you *do*?' I turned from looking at the imposing building in front of me where a queue was beginning to form. 'Are you a practising Sikh? Shouldn't you be wearing your hair long and in a turban? And not drinking? You had a beer at Daisy's?'

Daler smiled. 'I was born Sikh...'

'The same way I was born a Catholic?' I interrupted. 'Religion doesn't mean much to me, I'm afraid. It certainly doesn't define who I am.'

'Nor me. Or my family. I certainly didn't undertake the Amrit Ceremony when I was a kid.'

'The Amrit Ceremony? The Langar meal? I'm sorry to say that's stuff I've no knowledge of.' Lots of my mates at school had taken Religious Studies at GCSE, thinking it was a bit of a soft option but I hadn't. 'What I'm saying is, I've no idea what you're talking about. I mean, as a non-Sikh, and as a very lapsed Catholic, should I even be entering your temple?'

'Absolutely.' Daler smiled. 'Sikhs believe that all religions have different paths but ultimately reach the same God.'

'A bit like different little streams all ending up in one big river?' I rather liked this analogy.

Daler laughed. 'You could say that, but I have to say I've never thought of God being like the River Colne – bit polluted and full of chemicals isn't it?' He nodded towards the Gurdwara, which had become a hive of activity. 'If you look across there at the queue, there probably isn't one Sikh amongst them. Very religious, very fundamental Sikhs will undergo the Amrit Ceremony when they're about thirteen or so, and in doing so they make a commitment to the religion: you know, to keep their hair long out of respect to God who gave it to them, to wear the turban and abide by the five Ks, as a sign of that commitment.' Daler paused and smiled. 'Don't worry, I'm certainly not hugely religious, nor is my family. However, it's just something we've always done; we take our turn to help out at the Langar meal. And it's not just helping those worse off or less able than ourselves; it's a way for all of us, regardless of wealth and status, to prepare and eat food together and in doing so get together and have a good time socially. Sorry, I didn't mean to sound self-satisfied or give you an impromptu lecture on Sikhism.'

'Don't be silly. This is fascinating. I'm just amazed that this goes on every Sunday evening in Midhope town centre and I knew nothing about it.'

'Actually—' Daler laughed '—a meal is prepared every *day* in most towns in the UK. Throughout the whole world in fact. I suppose it's a bit like your traditional Italian family all getting together to eat.'

'Not really.' I frowned. It had been a big tradition that all of Nonno's family got together to eat every Sunday. I'd loved it as a kid, but Mum had hated the whole family-gathering set-up, everyone pitching in to help at Angelo and Consettia's place and, by the time I was ten and Mum already looking for a way out of both her marriage to Dad as well as the extended Piccione family, she refused to have anything more to do with it. Luca, being a particularly surly, somewhat arrogant adolescent at this point, took his lead from Mum and also dug in his heels, so it was just me and Dad who continued to meet up with our Italian family and friends at Angelo's house. But never once had there been anyone for dinner who wasn't part of the Piccione extended family. And, certainly, no one was ever invited in off the streets for a free meal.

'Everyone, and anyone, is welcome,' Daler went on. 'It's no different to helping out with the food kitchen that's organised every week for the town's homeless, or… or being a Samaritan or… or you know, a Street Angel.'

'I feel a bit ashamed,' I said, frowning. 'I've never even thought about helping out with *any* of those things. So, are you saying anyone can just pitch up for a meal?'

Daler nodded. 'Yep. We do get a lot of the town's

homeless – that's who're queuing up at the moment waiting to be let in. But that's fine. Sikhs believe everyone is equal, so that's why all the food cooked is totally vegetarian – and often vegan – so that those who don't believe in eating meat are not put at a disadvantage. And why there's no hierarchy about seating.' He laughed at this. 'Everyone just takes a place where they want – we sit on the floor.'

Daler took my hand and we walked through the car park and into the cavernous hall where a group of children were setting out plates and paper napkins.

'Darling, you're here.' A very stylish woman, a huge pinafore unable to camouflage the obviously expensive and upmarket pink sari she was wearing, headed in our direction.

Oh heavens, was this his mother? Was I being introduced to his mother on our very first date?

'Francesca, this is my *dadi*.'

I looked at Daler for help: this was his father? Was cross-dressing not frowned upon in the Sikh religion then?

'My grandmother,' Daler explained helpfully, when I didn't quite know what to say.

'Oh gosh, your grandmother?' I twittered, holding out my hand. 'Gosh, I thought you must be Daler's mother…'

'No, that's *me*,' a voice behind me laughed gaily as the older woman in the pink sari preened somewhat. 'My mother-in-law adores people thinking she's Daler's mother rather than his grandmother.' I turned to face one of the most beautiful women I think I've ever seen. If she was Daler's mother – and I knew Daler had just had his thirtieth birthday – then this woman had to be at least fifty. She honestly could have been Daler's big sister.

'Mum, this is Francesca. Frankie, my mum, Chuni.'

Chuni Dosanjh was tall, slim and with a figure to die for. Her long dark shiny hair was pinned up with a single clip, presumably in deference to the food preparation in which she'd been engaged, and her incredible face, which I was having trouble taking my eyes from, was beautifully made up, her dark eyes subtly outlined in soft kohl, her full mouth a perfect crimson bow. I felt totally at a disadvantage in my white denim cut-offs and navy T-shirt compared to the stylish – obviously expensive – white linen designer trousers and top Chuni was wearing. Her arms, slim and toned, were laden with gold bracelets, despite her being in the middle of cooking for the quickly moving line of men and women who were now being helped to the delicious-smelling food on offer. Some in the queue, it was apparent, from their dress and turban, were Sikh; others were from the growing numbers of those living on the town centre streets.

Chuni took my hands in her own before kissing me on both cheeks. 'I'm so pleased to meet you, Francesca. Now that Daler's moved up from Coventry, he's having to make new friends in the area…' She paused, her head to one side. 'I tell you what, Daler, when we've finished up here why don't you bring Francesca back to the house for a drink?'

'Up to Frankie.' Daler smiled, holding my eyes for what seemed minutes. He finally looked away and across at the queue for food that was showing little sign of diminishing, obviously remembering he was here for a reason. 'I'm on serving and clearing-up duty,' he said. 'Why don't you grab a chair over there, Frankie, and once I've served this lot, I'll bring us some food over?'

'Why don't I help you instead?' I asked. I certainly didn't

want to be sitting on the one chair in the hall like the Queen Bee holding court while everyone else was sitting cross-legged at my feet on the floor.

'Are you sure?' Daler frowned. 'I didn't bring you here to work.'

'Of course. Find me a pinny, tell me what to do and I'm all yours.' I felt myself go pink – again. What a stupid thing to say: *I'm all yours*. What the hell was the matter with me? Dr Daler Dosanjh was obviously what was the matter with me. This was all new to me, I realised, as I washed my hands, covered my hair as instructed and tied a large pinafore over my cut-offs and T-shirt; and I didn't just mean being introduced to a Gurdwara soup kitchen. I spent the next half an hour serving a pile of chapatis, together with a dhal made from pulses, as well as a kind of creamy rice pudding.

Those who were regulars to the Gurdwara – both Sikh and otherwise – obviously knew Daler to be a doctor and I could hear him doling out advice and sympathy on a variety of ailments alongside the food. What a heavenly man, he was, I thought as I continually took surreptitious glances in his direction, taking in every aspect of him. Every now and again, he'd look my way too, our eyes would lock and we'd both grin a daft sort of smile at each other. Once everyone had been served, those who'd been cooking and helping piled their own plates with food and went to join the others sitting on the floor.

Even though I'd eaten absolutely nothing back at Daisy's place, I found I could only nibble at the delicious-tasting food Daler handed to me as we sat together near a group of youngish women who had come in from the street to eat.

'Aren't you hungry?' Daler asked, concerned. 'Are you not used to eating this type of food?'

'Oh no, no, I adore this sort of food,' I said truthfully, taking a too-big mouthful of the vegetarian curry to show I meant it and then, dry-mouthed at Daler's presence, his arm brushing against my own as he lifted his food to his mouth, found I was unable to swallow. This was ridiculous.

'They have so little,' I said, once I'd managed to persuade my throat to relax and get the food down in as polite a way as possible without disgracing myself. The curry was truly delicious and I continued to eat, looking over at the five women, all in Middle Eastern black despite the heat of the English summer.

'Midhope has a growing community of people from the Middle East, especially those fleeing from the nightmare that's Syria as well as Iran and Kurdistan,' Daler said. 'The town has people claiming asylum from various countries in North Africa as well, but particularly from Eritrea and the Sudan. They know they can come to the Gurdwara for a meal. Most don't take advantage by treating it as a daily, free, open restaurant and we've had offers of help to prepare and cook the meals in return, even though their religion and possibly their beliefs might be quite different.'

'I feel very guilty that I know so little,' I said, laying my plate to one side. 'I suppose I've had such a privileged upbringing I've taken it all for granted.'

'The thing is,' Daler went on, waving goodbye to the group of women as they left the hall, 'refugees and asylum seekers have often left their own country with hardly anything. They're also sometimes here illegally and very frightened of the law and what might eventually happen to them. They're afraid to register with a doctor, even if a practice will take them on, and many won't. So, I often come down, not to help with the food but to be here to give medical advice where I can. Sometimes I can't.' Daler looked round, frowning. 'There's often another doctor down here; I can't see him today. Really nice bloke. Syrian. Older than me. I don't ask, but I think he's possibly here illegally. He helps where he can and has a meal with us as well.'

'I feel *very* guilty now.'

'That's silly. Guilt is a totally useless emotion. I guess you and I are a couple of generations down the line.'

'Down the line?' I didn't know what Daler was getting at.

He smiled, stroking my bare arm, sending delicious tingles through my whole body. 'Well, I'm assuming your Italian family left Italy at some point to find a better life?'

'Sicily,' I corrected. 'And yes, they did. My Nonno Angelo came here in the early 1950s and started work in one of the woollen textile mills round here.'

'As did my great-grandfather.' Daler smiled, pleased at the connection. '*Dadi*, over there—' he indicated his grandmother whose beautiful pink sari, now she'd taken off her apron, stood out like a summer rose amongst the darker clothing of the women amongst whom she was holding court '—*her* father came here from the Punjab in Northern India when the British Government invited workers from the Commonwealth to help rebuild Britain after the war. Native Brits do have a tendency to forget that they were actually *invited*.'

'Nonno Angelo started worked at Dobson's Mill in the mid-1950s.' I didn't add that my mother, Suzy née Dobson, was one of the elite Dobson family herself, and that *her* mother, my Granny Dobson, had never got over – as quite probably neither had my mother herself – her daughter marrying Joe Piccione, son of Angelo Piccione, Sicilian immigrant and purveyor of Italian pickles, vinegars and preserves as well as being one of their former mill workers.

'Balveer, my great-grandfather, worked up at Goodners' mill,' Daler said. 'I don't think it even exists anymore. Anyway, he did a couple of years there, saved up as much money as he possibly could, borrowed some more from his family back in the Punjab, and started selling footwear on the markets all over West and South Yorkshire, but particularly at Midhope Monday Market and Barnsley Market.'

'Footwear? Really?'

'Hmm, sandals mainly. Anyway, eventually he set up his own factory over in Leeds making sandals…'

I stared. Something was ringing bells here. 'Dosanjhs?'

Daler nodded, torn between obvious pride and slight embarrassment.

'Dosanjhs?' I said again. 'Your great-grandfather invented *Dosanjhs*?' Everyone had at least one pair of these sandals; I reckon my mother had at least four or five pairs. They were so comfortable, so stylish, so, so British I suppose. They were as ubiquitous, as well-known a brand as Scholl's, Birkenstock; even Ugg. I stared at Daler. 'Blimey.'

Daler smiled. 'You see, most people who start with absolutely nothing will fight to get more if they're given a chance to do so. Give people a chance, share some of what you have…'

'Darling, are you going to bring Francesca back with

you?' Chuni Dosanjh, her long black hair now unpinned and hanging in a mass of shiny waves to her shoulders, was making preparations to leave.

'Frankie?' Daler turned to me and smiled, whispering in an undertone, 'I understand if it's all too much for you in one day.'

I shook my head. 'No really, I'd really like that.' I wouldn't have cared where we were headed as long as I could spend just a couple more hours with Daler.

All the way out to his parents' house, Daler drove with one hand on the steering wheel while holding my own with the other, (a good job the car was automatic) stroking my skin with his thumb until I was a bit of a squirming mess. Before we actually reached the house, Daler suddenly pulled into a lay-by and, with the engine still throbbing, turned to me, took my face in his hands and looked deep into my eyes before kissing me with such expertise, and so thoroughly, my hands went automatically up to his hair, my fingers threading through his black curls as I kissed him back.

'What have you done to me, Frankie Piccione?' He smiled down at me, put the car into gear once more and carried on down the lane.

Daler's mother was obviously inordinately proud of her newly built house. I call it a house when really it was a mansion, a country hotel, a palace almost. While its style and interior were not what I'd have chosen myself, being almost hedonistically over the top, I totally understood Chuni's pride in her estate.

The approach to the house was through huge, black, imposing wrought-iron gates, a seemingly never-ending driveway leading through woodland, mature trees and borders to a walled courtyard in which were set several fountains all merrily shooting water skywards (regardless of a threatened hosepipe ban after the long dry summer we'd just had), a stone gazebo and what can only be described as a ten-car showroom. If it hadn't been for the cars, I might have fancied having lost my way (as well as my century) in a Jane Austen novel.

'Welcome, welcome. Do come in, Frankie.' Chuni was already waiting, drink in hand, at the top of the flight of stone steps that led to the entrance (it was far too grand to simply call it a door). Taking my arm in hers, she ushered me down a corridor towards a splendidly gracious sitting room, Daler bringing up the rear.

Halfway down the marble-floored corridor, I stopped at an open door. 'Oh, wow.'

'Go on, Mum.' Daler grinned. 'You're dying to show it off. You've obviously left the door open on purpose; let Frankie see.'

'I'm not showing off. What an idea, you ridiculous boy.' Nevertheless, Chuni leading the way, we did a detour into the kitchen. Kitchen? It was the size of an aeroplane hangar. And, in my job, I came across plenty of those. Chuni could probably have served the Langar meal for half the town in there, had she a mind to. Equipped with every possible gadget and gizmo from the top-of-the-range coffee maker to not one, but two central islands connected by a highly polished bridge of blonde wood, it was kitchen paradise. Bloody hell, who had an actual *bridge* in their kitchen?

I exhaled slightly, as I began to realise I was stepping into a very different world here in the Dosanjh kitchen.

'Gosh, I bet 25 *Beautiful Kitchens* would like to get their hands on this,' I breathed.

'They already have.' Daler laughed.

'Well, it wasn't a *big* feature.' Chuni pouted.

'Mum.' Daler shook his head. 'It was a six-page spread.' He turned to me. 'And the daft thing is, Frankie, she doesn't even cook in it.'

Oh, just let *me* in there then. Let me get my hands rolling pastry on that cold black granite; mixing and liquidising in that Thermomix (my Thermomix envy had lately surpassed even my current coveting of a Rick Owens' leather jacket); pounding and leaving bread dough to prove near that shimmering bank of ovens.

'You don't cook, Chuni?' I finally asked, coming back down to earth as both Chuni and Daler smiled at my wide-eyed stance.

'Of course I cook.' Chuni gave a little laugh, batting her hand towards Daler, slightly aggrieved. 'You *must* come over, Frankie, to taste my rajma masala or bhuna gosht. I'm going to put you in my diary before you leave.'

'Right, OK.' I glanced round at Daler, primarily to see his reaction to his mother's organising of his social life – I assumed Daler was also to be in on the projected curry evening – but also to find out where, then, the actual food was cooked.

'Curry kitchen.' Daler smiled, anticipating my question and nodding his head towards a far door. 'Through there.'

'Oh, pish.' Chuni pouted once again. 'You're making out I run a curry takeaway through there, Daler. Naturally I cook in here as well, Francesca. It's just that turmeric can stain so badly.'

'Right.' I was saved from responding further by a man's voice at the door.

'Ah, you're here.'

'Dad, this is Francesca Piccione, a friend of mine.' Daler appeared slightly tense as he turned to face his father. 'Francesca, this is my father, Manraj.'

'A friend? Hello, Francesca, how nice to meet you.' Manraj Dosanjh held out a hand and shook mine briefly with an accompanying nod that was almost dismissive before turning to Daler and saying, 'Sienna has called several times, Daler. Apparently, she hasn't been able to get hold of you the last couple of days. Would you ring her, please, before you do anything else?'

12

Frankie

Then

The day after the barbecue and my meeting his parents, Daler was on duty in A and E from 6am. It being the August bank holiday Monday, Daisy and I were free to clear up the abandoned beer bottles, the ketchup-smeared paper plates and half-eaten sausages, boot out a couple of post-revelry hangers-on and, after a good hoover round and a dog walk with Malvolio, were able to indulge ourselves with another morning of sitting in Graham and Kate Maddison's garden drinking coffee and eating toast smothered in Piccione's Raspberry Jam in the glorious sunshine. In the afternoon I left Daisy looking after Malvolio and awaiting the return of her parents. I popped in to see both Dad and Tammy and then Nonno and Nonna (Mum and Paul, to my guiltily felt relief were away in Sardinia for several weeks) and then drove out to a pub near the hospital where I'd arranged to meet Daler.

The place was so jumping with bank holiday revellers,

determined to make the most of the day, I didn't even attempt to park the car but, instead, left a message for Daler to meet me five miles or so away out on the moors. It was glorious out there, away from the drinking, celebratory hordes, and I parked up, crossed the deserted road and sat at the edge of the moorland where Daler would be able to see me.

I lay on the springy purple heather, sunshine dancing on my closed eyelids, just breathing in the pure air and being totally ignored by the devil-eyed sheep to my right, munching grass like there was no tomorrow. (Maybe for them, there *was* no tomorrow except lamb chops and mint sauce, whereas for me, a whole new future including Daler was, I felt, just beckoning.) I couldn't bear the thought of returning to the asinine world of commercial package holidays and wondered what would happen if I didn't. Return that is. There'd always be *someone* to step into my navy courts, someone who still thought being an air stewardess was exciting, glamorous, the chance to see the world and meet new people.

During the last year or so, I'd seen very little of that world apart from the insides of city airports themselves. And the people I'd met, I didn't have time to get to know anyway.

I'd spent a good hour on my laptop that morning, scanning website after hospital website researching the best way – and the quickest – for me to start nurse training. The germ of an idea, started in A and E just a few days earlier, was never far from my mind; in fact I'd go so far as to say it was becoming a bit of an obsession as I scrolled, googled and wrangled with where I wanted to be and where I could train. Student nursing places in Liverpool, Newcastle and Somerset were all taken it seemed and I would have to wait at least a year for my application to be considered. I couldn't *wait* a year: I was so full of excitement for my new idea ('That's the trouble with you, Francesca,' my mother had said, always cutting, 'your enthusiasm for yet another new project has fizzled out before you even start'), I wanted to start next week, tomorrow, now...

'Were you asleep?' I jumped as a cool hand reached for my own.

'I think I was,' I admitted. 'I was dreaming of lamb chops... in scrubs.'

'Oh? Do you often dream about them?'

'No, not a bit.' I laughed, sitting up to point out the sheep but they'd obviously moved on and I began to giggle at the thought that Daler, a committed non-meat eater, must think I was a rampant carnivore, dreaming about lamb chops. I turned to look down at Daler who was now lying beside me, still holding my hand. 'Tired? Been a long day?'

Daler nodded and tightened the grip on my hand but kept his eyes closed, giving me the chance to study his beautiful face in detail. Mauve smudges of tiredness lay beneath his closed eyes but, apart from that, his entire face was unblemished milk chocolate, leaching into long curly hair and the beginnings of a beard and moustache the colour of ebony. He was devastatingly good-looking and yet didn't appear overly conscious of it. His full bottom lip, slightly darker than the top, was waiting only to be kissed and, as I bent slowly forward to do just that, he smiled and I saw he'd been watching me from under his lashes all along.

'That's cheating.' I smiled as our lips met, the very scent of him making my senses reel. I was totally consumed with this man in a way I'd never felt before.

'What is?'

'Watching as I'm looking at you. Peeping's not allowed.'

'I need to take every opportunity to drink you in,' he said seriously. 'I need to carry your picture in my head when you leave.'

'Will you come over to Liverpool?' I asked, kissing his cheekbones, feeling my lashes skim his smooth skin.

'Of course.'

'When?'

'As soon as I can. Frankie, I know I've only just met you…' Daler trailed off, seemingly unsure whether to continue.

'And?' I prompted.

'And I'm not one usually to get heavy, but…'

'But?'

'But I've never felt like this about anyone before. I feel as if you've turned my whole world upside down.' He laughed, embarrassed. 'If I'm not careful, I'm going to be writing poetry next.'

'Good.' I smiled. 'That's really, really good.'

But Daler didn't come over to our flat in Liverpool for over a week after that bank holiday Monday. We kept missing each other. I was either 35,000 feet up over Belgium, Tunisia or Ljubljana doing the whole arm-waving thing and smiling benignly through my over-glossed lips, or he was on call, carrying out extra shifts.

Or just not answering my calls.

Daisy and I had returned to the Liverpool flat and another hellishly long stretch of flying non-stop, it seemed at the time, to every damned capital and holiday destination across Europe and North Africa. Late August saw every last man and his dog grabbing holiday deals before the return of school and the rain and grey skies of autumn.

I'd so had enough of flying.

Over a week later, both Daler and I finally managed to coincide our days off and he drove down the M62 to the flat with a bottle of wine, a bunch of yellow roses and a pack of lamb chops. Not having seen him for so long, I'd built him up into an absolute sex god: in my imagination he was Dev Patel crossed with Imran Khan (Daler had said he was big into cricket) with just a smidgen of Gandhi (I didn't, in all honesty, go for little bald-headed chaps in round glasses – it was because of his vocation to help others) so that when he arrived and rang the doorbell I was aware I'd set myself up to be disappointed.

I wasn't.

He was everything I remembered, including the beanie hat pulled over his dark curls, the smooth, unblemished skin, the well-muscled, quite heavenly body I could make out under the white T-shirt and scuffed black leather jacket. God, I thought as I led him into the kitchen, where Daisy was eating a late breakfast, he must have every nurse twitching to abandon her bed-making corners and tumble him into it.

'Yes, it's all OK.' Daisy grinned in my direction through a mouthful of cornflakes. 'He's even better than we remembered.'

I threw an abandoned pair of rolled-up socks in her

general direction and, grabbing my jacket, ushered Daler back out of the door and down onto the street to find breakfast.

'Right,' Daler said seriously, once we had huge mugs of steaming cappuccino and a pile of almond croissants in front of us, 'before we go any further, you need to make a phone call.'

'To whom?' I frowned in his direction.

'Sarah Vickers…' Daler had his phone out and was scrolling through.

'Who's Sarah Vickers?'

'She co-ordinates student nursing at Midhope General… Right, here you go. I've sent the contact details over.'

I felt my pulse race. 'What do you mean? Is this for *next* September?' The very thought of another year trundling my duty-free trolley down too-tight aisles was filling me with dread, but I'd known, in all reality, I had few options.

'No, for *this*. If you really want this, Frankie, then Sarah is prepared to have a chat with you. I've told her all about you. Apparently, there's a couple of places on the course at Midhope university because two people have pulled out. You've got a degree…'

'Yes, but in business studies. And—' I frowned '—not a particularly good one.'

'Doesn't matter. You've got the required maths and English as well as all the sciences at GCSE and you've got biology at A level. It's just whether you really want to take on the huge commitment of starting at the bottom all over again? Whether you want to come back to Midhope?'

I looked up and met Daler's watchful stare. 'Do *you* want me to?'

'Come back and be near me? Come back where I can see you all the time? I think that's pretty obvious, isn't it, with all this planning and conniving I've been doing on your behalf?' Daler took my hand over the plate of croissants, unintentionally transferring a smattering of icing sugar onto my wrist as he did so. He lifted it to his lips, removing the stickiness with his beautiful mouth, his huge dark eyes never once leaving my own. All I could think, as my insides lurched crazily, was what beautiful, brown-eyed babies, with their cappuccino-coloured skin, Daler and I would have between us. 'I know it's absolutely ridiculous, Frankie,' he finally said, 'you know when I've known you only such a short time and…' He replaced my hand, just when I thought I'd no other option but to rush him back to the flat and tumble him into bed. 'I don't mean to get heavy, but what do you think?'

I nodded in delight. Daler had done all this for me. For us.

'OK, eat up, go and ring Sarah – she's expecting your call – and then, Frankie, I'm sorry, but if I don't make love to you, I'll be forced to eat those lamb chops instead and that won't put me in the good books of Guru Nanak. Or my mother.'

I made the phone call, speaking for a good twenty minutes to a rather scary-sounding Sarah Vickers who tried every which way to put me off starting a nursing career. I realised later, when I actually met her, this was her way of finding out if I was really committed to the long haul ahead or was it that I was simply starry-eyed after meeting Daler? Was I merely imagining myself in the leading role as a nurse in nothing more than an old-fashioned Mills and

Boon (Medical) novel? I arranged an appointment both with her and the woman in charge of nursing studies at the university for the following Wednesday.

So that's how I started my new career as a student nurse just three weeks later. It was all done so quickly, and yet so smoothly, as if it had been part of my game plan for years. I went from being an air stewardess living in Liverpool with a decent enough salary, to being a penniless student once again and living at home, in the granny flat next door to Dad, Tammy, Matteo and Angel. Daisy hadn't been too happy that I'd abandoned her to her *fate above the clouds in troubled skies* as she so eloquently put it, as though she were Douglas Bader himself. And, although my line manager had a bit of a hissy fit, accusing me of leaving *him* in the lurch as though I'd personally thrown him out of the cockpit over Torremolinos without a parachute, it wasn't really a problem as the main holiday season was coming to an end and the airline was about to cut staff numbers anyway.

But none of that mattered: Daisy found a new flatmate within days and was talking to me once more; Dad and Nonno were happy to have me home and involved with something worthwhile and I got stuck into my studies, which I found fascinating after the dry content of statistics and business law I'd had to wade through when studying my first degree at Northumbria. But best of all, I was seeing Daler almost daily.

My *Daily Dose of Daler*. I would grin, flinging my arms

around him as he let himself, utterly exhausted, into the granny flat after twelve hours on the wards.

'Did you know,' I would offer, as he stretched his tall – utterly beautiful – body along the sofa, often too tired, initially, to do anything more strenuous than drink the ice-cold beer I kept in the fridge for him, 'your eyeballs are actually part of your brain?'

'No, really?' he'd say, his warm hands starting to explore the sensitive skin under my sweater.

'And that your heart circulates blood through your body one thousand times a day?'

'Well, fancy that,' he'd say, his eyes seemingly wide with amazement as his fingers concentrated on unhooking my bra at the back.

'Or, that the most flexible muscle in your body is…?'

'This one?' he'd ask, looking down at himself in fake surprise.

'I think you'll find, Doctor,' I said loftily, 'that a penis isn't a muscle. Mind you, I'm not sure *what* it is…'

And that would be it: supper, if it were suppertime, left to go cold; breakfast, if it were that time of the day, abandoned on the kitchen table. I was addicted to Dr Daler Dosanjh.

Totally, utterly and beyond redemption, addicted.

My family welcomed Daler with open arms. Even my mother who, let's face it, particularly after being married to Paul Stockwell for the last fifteen years or so, was not known for her ability to embrace multiculturalism, could see the advantages of my hooking up with the gorgeous doctor. Especially one from such a wealthy and well-known family as the Dosanjhs.

Not so my maternal grandmother.

'But, Francesca, dear, he's you know...'

'Gorgeous?'

'You know...'

'Exceptionally bright...'

Granny Dobson tutted. 'Now you're being evasive. Bad enough when your mother brought home that little *Eyetie...*'

'Granny, do you mind, that's my dad you're talking about. I do sometimes think you forget *I'm* a Piccione as well.'

'Oh, don't be so silly, Francesca. You're as British as I am. Now, as I was saying, this new boyfriend of yours, he isn't a *foreigner*, is he?' Granny Dobson lowered her voice and it was obvious she'd been watching reruns of *Downton Abbey*.

'Oh, for heaven's sake, I'm not having this conversation with you, Granny.' But I was. 'Daler is as British as you are...'

'Oh, have I got the wrong one?' She appeared to breathe a sigh of relief. '*Not* the one you're always apparently wrapped around? The doctor chappie?'

'Yes,' I said crossly. 'The doctor *chappie* – Dr Daler Dosanjh – he's as British as you are.'

'Oh, I don't *think* so, dear. So it's serious, is it, between the two of you? You're not going to have to wear one of those black post-box things over your head...'

'Right, that's it.' I was livid. 'I really am *not* having this conversation with you until you learn some manners. You're an irascible, racist old woman and when you apologise for your disgraceful show of misguided, outdated, utter *rubbish*, then I'll consider coming over to visit you again. And,' I added, determined to have the last word, 'he is utterly lovely.'

'Well,' she sniffed, just as determined *not* to let me have it, 'at least your children will never be short of sandals.'

The reaction of Granny Dobson to Daler was the direct antithesis to that of Aunty Pam.

'Is this him, Frankie?' Pam almost fell off her chair when I took Daler round to her place. 'You are *gorgeous*.' She beamed, grabbing him in a bear hug and almost squeezing the life out of him. 'Goodness me, you really are.'

The pair of them became huge friends, discussing all manner of political and social issues as well as their shared love of soul music. And once I started my first block of work experience on the wards at Midhope General and found myself on evening shift, it wasn't unknown for Daler to call round at Pam's where I would meet him later.

Daler was still living in the palace that was his parents' place. He had his own set of rooms in one wing of the house, but he preferred to stay in my little flat with me whenever he could. Chuni insisted on my joining the family to eat with them at least once a week. Daler's sister, Juneeta, was between university and actually finding a job that would interest her, but appeared to spend her days either with Chuni, adding to their extensive – and expensive – range of handbags and shoes or driving over to Leeds or Manchester for lunch with her coterie of friends who seemed to be all trained lawyers, medics or pharmacists, or flying off to London and even Dubai to attend yet another family wedding.

And it was at one of these family weddings that I first had an insight as to my position in the Dosanjh family.

13

Pam

Then
August 1974

Pam didn't want to go in to work the Monday morning after that weekend, mortification rising like cream on milk every time she remembered the events of Saturday night in which she'd been a willing participant in the dark shadows of that little dell behind Greenstreet Park.

Waiting in the rain for the 8.11am bus to Piccione's with her usual fellow passengers, Pam found herself hiding her face under Janet's insubstantial old pink Barbie umbrella – the only one she could find once she'd opened the back door and realised it was raining – and actually physically shaking her head as she tried desperately to obliterate pictures of herself in Marco's car.

Were Mr Ellis in Sales and Jean Thompson in Marketing, who'd both just joined the bus queue, looking at her strangely? Had word somehow got out? Would Miss Bryan in Personnel demand to see her before giving a warning about lewd (her mother's favourite word) behaviour with Mr Piccione's elder son? Could she even be asked to leave?

Piccione's was a family firm with strong Catholic values and there was no place for little slappers like her who'd thrown the honour of being crowned Miss Piccione 1974 right back in Mr Angelo's face by abusing (her mum liked this one too, but Pam wasn't totally convinced she herself was using it in the right context on this occasion) those strict religious and family merits. If Personnel thought she was no longer fit to walk the newly carpeted office floors upstairs, would she be banished down to Pickles with several of the girls from 5D at Westenbury Secondary Modern who'd joined their mums and grannies – their whole family in the case of Sheila Ackroyd – on the production line. And this time tomorrow would she be donning the green overalls and ridiculous shower cap before coming home stinking of vinegar? Her mother would have a fit.

The red double-decker arrived in a squeal of brakes and diesel fumes, splashing dirty water from the road onto Pamela's brand-new pair of pale-coloured tights. She shook her leg crossly, and then did the same with the tiny plastic umbrella before taking an unoccupied double seat near the back, hoping no one would join her so she could relive in peace the momentous occasion of Rob Mansell's unexpected turning up at the house yesterday.

But, to Pam's relief, nothing appeared too different from the usual run-of-the-mill Mondays apart from one of the silver-foil *Miss Piccione 1974* balloons someone had already tied to her chair waving a friendly welcome as she moved, embarrassed, over to her desk. She quickly filed what was left over from Friday (when, Pam mused, she was a different girl, a total innocent unaware of how very quickly she was about to throw overboard her most precious commodity as she sailed blithely off into the night with Marco Piccione) and made coffee for her boss, Mr Pickersgill. When a whole load of new invoices was dumped on her desk, she set to and quickly filed most before being asked to cover on Reception for an hour after Dorothy Saunders, the elder of the two receptionists, bit down too enthusiastically on a Piccione Cantucci, cracking her dental bridge and being given time out for an emergency appointment at the dentist down the road.

Just before the dinner break, Mr Pickersgill suggested Pam might like to come into his office in order to practise some of her newly acquired shorthand skills.

'Oh, but I haven't started yet,' Pam protested. 'My day release doesn't start until the middle of September when tech goes back.'

'Oh.' Trevor Pickersgill appeared slightly put out. 'Well, I tell you what, Pammy, (Pammy?) grab one of the shorthand pads, and I'll dictate a letter. I'll go slowly so you can get it all down in longhand and then you can have a go on Kathleen's typewriter. It's sitting there doing nothing while she's on holiday and it will be good practice for you.' He'd smiled wolfishly, glanced down at Pam's long legs in their pale tights and disappeared into his office.

Feeling foolish, Pam had left the filing, found a brand-new shorthand pad (Kathleen Tucker would be furious, Pam knew, if she could see her furtling around in the older woman's desk drawer from her deckchair on the beach at Bridlington) and followed him in.

'Close the door, Pammy. So,' Mr Pickersgill said slowly as, pencil at the ready and head down, Pam prepared to write, 'just be careful with Marco Piccione.'

Pam had already written down the words in her neat handwriting before she realised Mr Pickersgill wasn't dictating an actual letter, but issuing a warning. Her head shot up, her face scarlet.

'Pretty girl like you, Pam. Got a bit of reputation has our young Mr Piccione. I'd be very careful before you get in that car of his on your night out with him.' Trevor Pickersgill's porcine eyes slid from her own down to her breasts in their white and blue striped cotton shirt, and Pam had the horrible sensation he could see beyond the fabric to her sensible M&S bra. He stood up, apparently forgetting he was supposed to be dictating a letter, and moved behind her, planting a moist hand on her shoulder, his fingers actually coming to rest on the swell of her right breast, his halitosis nearly knocking her sideways as he leaned in, breathing heavily through his mouth.

'I have a lot of filing to get on with.' Pam jumped up hurriedly, knocking his hand off as she swivelled back in the chair and made a hasty retreat to the safety of the outer office. 'Mrs Bennet will be after me if it's not done before dinnertime.'

More angry than upset at Trevor Pickersgill's success at getting his sweaty hands on her – she had been warned by several of the other young office girls not to be left alone with Pervy Pickersgill in his office – Pam was now in fighting mood to take on Maureen Cooper in the canteen.

She found Maureen sitting with a group of her cronies from the typing pool, Tupperware box open in front of her from which she was just about to lift one half of a sandwich, its interior of Day-Glo pink ham pulsating a sharp contrast with the flabby white sliced bread it cushioned.

'Can I have a word, Maureen?'

'A word?' Maureen asked, but nevertheless making any further response on her part at least less viable as she bit deeply into the sandwich.

'Hmm.'

'Have a seat, sit down.' Maureen finally managed to nod before reaching for her cardboard carton of thick greasy chips – a Piccione canteen speciality – and waving a hand at the already occupied chairs. 'Go and grab another chair.'

'I just want a word, Maureen, I don't particularly want to eat with you.'

That stopped Maureen in her tracks, but only temporarily. 'Oh, too good for us now you're Miss Piccione?' Maureen sneered through a mouthful of fried potato.

'I've already got a seat with Jane over there,' Pam said patiently, although standing up to Maureen Cooper, surrounded by her mates, was making her heart pound.

'What's up?' Maureen asked, swallowing and standing. She indicated with a nod of her head towards the entrance, picked up her can of Fanta and, swigging from the can as she walked, led the way out.

'What did you put in my drink?' Pam asked, turning to face Maureen.

'Drink? You don't have a drink.'

Pam tutted. 'On Saturday night. At the RAFA club.'

'Don't know what you're talking about.' Maureen affected nonchalance.

'Yes, you do,' Pam said crossly. 'I know exactly what you put in my champagne.'

'Ooh la-di-da, champagne, listen to you. If you know exactly what I put in your drink, why are you asking then?'

She had a point there, Pam conceded. 'Listen, you do anything like that again, and I'll have the police on you. Tell them you do drugs.'

Maureen actually laughed at that. 'Oh, grow up, you daft cow. Don't come all high and mighty with me just because you're off out with Marco Piccione…' She trailed off as the man himself, accompanied by his father, walked towards them and the main entrance to Reception.

'Ah, *Miss Piccione* 1974,' Angelo called over, beckoning. (She was, Pam realised, already getting sick to death of the damned handle.) 'A word, a word, *cara*…'

Pam gave Maureen one last glare, reciprocated three-fold by the other girl and, feeling her face flush at the sight of Marco as he stood silently waiting at his father's side, walked over to meet them.

'Now then, Pamela, table is booked and waiting for you on Wednesday night. That alright with you, *cara*? Marco pick you up seven o'clock?'

Marco hadn't said one word during his father's greeting and Pam found she couldn't even look across at him, never mind meet his eye. Thank goodness it hadn't been arranged for Friday, her birthday and date with Rob. She'd get this damned silly prize dinner with Marco over and done with on Wednesday and be able to look forward to the proper prize with Rob on Friday.

'That will be lovely, thank you.' Her mother's mantra on good manners ensured politeness. What the hell she and Marco were going to talk about for three hours over pizza she couldn't imagine, but she'd get through it.

Marco gave her a wintry smile and, without one word spoken, walked ahead of his father to the main entrance.

'Let's have a look at you, Pamela.' Mary Brown cast a critical eye over Pam's flared trousers. 'Do you think you should be wearing those? Wouldn't a nice skirt be more appropriate for a restaurant?'

'These are fine, Mum. Really.' No way was she letting Marco Piccione have another look at her legs.

'I'll go, I'll let him in.' Mary dashed off in high excitement down the hallway as the doorbell sounded and Dennis Brown grinned, tutting and exchanging a sympathetic look with Pam.

Marco looked quite different out of the black dinner jacket of the previous Saturday as well as his usual black suit, shirt and tie he wore when he was at work and Pam, understanding just how Mary Brown's mind worked, knew her mother would feel somewhat let down at Marco's appearing on their doorstep in jeans and a casual shirt. Mind you, they were smart, expensive-looking jeans and the lack of collar and tie was, Pam could gauge, almost forgiven on Mary's part by the addition of an obviously expensive navy jacket.

'Do come in, Marco,' Mary was saying. 'Would you like a drink while you're waiting?'

'No need, Mum, I'm here,' Pam shouted down the hall. She shoved a hovering and grinning Janet out of the way – desperate to actually set eyes on the man himself rather than his bunch of flowers – kissed her father goodbye, picked up her bag and, smiling at Marco, who was about to step over the entrance, said, 'Shall we go?'

Pam felt her pulse race a little as Marco held open the

passenger door for her and she slid into the seat in which she'd lost her head and her virginity (there she'd said it, albeit to herself) only four days earlier, but she thanked him politely, sat bolt upright with her trousered legs held demurely together while he turned the car and shot off quickly in the direction of Midhope town centre.

Bennani's was one of the new Italian restaurants springing up seemingly all over the town. There'd always been a number of Italian as well as Greek-run coffee bars in town – The Alassio, The El Greco, The Acropolis – but these had now expanded into proper pizza and pasta places with their mandatory wooden floors, tiled tables, oversized pepper grinders, as well as Italian flags and scenes hanging on every wall and the heady garlic overload Pam felt she could cut with a knife.

Marco appeared to be on first-name terms with all the smiling, confident waiters, greeting their smouldering brown eyes, abundant black hair and dazzling white teeth with a Latin-type hug and kisses rarely seen – actually, *never* seen, Pam amended – between two Yorkshiremen. She'd never seen her dad hug another man, all forms of male introduction carried out with a quick manly handshake, the symbolic *pint?* gesture of the right hand or simply a brusque nod accompanied by the recipient's name: 'Eric/ Fred/ Jack.'

And the Italian waitresses: oh, but they were beautiful. Pam gazed in wonder as Marco kissed each of the dark-eyed beauties in turn, conversing in fluent Italian with each one, sharing a joke and making them laugh. Feeling pale and uninteresting in comparison, Pam began to see why Marco might feel resentful at being forced out with her when he could obviously tumble any one of these gorgeous creatures into his bed with just one click of his fingers.

She felt gauche and provincial especially when the menu arrived in front of her and she didn't understand one word on it. She'd loved French at school, had been able to converse at length with Mr Bradbury, the French teacher, but this menu was beyond her. *Pollo?* Was that like the French *le poulet* for chicken? She was on safe grounds with chicken. But what the hell was *primi piatti di mare* or *penne allo scoglio?*

Pam glanced up to see Marco watching her intently and with some amusement. She flushed, wishing she could get the evening over and done with and be back at home in bed reading *The Rainbow* which, she'd just discovered, was the prequel to *Women in Love* and which she'd taken to reading in the canteen at work if Jane wasn't there. She was finding it totally absorbing. Lawrence would, she reckoned, have understood her *swooning* the other night in Marco's car, although he might have frowned at the Quaalude that had encouraged it.

'Turn over,' Marco commanded.

'I beg your pardon?' Pam stared, unable to dispel all images of her having sex with this man.

'The English menu. It's over the page.'

'Oh right. Lovely.' Embarrassed, Pam did just that but, not knowing her *tagliatelle* from her *linguine*, *tortellini* or *pappardelle* and with a very lovely waiter hovering somewhat impatiently at her side, she quickly ordered the chicken and closed the menu.

'Would you like me to order for you?' Marco asked. 'It

can be a bit confusing at first, you know, all the different pastas and courses.'

'OK, thank you.'

Marco spoke in rapid Italian, pointing with an olive-skinned rather stubby finger to various things on the menu and then, once he'd left, sat back and looked at Pam but said nothing.

'Look,' Pam eventually said, blushing furiously. 'There's something I have to say, something you need to know... the other night... in your car...?'

'I'm sorry...'

'You're sorry?'

'Hmm, you'd obviously had too much to drink...'

'I hadn't actually...' Pam took a deep breath. 'Someone had slipped a drug into my drink.'

'Drugs?' Marco appeared shocked. 'You don't think it was me, do you? I promise you, I...'

'No, no, no, I know it wasn't you,' Pam assured him. 'I didn't realise it at the time, didn't know why I was behaving like I did. I know exactly who it was. I just need you to know that I would never have... you know... if I hadn't been slipped something.'

'OK, right.'

'Marco, I'm horribly embarrassed about the whole thing. I'm just asking you to please not tell anyone, particularly at work, what I did.'

'What *we* did.' Marco smiled. 'I don't think it would show me in a particularly good light either, do you, if it came out that I'd taken advantage of you like that?'

'Well you *did*, didn't you? You know, *take advantage* of me.' Pam lowered her voice as an elderly couple looked across in her direction. 'You *did*,' she insisted for good measure.

'I'll be honest with you, Pam, I just thought you were, you know, *desperate* for it.' Marco raised an eyebrow and Pam felt a sudden creeping anger begin at her toes and work its way upwards until it became almost a physical pain in her chest and she had to stand in order to remove it.

She shoved back her chair, almost stumbling as her foot caught in the strap of her shoulder bag and the hovering waiter raised his hands (overly dramatically, Pam would later recall) and actually *jumped* out of her way. She pinballed off a couple of tables and another two Italian waiters (hell, they were lurking everywhere) in her desperate search for the loo and eventually saw the signs: *Signori* and *Signore* towards the back of the restaurant. Luckily these were both accompanied by the universally understood images of a man and woman and she pushed open the door of the second and stood at the mirror, examining her flushed face as she held her wrists under the running cold water.

'*Desperate* for it?' she snarled at her reflection. '*Desperate* for it?' she snapped once more before drying her hands and running one through her blonde bob. She was going home. If she hadn't left her bag, with its contents sprawled under the table, she'd have walked out, found a taxi and gone straight away. Except, Pam thought, as her face began to regain its usual colour, her mum would want to know what had happened and, to be fair, she *had* wanted it. She *had* been more than a willing partner in what she'd allowed Marco to do.

I was drugged, she argued with her reflection, *drugged*,

and, holding her head high, she exited the restroom and walked as calmly as she could back to their table.

'Marco, I most certainly was not *desperate* for it,' Pam said through gritted teeth as he stood and she sat once more. 'I have never, ever done *anything* like that with anyone before. It was a total and utter mistake on my part and you *did* take advantage of me, whatever you might think. Now, for your father's sake…' she paused '…and my mother's sake (Pam thought that sounded very grown up) could we just get on with this meal, then you can take me home and we need never see each other again?'

Marco nodded. 'Except at work of course.'

'Sorry?'

'I'll see you at work.'

'Well yes, of course.'

'I *am* really sorry, Pam. That was a crass and vulgar thing to say just now…'

Pam nodded. While she wasn't quite sure of the meaning of crass, *vulgar* was another of Mary Brown's favourite words, rolled out with an accompanying pained expression on a fairly regular basis when her dad broke wind or Sybil next door showed too much of her well-endowed chest.

'My father will be very disappointed. He's taken quite a shine to you.'

'As has my mother to you.'

Marco grinned across at Pam and moved the glass of Coke in her direction. 'Friends?' he asked.

'Suppose so,' Pam conceded, glancing at the huge clock on the wall opposite. She turned back to Marco who was still smiling, his dark eyes softened with amusement. He was quite good-looking really, she thought. If a little small. Well, very small, really. She could get through this evening and they could be friends. 'So, what's this?' she asked, poking with her fork at the mound of pasta placed in front of her and lifting it tentatively to her mouth. 'Wow,' she added, before Marco replied. 'This is *heavenly*.'

PART 2

14

Frankie

The Saturday before I started my new job working at Piccione's, Dad had come up trumps, giving me a lift, very early, down to the station and, handing over his credit card, telling me to treat myself in Manchester. When I'd protested, arguing that I was no longer his little girl and no way was I about to rely on him for handouts, he'd tutted loudly, hugged me fiercely and said I would always be his little girl. If I was so concerned at feeling beholden to him, he reminded me I had two years of birthdays and Christmas owing to me while I'd been away. I was sure he'd sent me a cheque on a couple of these celebrations, but he said he was sure he hadn't and, if he had, well then, fair play to me, I'd come out on top.

To be honest, he wasn't quite as chipper when, just before I got out of the car, I told him about the possibility of my moving into Daisy's cottage down at Holly Close Farm.

'What do you want to do that for when you can live rent

free in the granny flat with Tam and me?' He was really put out. 'You can eat with us whenever you want as well; you need fattening up a bit and you know what a good cook Tammy is.' He paused, patting his own stomach somewhat ruefully. 'I must get down to the gym more often,' he said, almost to himself before adding gleefully, 'I see that stepfather of yours has put on a bit of weight too. I hear the fool thinks he can come back as MP as well. *Whoever* it is standing against the pillock – could be Genghis Khan for all I care – he's got my vote. Now, don't make any decisions yet about where you're going to live; leave it a couple of weeks...' He shut up when I began to laugh. 'Alright, alright, I know, I know,' Dad sighed and patted my arm briefly. 'Tam keeps telling me to give you some space. It's just, you know, you were so beside yourself when you and Daler... you know, last time...' He trailed off not quite sure how to handle what he was saying. 'I threw away all my bloody Dosanjh sandals, you know,' he said fiercely, 'even though they were the best things for my plantar fasciitis. The thing is, Frankie, now you're back, we don't want you running off again.'

I kissed his cheek. 'Dad, you can't protect me from life. Life happens. It won't happen any the less by my living with you rather than Daisy, you know.'

'Yes, but I can be *there* for you, Frankie.'

'Dad, I'm going to see you every day at work, and Daisy's place is only a fifteen-minute drive away. Anyway, I've not decided I *am* living there yet. I'm going to go over with Daisy tomorrow and see what I think.'

'Do you want me to come with you, love? You know,

check it out: sort out what rent and bills you'll be paying. Make sure you'll be safe there?'

'Dad, stop it. I'm nearly thirty.'

'Are you really? Goodness. To me you're still my little girl in your white ankle socks and red sandals, falling off your bike; crying when your mum left...' His face darkened for a moment. 'Right, go on or you'll miss your train. Buy yourself what you want. And merry Christmas!' I laughed at that, jumped out of the car and ran for the train.

I'd not actually planned on doing anything with my hair but, apart from Aunt Rosina taking her huge kitchen scissors to my one plait every couple of months or so while I was in Sicily, I'd done nothing else to it and I suddenly decided I'd had enough. Mum's scornful – and, I felt, unnecessarily unpleasant – comment at my being an ageing hippy had hit home. I wanted some of the horribly expensive shampoo and conditioner I'd always bought from my hairdresser in Liverpool and as I walked down towards King Street in the city centre, I popped into one of the upmarket salons to buy some.

'You haven't any spare appointments, have you?' I asked the pink-haired receptionist who was simultaneously chewing on some sort of granola bar and taking my money for the shampoo. I suddenly longed for a good haircut.

'Spare appointment?' She laughed with some derision. 'On a Saturday morning? In the middle of Manchester? You need to book at least a month ahead. Who's your stylist here?'

'No, no, I've never been before. Just asking, you know, on the off-chance...'

'Off-chance?' More derision. 'Sorry we don't *do* off...'

'I can do you,' a voice interrupted Pink-Head from its owner's reflection in a mirror behind me. 'My lady's just called to say she can't make it. Prolapse problem again, I think,' he added, somewhat unnecessarily.

'Well, she didn't let *me* know,' Pink-Head retorted. 'Anyway, there's a whole *queue* of customers just waiting by their phones in case of a no-show.'

'Well they're not here now, ready to go, are they?' The stylist frowned. 'First come, first served. We could have you done while *she's* ringing round.' There was obviously no love lost between the two of them.

I nodded in agreement.

'Come on, sit down. Let's take this plait out; tell me what you're thinking.'

'I'm thinking I don't want to look like an ageing hippy.' I smiled. 'I've not been to a hairdresser for over two years.'

He didn't flinch dramatically as was my expectation – and probably his right – but instead ran his hands through my past-shoulder-length dark hair, lifting, twisting and pulling with such intensity – almost passion – I wanted to laugh. What was that poem about the *Rape of the Lock*?

'It's only hair.' I smiled again as he finally let go of my tresses and twisted me round in the chair to face him.

'No such thing as *only hair*,' he said crossly. 'Right, there's far too much of it: it's pulling your entire face down and hiding your best features. We need a whole load off, quite a bit of layering and some rich red and copper lowlights running through the lot of it.'

'Sounds expensive and time-consuming,' I said nervously, my eyes meeting his in the mirror.

'Both.' He nodded, reaching for a black plastic protective shawl before tying it decisively round my shoulders. 'But I tell you, absolutely worth it.'

Oh, and it was. Sid coloured, cut, layered and blow-dried my hair with equal measures of interest, determination and expertise, hardly speaking as he transformed my long, straight hair into a work of art. 'Right, stand up,' he finally ordered. 'Pull your hands through your hair, bend over and give it a shake. I want it to look natural; I want you to be able to handle it yourself. It needs to flow. No stiff helmets here…' I wanted to laugh at that '…Jesus, although I say it myself, that is wonderful. Now, for whatever reason you've been hiding yourself behind this curtain of hair, let it go. Let it go.' He was beginning to sound like something off *Frozen*. 'Just let it go and start again.' Sid gave my hair one last rake with his fingers and stood back to admire his handiwork.

'What are you?' I smiled, but felt tears threaten. 'An amateur psychologist?'

'Psychotherapist, probably, in this job,' Sid said seriously. 'New clothes now?'

I nodded as I handed over Dad's credit card, wincing slightly as I saw the amount ring up. Several Christmases this, I reckoned, as I headed for the door, a coffee and almond biscotti and then, the shops.

'Hang on, stop right there.' Daisy held up a hand, shook her head and then closed the front door of her cottage on me again.

'Daisy!'

'Not today, thank you,' Daisy shouted from behind the closed front door. 'The room's already let to my mate, Frankie. I don't know who *you* are or how you know there's a room to rent but…'

'For feck's sake, you daft bint, stop messing around and let me in.'

Daisy opened the door and sighed. 'Oh God, I'd forgotten how gorgeous you can look once you've scrubbed up. How am I supposed to compete with this now? The neighbours will be flocking in droves, wanting to come and look at you and take you out; I'm not going to get a look-in. Or a minute's peace.'

Daisy sat on the wall that divided the pair of semi-detached cottages she and her sister Charlie had inherited from their great-grandmother, Madge, looking ridiculously morose.

'Daisy, I hate to tell you this, but there *aren't* any neighbours.' This was the most beautiful spot on God's planet and, as I breathed in the chilly Yorkshire air, closing my eyes against the weak sunshine, I knew for certain that I wanted to live here with Daisy. The actual farmhouse, Holly Close Farm, which had belonged to Madge together with the cottages, had been given over to the Maddison sisters for its development just as I'd packed my bags and run away to Thailand. I think, if the opportunity hadn't arisen for Daisy to work with her architect sister, Charlie, on the project, then once Daisy had finally given up working as an air stewardess – she continued to do so for a few months once I'd started my nurse training – she might have travelled to the Far East with me. Instead, she stayed here in Yorkshire, working with Charlie and living, slightly nomadically it appeared, at either or all of her parents' house, her great-grandmother Madge's bungalow, and with Matis Miniauskiene, whom I'd never met, but who had been one of the Lithuanian builders working on the development with whom Daisy had had quite a thing; before, not really knowing what else to do, she'd set off back on her own travels, returning to Australia and New Zealand.

'Oh, Daisy.' I was actually lost for words.

'You've not seen it yet.' Daisy smiled, affecting nonchalance but obviously desperate to show me around. 'Inside or out first?'

'In. Just lead me to my bedroom.'

'Don't make any decisions until I take you round. I'm not going to force your hand, Frankie. The decision has to be yours...' She paused and said seriously, 'But if you turn me down, I'm going to have to kill you.'

We went through the hallway, Daisy acting as estate agent, pointing out each room: 'Downstairs loo, sitting room, kitchen.'

'Oh, my God, Daisy, the kitchen, the *kitchen*.' I stood in awe, simply taking in every aspect of the light, airy extension Charlie Maddison had so cleverly and professionally added to the cottage's original footprint. Long, bifold doors (similar ones, at Mum's place, overlooking the next modern monstrosity on the estate, reminded me of being imprisoned in some sort of dystopian watchtower) led out onto a kitchen garden already, thanks to Daisy's diligence, alive with the start of the new season's pots of rosemary, sage, thyme and mint and then onto the amazing view beyond.

I was already imagining myself baking the *focaccia al rosmarino* and the *cassata alla siciliana* as well as the *crema al limone* to which I'd become addicted and which had been raised and pinpointed as a possible start to my new career in marketing and development at Piccione's.

'Charlie's cottage is identical,' Daisy said proudly.

'I can't believe that the pair of you actually own these and yet neither of you have ever lived here.'

'Circumstances: men, relationships, travel, money. You know how it is.'

I did.

'You can have almost free access to the kitchen, Frankie,' Daisy said persuasively. 'Just give me the microwave to heat up my dinner-for-ones.'

'Burgers?'

'Not had one burger pass my lips since the night of my appendectomy.' Daisy shuddered.

'Wind.'

'Terminal food poisoning.'

We both laughed at the memory. It seemed such a long time ago; so much water under the bridge since that morning in Midhope General A and E.

'Come on,' Daisy said knowingly, taking my arm to stop me remembering. 'Come and see your bedroom.'

'OK,' I said, as I walked into the south-facing bedroom that would be mine, a room so light and airy one could almost feel it rising like a Victoria sponge, 'you don't have to sell it to me anymore. I'm sold.'

'Yes, but you haven't seen *this* yet.' Daisy smiled in excitement, opening one of the doors to the right of the window.

'Oh. Oh.' I gasped.

'Good God.' Daisy grinned. 'Is that how you orgasm these days...?'

'No idea, it's been a long time...'

'Because if it is, I'm going to have to get the police.'

'The police?'

'You know, to tell you to come quietly.'

'Sorry?' I wasn't listening to a word Daisy was saying as I gazed in wonder at the clever architectural planning Charlie Maddison had come up with in order to go from the bedroom straight into a walk-in wardrobe. This wasn't just a wardrobe; the tiny, fitted walk-in cupboard trumpeted by the salesman of a newly designed, modern house as the ultimate in upmarket storage. This was wardrobe *heaven*; St Peter himself couldn't have such a space for his robes and keys.

'Charlie could easily have gone for three bedrooms for each cottage,' Daisy was saying at my side, 'and she's so clever. This lot can actually be removed fairly easily and we can – if we ever do sell – sell them as such. But we'd both always dreamed of an actual walk-in wardrobe for ourselves. When other kids at school were drooling over photos of Orlando Bloom and Brad Pitt, we had pages ripped out of *House Beautiful* showing wardrobe space...' she broke off, laughing '...before fantasising about Orlando Bloom, in his undercrackers, choosing a shirt from one of many on the rails.'

With meticulous, if not miraculous, attention to detail, Daisy's sister had created stylish storage for each of the two bedrooms in both cottages. Double hanging rails, slide-out shoeboxes and shelving towers in a beautiful soft-blonde wood stood haughtily to attention as I stood and just gaped. 'Wow. I'm lost for words.'

'Just one word will do.' Daisy grinned.

'Just one?'

'Uh-huh.'

'Which is?'

'Yes.'

'OK.' I laughed. 'Yes. Yes please. I love it. When can I move in?'

'I can't believe this is all yours, Daisy, and you've never lived here,' I repeated as, ten minutes later and mugs of hot chocolate to hand, we braved the chilly March breeze and made our way down to the edge of the garden to a fossilised stone table and bench that must have been in situ as long as the cottage itself. A mass of daffodils, ranging from acidic yellow to a creamy lemon, were putting up a good show of defiantly taunting the breeze, intent on tossing their heads westwards to the Pennine hills whose backbone could just be made out under a lowering sky.

'Couldn't afford it. Needed the exorbitant rent money from this place to live while I was off, or while I was back at Mum and Dad's place.'

'What about Matis?' I asked gently. 'You've never really said. You know, you were so into him just as I was setting off to go to the Far East? When you and he were working together on this place? And then you just stopped mentioning him in your emails and texts.'

Daisy took a deep mouthful from her mug before wiping away a chocolate moustache. 'Pass those biscuits,

Frankie.' She took two, munching solidly through one before attempting to explain through the second. 'I really didn't think it was tactful, you know, to be extolling the virtues of Matis when you had had such an awful break-up with Daler. It might have meant you never coming back to England.' She added, 'And I missed you.'

I stroked Daisy's arm, suddenly feeling more at home and glad to be back than I'd done in the past few days either at Mum's or when visiting the factory.

'Anyway, I messed up,' she went on.

'Oh?'

'Matis wanted more. The whole marriage and baby thing.'

'Oh? Really? Gosh.'

'Hmm.'

'And?' I prompted her as she drained her cup, wiping at her mouth once more.

'And nothing. I turned him down; didn't want to be trapped here in the small village I grew up in. Once the building work down here was completed, and he and I had made some big decisions, he went back home.'

'To Lithuania?'

Daisy nodded. 'As I say, I messed up. Frightened of commitment, I guess. I miss him terribly,' she added.

'Well it's not too late,' I urged, giving her a hug. 'Text him, email him, ring him. Tell him you miss him...'

'Too late,' she sighed. 'I missed the boat on that one. I still see a lot of Deimante, his sister, and she keeps me informed. Matis is married with a lovely fat bouncing baby and is settled back near his parents just outside Vilnius.' Daisy rubbed at her eyes and then smiled. 'No, I shall go up to

Edinburgh in the autumn, train to be a vet and eventually take over my dad's practice. I'll live here and go down in local legend as The Woman With Healing Hands, mending every woodland creature that drags its injured leg or trapped paw to my doorstep; every bluebird that hops its way here with a broken wing.'

'And will the seven dwarves be on hand to do your cleaning and cooking?' I laughed.

'I hope so,' she nodded sagely. 'I bloody hope so.'

15

Frankie

'Give us a twirl, love.' Tammy, fully made up at 7am, a huge frying pan to hand like some warring Amazonian, paused for a moment from adding rashers of bacon to said weapon and batted her elongated lashes in my direction to nod her approval. 'Yep, you'll do. You look fabulous, Francesca. Doesn't she, Matteo?' She turned to Matteo who, with a full mouth, was attempting a close examination of a burgeoning pimple on his chin in the back of his cornflakes' spoon.

'Huh?' Matteo didn't look up.

'Frankie. Doesn't she look absolutely right for the job? New director at Piccione's.'

'Huh?' My half-brother bent his head, elbows splayed as he shovelled another truckload of cereal into his already-crowded mouth.

'You look lovely, Frankie.' Angel continued to feed pieces of toast soldier to the almost life-sized baby doll sitting on a chair of its own, rather than to herself. 'Nonno says *I* can be a director too one day.' Angel was immaculate in her navy school uniform, and so utterly cute I wanted to go over and pick her up by the two handles of dark hair sticking out at right angles to her head. She reminded me of Felix, the wooden pony I used to ride round the kitchen when I was a kid myself, hanging on to his sticking-out black handles and urging him forwards.

'You get in there, love,' Tammy said determinedly. 'Shake things up a bit. Show 'em what a woman can do.'

I laughed, sitting down and helping myself to juice, feeling nervous at the thought of the new venture ahead of me. A huge part of me was wishing I was still sitting down to breakfast in Aunt Rosina's kitchen in Sicily rather than this one where the juice was sweet and cloying and the bread was sliced and in cellophane. I wondered where I could get *pagnotta del Dittaino* – the freshly baked sourdough bread I'd feasted on every morning (with unsalted butter from the dairy in the village and Rosina's *crema al limone*) before joining the men out in the olive and lemon groves and wheat fields. The workers on Rosina's smallholding continued to do much of the agricultural work by hand rather than embracing the mechanisation neighbouring farms had begun to employ, and I'd loved the sheer physical labour of it all.

'Are you talking to me or Angel?' I asked, declining with a shake of my head the full English Tammy endeavoured to feed her family every morning of the week. Dad really was going to have to watch his cholesterol.

'Both of you,' Tammy said, determinedly breaking eggs into the frying pan where they hit the hot fat with a loud crack. 'It's your heritage, both of you and, since Pam's retiring, the place is going to need another strong woman at the helm. She's back from her holiday today, you know.'

'I know, I can't wait to see her.' I adored my Aunty Pam, my dad's elder brother Marco's wife. Ex-wife. She'd been a major part of Piccione's for years – since she was in her teens apparently – and, although she rarely talked about either her short marriage to Marco or how, because she was married to Angelo's elder son, she'd gone from being office girl to virtually running the place, Angelo, I knew, was going to miss her presence and know-how at the factory immeasurably.

Tammy lowered her voice. 'Somebody needs to keep that Margaret Holroyd in her place…'

'Is Nonno still at it with her?' The mention of anything slightly sexual had obviously roused my half-brother Matteo out of his semi-supine stupor, provoking his interest as nothing else could.

'At it with her?' I laughed. 'God, what a revolting expression, Matty.'

He blushed scarlet and glared at me in turn before hiding his red face in his cornflakes. I felt chastened, and, remembering the horrible highs and lows, the spots and greasy hair of my own adolescence, reached over to pat his hand which he studiously ignored.

'Morning, *bedda mia*.' Dad, arriving at the breakfast table in a waft of aftershave and bonhomie, kissed Tammy's cheek and patted her ample tight-jeaned bottom somewhat lasciviously, much to the disapproval of Matteo, who gave a grunt of disgust in his father's direction. Anything overtly affectionate between his own parents was obviously uncalled for and to be avoided at all costs, whereas between his grandfather and his PA it was nothing short of compelling.

'Oy, less of that.' Dad gave Matteo a playful clip around the head before kissing him on both cheeks.

'Gerrofff.' Apart from rubbing at his face, Matteo ignored Dad, attacking his cereal again with gloomy inexorability.

Tammy lay a heaped plate of bacon, eggs, mushrooms and some sort of black pudding in front of Dad, tucked his napkin into the top of his beautifully ironed blue striped shirt for him and patted his bald patch affectionately. He really did appear to have lost a lot more of his hair in the two years I'd been away. Maybe it was the testosterone. Didn't they say the more sex you had, the more testosterone you produced, and the less hair you ended up with? Wasn't there a correlation between no hair on a man's head but a thatch of it on his chest and the amount of sex he was getting? I glanced over at my dad, where a mat of dark chest hair was already making a bid for freedom through the straining buttons of his shirt showing below the starched napkin. Or had I totally made that all up? Whatever. All I knew was that Dad and Tammy were still, fifteen years on, totally in love with each other; couldn't keep their hands off each other. I sighed. Would *I* ever feel the same way again?

'You OK, Frankie? You look lovely.' Dad smiled through a mouthful of food while Matteo, obviously having endured quite enough praise being cast in my direction, stood and, sighing loudly, ambled off.

'Clean your teeth and brush your hair!' Dad shouted after him.

'Didn't do yours much good, did it?' he retorted under his breath as he began to plug himself into some music whilst Tammy laughed uproariously, patting Dad's shiny pate once more.

I didn't ever remember such jolly banter between Dad and my own mother when I was growing up. Constant bickering, leading to full-blown rows where Mum would be demanding more, always more: a new car, the sitting room decorated, a cruise, the paying off of her ridiculously high debt on her credit card, *another* pair of Jimmy Choos... The list was endless, the rows seemingly the same until Mum finally walked out, taking Luca, leaving Dad devastated and my world imploded.

'So,' Dad said, wiping his mouth on his napkin and laying it down on the table, 'you're off tonight then? To Daisy's place?'

I nodded. 'After work this evening. I took most of my stuff over yesterday and the car is full now as well. Once I'm settled, come over and I'll cook for all of you. You should see the kitchen; it's out of this world.'

'OK, OK.' Dad was clearly still put out that I was going. 'But listen, if you don't like it. You know, if you don't get on with Daisy...'

'Come on, Dad, you know Daisy. Everyone gets on with Daisy.'

'I know, I know, but you know there's always a home for you here. Now, before we go, just a couple of things. Luca is obviously going to be your boss...'

'Right.'

'...but don't let him boss you. And then there's this Cameron Mancini chap as well. I didn't think it absolutely necessary to have him on board, but Luca and Angelo are quite taken with him, and now that Pam's retired...' He trailed off. 'So, Miss Piccione—' he looked at his watch, patted his stomach and belched discreetly before standing '—see you for Monday morning briefing at nine-thirty.'

'Francesca,' Luca started, somewhat pompously I thought, 'you'll report directly to Cameron here. You'll be working together on both the marketing as well as the R and D of Piccione Preserves which, unfortunately, have been losing favour quite dramatically with the British public.'

R and D? I was momentarily lost as to its meaning once again. And me with a business degree, for heaven's sake. Aunt Rosina's lemon groves, languidly basking in the hot Sicilian sunshine, flashed before my eyes and I had a real urge to tear off my new black pinstriped suit, push away the myriad incomprehensible facts and figures dancing in front of my eyes and head back down the M62 to Manchester airport.

'Research and Development, Frankie,' Dad was saying kindly, obviously reading my mind.

'Of course,' I answered in my most professional voice. 'Now,' I stabbed at some arbitrary figures with my pen. 'Line five, Luca? In red? If you could take us through what those represent?'

Luca hesitated and then looked across at Cameron Mancini. We *all* turned to look at Cameron Mancini.

He looked right back at us for several seconds: from Luca, to Angelo, to Dad and finally to me, scrutinising every facet of me for what seemed an eternity. And just when I was on the point of shouting, 'Yes, it's a fair cop – I'll talk,' and Dad was clearing his throat in empathetic embarrassment, Cameron launched. And boy, did he launch. After forty-five minutes of an intense dressing-down in his cultured New Hampshire accent as to where Piccione's was going wrong and what we must do in order to not only get back on track, but also overtake our competitors in an increasingly sluggish market (at which point I was doodling slugs happily slurping up raspberry jam on my notes) I'd given up the will to live.

I took myself off back to Sicily until I could almost feel the heat beating down through my hat as I worked. The olive harvest had been only several days' work, but it was a total labour of love, an ancient rite that has been going on since biblical times and before. The majority of the neighbouring farms to Aunt Rosina's brought in the automatic machines that drove up to each tree, shaking them maniacally in a sort of epileptic dance, until every last olive was off. Absolutely fascinating to watch, but I loved that in the small groves that continued to harvest by hand, there was something akin to getting right back to nature when, with beating pole to hand, we toiled in the September heat, working in teams to knock off the ripe seeds into the *lenzi* nets below...

I came to with a start as Cameron emphasised what he was saying with several hits of his (expensive-looking) fountain pen on the polished boardroom table and realised it wasn't just me who was having difficulty concentrating: Angelo was fidgeting, rubbing at his arthritic fingers, Dad was reaching for his heartburn medication (I really would have to have a word with Tammy as to what he *should* be eating) and even Luca appeared to be wondering how much longer we were going to be at the mercy of his new protégé.

'So, there you have it,' Cameron eventually barked, closing his file. 'You gotta long road ahead of you. Luckily, Piccione's Caponata is still the world's number-one most recognised product in its category – much the same, I guess, as Heinz baked beans and Oreo cookies – (oh, give me a Fox's Custard Cream *biscuit* any day, I thought idly) and that will continue to carry you through. I spent most of my first day here down on the Preserves production line. You've gotta whole load of updated equipment down there, Angelo, but you're not putting it to the best use. Francesca.' He suddenly turned his attention back to me. 'I suggest you spend some of today down there getting to know what's going on and how *you* see the way forward.' He looked at his watch and then back at me. 'If we say 5pm? Back here…?'

Wasn't 5pm home time? Cameron Mancini obviously didn't realise most folks round these parts wanted their tea on the table by 5.30pm sharpish.

'…so you can report back?' With a dismissive nod of his head in my direction, he turned to Dad and Angelo. 'We're going to have to get a time-and-motion study in operation at some point.'

Dad shot an exaggerated look of terror in my direction before meekly following the others into Angelo's office.

Luca's laptop was still sitting where he'd left it on the boardroom table and I turned as he retraced his steps from Angelo's office in order to retrieve it.

'I hope you don't think you're just going to float around looking pretty.' Luca scowled in my direction. 'Pam's retiring has left a big hole that needs filling, but unfortunately I don't see you having either the zeal or the capacity to do that.' He looked me up and down. 'I give it a couple of months before you've had enough: enough of working nine-to-five for a living; enough of being back here in Westenbury.'

'I don't suppose any of us appreciate just what Aunty Pam has achieved here the last fifty-odd years.' I smiled, trying to stay calm, when really what I wanted was to give my brother a bloody good kick in the shins.

'Yes, well don't think you're just taking over where she left off.'

'I wouldn't presume...'

'No, don't you presume *a thing*, Frankie.' Luca picked up his laptop and made to join the others once more, but turned with a parting shot. 'If I'd had my way, you wouldn't have been given this opportunity to join us. Now you appear to have got what you wanted, don't think you can fanny around doing nothing. And, don't go running off telling tales to Dad or Nonno when the tough gets going.'

When the tough gets going? If I hadn't been feeling homesick for Sicily as well as totally out of my depth in a new job I didn't really want anyway, I'd probably have laughed out loud at Luca's pomposity. So, instead I had to pretend I knew what the hell to do next. Taking a deep breath, I pushed away all images of that September harvest and picked up my bag and file. Cameron Mancini was absolutely right: my first job (once I'd found coffee) was to head down to the factory floor and see what was going on since I'd last worked on it myself years earlier.

'Hey, Frankie, get you.' A disembodied woman's voice fought with the hum and clatter of the machinery and the inevitable banality of Radio 2, and I wondered idly if the radio was ever tuned to any other station as Chris Evans – or had he been replaced? – Jeremy Vine and Steve Wright made their daily, ritualistic appearance over the air like something from an Orwellian dystopia. 'You've come to slum it down here with us lot again?'

The next second I was enveloped in a huge, warm, perfumed hug – the perpetrator had been wearing *Rive Gauche* since her youth in the Seventies – that went on for a good few seconds.

'Sorry, love.' Carol eventually grinned. 'Just making up for lost time. By 'eck, Frankie, you're looking good. You've finally crossed over to the dark side then?'

I laughed at that. 'I don't know about that; I might be back down here with all of you lot if my new boss isn't impressed with what I come up with.'

'Who? Luca? He's your brother – he can't sack you.'

I think he probably could.

'She means the new fella, don't you, Frankie?' Carol and I were joined by her sister, Linda, their mother Mavis and sister-in-law Debs. 'He's a bit of alright, isn't he? Where did Angelo find *him*?'

'New Hampshire, I believe.' I smiled, really pleased to be back in the company of these women who'd taken me under their wing when I'd spent day after monotonous day on the Pickles production line during school and some uni vacations, sharing their gossip and their warmth, as well as their crisp sandwiches.

'Oh, I thought he was *American*.' Linda seemed disappointed. 'Not another *Southerner*.'

'He is.'

'But you said he was from Hampshire…'

'*New* Hampshire, Linda,' Carol tutted. 'You know, like we've got York up here in the north and the Americans pinched it and called it *New* York, and down south they've got Hampshire and the buggers pinched it and called it *New* Hampshire. Were you away when they did geography at school?'

'Probably legging it down in town with Debs at the time.' Linda grinned. Both Linda and Debs were pregnant and married at sixteen, and were still married to their respective men who were now line managers, one in Piccalilli and one in Cantucci.

'*New* England,' Mavis was saying thoughtfully. '*New* Jersey, *New* Orleans…'

'Nova Scotia,' I said, joining in with the game. God, I should be looking at raspberry jam and marmalade output instead of gossiping. I looked nervously over my shoulder to make sure Cameron Mancini wasn't hovering.

'No, love,' Linda said kindly, 'it has to start with *New*…'

'It's Latin for New Scotland,' Carol tutted impatiently. She turned back to me. 'So, you OK, Frankie?'

'OK?'

'I heard you rushed off to the Far East because of one of the Dosanjhs? Shame, you'd have been kept in sandals for the rest of your life.' Carol looked down at her own feet, which were sporting a pair of trainers with the telltale, ubiquitous Dosanjh logo. I didn't realise Dosanjh's had expanded into sportswear, and wondered if that was Daler's doing. 'Only things that help when the old varicose veins are playing up,' she added.

'How come you're all in Preserves now, rather than

Pickles?' I asked, desperate to get off the interrogation re Daler and the Dosanjh family.

'Your dad promoted me to line manager down here when Audrey Blackburn retired,' Carol explained. 'I said I'd only move over if I could bring my team with me. There was a bit of a shuffle-round and here we all are. Right, you lot, back to work. Come on, Frankie, there's been quite a few changes since you were last here. But there's room for so much more.'

'Wow, this is amazing,' I enthused, genuinely impressed with what was going on down here in Preserves. 'It's all so different from Pickles.'

'The main difference is you go home with your hair smelling of sugar rather than vinegar.' Carol smiled. 'And yes, I agree with you. I'm very proud of our jam and marmalade; it's fabulous stuff, full of big chunks of real fruit and not too sickly sweet – that's because the ratio of fruit to sugar is higher than a lot of brands. That makes it more expensive to produce, obviously, but I hope your new boss keeps to that ratio. He was down here all Friday, poking about into everything as well as up in the lab with quality control, tasting and testing.'

Carol gave me a whistle-stop tour of the whole Preserves section where a lot of updated, shiny new machinery had been installed while I was away; because I'd only really ever worked in Pickles, it was all totally new to me. We started with the fruit: both frozen and aseptically produced puree, taking in the mainstay raspberry, strawberry, and blackcurrant as well as the less popular peach and pineapple whose sickly-sweet, heavily perfumed odour was almost overpowering.

She took me through the washing and sorting departments, pointing out proudly – and without me really taking it in – the (mediaeval torture-sounding) turn-screw pumps, something called the exchange piston batcher and a brand-new labelling machine of which, Carol said, they were all a bit frightened. I plunged totally out of my depth when the boffins in the labs and in Quality Control tried to take me through an analysis of the organoleptic parameters of the odour, colour, taste and consistency of *each* of Piccione's Preserves in turn, and was on the point of jumping into the machine and becoming jam myself when the chief scientist – a gingery looking man called Marcus – started on mass total extract.

Or some such thing.

By 5pm, having totally forgotten all the statistics I'd had thrown at me during the day – which made little sense anyway – I was ready to face Cameron Mancini.

'Ah, Francesca, how's it going?' Was there a kinder tone to his voice than earlier in the day? He looked tired, his tie had been loosened and the beginning of a five o'clock growth was starting to shadow his handsome face. Handsome? Did I think him handsome? Well yes, no one could argue he wasn't attractive. If you liked that sort of thing. He was a bit too smooth for my liking, a bit too conservative and sure of himself. And, at the end of the day, he was in my brother Luca's pocket. I decided I wasn't going to pussyfoot around with this man. I was a Piccione, for heaven's sake. He was the hired help.

'OK, Cameron, in a nutshell?'

'Sure. Go for it.'

'Right. It's boring: the jams are boring. The raspberry, strawberry and blackcurrant taste fabulous and *are* fabulous. Full of fruit and not too sweet. I wouldn't change a thing there.'

Cameron raised an eyebrow. 'OK. But?'

'We're way out of date with the rest. Where's the fig jam? The rhubarb and ginger jam – for heaven's sake we're two minutes away from the Rhubarb Triangle in Wakefield – the strawberry and rose petal? Why aren't we resourcing home-grown Yorkshire gooseberries? Every allotment from Mirfield to Marsden grows gooseberries. Chilli jam? *Chocolate* and chilli jam...?'

Cameron raised the other eyebrow,

'Alright, alright, maybe not that,' I said hastily. 'Get rid of the peach and pineapple jams. They're foul and, according to Sales, not a bit popular. We need to be coming up with different jars, different packaging, jams Harrods will be fighting over to stock in their food hall. Next and most importantly...'

Cameron leaned back in his chair and, very impressively, raised both eyebrows simultaneously.

'...we totally alter the recipe of the lemon curd and actually call it *crema al limone*. I know we've been promoting the stuff as traditional Yorkshire lemon curd with its gingham-designed lid, but what we have now is horrid.' The acidly sweet and gelatinous mess I'd tasted up in Quality Control had been repeating itself on me constantly, all afternoon. 'If a real lemon – a beautifully sun-kissed, *Sicilian* lemon; we Picciones are *Sicilian* for heaven's sake – has ever come within fifty yards of a jar of that stuff downstairs, then I'm a… I'm a…' Oh bugger, I couldn't think what the hell I was as Cameron Mancini sat forward, steepled his long, tanned fingers and fixed me with his shrewd blue eyes.

'Is that it?'

I quailed somewhat under his continued gaze. 'No, actually,' I said. 'That's not *it*: Piccione's Honey is pretty disgusting too. The bees that produced that stuff need firing. Give them their marching orders, send out their P45s, and find some new ones.'

16

Frankie

Now

I could hear Marvin Gaye belting out soulfully from behind Aunty Pam's shiny red-painted front door as I stood waiting on the doorstep in the bitter cold. I shivered, longing for some warmth, some sunshine, some relief from the grey, scudding clouds that obliterated the sight of any blue sky as well as the realisation that spring was actually here but yet seemed unable to take away my need to see Daler again.

'Aw, sweetheart, you're back.' Aunty Pam enveloped me in a hug that surpassed even the one from Carol in Preserves earlier that day. 'I've missed you so much. Over two whole years without you. I can't tell you the number of times I nearly got on a plane to surprise you in Sicily.'

'Why didn't you then?' I smiled, when I finally managed to untangle myself from her grasp.

'Too busy winding up things here, I suppose. And I

wasn't convinced you'd want your elderly aunt encroaching on your new life out there.'

'Elderly?' I laughed at that. 'Anyone would think you were in your dotage. What are you now? Sixty?'

She grinned, ushering me into the warm and welcoming kitchen. A pile of ironed summer holiday clothes – T-shirts, shorts and flimsy swimwear – was tottering manfully on the kitchen granite while several pastel-coloured cotton dresses swung on hangers from the *batterie de cuisine* above the central island. The ironing basket remained steadfastly half-full despite Pam's obvious administrations to the contrary. 'Sixty-two last August – not that I'm shouting *that* out to all and sundry. You forgot it,' she added accusingly.

'I'm sorry,' I pleaded. And I was.

'Tttsss,' she tutted. 'Birthdays. *I'd* rather forget all about them these days. Anyway, I'm still fifty on the dating sites. Otherwise I'd end up with old codgers over seventy who have to get up several times in the night to pee or who're on the lookout for a nursemaid in their old age. And I tell you, Frankie, now I'm retired, I'm not spending it catering to an old bloke's prostate or being sent out to fetch his bad back and Viagra prescriptions because he's either unable or too embarrassed to go himself.'

I laughed at that. 'Honestly, Aunty Pam, you don't even look fifty.' And I wasn't being sycophantic: Pamela Piccione, at sixty-two, looked at least a decade younger than her birth certificate said. She was tall – easily a good six inches above me – and beautifully slim, and her plentiful blonde hair was to her shoulder. She was sassy and funny and I'd never understood why she'd spent so many years single after she and my Uncle Marco, Dad's much older brother, had divorced. 'How was Lanzarote?'

'Warm. Fabulous. Energetic. Bev and I danced until we dropped: Soul and Tamla hour every night at nine. Great DJ...' Pam trailed off. 'So, you're back? For good?'

I nodded. 'Well, we'll see how it goes. The meeting I've just had with Cameron Mancini could mean I'm out on my ear before I've even started.'

'Oh, they've actually taken him on, have they?'

'Hmm. Did you meet him? Did you have a say in whether to employ him or not?'

Pam shook her head. 'Luca brought him up into the offices when he was showing him round before Angelo and your dad decided to take him on, while I was away. Nothing to do with me anymore. I've retired, Frankie. I've finished at Piccione's.'

'Surely you're still going to have some say in what goes on?' Aunty Pam had always been there, always been a big part of the company.

'Well, yes, I've obviously still got shares, and there are some board meetings I'll be invited to. But I'd done over forty years – forty years, Frankie; hell, where did that go? – and, much as I love the place and Angelo, I want to do other things. I want to travel more; hopefully spend more time with Carla.'

My cousin Carla, Pam's only child, was much older than me and had settled in Vancouver after completing her French and Italian degree and falling in love and marrying a Canadian national. As far as I could remember, I'd only met Carla a couple of times, once when I was tiny and again when she was over with her husband and two children, just as Mum and Dad were divorcing when I was eleven and about to be shipped off out of the way to prep school a hundred miles or so down the M1.

Aunty Pam had always been there. She'd babysat for Luca and me when we were little kids and Mum and Dad were out socialising, of which they did a huge amount, Mum still being a big part of the old Midhope Textile Mill Owners' social circle. Pam regularly had me over with her for whole weekends, letting me bake when Mum never had. Mum had never actually baked, never mind letting me *help* her bake. Far too messy having flour, syrup and oats on her spotless kitchen units for Mum to even consider making flapjacks, with or without my help. Especially when you could buy far superior stuff on trips out to Waitrose and, heaven be praised, to Harvey Nicks as well, once the store had opened in Leeds, complete with its own food hall.

'Lovely, Francesca,' Mum had said, peering, with what can only be described as a pained expression, into the tin of biscuits Aunty Pam and I had made her for Mother's Day. Mum had looked in some disdain at the luminously red hearts and MUMMY shakily engraved on each biscuit by my seven-year-old hand and said, 'Your dad will enjoy these.' And he had, scoffing the lot, much to Mum's disapproval as she sipped at her glass of PLJ, her mouth pursed as tight as a dog's bum, as much at the sight of Dad's expanding waistline as the tart lemon juice she forced down her throat before every meal in the apparent hope it would dissolve and gobble up the calories she was about to consume.

It was Aunty Pam who'd argued vociferously for my not being sent away to school. Who'd even suggested I go and live with her for a while – I learned years later – until the arguments and the downright nastiness over the divorce had settled down. But Mum was having none of it. No way was I to be allowed to live with 'that woman', even temporarily, when I'd been offered a place at a boarding prep school near Nottingham and where I was to be hot-housed academically in order to sit common entrance for Millfield, her father's old public school where, apparently, he'd excelled at sport and not much else. It was Aunty Pam who wrote to me without fail every week when I was paralysed with homesickness those first few months away, and it was Aunty Pam who regularly drove all the way down to Somerset once I was there, staying at little B and B places on the way down and making quite a holiday of her visits to me. It was Aunty Pam who encouraged me when football was all I lived for and when Mum utterly disapproved of my involvement in *the totally ridiculous idea* of football for girls.

And it was Aunty Pam who was there for me in the days after Daler did what he did and I made the decision to run from it all.

'So,' Aunty Pam was saying, bringing me back to the present. 'What have you done to upset the American Boy Wonder?'

'Well, no one was telling me what to do, no one was asking me to focus on any particular area, so I just went down to see Carol, Linda and Debs and took it from there. I decided to have a good nose round all aspects of Preserves and try and see what was going on from a totally objective viewpoint. You know, no emotional ties clouding my judgement and getting in the way of what was actually happening down there, which I assume was what Cameron

Mancini was doing himself before the weekend. Does he have Italian ancestry himself, do you reckon? You know, with a name like Mancini?'

'No idea. Didn't you ask?'

'Oh, I'm nowhere near finding out anything *personal* about him.' I smiled and started singing: '*It's all about the jam, 'bout the jam, no trouble...*'

Laughing at my dreadful rendition, Pam asked, 'Is he dishy though?' She did something strange with her lips that was obviously her interpretation of sexy and just made me want to laugh in turn.

'No idea,' I lied. 'I wasn't looking.'

'And what was your overall impression of Preserves? I'd been there so long myself, I'm not sure *I* was actually able to look at it objectively any longer. Definitely needs new input; it'll do the place good to have you and this Mancini chap there.'

'My gut reaction is to leave well alone what is working well – you know the strawberry, raspberry and blackcurrant jams. Get rid of *everything* else and start again, concentrating on both a brand-new lemon curd recipe and packaging, and the same goes for honey.'

'Blimey.' Pam looked a bit taken aback. 'And on your first day as well? Have you told Angelo this?'

'Do you want to finish him off? You know how he hates change. And spending money. It's taken both Dad and Luca to get him to shell out on new machinery. It's now another job to actually use that machinery with totally different products.'

'So, Daler?' Pam said, patting at my arm as she poured us both a glass of wine. Have you heard anything?'

'Anything?'

'You know.'

'You mean, was he in touch while I was away?'

'Hmm.'

I hesitated. 'He texted me when I left. And then at Christmas and on my birthday. And on the anniversary of the day we met. I had to tell him to stop.'

'Hard, I know, sweetie. But for the best. You've managed over two years without him. Move on, Frankie.'

'Much easier to say and do when you're thousands of miles away. You know, Pam, I'm not sure how much of a good idea this was… coming back… What if I bump into him? What if I see him? What do I say?'

'Frankie, why would you bump into him? He's in London now. And this is where your friends and family all are. You can't be hounded out of your own village – and the nursing job you loved – through no fault of your own.'

I actually laughed at that. 'I think *being hounded out of the village* is being overly dramatic. It was my choice to leave both. And I'm glad I did. I've learned a lot about myself while I've been away.'

'You gave up your nursing career.'

'Yes, well, who knows? If Cameron Mancini – and Dad and Angelo – all think I'm talking rubbish when it comes to jam, maybe I can pick up where I left off.' I glanced across at Pam. '*You* managed to move on once your marriage was over.'

'Big difference, Frankie: I never loved your Uncle Marco. I'm not sure I even liked him much.'

'You've never said that before,' I said, really surprised.

'Well no, it's never easy admitting to anyone that you never even liked the man you were married to, you know.'

'Dad's never really talked about Uncle Marco although Mum's always hinted at things about him. She's told me quite a lot about what happened.'

'Oh, your mother doesn't know everything, even though she likes to think she does.' Pam pulled a face. There was absolutely no love lost between my mother and my Aunty Pam. 'Are you dashing off? Will you stay and eat with me? I've made plenty.'

I smiled at that – Pam *always* made plenty, always had enough for anyone dropping in, which, with her having so many friends, both male and female, they often did. 'Actually, Daisy's doing an evening shift down at the vet practice and won't be in until after nine. It would be nice to move in if she's actually there, rather than scrabbling about in the dark.'

'She's given you a key, hasn't she?'

'Yes, of course. And her mum and dad helped us move lots of things down there yesterday. We've got a bed apiece all made up, a couple of beanbags in the sitting room and my lovely clothes I've not worn for two years all hanging up in my own personal walk-in wardrobe. Trouble is, it's really dark down there and I don't really know my way round yet, so it would be good to wait until we arrive back together.'

'Lovely. Well, you can have at least one glass of wine and the chicken's just about done.' Pam moved over to open the oven door.

'Thank you. And will you tell me all about it?' I looked across to gauge Pam's reaction.

'*It?*' She gave me one of her looks.

'Well, you've just admitted you married a man you didn't like. So, go on, you've never really told me much about how you met Uncle Marco. Or why on earth you married a man you didn't love and, after you divorced, spent the next years alone.'

'Erm, I've not exactly spent it *alone*.' Pam grinned. 'I think you should get it out of your head I've led the life of some sort of nun, Frankie.'

'Tell me then.' I smiled. 'I'm a big girl now. Go on, right from the beginning.'

17

Frankie

Now

'Goodness.' I laughed, momentarily distracted from Pam's tale by the headily aromatic chicken and roast potatoes she placed in front of me. 'You were actually a Miss Piccione beauty queen? I never knew Piccione's did that sort of thing back in the day.'

'You must have seen the black and white framed photos taken every year? In the boardroom? As far as I know, I was the last Miss Piccione. I'm actually amazed it carried on as long as it did, you know? Once those wonderful women had sabotaged the Miss World contest, when Bob Hope was compering it back in... 1970, I think it was... the unions and the women workers tried to ban it. Eventually they did, and good for them. It was all a total nonsense anyway.'

I shook my head, helping myself to a too-big portion of the caramelised-topped cauliflower cheese. 'I always love the way you do this,' I said, pulling off a stringy nodule of burnt, melted Emmental before popping it in my mouth.

'Nope, I can't remember seeing any photos. Do you cook like this for yourself every night?'

'Every two or three days.' Pam smiled. 'And then I've always got some leftovers to feed myself. Having said that, now I'm no longer going to be at work, I'm certainly going to be experimenting with some new recipes. Actually,' she went on, 'thinking about it, those photos were taken down years ago. Angelo didn't agree with him of course, but your dad – probably under Tammy's influence – thought they were *infra dig*, you know, demeaning to women. They were replaced by photos of all the prizes Piccione's *Caponata* and strawberry jam have won over the years at different national and international food fairs. The photos will be in a cupboard somewhere, unless Luca's thrown them out when he's been updating the place.'

'So, go on then,' I said, putting down my knife and fork and reaching for my glass of wine. 'That was the first time you saw Uncle Marco? That night at the RAFA club? I don't think the place is there anymore is it?'

Pam shook her head. 'It was turned into a McDonald's years ago. More chicken?'

I shook my head.

'Potatoes?'

'No, really.'

'Cauliflower? I know it's your favourite.'

I laughed at that. 'Are you trying to avoid telling me how you ended up with Marco?'

'Well, it's a bit… well, you know, it doesn't really put me in a very good light.'

'Oh?' I reached for my cutlery and dug in once more, largely to avoid Pam's slight embarrassment.

'You have to remember I was only sixteen. Actually, a week off being sixteen, although I certainly looked a lot older; I think it was with my being so tall. I was much taller than most of the other girls and I was never asked my age in pubs at a time when they were so strict about underage drinking. You could be hauled off home by the police to face your parents if you were caught in a police raid. And then end up in front of the magistrates. It was my mother's biggest fear, my being brought home in a panda car and having to face the gauntlet of the street watching behind their lace curtains.' Pam laughed at that. 'Apart from *Coronation Street*, the old biddies down our road didn't have much else to gossip about.'

'Well, I think I've pretty much worked out you ended up married to him not much later on. So, Marco either swept you off your feet or you got pregnant?'

'I bet you knew that. I bet your mother told you that?'

'Yes, of course she did. One of her favourite stories.' I grinned. 'You know, how the sixteen-year-old baggage from the council estate ended up getting pregnant and marrying the elder Piccione son.'

Pam tutted. 'She's a cheeky mare that mother of yours. She doesn't know half of it. We *didn't* live on a council estate. And it certainly wouldn't have mattered if we had. My mum and dad had scrimped and saved for a mortgage for our house before they considered getting married; Dad worked at Balmforths' Foundry all his life and mum worked part-time as a school dinner lady and also down at the little supermarket in the village filling shelves. *Thrifty*, it was called...' Pam started laughing as she remembered. 'My dad used to call it *Shifty*. That's gone too now. Janet was the first in our family to go to university when, just a few years earlier, it was totally accepted that we girls left school at sixteen to go into the offices of the big companies round here, while the boys got the engineering and textile apprenticeships.' Pam smiled as she cleared the plates. 'All changed now of course: not a damned apprenticeship to be had for love nor money.'

'Hey, maybe that's something I could bring up with Luca. You know, start the whole apprentice scheme again. For both boys *and* girls.'

'I can't imagine any sixteen-year-old would even consider being apprenticed to a pickle production line, these days,' Pam sniffed. 'Far too busy filling in their UCCA forms to study media or body contour technology or... or underwater basket-weaving.'

I laughed at that. 'Stop it, Pam, cynicism doesn't suit you. So, was my dad there? That night you met Marco?'

'You have to remember your dad is so much younger than Marco. I do remember Joe being there, that night. You know, at the RAFA club when he should have been tucked up in bed. But that's Italians for you: Angelo liked to show him off. I just remember this little boy with big brown eyes and hair Brylcreemed to one side of his lovely little face.'

'Brylcreem?'

'Before your time. So, your dad would have been about eight or nine at the time. He was really cute in his own customised little dinner jacket and dicky-bow, on his best behaviour, trying to be all grown up. He adored his big brother.'

'So how old was Marco then?'

'That night?'

I nodded.

'He was twenty-one and very, very handsome.'

'I bet he had all the girls after him?'

Pam nodded. 'But the thing was, Frankie, I wasn't at all interested because I had such a thing about this guy called Rob Mansell.' Pam's eyes took on a faraway look as she laid down her knife and fork and picked up her glass, sipping at her wine, obviously lost in thought.

'And?' I prompted.

'And I'd been going out with Rob a month or so, hiding the fact I wasn't yet sixteen and certainly shouldn't really have been able to get into the town's nightclubs as Jane and I were doing at the time. I just *loved* soul music as Rob did. Tamla Motown, Northern soul, Stax...'

'Stax?'

Pam waved a hand as if I should know exactly what she was talking about. 'Stax record label. They had Otis Redding, Booker T...'

'OK, OK.' I knew from past experience, if I didn't move Pam on, she'd go through the whole lot, get out her 45s and even demonstrate a few spins and backdrops on the kitchen floor. As it was, she jumped up to find her iPad, fiddled around with her Sonos and, once she'd set Martha Reeves free in the kitchen, went to the fridge to do the same with a cheesecake she'd made earlier that day.

'So, if you weren't interested in Uncle Marco, only had eyes for this Rob Mansell bloke, how come you ended up pregnant?'

'Too much champagne, I'm afraid, as well as Angelo's determination to stop Marco "catting around" as he called it. *Come un cane in calore...*'

'Like a dog on heat?' I translated, laughing. 'Dogs as well as cats? Nice!'

'You have to remember how it was back in the Seventies. Marco was twenty-one, he'd never brought home a decent steady girlfriend and Angelo, who was himself married to Consettia – like the good Italian Catholic he was – at the age of eighteen, wanted his eldest son married, settled and producing Piccione bambinos to carry on the Pickles dynasty.' Pam started laughing at that. 'What he got up to once he *was* married, didn't, I'm afraid, concern Angelo too much.'

'Blimey, sounds like *The Godfather*.'

Pam laughed again. 'I'm *convinced* Angelo had been watching the film and saw himself as the big boss. He and Consettia and the boys had recently moved into High Royd and he did lord it about up there. He sported a new moustache just like Don Corleone, wore his dinner jacket whenever he got the chance and was beginning to invest heavily in the new Italian restaurants that were suddenly springing up everywhere. People had had enough of awful British food in staid restaurants in the early Seventies, and Angelo was certainly the money behind several new Italian places in town. I think his aim was to open his own restaurant – you can just see it, can't you? – *Angelo's* or *Piccione's* – but the pickles and preserves were totally taking off and he just didn't have the time to get personally involved. He'd also just set up another company – *Piccione's Italian Food and Wine* – and started importing Italian foodstuffs wholesale at a time when we Brits began to realise pasta meant more than a tin of glutinously orange spaghetti hoops, but were unable to find the pasta and virgin olive oils we wanted in

Tesco.' Pam laughed again. 'You have to remember, Frankie, this was West Yorkshire, not London: the only olive oil you could get at the time was a tiny bottle from the chemist you bought in preparation for having your ears syringed.'

'I didn't realise.' I smiled. 'I suppose having always been in a family that's cooked and adored Italian food, I assumed everyone round here had always eaten like us.'

'You're joking.' Pam raised an eyebrow. 'Until I met Marco, meals at home were my mum's neck of mutton stew...' she actually shuddered at the memory '...my dad's favourite oxtail and cow heel and, for a treat, a Fray Bentos Steak and Kidney pie from the corner shop. I loved those,' she added dreamily.

'I'd have thought Angelo would have had his eye on a daughter from one of the other Italian families in the area for Marco? You know, the Colettas, the Longos, the D'Agostinos?' I recalled the huge Sunday lunches when other Italian families had sat round the laden table presided over by Angelo, feasting on mountains of pasta and lamb. 'There were so many different Italian families he could have chosen a wife for Marco from. Why you?'

'If Marco had married the daughter of one of Angelo's Sicilian friends then, in effect, he'd have been joining the two families together, allowing access, to some extent, to his burgeoning empire, and Angelo didn't want that. Also, knowing Marco as he did, Angelo didn't want a girl's angry father on his doorstep once Marco wandered which, Angelo knew, he eventually would.'

'Really?' It all seemed a bit dramatic. Like a Sunday evening TV drama. 'Was Angelo really so manipulative?'

'Really. You can imagine how delighted Angelo was when

your dad started going out with Suzy Dobson. His younger son marrying the daughter from Dobson's Mill was right up Angelo's street, and he encouraged it every bit of the way. Not only was Joe stepping into old Midhope society but, by doing that, he was keeping another Sicilian family's mitts off the Piccione Empire.'

'I never knew any of this.' I smiled again. 'Angelo has always just been lovely old Nonno to me.'

'Sicilian politics. Fascinating stuff, isn't it?' Pam attacked the cheesecake with a huge knife, and part of me wondered if it wasn't Nonno she had in mind as she thrust the sharp metal into its soft centre. 'And if you, Frankie, as part of his family, haven't really got much insight into Angelo's mindset, then you can understand how a daft sixteen-year-old from Westenbury village had none. It took me quite a few years to realise why I'd ended up with Marco,' Pam said shortly. 'But, suffice to say, I filled a slot: bright, pretty local girl working at Piccione's. I fitted the bill.'

18

Pam

'Where are you going all dolled up?' Mary Brown looked Pam up and down before asking hopefully, 'Is Marco coming to pick you up again? Is he taking you out for a birthday treat?'

Pam shook her head. 'No, I'm going out with Rob. *He's* taking me out for a birthday treat.'

Mary stopped wiping down the sink with Dennis's old Y-fronts and turned, throwing the cloth onto the draining board. (The thought of her dad's underpants, now utilised as a dishcloth and getting into the corners of every teacup and plate, made Pam feel slightly queasy and she looked away, knowing what they'd once covered.) 'Rob? Rob who?'

'You know perfectly well who Rob is, Mum. He was here in the garden last Sunday.'

'The one with the holes in his jeans? The one who does the funny dancing to black man's music? I'm surprised at you, Pamela. What does Marco think about it?'

'Marco? What's it got to do with *him*?'

'Well, you know, I thought you were going out with him? He's a real catch, Pamela. Look at that car of his.'

'Mum, I won the prize of dinner out with Marco. He took me out. It was very nice. But that's all it was.'

'Did he ask to see you again?'

'No. Why should he?'

'He sent you flowers.'

'So did his dad and I've not heard Angelo Piccione on the phone wanting to take me out, have you?'

'Now you're being silly.'

'So are you, Mum. Marco did his duty to his dad and the company and took me out for my prize. End of story.' Pam examined the newly painted pink nails she'd forked out for at the beauty parlour on the way home from work, using the five-pound note her Granny Brown had included in her birthday card which, as always, had arrived a week early.

'You should be saving that money,' Mary said waspishly as Pamela held up her hands to the mirror over the sideboard.

'Why?'

'For a rainy day. Or your bottom drawer. Our Lynne didn't spend a penny on herself once she got herself engaged on her seventeenth birthday. Every bit of her Christmas and birthday money went towards buying that orange Bacchus dinner and tea set of hers... I have to say it's far too modern for *my* taste, but if *she* likes it...' When Pam didn't respond, Mary went on, 'And tea towels; and all those spice jars she insisted on having.'

'I bet she's never used *any* of that coriander or cumin stuff,' Pamela said vaguely, her mind only on Rob.

'That's not the point,' Mary said.

'So what is?'

'Well, she had a fiancé and a ring on her finger by the time she was a year older than you. You don't want to get left behind, Pamela.'

'Yes, but *I'm* not engaged,' Pam reminded her mum. 'Nowhere near being, thank you very much, so I'm certainly not wasting my money on tea towels.' Mind you, ever since Rob had arrived last week with the gladioli, she'd been having little dreams, little fantasies, of walking down the aisle towards Rob as Stevie Wonder sang 'You are the Sunshine of my Life'.

'Are you listening, Pamela?'

'Hmm.'

'If Marco Piccione asks you out again, you make sure you go.' A sudden thought obviously crossed Mary's mind. 'You could invite him here, Pamela. For his Sunday dinner. I bet he'd appreciate a bit of Yorkshire home cooking after all that foreign stuff he'll be forced to eat at home.'

'I can hear Rob's car, Mum. I'm off.'

'Just you be careful in that car,' Mary shouted at Pam's departing back. 'Don't let him drive too fast. And watch what you're up to as well...'

Too late, that boat's already sailed. Pam frowned to herself, remembering the previous Saturday evening. She opened the front door and set off down the garden path to meet Rob.

'Where are we going?' Pam was surprised when Rob didn't take the main road leading into the town centre as she'd anticipated but instead turned right at the ring road and headed back out of town in the opposite direction.

'You'll see,' he smiled. 'Happy birthday. You look gorgeous, Pam.' She glanced down at the white T-shirt she'd teamed under the pink and white striped blazer with its huge lapels, and knew she'd made the right choice. Rob himself wore a white T-shirt tucked into the usual bleached Levi's (*to go out for dinner, Pamela?* she could hear her mother's critical voice) topped with a beautiful black formal jacket that she would have liked to have stroked.

'Thank you,' she said, happy to sit back and filch surreptitious glances at his profile, taking in the thick blond hair and, when he turned to her, the lovely brown eyes that had so attracted her to him in the first place, enjoying seeing his hands dependable on the steering wheel of the old Morris Minor.

Rob drove on through dusty country lanes overhung with boughs of huge oak, sycamore and beech, their leaves still green and lush even though it was late August and the new season was already waiting in the wings for its succession. A tang of farmyard drifted in through the open windows and the heat of what had been a very warm day rose and curdled and drifted in alongside the smells. Acres of grazing sheep, the spring lambs now unidentifiable in size from their parents, gave way to fields of brown-horned cattle, indifferent to the occasional cars or the evening walkers making the most of the fading light.

'I still don't know where you're taking me.' Pam smiled. 'Are there many places to eat out here?'

'There's just the one as far as I know.' He grinned back and, almost immediately, pulled up at and then through what appeared to be a farm gate. 'Here we are.'

'Where? A farm restaurant?'

A tall, slim woman in dungarees, blonde hair piled up messily on top of her head, a handful of dusty-looking leeks in one hand, appeared at Pam's side as she got out of the car.

'Mum, this is Pam.'

Mum? She was having a birthday dinner with Rob's mum? She turned to look at Rob who appeared slightly sheepish.

'Hello, sweetheart.' Mrs Mansell smiled and waved the leeks in Rob's direction. 'Lovely to meet you. Everything's ready for you, Rob. I need to do something with these; they are absolute beauties, aren't they? I'm definitely going to beat Arnold with these.'

Literally? Pam wondered. What on earth was going on? Who was poor Arnold and what had he done to be in line for a bit of ABH with a giant leek?

'The Heath Green Harvest Festival.' Rob grinned, seeing Pam's face. 'Mum has a love-hate relationship with Arnold Crawshaw, one of the guys on the allotments.'

Rob's mother turned once again to Pam. 'Happy birthday. I do hope you enjoy your meal.' With her thick blonde hair and doe-like brown eyes, there could be no doubt as to whose son Rob was. Except his mother spoke with an accent Pam couldn't quite work out.

'Is this where you live?'

'Hmm, I told you we lived out here. Come on.' Taking Pam's arm, Rob led her across the yard – which she realised wasn't attached to any farm and so, in effect, wasn't a farmyard at all – and down the garden path before helping her climb over a stile into a field.

Pam looked back over her shoulder at the one cottage where the Mansells lived surrounded as it was by seemingly acres of land, and then looked across at the myriad allotments in front of her.

'Here.' Rob led the way to a huge green garden shed, not particularly attractive from its exterior but, inside, a veritable haven from the outside world. He switched on a couple of lamps and the shed's interior was suffused with a warm glow.

'Oh, wow,' Pam exclaimed looking round at the large pine table laid with a white starched cloth, candles – which Rob immediately went to light – crockery, cutlery and a picnic for two. 'Have you done all this?'

'The picnic? Hmm, I called at Sainsbury's on the way home from work yesterday. And there's a fabulous little deli just opened in the village. Very trendy.'

Pam wasn't quite sure what a deli actually was but, if it sold goodies like this now waiting for them on the table, she wanted to know more.

'I hope this is OK?' Rob seemed nervous, his usual confidence, now that he was off the dance floor, missing. 'Not everyone would think it a treat having their birthday dinner in a shed in a field…'

'Honestly, I think it's fabulous.' Pam went over to Rob and kissed his cheek. 'Thank you. It's just not what I expected, especially from you.'

'No, don't tell my mates *anything* about this.' He grinned. 'They'd really take the piss. The thing is, I'm desperately saving up to go to uni. I should get a fairly good grant having worked for several years, but I want to be in London, and you know what London's like.'

'Really? London?' The very thought of him leaving, just when she'd been hoping Rob was wanting their relationship to go further, sent a sudden shock of despondency through Pam.

'I love the countryside round here, but I love big cities too. You know, the clubs...? If I'm going to live in a city, I may as well choose the biggest and busiest.' He glanced across at Pam as he poured her a small glass of cider and reached for a beer. 'Wherever I end up studying – if I do manage to get a place – I'll be home a lot. I might actually try Manchester or Leeds. Both do the course I want. Then I'll be a lot nearer.'

Pam understood, just from the way he was looking at her so intently, what he was trying to say.

'What do you want to study?'

'Politics, social sciences. I want to be a social worker eventually.'

'Really? You've never told me any of this before.'

'Too busy dancing.' He grinned again. 'Come on, sit down and help yourself.'

'Gosh, I don't know where to start.'

'This would be good.' Rob handed her a plate. Then he laughed out loud. 'It is a bit cheeky I suppose, you know, inviting you out for dinner and then bringing you to a field.'

'Does it all belong to your mum?' Pam knew Rob's dad had died a couple of years earlier.

Rob nodded. 'Mum had it as a smallholding for years before she divided it up for allotments that she lets out. You know, chickens, organic fruit and vegetables.'

Pam wasn't sure what organic meant.

'Mum doesn't believe in spraying her stuff with pesticides or weed killer.'

'Oh.' Pam had a sudden vision of her own mother, a

huge can of slug pellets to hand, exorcising and executing anything that had the temerity to venture anywhere near her dahlias. 'How does she get rid of the slugs then?'

'Beer in an orange-peel trap. They get drunk, fall in and die a happy death.' Rob passed over a long crusty stick of French bread.

A bit different from the Hovis her mum always bought from the bakery in the village, eschewing the white-sliced Mother's Pride she vocally condemned (along with tomato ketchup) as 'common'.

'Just break it with your hands,' Rob instructed as she reached for a knife. 'And try the Brie. It needs eating before it runs off the table.'

There was only ever a choice of Cheddar or Cheshire at home (or occasionally her mum would succumb to buying some of the Gorgonzola her dad loved but to which all the females in the house referred to as his *sock cheese*) and Pam wasn't quite sure if she liked the buttery, earthy taste or runny texture of the Brie. Rob piled her plate with different garlicky pâtés (much, much nicer than the potted meat that went into sandwiches at home) more types of cheese, a creamy coleslaw, ruby red tomatoes bursting with juice and flavour ('my mum's from the greenhouse,' Rob said) and a huge bowl of green salad (including what looked suspiciously like dandelion leaves) onto which he was pouring oil. Oil? Pam was confused. Where was the Heinz salad cream?

'Oh, hang on.' Rob jumped up. 'We need music. Mum's just treated herself to a new cassette player. She loves Fats Domino and Little Richard – in fact any black American stuff from the Fifties and Sixties.' He grinned. 'I've seen her up here, when she thinks she's not being watched. She turns the music as high as she can and just goes for it.'

'Goes for it?' Pam couldn't imagine her own mother *going* for anything unless it was to decry all of them for not putting their pants and towels in the linen basket for washing.

'Singing. And dancing as well.'

'Obviously where you've got your love of dancing from?'

'More than likely. She's always danced.' Rob smiled and inserted a cassette. 'I'm not convinced about these.' He frowned, holding up its plastic case. 'I'd much rather play my 45s, but these are fine for out here. Just listen to this – the latest from Martha Reeves.'

'Where's she from?' Pam asked, once Martha was singing and Rob was breaking off more bread. 'Your mum, not Martha Reeves, I mean. She's not from round here, is she?'

'She's German.'

'But your dad is – was – English?'

Rob nodded. 'Dad met her and totally fell in love with her during the war. He was in the D-Day landings and then his regiment eventually moved up through Germany. Mum's family lived on a farm near Berlin. They'd already been forced to give over most of their food and livestock to the retreating German army. Then the allies came along and took what was left.'

'Really? I thought the Brits were the good guys?'

'They were fighting an enemy. I guess they thought nothing of turfing a German farmer's family out of their own beds and raiding their food cupboards when they'd seen what Hitler had done to the rest of Europe. Anyway, my mum was just sixteen and Dad fell head over heels in love with her.'

Just sixteen, Pam thought, pleased. *My age*.

'And she with him. Dad was sent over to Burma for a year but they wrote to each other, with a mate of Dad's translating into German for him and as soon as the war was all over and he was able to, he took the train back to Germany and brought her back to England and they got married.'

'How romantic. What a wonderful story.'

'It is, isn't it?' Rob looked at her, smiled and Pam knew what she'd known ever since she'd first set eyes on him in Moonlight several months ago now: she really, really fancied him and she wanted this relationship to go a lot further.

'So, what did you get up to once I'd left you on Saturday evening? I'm sorry, I meant to ask you when I saw you on Sunday.' Rob lifted salad leaves onto a side plate, but didn't eat as he waited for Pam to reply.

'It was Piccione's summer ball at the RAFA club. I went on there with Jane. And...' Pam hesitated '...I was crowned Miss Piccione 1974.'

Rob frowned. 'Oh? Really? I'm amazed antiquated rituals like that still happen. Mind you, you had to have won it – you must have been the most gorgeous girl there.' Rob leaned across and stroked her hand before going back to the salad. 'So, what was your prize? A day trip to Blackpool?'

Pam laughed at that. 'No, a bottle of cheap fizz...' She hesitated once again. 'And dinner out with Mr Piccione's son.'

'Really?' Rob said once again. 'And have you been? Have you claimed your prize?'

'Yes, we went to Bennani's in town on Wednesday.'

'With *Marco* Piccione?' Rob put down his fork and glanced across at Pam.

Was Rob jealous? 'I didn't know you knew him,' Pam said surprised. 'Anyway, it was nowhere near as lovely as this,' she reassured him.

'I don't know him at all,' Rob said. 'Just heard of him. Everyone's heard of the Picciones. Angelo Piccione's got a bit of a reputation as a womaniser and I'd always heard that Marco was going down that road as well. Did you feel safe with him? He didn't try anything?'

'No, no, no,' Pam said, hearing her voice rise as well as the colour in her face.

'I'd hate to think that, Pam.' He laughed self-consciously, raking a hand through his blond hair in a way Pam had come to know and to love. 'I don't know what the hell you've done to me...' he gestured round the shed as if to say: *you made me do all this* '...but I tell you what, I want you to keep on doing it.'

19

Frankie

'I assume you know about this?'

'What's that?' Daler spread Piccione's Lemon Curd thickly onto his toast and without cutting the slice in two lifted the whole piece to his mouth and took an enormous bite. 'God, this stuff is good,' he managed to get out before going in for a second attempt.

'Do you think so? It's far too sweet for me. It's the one thing I reckon Piccione's have never got right. I can't bear the stuff.'

'It's wonderful,' Daler reiterated, demolishing the remains of the toast and licking at the splodge of escaped lemon curd on his fingers. 'Just lock me up in a tower with you and a vat of this stuff and I'll die a happy man.'

'You're not dying, are you?' For a split second I had an awful vision of life without Daler. It was unthinkable. 'You do eat far too much sweet stuff, you know.'

'Leave me alone.' Daler grinned, scraping the remaining

lemon curd from the bottom and sides of the jar and spooning it directly into his mouth. 'It's the only pleasure I have in life when I'm denied lamb chops, and shouldn't really be drinking alcohol.'

'The *only* pleasure? Are you sure about that?' I wriggled my hips seductively and ran the tip of my tongue around my lips in parody of a porn star and moved towards Daler. It was Saturday morning in mid-October and we were sitting in my tiny kitchen in Dad's granny flat listening to the Rev Richard Coles and Aasmah Mir on the radio. While I had a pile of university coursework to get through – I did hope Daler was going to help me with the bits I couldn't quite get my head round – Daler himself was revelling in the fact he had two whole days off.

'What do you assume I know about?' Daler finally asked as I allowed him to come up for air from my ministrations. He tasted of sugar, lemon and coffee.

'Sorry?'

'You were showing me something? You know, before you started perverting me.'

I reached for the stiff cream envelope on the table. 'This?'

'You're not being very helpful, Frankie. I may be a man of many talents...' he moved a warm hand towards the cord holding up my pyjama bottoms '...but even I can't see through paper.'

'*This.*' I took the rectangular card from the envelope. It was as heavy and expensively embossed as the envelope in which it had arrived. 'It's an invitation to your cousin's wedding in Leeds.'

'Right.'

'So, did you know about it? Did you know I'd been invited?'

Daler nodded. 'I asked Mum to sort it.'

'But it's next week. Next Friday. Surely, it's too late for an invitation to go out? What do I wear? I should be in lectures.'

'Well, yes,' Daler conceded, 'obviously, the invitations went out months ago. Literally months ago. But I wanted you there, Frankie. With me. So I asked Mum to sort it.' He shrugged. 'End of.'

'And your mum was OK with it all?'

'Hmm.'

'And your dad?' I found Daler's father somewhat distant. Actually, more than that: distinctly chilly. Manraj Dosanjh was polite in the extreme but, compared to Chuni's exuberant friendliness, he had the ability, whenever I was round at *Dosanjh Towers* – as I'd dubbed their sprawling pile – to make me feel slightly uneasy, and even, at times, unwelcome.

'Hmm.' Daler replaced the card in its envelope and, draining his coffee cup, reached once more for the cord holding up my pyjamas. 'Like I said. Everything's OK.'

I couldn't get out of the following Friday morning lecture – I didn't want to get out of it – as it was timetabled for one of the many simulations used by the university to reflect real-life situations in the safety of the classroom rather than actually on the ward, and we were being taught the intricacies of understanding the science behind, as well as the practical skills of, taking blood pressure. Whenever I'd had my own blood pressure taken for whatever reason, it had never been explained to me what the top number over the bottom number meant. You could have told me I was 200/120 and I wouldn't have any idea I was about to – literally – blow a gasket. I was looking forward to it.

Luckily, this was just in the morning, the afternoon being given over to self-directed study. Knowing I'd have to self-direct myself at the rate of an express train (and in doing so probably send my blood pressure up to those dangerous levels I'd just been learning about) over the weekend to make up for my going AWOL on the Friday afternoon, I was able to join Daler in Leeds towards the end of the afternoon.

The *Anand Karaj* (or blissful union as Daler had explained it to me) of the happy couple had started the day before with celebrations at the bride's parents' home in North Leeds. The actual religious ceremony and solemnisation joining Parmit Dosanjh, Daler's cousin, to Deepan Bhasin had taken place earlier that day in the large Gurdwara on Chapeltown Road just out of the centre of Leeds. The real celebrations, and boy, was this an amazingly colourful fanfare of a celebration, had then moved on to the banqueting suite at the Royal Armouries.

By the time I'd driven over and found somewhere to park my Mini, the pre-dinner party was well under way. Feeling terribly shy and out of place amongst the beautifully attired guests who, together, resembled nothing more than a glorious, technicolour flock of tropical birds, I hovered around the periphery of the fabulously decorated hall, desperately trying to find Daler. Everything from floor to ceiling, including the floor itself, was decorated in hues of red, ivory, gold and navy blue. With the majority of the guests adorned in similarly strong colours leaching into the decorations themselves, I had the ridiculously fanciful notion I'd fallen into the kaleidoscope Aunty Pam had given me for my seventh birthday, and which I still wasn't averse to squinting through when the mood took me.

Trays of canapés – *raja chicken*, *chilli paneer*, *mogo masala* – and all explained to me by the traditionally dressed waiters – appeared to descend on me non-stop so that, at one point, I had two in one hand and one in the other. It seemed almost an impossibility to find Daler amongst all this colour and adrenaline-filled, intense pizzazz: there must have been a thousand guests in the process of acquainting and reacquainting themselves with long-lost friends, relatives and business associates and the chattering and excited greetings were literally almost deafening. Certainly, the loud bhangra music was fighting a losing battle with the enveloping sound, being almost totally drowned out by the plethora of loud squawks, delighted shrieks and general bonhomie washing in ever-increasing waves around me.

'Darling Francesca, you found us? Well done.'

Just as I was about to give up the ghost and retreat back to my car with my two *samosa chana chaat*, Chuni was advancing upon me, hands held out in welcome as she turned simultaneously to the three women in her wake. 'You *must* come and meet Francesca,' Chuni was gaily singing as I desperately popped the final delicious morsel into my mouth and wiped my hands surreptitiously down my dress before holding out my own hand. 'She has been *such* a darling, helping Daler to readjust to life back up here in the grey, miserable north.'

Miserable north? Wasn't Chuni herself from Dewsbury? And surely, Daler had only been working in Coventry, the grey, miserable midlands? She was making it sound as if she was from somewhere far more exotic and had been dragged up to Yorkshire kicking and screaming. I was tempted to remind her that *Dosanjh Towers* overlooked the incredibly gorgeous Norman's Meadow, one of the most beautiful places on the planet.

'You're a friend of Daler?' the elder of the three asked, pressing my hands into her own.

'She's Daler's *best* friend at the moment...' Chuni chirruped.

At the moment?

'...and has been an absolute poppet taking Daler out of himself when he's been so involved with this new job at the hospital,' Chuni went on. 'All work and no play and all that.' She sighed heavily. 'I do sometimes feel he's taken on far too much with all this doctoring.'

'And I hear you're going to be *a nurse*? At Midhope General? Well done you, getting down and dirty.'

Down and dirty?

'You'll be doing your fair share of swilling out bedpans, I would imagine?' The heavily made up and bejewelled matron in the middle of the three smiled, somewhat condescendingly, the question obviously rhetorical as she added, 'My two daughters are both medics.' I was almost blinded by the flash of diamonds and emeralds as she blithely indicated with her hand to somewhere behind her in the almost seething crowd of guests. 'Jasmine is professor of obstetrics in London and Abbey is a consultant paediatrician near Bristol.'

And I – just about – understand the intricacies of blood pressure, I nearly replied but, instead smiled. 'You must be very proud.'

I was rescued from Chuni and her gang of three by a warm hand on the back of my neck.

'Ah, Daler, there you are,' Chuni admonished. 'Poor Francesca has arrived and is *totally* lost. You must look after your friends better than this, darling. It's so good of you to give up your time again, Francesca.' She linked my arm somewhat possessively as she turned to the other women. 'This gorgeous girl has helped out at the Langar meal as well, you know…' before smiling back at me '… to keep Daler company. Right, you two, off you go, enjoy yourselves.'

'Golly.' It was all I felt able to say as I followed Daler towards a waiter with a tray of drinks. I could have knocked back the whole lot in one go.

'A bit overwhelming?' he asked, smiling down at me worriedly.

'Just a bit. There are *so many* of you.'

'Of us? Sikhs, you mean?'

I hadn't meant that. Or perhaps I had. 'So many of your friends and relatives all in one place,' I amended.

'I don't know half of them.' Daler frowned. 'It's the custom to show hospitality to as large a gathering as one is able.'

'You look gorgeous,' I said, my eyes taking in the light-coloured, beautifully cut jacket worn casually over yellow waistcoat and formal dress trousers. I'd only ever seen Daler wearing jeans and T-shirt – or scrubs – and I felt quite dazzled by his beauty.

'So do you.' He smiled.

'Hardly,' I said, crossly. 'You said as long as I wore something bright – never black or white to a Sikh wedding – I'd be fine. I wish you'd told me, Daler, that this dress would be an absolute no-no. Verboten.'

I'd chosen this favourite red dress of mine – accompanied by my one pair of Louboutins (a Christmas present from Mum and Paul a couple of years previously, they were shiny, red, patent and bloody uncomfortable) – with the help of Tammy who'd rifled through my wardrobe with a triumphant, 'yes, this is the one,' before pushing me into the shower. Tammy had taken the dress off for 'a quick sponge down' (like a geriatric having a bed bath) and 'quick once-over with the iron' as well as a stitch to the hem where, if I remember rightly, I'd caught it in the heel of my shoe on a somewhat drunken night out with Daisy and the rest of the Liverpool-based air crew.

That I'd got it all wrong was confirmed when, looking round I could see no other, amongst the brightly coloured saris and lehengas, actually in red. And doubly confirmed when the bride, Parmit, made her entrance wearing the devastatingly beautiful bright red, jewelled and embroidered wedding sari. I gazed in awe and wonder at her. She looked so beautiful, so happy.

'Don't worry,' Daler soothed, but I could feel his discomfort. 'You weren't to know.'

'No, but *you* did.' Was this our first row?

'It's fine. You're not a Sikh in traditional dress. It's not the same.'

★

I'd have felt a whole load better, more at ease, if I could have downed more than the one glass of champagne, but not only were a large majority of the guests – including Daler – drinking Coke or orange juice, and the last thing I wanted was to appear a lush in front of his family and friends, I was also mindful of having the car with me. I was quite relieved, after being introduced to, and making conversation with, a whole load of different people when we were invited to take our places to eat in the vast banqueting hall. Daler had told me that, traditionally, Sikhs had eaten the wedding breakfast in the Langar hall of the Gurdwara, prepared and served in the same way as the daily Langar meal, but there had been a shift, for those marrying in the larger cities of London, Birmingham, Manchester and Leeds, to celebrate in style in the more commercial venues of hotels and dedicated halls.

I took Daler's hand as we attempted to join the crowd jostling to see one of several table plans, but left him to it when that seemed an impossibility. He finally got through and, after a good five minutes' perusal he returned to my side.

'I'll take you to your table,' he said, not quite meeting my eye.

'*My* table?'

'I'm on the top table with my family,' he said. 'Sorry, I should have thought…' He frowned, looking round almost in desperation. 'No, that's daft, come on, I'll come and sit with you at the back. We'll ask for another chair, another table setting…'

'No, really, Daler, please, don't make a fuss.' I was mortified when several of the guests turned at Daler's raised voice to see what was going on. 'I was very last-minute if you remember. Honestly, it's fine…'

'Come on, Daler,' Manraj Dosanjh urged his son, one hand firmly on Daler's arm. 'Help your friend to her place and then come and take your own down at the front with us.' All said, on his part, without a glance in my direction.

The noise emanating from each beautifully and cleverly decorated table was immense, each vying to compete with the next, it seemed, as hands were shaken and more kisses and hugs thrown out to new guests joining each one. I knew, if I could just have a couple of drinks, I'd be able to relax and even enjoy myself. *What wasn't to like?* I admonished myself, sternly. For heaven's sake, I was at a fabulous party, about to get to know a whole load of Daler's friends and family – although, to be honest, Daler himself didn't seem to be acquainted with the majority of them – and wine was flowing.

Oh, sod it. If I was going to get through this, I needed a drink. I made the decision to leave my car overnight and get a lift back with Daler. He – or I could always beg a lift from Dad or Tammy – would just have to run me over from Westenbury at some point the next day.

'White or red?'

'White please.' I downed a good half-glassful and, feeling the soothing liquid begin its magic and myself relax, sat back for a good look at my table companions. 'Hello.' I held out my hand to the guy on my right, delighted that there was someone, like me, who not only was obviously non-Sikh, but who was wearing, also like me, the forbidden colour of red.

He loosened his tie around the collar of his red shirt and grinned back in my direction, obviously pleased to see a fellow rule breaker. 'Hi, Anthony – call me Tony,' he amended, shaking my proffered hand. 'Bride or groom?'

'My boyfriend—' I indicated with a nod of my head the top table '—is the bride's cousin. You?'

'Oh, I just happen to work in the same legal firm as Deepan.' Tony smiled. 'Isn't this absolutely fabulous?' He swung an arm expansively. 'All of this, I mean?'

And it was. Now I had someone to talk to, now I had the crutch of a few glasses of Sauvignon Blanc – and an exceptionally good Chilean one to boot – I was able to take in the whole fabulous madness and was starting to enjoy myself. 'I never imagined anything like this,' I said. 'My lot are Sicilian and know how to throw a good party.' I beamed. 'But nothing on *this* scale. It's so colourful, so... so *vibrant*.'

Tony refilled my glass from one of the many bottles cooling in the huge red-and-gold-coloured bucket packed with ice and I reached forwards to read the glittering gold-bordered card placed on a tiny gold easel in the centre of the table. 'Dior?'

'That's us – our table,' a beautiful girl with mesmerising eyes in the most heavenly midnight-blue sari to my left explained. 'Hi, I'm Moneek. Parmit has gone for a designer theme for her do.'

'Designer theme?'

'Oh yes.' Moneek nodded sagely. 'It's the total done thing these days; it makes it so much easier for the guests to associate and remember your wedding if there's an actual theme. Gives the wedding planner something to work on as well. I thought she was going for *Fairy Tales* or

– heaven forbid – even *Rajasthani* when I saw all the red, gold and blue, but that's so last year. No, I think this is very good. Look…' She waved a hand in the direction of the surrounding walls where images of different men and women were in the process of being flashed up. 'See?'

I didn't really.

'St Laurent, Westwood, Stella McCartney…' she chanted as designer after designer replaced the one before and tables whooped in delight and in turn as their particular designer hit the screen. *Golly*, I thought, as I dutifully stood and cheered, following the others' lead as we hollered in turn once Christian Dior made an appearance. I knew very few clothes designers: apart from my Louboutins, I was a bit of a Zara girl at heart. So, if we down in the cheap seats were Dior, what on earth was the top table where Daler was seated? I glanced across the room, trying to catch his eye, but he was fully engrossed in conversation with an exceptionally attractive girl in a simple and yet beautifully cut green and gold lehenga. No one on the bride and groom's raised table appeared to be jumping up at their designer of choice and I came to the conclusion the whole thing must simply be a party game for the masses rather than the superior beings at the front.

'Deepan has been worried about his father, you know.' Tony leaned in to speak in a confidential whisper. 'He has a bum ticker he's been trying to keep a secret.'

A bum ticker? What in God's name was a *bum* ticker? Was this something I was going to come across once I was actually on the wards? Or was it similar to a *chicken tikka*…?

'Right.'

Tony nodded sagely in the older man's direction on the top table.

I glanced across once again, trying to evaluate the seriousness of the inflicted man's poorly arse but was immediately diverted from his worrying backside by the green and gold girl's hand lying possessively on Daler's arm.

Oy, back off, Greeny, I wanted to shout. *He's mine*.

'Hmm,' Tony was saying into my ear, 'there was some concern that his father's heart might give out before the wedding.'

'Oh, his *heart*? He's having problems with his *heart*...?' I gave a whoop of laughter that ended in those dreadful giggles that once afflicted with, are hard to stop. 'His heart...?'

'He's actually very ill, you know, not really *funny* at all,' Anthony – call me Tony – said giving me a funny look before turning to speak to the girl on his right.

Oh blimey, second faux pas of the evening: not only was I dressed in a manner to offend the bride and all Sikh sensibilities, I was now laughing like a mentally defective hyena at her new father-in-law's heart problems.

The only food I'd eaten all day was the remaining – insubstantial – crust from a loaf of Hovis at breakfast and the six delicious – but just as insubstantial – tiny canapés an hour previously, so was relieved when steaming fragrant dishes of *raada lamb*, *jeera pulao*, *tava paranthas* and *kadai paneer* were placed on the table in front of us.

'Oh,' Moneek, on my left, sounded disappointed, her eyes following the waiters as they finally retreated.

'Are you OK?'

'I was hoping for maybe just a little beef,' Moneek

admitted, lowering her voice in my direction. 'We're not allowed it at home and I do like a juicy steak occasionally… but don't let my dad hear that.' She passed the various side dishes down the table, piling her plate with a mound of food that belied her tiny frame.

More wine was poured, more whooping ensued as Dior made several comebacks on the screen putting our table, apparently, in the lead, and then we all dived in to the delicious food.

'I see Sienna's back in favour.' A very large girl in a rather too-tight gold and yellow sari nodded across to Moneek through an obviously too-large mouthful of food.

'Was she ever out?' Moneek yelled back. 'I don't *think* so.'

'Look at old man Dosanjh trying to get the two of them back together.' The girl in gold and yellow smirked, turning towards the top table.

My head shot up, the food turning to ashes in my mouth. I swallowed hard and reached for my glass of wine.

'She's obviously heard he's been messing around with some *ciṭī kuṛī dī samasi'ā*.' The girl's tone wasn't kind.

I swallowed again and asked, as pleasantly as I could, 'Who are you talking about?'

Both girls turned in my direction and stared, realising they'd been talking over me. 'Oh, the gorgeous Dr Daler Dosanjh up on the top table. You won't know him: he's Parmit's cousin. If you look – no,' she tutted crossly. 'Don't both turn and stare at the same time – if you look, you'll see him. He's talking to the girl next to him in the green lehenga… God, who would ever wear green at a wedding…? Anyway, Daler has been in love with her for years…'

'It's always been assumed they'd marry,' Moneek interrupted. 'Daler's dad, Manraj, has been trying to bring the two families together for *ever*.'

'But Sienna, I think, was looking for a better option.'

'A better option than the Dosanjhs, for heaven's sake? Who's she after, Prince William?'

'A bit too Yorkshire for Sienna, I reckon; she'd rather be living in London.'

'What was the phrase you used?' I asked, forcing a rictus of a smile.

'Phrase?' Yellow Sari had loaded both her fork and her mouth once more and couldn't utter more than one word. She chewed and swallowed and eventually repeated: '*Ciṭī kuṛī dī samasi"ā?*'

I nodded.

'White girl,' Yellow Sari translated. 'No offence, and all that,' she added, looking me up and down. 'It just means White Girl Problem.'

'Thank you,' I returned, laying down my fork.

'Any time.' She beamed, turning back to her plate of food.

20

Frankie

Then

Driving home in the early hours of Saturday morning from the wedding in Leeds, Daler was quiet, uncommunicative even. The wedding do had gone on and on and, once I'd decided to leave my car in the car park and been told I was a *white girl problem*, I'd spent most of it knocking back wine with the rest of the drinkers on the table. And could they drink. The music, the eating, the speeches, the fabulous displays of bhangra dancing, the drinking and the almost deafening chat seemed to go on for ever, and after five or six hours of this intense celebration I just wanted to go home.

It wasn't that I was against such exuberant festivity as this: I felt honoured to have been invited and to be part of the experience – even though I knew it had been Daler who had manipulated my invitation – and normally, especially once I'd made the decision to get stuck into the alcohol, I'd have been completely taken up by the whole madness of the evening.

I was absolutely fascinated by the all-male bhangra dancers in their turquoise, pink and white *pag* turbans and *kurtas*, their singing, shouting, beating the double-headed *dhol* drum and hypnotically throwing their stick thing (*daang*, Moneek instructed me) into the air and towards the tables as they danced. Moneek also informed me, somewhat sniffily and in a voice loaded with too much red wine, that 'bhangra originates from a very *patriarchal* society – you know? – connecting to a much deeper set of masculine values that are quite *outmoded* in today's world...' I didn't care. I absolutely adored the whole thing and if Daler and Sienna hadn't been up on the top table, coolly watching but not joining in at all, I had an awful feeling I'd have been up there with the gorgeous dancing men, demanding a *daang* of my own and getting stuck in with them.

But, apart from the dancing, most of the time I felt like I was on the outside looking in; that I wasn't really involved in what was going on and the more alcohol I drank in order to feel myself a cohesive and organic part of my whooping and celebrating fellow table companions, the more I was unable to shake off the feeling of being on the periphery of it all.

I did try. I was up dancing with Moneek and Gold and Yellow Sari (I never did get to know her name) at every opportunity, even kicking off my high heels in order to stay on the floor as long as the others, before introducing myself and chatting with each one in turn of the other nine on the table. And yet not one person there asked anything about me. Why I was there? Who I was with? It was assumed, I think, because I was on the table with a whole load of workmates of both the bride and groom, I must be just another fairly unimportant colleague, invited because that was the way of Sikh hospitality at society weddings such as this.

No one, it seemed, made any connection with myself and Daler Dosanjh and, after the comment by Gold and Yellow Sari, I didn't feel I could either, especially as Daler appeared fully occupied with Sienna. Every time I looked over to the top table – and I found myself doing it constantly during the long interminable hours – Daler was either talking with her, laughing with her, dancing with her or – and this was worrying – the pair of them had disappeared.

On the drive home I was physically and mentally exhausted but as I sat in the passenger seat of his car, my eyes closed, I was also totally attuned to every aspect, every little nuance of Daler as the car ate up the miles down an almost deserted M62.

I know he thought I was asleep, but I was able to watch him from under my lashes as he drove – probably too quickly – down the motorway back to Midhope. His beautiful face seemed rigid – brittle almost – but at one point, as he slowed down for traffic lights, he turned to me and mouthed, 'I love you, Frankie,' and relaxing into the assurance of his love for me, I drifted off to sleep.

I was frightened to ask about Sienna, frightened to hear of Daler's past love for the beautiful cool girl in green.

'That was such an amazing experience,' I lied, feigning tiredness and yawning loudly as I pulled off my clothes in my tiny bedroom, scrubbed at my make-up and jumped into bed. 'Let's have a full post-mortem of the whole thing tomorrow.'

Daler, who was still fully dressed and drinking an ice-cold

beer he'd found in the fridge, came to stand by the bed and I could sense him looking down at me.

'Come to bed,' I whispered, needing him next to me.

'I'm up in a couple of hours,' he said quietly. 'On the 6am shift in A and E. I ought to go home.'

'Well then, you've got...' I squinted at my bedside clock '...four hours. Come on, Daler.' I pulled back the duvet. 'Come and sleep.'

I feigned sleep once more. I wanted to know more about Sienna – he'd never once mentioned her in the three months we'd been together – but I didn't want to get into an alcohol-fuelled argument with him when I might hear something I'd rather not. I knew I was being pretty ostrich-like, but I also knew Daler had been, to all intents and purposes, acting out his role as dutiful son and relative at his cousin's wedding. He might once have been in love with this Sienna woman and, yes, his father, who I knew wasn't that impressed with Daler's relationship with me, might have been trying to rekindle that – hopefully – dead relationship, but at the end of the day Daler loved me. I knew he did, and not just because I'd seen him mouth the words as we drove home in the car.

Anxious and uptight as I was, I pulled Daler into my body and, the alcohol getting the better of me, I slept only to be awakened, an hour or so later, by Daler's warm hands pulling down the flimsy straps of my nightgown, his mouth on my neck and then moving down to my breast. In my half-awake state, my body responded automatically and deliciously to his every move and as we made love, silently and incredibly movingly, I knew that if I were to lose Daler I would also lose myself.

As he reached his climax, Daler pulled my hands above my head and breathed, 'Frankie, I love you. You are, and always will be, the other half of me.'

I knew Daler would be absolutely shattered after twelve hours' duty in A and E on a Saturday, especially after a shift on only a couple of hours' sleep. I'd kissed him goodbye in the gloom of a late November morning and, after catching up on a few more hours' sleep, went round to cadge coffee and one of Tammy's fabulous blueberry muffins before heading off to the supermarket. I'd decided I was going to cook Daler a fabulous curry as well as make lemon meringue ice cream in order to indulge his sweet tooth.

'There's a few jars of lemon curd in the pantry,' Tammy said as I closed my eyes in over-the-top ecstasy on the final bit of muffin. 'Just help yourself.'

'Don't tell Dad—' I lowered my voice '—but I actually find Piccione's Lemon Curd far too sweet. Although Daler absolutely loves it.'

'I know what you mean,' Tammy whispered in return. 'I buy Sainsbury's own, but don't tell your dad that either. He'd go ballistic.' We grinned conspiratorially. 'So, special supper for Daler then? Any occasion?' She raised an eyebrow hopefully.

'No, not at all. We've been seeing each other three months now and I just thought I'd tell him... you know...'

'You fancy the pants off him?' Tammy grinned. 'Frankie, he *is* absolutely gorgeous. Dad and I watched *Lion* last night. Your dad went through a whole box of man-sized Kleenex, but all I kept saying was, "*Are you sure Daler wasn't Dev*

Patel before he became a doctor?" Daler, I mean,' she added seriously through a mouthful of muffin. 'As far as I know, Dev Patel never trained as a doctor.'

'I know exactly what you mean.' I laughed.

'You're so much happier now than I've ever seen you,' Tammy went on. 'Get that curry cooked and bubbling then meet him at the door with a great big gin and tonic…'

'He only drinks beer.'

'OK, meet him at the door with an ice-cold beer, have your evil way with him and then feed him curry and lemon meringue ice cream. He'll never leave your side after that little lot.'

'I don't have any intention of letting him.' I grinned, dotting the remaining muffin crumbs with a wet finger and going off in search of Tammy's reusable shopping bags.

I *was* so much happier, I admitted to myself as I trailed up and down the supermarket aisles looking for the spices and vegetables I needed to make *dahl* and the ingredients for lemon meringue ice cream and then, remembering I'd a whole load of university work to do, put my foot down, grabbed what I needed, braced the cold and wet outside, and shot home.

I *was* happier, I thought again in the car. I was really enjoying my nursing – pretty broke of course, but Dad and Nonno were not averse to helping me out now that they could see I was really embracing my new career. I'd often find Dad had taken my Mini and filled it with petrol and Nonno was always sending over food parcels of pickles and preserves with an envelope containing £50 '*to tide you over, cara, while you become next Florence Nightingale*' nestled between the jars. I missed Daisy more than I ever thought I would as she continued to work for Flying High. But I had Daler. I had Daler and I loved him.

I spent the afternoon cooking and finishing an essay on *Reflection on Communication in Practice* and, feeling pretty proud of my efforts on both scores, went to shower away curry cooking smells and pamper my body a bit, laughing out loud to myself, and determined to relate the mistake I'd made over the *bum ticker* to Daisy who, I knew, would really appreciate the tale.

So immersed was I in shampooing, conditioning, defuzzing and moisturising in the shower I didn't realise how late it had become. By the time I'd dripped from the shower and found my favourite black leather skirt and grey cashmere jumper, it was going up to seven.

And then it was eight and no Daler.

This didn't worry me. I knew now, having already spent a couple of weeks on the wards of Midhope General, just how frantic the pace can get if several emergencies come in at once, or if, for whatever reason, a ward is short-staffed.

And then it was nine and still no sign of him.

I nibbled at a cantucci, as much for something to do while I waited as to stop me taking 'taster' samples of the dahl which, though I say it myself, was really quite delicious. I was dying to have Daler sit down, kick off his shoes and just relax with a beer and eat.

At nine-thirty I checked my phone for the hundredth time and then tried ringing him.

Nothing.

Then I began to imagine all sorts of things and, of course, Sienna was playing a leading role in the main drama running through my head. Wasn't she living in London? I supposed she was still up in the north staying with her family. Had she waited outside the hospital until Daler came off duty and whisked him away somewhere? Was he more than happy to be whisked?

My phone rang. Thank goodness. I grabbed it and, although I was delighted to hear from her, it wasn't Daler.

'You OK?' Daisy asked. 'You sound a bit, you know, *fraught.*'

'No, I'm fine. Really. It's just that I've made this really lovely meal and dolled myself up – the whole works – and Daler has obviously been caught up in an emergency at the hospital again.'

'Well, he does work in Accident and *Emergency.*' Daisy laughed. 'You know, the name's on the tin. Anyway, listen, I'm back home.'

'For the weekend?'

'For good. Been sacked.'

'Oh?' Daler was momentarily forgotten at this little bombshell. 'What did you do this time? Drop a cabin bag on some old dear's head again?'

Daisy laughed, remembering. 'Something like that. It's a good story, so I'll tell you when I see you. But listen, I'm going to be here for a while. Charlie's back as well...'

'Oh, your poor mum and dad.'

'...and we're going to work together on a building project on an old farmhouse my Granny Madge has just told us she owns. Unbelievable, but all really exciting...' Daisy's enthusiasm was palpable as she continued to speak, telling me in great detail about the whole thing. I looked at my watch. It was almost ten. '...and the best thing about it is Granny has actually given us – can you imagine, Frankie – *given* Charlie and me an old cottage on the site. For us to develop. I've got a house... I own a house...'

'Daisy, that's wonderful. Can I talk to you tomorrow? I'm getting a bit worried about Daler. I need to ring him...' Basically, get off the phone, Daisy.

'Oh, OK, sorry, it *is* late. Come over tomorrow. Come and see it. I'm dying to show you...'

The second I pressed the end call button on my phone, it sprang into life once more.

'Daler? Where are you?'

'A and E.'

'You're still there? Oh, for heaven's sake, Daler? Shall I bring the damned curry there? Bring you a takeaway?' Although I was fed up, cross that our evening was ruined, the thought of me becoming a curry takeaway service in my Mini was making me giggle.

There was a strange noise coming down the phone and I couldn't work out what it was. And then I realised it was actually Daler. 'What is it? What's happened?' When he didn't reply and I realised he was crying, I soon stopped. 'Oh, Daler, I'm sorry I was laughing; I was just imagining me as a curry service. Has someone died on you?'

'It's Dad.'

'Your dad? What?'

'He was attacked at the temple this evening. It was his turn to help with the Langar meal. Dad was helping to clear up and came across some guy where he shouldn't have been, shooting up. Dad told him to get out – the temple mustn't be sullied by drug use; I've told you that – and the guy went for him. Stabbed him...' The awful sound of Daler, my lovely strong man, crying, came down the phone again, unable to get his words out.

'Oh Daler, no. Is he... OK?'

'OK? Frankie, he's just been... *attacked* with a huge machete by a fucking drug addict who shouldn't have been in the Gurdwara to begin with.'

'I'm sorry, Daler. I'm so sorry.'

'He's in surgery now.'

'I'll come over. Over to the hospital.'

'No, no. Really. Please don't. Mum and my grandmother are both already here and Juneeta is on her way. There's all sorts going on with the police taking statements and Mum having absolute hysterics. Look, I'll come round tomorrow...'

And he rang off.

I cleared the table, put foil over the curry and cling-filmed the cold, cooked basmati rice and then, not quite knowing what else to do, unlocked the door that led to the main house to find my dad. As well as Aunty Pam, Dad was, and always would be, my go-to for love and comfort when it was needed.

21

Pam

Then

Pam knew her whole world was about to come crashing down around her ears. Whoever it was said you couldn't get pregnant the first time you had sex or just after you'd finished a period obviously hadn't met Pamela Brown: a double whammy; a full house; Plague and Pestilence about to descend on the house of Brown in Westenbury village.

Years later, Pamela was still unable to work out why she hadn't just kept it all quiet, gone off to London or Manchester for 'a few days' break' with Jane and had a termination. She just didn't know how to go about it. Would she have to sit in front of Dr O'Bryan, their elderly Irish-Catholic family GP and ask/demand that he sign one of the two forms to say she was mentally unstable and couldn't possibly continue with a pregnancy? She'd known him since she was a baby herself, hiding under the bedclothes as a child, heart pounding as he'd slowly creaked his way up the stairs to her bedroom (she'd visualised him as the child catcher: *There are children here somewhere. I can smell them. Come along, kiddie-winkies!*) whenever she'd had yet another bout of bronchitis or tonsillitis to which she was prone, or the yellow jaundice that had really frightened her mother.

In the end, when she'd missed two periods, she confided in Jane who, at first aghast, had come up trumps and gone with her and a Horlicks jar containing her early morning pee to Raynor and Sons' Pharmacy in the High Street where their *Ladycare Pregnancy Test and Information Service* poster was discreetly sandwiched between an advert for Truss Support and details of the local Alcoholics Anonymous.

There was, it seemed, no going back.

Eventually, with heart pounding, blood racing in her ears and the metallic taste she couldn't get rid of in her mouth making her stumble over her words, she got her mum alone in her bedroom when everyone else was out of the house. Mary Brown was on her hands and knees hunting for Janet's grey school sock that had gone AWOL from the newly ironed clothes she was in the middle of sorting into piles on her bed before dispensing to their rightful owners.

'Where's Dad?'

'In the garden. Been having problems with his morning glory. Says it just won't grow big enough or something…'

'Mum, I'm pregnant.'

Mary, intent on running the recalcitrant sock to ground wasn't concentrating. 'I had the both of them two minutes ago… Sorry, love, what did you say?'

Oh God, wasn't once enough? She now had to speak out and repeat the words? Pam took a deep breath, focused her attention on the print of the *corps de ballet* from *Swan*

Lake that had been a feature of Mary's bedside table for ever and said loudly, 'I said: "Mum, I'm pregnant."'

The colour drained from her mother's face as she sat – comically, Pam thought, with her legs splayed out in front of her – at the side of the double divan, and then almost immediately reappeared, starting at the base of her neck and spreading northwards in a mottled flush.

'What do you mean, you're pregnant?' Mary stared, her eyes moving from Pam's face to her middle.

'I mean, *I'm pregnant.*'

'It's that scruffy dancing German, isn't it?'

'German?'

'You told me his mother was German.'

'Well, yes, she is.' Pam frowned. 'What's that got anything to do with it.'

'Germans? Your father fought a war against bloody Hitler and now you're bringing one into the family?'

'Mum, first of all, the war was just about over when Dad was drafted into the army. I don't think he even had a sniff of a German...'

'You tell that to those who were bombed, over in Sheffield.'

'What are you going on about, Mum? Secondly, this has nothing to do with Rob.'

'What, the bombing in Sheffield?'

'No, my being... you know... pregnant.'

'Oh, right, so he knows, does he? And says he'll have nothing to do with you? Won't put a ring on your finger and make it right? Typical German.' Mary Brown was actually crying now, furiously wiping at the tears with Janet's one grey school sock. 'They did this to a whole load of girls they got pregnant in France. Left them high and dry once they retreated. The locals tarred and feathered the trollops, you know.' Mary gave her such a furious look Pam knew her mother wouldn't be averse to meting out the same punishment.

'Mum, I don't want this any more than you do...'

'Then you should have thought about that before you... you know...'

'It's nothing to do with Rob. It's not Rob's.'

'Well whose is it then?' Mary stared, still seeming unable or unwilling to get up off her bedroom floor.

'Marco Piccione's.'

'Marco Piccione's?' That shut her mother up like nothing else had. 'But you've not been going out with *him*.'

'Mum, the night of the Miss Piccione contest, I was slipped some drug into my drink.'

'Drugs? Drugs?' Mary actually brought the school sock up to her open mouth. 'Marco *drugged* you?'

'No, no, not at all. Honestly, Mum. It was a girl at work who did it. She doesn't like me.'

'Well, we'll get your dad onto her dad for a start. Where does she live...? But Marco Piccione still had to... you know... do the deed. He took advantage of you?'

Pam was very tempted to say, yes, she'd been knocked out cold and the next thing she knew Marco was on top of her and none of it was her fault. But it hadn't been like that: she'd actively encouraged him, had wanted to know what it was all about, the whole sex thing. Instead she said nothing.

'Have you told him? Does he know?'

Pam shook her head, fat tears rolling down her cheeks.

'Well, he's going to have to know, Pamela. If you're

pregnant to Marco Piccione, then he needs to know. And we need to know what he's going to do about it.'

It took all of Pam's nerve to make her way up to the inner sanctum of Piccione's directors and knock on Marco Piccione's office door. Over the past couple of months, when all she'd thought about was Rob and as much of her time as possible – after work and tech – had been spent with him, getting to know the real Rob (so different from the one he portrayed in the nightclubs) falling more and more in love with him, she'd seen Marco from a distance and they'd waved, or he'd walked through her office in order to have a word with Trevor Pickersgill and he'd smiled and laid a hand briefly on her arm before closing the door on himself and Trevor.

And that had been fine. They were friends – well, *friendly*, if not actually friends. Pam didn't know how friendly he was going to remain once she'd landed this little bombshell.

'Hi, Pam. Are you OK? Have you brought something up from Trevor for me to sign?' Marco looked up from the small black diary on which he was intent, rapidly closed it and popped it into his desk drawer before locking it and standing up.

Pam shook her head, frozen with terror at actually trying to find the words. Eventually she said, 'Look, Marco, there's something…'

Marco frowned. 'What is it? Are you OK?'

'I'm pregnant.'

'Right. OK.' Marco folded his arms, his face pale.

'It's yours, Marco. I'm really, really sorry, but there it is. I'm going to have… you know… a baby and my mum and dad know, and need to see you to see what we're going to do about it. Look, I've only ever done it that once, with you… with anyone…' The words came tumbling out and Pam didn't know if they made sense, didn't know if the words were even in the right order.

'What would you like me to do about it, Pamela?' Marco gave an almost weary sigh and exhaled.

'I don't know.'

'What do your mum and dad want?'

Pam shrugged. This was all so stupid. What the hell was she doing here, telling this man who wasn't interested in her, or the fact that she was having his baby? Well, she'd just have to go to one of those mother and baby places and have the baby and have it adopted and then start all over again. She'd just disappear and not tell Rob and then…

'Pamela, *cara*. How is Miss Piccione 1974?' Mr Piccione himself was suddenly in front of her, smiling, blocking her way to the door as she tried to exit and start on this new plan of hers. 'Everything good? Alright?'

Pamela nodded and then shook her head and, unable to speak, reached for the open door.

'Dad, come and sit down. You too, Pamela. Close the door and come and sit down. Dad, Pamela is going to have a baby…'

'You are engaged, *cara*? Going to be married? You're coming to hand in your notice?' Angelo tutted, his eyes moving to her abdomen as had anyone else's to whom she'd told the news. 'Oh, that is shame.' He tutted once more.

'Dad, Pamela is having *my* baby.' Marco spoke quietly but didn't seem too fazed at breaking such news to his father.

'*Your* baby, Marco?' Angelo appeared stunned and, as he turned back to Pam, now hesitating and hovering by the closed office door, she waited for his Sicilian wrath (she and Rob had been to the cinema to see *Godfather II* only a couple of weeks previously) to descend on the pair of them.

'A little Piccione bambino? Well, that is *wonderful*, Pamela.' Angelo enveloped her in a huge – garlicky – bear hug, kissing each cheek in turn. 'My first grandson to such a beautiful girl as you.' He paused, flinging his arms wide. 'Congratulations, Marco.' He beamed. He actually *beamed*, Pamela would later report back to Jane. 'Now, let's think about this. Your mama and papa know? They not too pleased I suppose? OK, this what we do. I ring your mama and papa; I ring your mama right now, this minute. Make it all OK and stop poor lady worrying. We have wedding before all world know about bambino. Make it all alright…'

'Is this it? Hell, it's a bit, you know, over the top, isn't it?' Dennis Brown slipped into a low gear and drove slowly through the huge black metal gates that opened jerkily at their approach. 'How did they know to do that then, do you reckon? Is someone watching, ready to open them?'

Pamela was feeling not only was she on the set of either *The Addams Family* or *Haunted House of Horror* but also incredibly nauseous, her mother's famous (famous to whom?) steak and onion pie threatening to make an untimely reappearance if she didn't get out of the car pretty damned quick.

'It's a bit dark, isn't it?' Dennis added, pulling up in a space at the start of a drive of great oak trees.

'It's November, what do you expect?' Mary Brown frowned, determined that Dennis shouldn't spoil this much-anticipated first visit to meet Pamela's prospective in-laws, the Picciones.

'Well, I'd certainly cut back a few of these trees...' Dennis broke off as Angelo Piccione opened the huge front door and, arms wide, almost ran down the flight of steps toward them.

'Welcome.' He beamed (did Angelo always *beam*? Pam thought irritably. Was there really anything to damned well *beam* about?), throwing his arms around Dennis who stepped back in alarm onto her mother's high-heeled toes, and kissing both his cheeks. Angelo turned to Mary Brown, taking both her hands and peering across at her in the dark. 'Oh, now I see where Pamela get her looks, Mrs Brown,' Angelo purred, kissing both her cheeks in turn.

Dennis snorted, turning it into a protracted cough and, despite feeling sick and suddenly very tired at the whole ridiculous situation, (maybe *because* of the whole ridiculous situation) Pam started to giggle. Mary elbowed Pam none too gently in the ribs, glared at her meaningfully and they all dutifully followed Angelo up the stone steps.

A diminutive woman with an eye-openingly bountiful chest stood at the end of the hall and said something in rapid Italian to Angelo before disappearing into another room.

'Come in, come in, is cold out there. I never get used to cold Yorkshire winters. Marco is through here...' Angelo led the way into a small oak-panelled sitting room where a modern gas fire was belting out heat into the already over warm and stuffy atmosphere. 'This is my snug,' Angelo said proudly. 'The lounge too big and cold to sit down for a talk.'

Marco stood as they trooped in and Mary glared in his direction, making Pam go hot with embarrassment. While she might be thankful that it wasn't the *scruffy-jeaned dancing German* who had ruined her daughter and brought dishonour to 23 Bellevue Terrace, her mother, Pam knew, wasn't prepared to descend from that elevated horse onto which she'd positioned herself without some apology and deference as to her daughter's honour.

'Very unhappy circumstances,' Mary was saying in her best visitor voice. 'You do know, Mr Piccione, Pamela was slipped narcotics (Narcotics? Had her mother been watching *Kojak* again?) or she most certainly would not have ended up in this situation.'

'I think we must all make best of bad work,' Angelo said sagely, shaking his head. 'We delighted to have Pamela join our family. Lovely girl... Where's the drink?'

The same little woman who had been in the hall on their arrival now carried in a tray, which neither Marco or his father appeared to be taking from her. This must be the housekeeper, Pam thought, noting the apron straining over the woman's huge bust.

'This Mrs Piccione,' Angelo said somewhat dismissively. 'Consettia, pour drink out for our guests,' he ordered, while Dennis moved forward to take the tray from her.

'Here, love, let me take that.' Her dad smiled and Pam suddenly wanted to cry. She didn't want to get married and leave her dad. He might say very little at the best of times, but he wasn't averse to slipping her a couple of quid towards some new shoes or coming out in the cold to pick her and Jane up from town if they'd missed the last bus home. Or helping a woman with a heavy tray when no one else seemed to consider they should. Consettia Piccione didn't appear overly grateful to her dad, clicking her tongue somewhat scornfully in his direction before turning to take a good look at Pam.

'So, you come live here with me,' Consettia said in very broken English, and Pam wasn't sure if it was a question or an order. 'With baby?'

No, no, no, Pam thought. *Please, God, no.* She turned, helplessly, to Dennis, her face white. She'd rather be incarcerated in a mother and baby home, on her knees scrubbing floors, doing the nuns' laundry and being flagellated with dry sticks than living with this hostile little woman in this gloomy great house. Marco, Pam noted, hadn't said a word throughout all this. Terrified of her mother, Pam concluded, wondering if she herself was going to throw up all over the uncomfortable chaise longue Angelo was now pressing her to sit on.

'That won't be necessary,' Marco said, speaking for the first time. 'Dad says we can have the gatehouse at the bottom of the garden. It's a bit near the road, obviously, but it's not a busy road and we can make it really comfortable. You know, to begin with.'

Pam shot him a grateful look, even though she was already feeling totally homesick as well as just plain old sick.

'Yes, I tell you all this yesterday, Consettia.' Angelo gave his wife a hard stare. 'No problem...' He turned back to Pam's mum and dad, smiling as he made to top up Mary's champagne glass.

Her mother accepted more bubbles with, what appeared to Pam, an almost flirtatious, 'Oh, don't mind if I do...' and her dad shared a look with Pam, raising an eyebrow in his wife's direction.

'The roof need looking at,' Angelo went on, 'but it has the two bedroom. I fix it, I sort it all. No problem at all.'

'Well it's not what we anticipated for Pamela.' Hell, Pam thought, the vowels of her name were being extended in direct proportion to the amount of champagne her mother was getting down her neck. 'She's a bright girl – passed all her CSEs at grade 1...'

Grade 5 for Physics, Mum, you've conveniently forgotten the damned Physics.

'...and already getting stuck into the shorthand and typing. We're sure she'd soon have been applying for full secretary jobs...'

What was a *full* secretary? Someone taking dictation after eating too much dinner?

'...or even PA to the director.' For a moment, Mary appeared to have forgotten Angelo *was* the director. 'Anyway...' her mum drained her glass '...goodness these bubbles don't half get up your... *one's* nose, don't they? Anyway,' she said once more, 'the damage is done. We'll all just have to make the best of a bad situation.' Mary reached for a hanky up the sleeve of her M&S cardigan.

Oh God, her mother wasn't about to cry again, was she? She'd cried on and off since Pam had told her the news, alternating with, 'You've thrown your life away, Pamela,' and not averse to adding a sneaky refrain of, 'What will the neighbours think?'

'This God's blessing,' Angelo purred, glancing across at the wall where Jesus was oozing cream-soda-coloured blood from various parts of his anatomy while hanging precariously from his crucifix at a forty-five-degree angle. Angelo crossed towards it, twitched the crucifix to its rightful ninety degrees, blessing Jesus with two fingers.

Like the pope? Pam panicked: would she too be expected to bless Jesus every time she came in from Sainsbury's?

'Bambino is always a blessing,' Angelo went on, smiling. 'And to my first son: my *first* grandson.'

'Actually, it will be *our* second,' Mary said proudly if not a little pointedly.

Oh, Jesus – sorry Jesus, Pam amended glancing over at the almighty who appeared to be looking directly at her now – was her mum in competitive mode again? She'd already gone down the one-upmanship road with Mrs Blackshaw at Number 27 whose daughter, Denise, had been married five years with 'nothing to show for it'.

'My elder daughter...'

Eldest, Mum, Pam thought recalling past English grammar lessons at Westenbury Sec Mod.

'...Lynne is... is *bearing* our first grandchild.'

And unto Lynne, a babe is born. Pam glanced across at Jesus who appeared to have given up the ghost. She placed a hand on her middle. She doubted whether her mum was heralding the coming of *this* grandchild down the length of Bellevue Terrace.

Marco walked over to Pam and took her hand. 'It will be alright,' he whispered kindly, producing a black velvet ring box and taking out a ring, which he placed on her finger to the accompaniment of a delighted *oooohhh* from her mother.

It will never be alright, Pam thought bleakly, *now that I can't have, and never will have, Rob.*

22

Frankie

December literally blew into Westenbury village. The month arrived with a sneer at the coming festive season, bringing cold, miserable and intense blustery weather that charged delightedly at the Christmas decorations hanging on the fascia of the village shops, fusing the lights and bringing down the large spruce Christmas tree recently erected in its usual spot just outside The Jolly Sailor.

For days, I battled my way out of the front door of my granny flat for the final weeks of term at uni, the fringe of my scarf irritating my eyes as the wool was flung back onto my face and wet sleety stuff settled on my hair and my car. In the end I abandoned scarves and broken umbrellas, relying on Daler's beanie hat, left behind in the flat the day before the attack on his father, to offer some protection from the elements.

The weather was miserable and, not having seen Daler for over a week, I was miserable too. Manraj Dosanjh had survived the knife attack but had endured a five-hour surgery and was now out of intensive care and recovering on the ward. I was surprised the Dosanjhs hadn't opted for a private hospital but, when I'd brought this up in one of our few phone conversations over the following week, Daler was somewhat dismissive, assuring me the NHS hospital was the best possible place for his dad and, as a prospective nurse, he hoped I wasn't going to be one of these people who were trained by the government and then sneaked off to an easier life in a private hospital. I was a bit put out at that – somewhat pompous – accusation, but bit my tongue, assured him that was certainly not my intention, and assigned his bad temper to the long hours he was working and worry over his dad.

'Are you going to come over to the flat, Daler?' I'd caught him just as he was leaving work and returning to Dosanjh Towers, his mother, he said, having totally broken down and needing him back at home. 'It's just that I really miss you…'

'Frankie, you can't know how much I'm missing you. And need you. Everything is just getting out of hand…'

'It's OK,' I soothed. 'I'm here for you. I'm not going anywhere.' I didn't add that both Dad and Nonno had been on at me to confirm whether Daler would be spending Christmas day with us all up at High Royd. Christmas had always been a big deal to the Picciones (*total bore really*, Mum used to sneer) and Nonno started planning the day as early as October, ordering in vast amounts of food and alcohol and demanding that all family should be present, as well as a large number of guests. Well, Nonno would just have to be less demanding, I thought, not daring to even bring up the subject of Christmas with Daler.

'I need to see you, Frankie,' Daler said.

'Oh, God, Daler, I can't tell you how much I need you too.'

There was a bit of a pause before Daler said, 'Can I come and see you tomorrow evening?'

'What do you mean, *can you*?' I laughed. 'Of course you can. Having said that, don't think you're having your beanie hat back; it's mine now.' I laughed again, waiting for a response, but Daler had already gone.

My granny flat might have been tiny, being really little more than a studio with a tiny snug overlooking Dad's south-facing garden, a separate kitchen in which was a table for three up against the wall, and a bathroom and bedroom, but it was cosy and I was rather attached to it. I'd not seen Daler for ten days and now that I knew he was coming around that evening I was in a state of high excitement. I made a fish pie filled with smoked fish, prawns, cream and wilted spinach topped with a golden cheesy mashed potato and then panicked whether Daler ate fish. Or cream. Or cheese. Well, there was at least spinach in there.

My Christmas decorations – traditional, but admittedly somewhat vulgar paperchains that Angel and I had made at the weekend – were snaking their way across the tiny flat giving the place a feel of rampant claustrophobia rather than their intended proclamation of the new-born son. I was just on the point of pulling the whole lot down – I'd tell four-year-old Angel they *fell* down – when the doorbell rang and, taking one final look at my reflection in the mirror, dashed to the door and flung my arms round Daler, bringing him in from the bitterly cold elements outside.

'Where's your key? Did you forget it?'

'No, it's here.' Daler looked pale. 'You know, with me not seeing you for ten days or so it seemed a bit, I don't know, intrusive... rude... just letting myself in?'

'Did it? Why?'

Ignoring my question, which I assumed Daler thought was rhetorical, he took off his warm woollen navy overcoat and unwound the red scarf from his neck. I was very tempted, there and then, to rush him into the bedroom, rip off the rest of his clothes and indulge myself in the latent fantasies I'd been storing up all week. Instead, I went to fetch Daler a beer, poured myself another glass of wine and put the fish pie in the hot oven.

'I'm getting married,' Daler said from the depths of the sofa, his beautiful face in my lap as I stroked his dark curls and the soulful voice of Adam Levine worked its way into my senses.

'Is that a proposal?' I asked, holding my breath in anticipation as, pulse racing, I wiggled my toes in delight underneath his jeaned backside.

'No.' He was having trouble actually speaking and as I felt him shift his body slightly, but appeared unable to turn to look at me, he repeated, 'No, Frankie, it's not. God, that it was...'

My first, ridiculous, thought was: I'll never be able to eat fish pie ever again now because I won't be able to separate its wonderful, homely smell from the pain that is slowly making its pernicious way along every part of me. Every vein, every tendon, every hidden place, every single bit of me cracking open in raw abandon as, in one fell blow, Daler blew apart my world.

Daler turned then and, taking my face fiercely in his hands, stared into my eyes. 'I love you but I can't do this.'

'Do what?' I finally managed to say through dry lips. 'Because you're Sikh and I'm not? Because I'm Catholic? I'll convert. Daler, I'll become Sikh…' I'd have promised to become a Tibetan monk; an orange person; even a convert to the Prince Philip Movement apparently started by the Kastom people in the Yaohnanen village on the island of Tanna, if it meant not losing Daler.

'No, Frankie.' Daler sighed, tiredly. 'It's because another woman is having my child.'

'What? What other woman?' I'd jumped out from beneath him and was standing at his side as he sat on the sofa, head in his hands. I slapped away his hands. 'You've been sleeping with some other woman since you met me?' I slapped at his actual head this time.

He shook his head. 'No.'

'What do you mean, *no*? Is this the immaculate conception once more? Oh no, of course, sorry, *wrong* sodding religion. This Sienna woman, I suppose?'

Daler nodded and then took my hand. 'Frankie, do you remember when we first met?'

'Of course, I remember when we first met, you pillock. It's totally and utterly ingrained in my *mind*.'

'And do you remember after that weekend you went straight back to Liverpool and we arranged that I should come over as soon as I was able?'

'Yes, and you didn't come over for more than a week. I assumed you were busy at work...?'

'I went straight down to London to see Sienna. I needed to sort out in my mind how I felt about her. As soon as I saw her, I knew.'

'Knew what? That she was pregnant? She didn't look very pregnant to me in that slinky little green sari the other night.'

'No, no.' Daler shook his head almost irritably. 'I knew that it was finally over between us and that I wanted to be with you.'

'Oh, a bit like a little competition? You had to actually see her in front of you to work out the answer of who's going to win the contest? Who turns me on the most? Who's got the most to offer...?'

'It wasn't like that, Frankie.'

'So what the fuck was it like then?' Big fat tears had arrived, seemingly from nowhere, and I brushed them away furiously. 'And how come you never mentioned this Sienna woman until she magically appeared on the top table with you at the wedding?'

'I didn't mention her because there was no need. It was all over with her – I wanted to be with you.'

'I'm sorry, but that's utter rubbish. I've always asked you about your past, about previous girlfriends and you've just shrugged it off as unimportant.'

'I know and I'm sorry.' Daler ran a hand through his dark curls but didn't look at me. 'I should have told you more.'

'Yes, you damned well should.'

'When you insisted on knowing, I did say there'd been

someone but, if you remember, you then said you didn't want all the details, that it would make you jealous.'

'And that was your cue to tell me her name and reassure me that yes, you *had* loved her, but it was all over and nothing could compare with what you had with me.'

'I'm sorry, I'm not very up on the female psyche.'

'You're a doctor, for heaven's sake. You should be totally up on *anyone's* psyche: what makes women tick, what we're really thinking when we say one thing but mean another. Of course I wanted to know about your past loves if only to google them, find them on Facebook and work out the competition...'

'But...'

'...which *you* were obviously doing when you went down to London to see her.' I glared at him. 'And I suppose it was *let's just do this once more for old times' sake?*'

Daler shook his head miserably. 'It wasn't like that. Once I'd met you, I didn't want to be with anyone else. I told Sienna this. The thing was, we'd been at a wedding together the weekend before in Bradford...'

'Another effing wedding? What is it with you lot and weddings?'

'Us lot?' Daler frowned.

'You know what I'm saying, Daler. Don't turn this on me and accuse me of playing the race card.'

'I wasn't about to.'

'But, Daler, that must have been at the end of August. It's now December.' I started to count the weeks on my fingers.

'Only just December. Sienna was eleven weeks pregnant when she told me at the wedding.'

'What? She's *not* three months pregnant, Daler. She'd have a bump by now.'

'She has, albeit tiny – her sari was very cleverly cut to hide the fact. First pregnancies don't often show at all until the second trimester.'

'Oh, don't go all medical on me, Daler.' I was really crying now and Daler reached out for me, pulling me into his arms and kissing my hair. He was, I realised, near to tears himself. 'Are you really saying, you knew nothing about this until this weekend at the wedding? Why on earth didn't she tell you when she found out she was pregnant?'

'She didn't know until a week before the wedding.'

I stared. 'The woman is three months pregnant and didn't know? Come on, Daler…'

'She was on the brand of pill that you can take continuously without having a breakthrough bleed…'

'You're doing the medical bit again, Daler.'

'I'm just trying to explain. So, even though she was on the pill, she got pregnant. It happens. It shouldn't, but it does. She started to experience the usual symptoms of early pregnancy: sore…'

'Don't!' I held up my hand, furiously. 'I'm a nurse – well slightly – I *know* the symptoms of early pregnancy.'

'OK, OK.' Daler put his head back in his hands. 'She took a pregnancy test, went to her GP and had it all confirmed, dates and all. Sienna said knowing she was going to be seeing me at the wedding at the weekend, she needed to tell me in person rather than over the phone.'

'Daler, girls get pregnant all the time. It's 2018, not some Victorian melodrama where the girl's father is going to come after you with a gun to get you down the aisle.'

'I know all this, Frankie, and seeing you at the wedding, dancing and enjoying yourself, I wanted nothing more than to be with you. But Sienna knew exactly what she was doing at that wedding: at one point she got her parents and my parents in another room together and broke the good news.'

'*Good news?*' I stared, taking my hand from Daler's.

'For our families it *was* wonderful news. They – particularly my dad and Sienna's dad who are distant cousins – have been working to this end for years. OK, a wedding should come before a child, but at least the news meant we'd be married pretty soon.'

'But, Daler, you came back to the flat with me after the wedding. You stayed with me. You made love to me, knowing you were going to be married to someone else.'

Daler shook his head fiercely. 'No, I *didn't*. I decided, driving home that I couldn't do it. I couldn't lose you. I'd rather lose my family than you. I actually made that choice.'

'Oh, Daler.' Hope flared in my heart.

'Abandoning Sienna to be with you would mean just that, I can tell you now. I'd be ostracised – lose my family, but I was prepared to do that.' Daler lay back and stared at the ceiling as tears ran down his cheek. 'And then I thought my dad was going to die this week. The hospital was telling us it was touch and go…' He broke off unable to continue. Eventually he said, not looking at me, 'He made me *promise* I'd marry and take care of Sienna and the baby. And I promised.'

All hope died.

Daler looked at me, unblinking. 'I also promised him something he's been wanting me to do since I was a kid.'

I stared in turn.

'I've handed in my notice at the hospital. I'm going to take over the reins at the London Dosanjhs factory in Southwark.'

I stood up and walked into the kitchen.

The fish pie had burnt. I took it out of the oven and threw it in the bin.

PART 3

23

Frankie

'Frankie...' Daisy was bounding down the stairs as soon as I got in, red-faced and sweating from my bike ride. I'd been living with Daisy two weeks and I felt totally at home in just the same way I'd felt when we'd lived together in the flat in Liverpool. But whereas we'd then been just a five-minute drive away from the airport in Speke, and not in the most salubrious of areas, this cottage of Daisy's down at Holly Close Farm was total heaven on earth.

I was already panicking about having to leave it in six months or so when Daisy left to go up to Edinburgh to start her veterinary course, which was ridiculous of me. I had to take deep breaths, tell myself to live for today, that I must enjoy the moment and stop both reliving the past as well as worrying about my future, but I wasn't that sort of person. 'She's always been a worrier has our Frankie,' Tammy would say to anyone listening, which made me want to laugh, the possessive 'our' making me feel both loved and part of my dad's second family, but at the same time the same age as six-year-old Angel who, according to her mother, was also 'a bit of a fretter'.

I spent each day of the Easter break out on my bike in the weak April sunshine. Bike riding helped enormously to focus my mind on the here and now as all my concentrated efforts went into the required pulling up out of the lane from the cottage, negotiating the twisting, pothole-ridden country lanes before joining the main roads with all the dangers of speeding cars and huge lorries that bore down on me from behind until I was actually squeaking with fear and about to give up the whole thing. The pull and burn in my legs and thighs, as well as my backside as I tackled the steep hills around Westenbury and followed the roads out to nearby Norman's Meadow and then out to Holmfirth and the moors beyond – the catchment area of the beautifully soft water for which this part of the world was famous – became easier the more hours I spent in the saddle and the further afield I roamed. I even cycled out onto the long stretch of road that eventually led out to Glossop and the Peak District, revelling in the beautiful scenery; the fresh, chilly air; and in the sure knowledge I was becoming fitter and stronger than I'd been for years.

At first I'd avoided the area of the sheep-strewn moors where I'd arranged to meet Daler on that wonderful bank holiday Monday almost three years earlier, but you can't cry and be miserable when you're out in the first sunshine of the year, on a bike that will have you off it if you don't show it who's boss (I'm sure someone would prove me wrong on that score). I'd actually cycled by the very spot with my head up, shouted, 'Fuck you, Daler,' to the duck-egg blue sky and the hoary-looking old ewe who gave me a look of utter boredom before carrying on chewing the coarse moorland grass.

I'd always biked, especially when I was at school and university and into football-fitness training and so had been delighted when I'd found an old bike belonging to Aunt Rosina on the farm in Sicily. It had, I think, just four gears and only half of them worked, but it got me around the fields and onto the neighbouring olive and lemon groves and I reckon that bike, as well as Aunt Rosina's *crema al limone*, kept me going when all I wanted to do was ring Daler from Italy just to hear his voice or, better, for him to tell me it was all a mistake; he was no longer married. That the relationship hadn't worked; there wasn't a beautiful little baby girl with her father's huge dark eyes and her mother's green, slinky sari. Sienna had fooled us all with that beautifully cut green sari, hadn't she?

'Frankie, are you listening?' Daisy was brimming with either news or gossip. 'Take that sodding helmet off. I can't take you seriously when you look like Marvin the Martian. Charlie's rented out her cottage again.'

'Charlie has? Is she here then?' I'd always found Daisy's big sister a bit scary. She was so clever and attractive and confident.

'Well, the *estate agent* has,' Daisy said with slight irritation. '*And* to a single man.'

'And it is a truth universally acknowledged, that a single man in possession of Charlie's cottage must be in want of a woman?'

'Sorry?'

'Sorry, I forgot you don't read.'

'I think you'll find, Francesca, I've read both *Vet Today* and *Gardeners' World* from cover to cover this morning. Given me a great idea for that patch of garden down by the fence. So, there's a very promising neighbour next door now.'

'Have you met him?'

Daisy shook her head and her blonde ponytail bounced. 'Seen the back of him, that's all.' She pulled the binoculars from behind her own.

'You've not been spying on him, have you?'

'Absolutely. We don't want to find we're living next to any old axe murderer or pervert.'

'Pervert?'

'You know, once the weather gets better and you're out in the garden in your skimpy little bikini out the front, I don't want to feel, as your landlady, that you're being watched through a pair of binoculars by some pervert. It's a bit lonely down here you know.'

'And by you looking at him through your binoculars, you'll know, will you?'

'Know what?'

'If he's a pervert. Come on, Daisy, I need a shower and breakfast. I'm starving.' I'd brought home a whole raft of jars of the nation's top-selling brands of lemon curd and wanted to try them out with the sourdough loaf I'd baked the previous evening. I'd spent the last month working with the R and D team at Piccione's, sourcing Sicilian lemons, local free-range eggs and sugar and now wanted to see what made other brands so successful, when Piccione's blatantly wasn't.

'Just come outside with me. See if you can see him over the fence.'

'You go. Go and put your gardening gloves on.'

'You know I never wear gardening gloves.' Daisy held up her dirt-engrained fingers in my direction as a reminder of her *bare-backed gardening* as she called it.

'OK, go and put your gardening *hat* on then and get your rake out. Look as if you're not spying on him. I'll make some toast and then you can tell me which lemon curd you prefer.'

'Maybe we can eat it out in the garden?' Daisy asked hopefully. 'You know, drape ourselves nonchalantly over the garden table so he can see us from his bedroom window?'

'Whatever.' I was already heading for the shower.

'Erm...' Daisy was laughing as she walked back into the kitchen, trailing dirt from the garden, a couple of unidentifiable (to me anyway) plant cuttings in her hand.

'What?' I looked up from the notepad on which I was meticulously recording the texture, taste and dropping consistency of the most expensive jar of branded lemon curd I'd sent away for.

'Slimy.' Daisy was still laughing as she shoved two of my neatly laid out and numbered pieces of lemon curd-laden toast into her mouth and chewed.

'The new neighbour? Slimy?' For some reason, I felt disappointed. 'This isn't a fair test now, Daisy,' I said crossly as her cheek bulged. 'All the toast pieces were exactly the same size, and the lemon curd exactly five mil.'

'God, you sound like Miss Mallinson, our science teacher at Westenbury Comp. She was always going on about bloody fair tests in science experiments. No...' Daisy laughed again, coughing superfluous crumbs of toast and lemon from specimen numbers 4 and 5 in my direction as they went down the wrong way '...*this* one: it's slimy. Don't like it at all.'

'Oh, I thought you'd met the new neighbour.'

'That's what I was trying to tell you. I have.'

'And?'

'And so have you.'

For one wild, ridiculous second, hope flared that it was Daler. Daler who'd left Sienna and moved back north from London, moving in next door to be near me.

'Erm.' Daisy was laughing again. 'Your boss?'

'My dad?'

'Oh, don't be so daft. Why would your dad have moved in next door? The American?'

'Cameron Mancini? He's living next door? Oh, for feck's sake, Daisy, that's all I need.'

'He's charming. You didn't tell me how good-looking he was. This is brilliant. You could have warned me he was so gorgeous and I'd have put on my lippy and Wonderbra before I went out there with my trowel.'

'Daisy,' I said patiently, 'Cameron Mancini is *not* charming. OK, good-looking, I'll give you that, if you like your men short-haired and booted and suited, which I don't.' (I'd been spoilt for ever, it seemed, by Daler's longish black curls, jeans and beanie hat.)

'Well...' she said, spooning out instant coffee.

'How can you drink that stuff? There's proper Italian

coffee in the pot.' I indicated the coffee jug – the only way to make coffee – I'd brought back from Sicily with me.

'Well,' Daisy said again, totally ignoring me as she poured boiling water onto the powder, 'your boss was totally charming when I invited him over for dinner next Saturday.'

'You are joking.'

'No, honestly, totally charming.'

'Daisy, I don't dispute that,' I snapped. I'd seen Cameron Mancini in action, schmoozing his way with any visitors and inspectors he'd shown around the production lines. 'I can't believe you've invited him round here? What are you giving him from your repertoire of baked beans, corned-beef sandwiches and dinner-for-ones?'

'No, that's your department. You're cooking.'

'Sorry, I'm washing my hair that night.'

'Which night?'

'Whichever night you've invited him. He's my boss – well, one of them – I don't want to sit like a lemon while you two eye each other up.'

'You've lemons on the brain. Right, this one, I love this one,' Daisy said, distracted for the moment from Cameron Mancini as she chewed thoughtfully, like a wine taster, on lemon curd specimen Number 2. 'Copy the ingredients from this one, stick *Frankie Piccione's Lemon Curd* on the jar and you're good to go. Now, I wasn't just planning on a threesome with you, me and your boss, Frankie – sorry, I've never fancied you. I thought we should have a party: you know, a moving-in party? But then I had another thought; I mean we're almost thirty and grown up. People have dinner parties, don't they, when they're our age?'

'Who would we invite?' I asked doubtfully. Daisy's parties had a tendency to get out of hand; irate neighbours and the police had often been a feature.

'I hadn't really thought,' she said airily, which meant she'd done nothing but think about it while she was tying up the ancient yellow rambling rose that had come down after a particularly high wind the previous week.

'You don't want to be disturbing the neighbours,' I said, eating the rest of the toast and lemon curd regardless of any scientific testing. I'd have another go in the morning when I wasn't so hungry.

'What neighbours? If we're inviting Cameron Mancini, it's a done deal.'

'What about the couple with the toddler up at Holly Close Farm?'

'Oh yes, good idea. Libby and Seb are great fun. He's pretty gorgeous but, unfortunately, has only got eyes for her, so you'll have to keep your own eyes on your plate. Anyway, *you'll* be in the kitchen cooking most of the time... Don't worry I'll do all the serving and clearing away. Right, who else? Problem is, so many of the people we were at school with have moved away. And those who haven't are all boring.'

'Are you including us in that category?'

'Oh gosh no. *We're* not boring. And, we've been away most of the time since leaving school; you know, travelling, working, so we certainly don't come into the boring bastards' category. *We've* a whole lifetime of experiences between us to bring to the table. You can talk about your football career...'

'Which didn't get very far,' I said ruefully. I really missed playing football.

'Got it.' Daisy jumped up reaching for her phone. 'I'll phone Deimante.'

'Deimante?'

'Matis's sister-in-law. She's married to Gatis, Matis's brother.'

'Blimey, all sounds a bit complicated. As in your ex, Matis?'

'Yep. Deimante used to play for the Lithuanian national women's football team.'

'Really?'

'Really, yes. You'll have loads in common. Right, your turn.'

'My turn?'

'To invite someone.'

I paused. How sad was this? I could think of no one. All my friends from school in Somerset, and university in Newcastle, were spread around the country – mainly in London – and actually around the world. I hadn't realised just how much I depended on Daisy for friendship. It made me feel a bit unloved. A failure that, at nearly thirty, there was no one in the vicinity who was there for me. I did a quick mind tour of people I knew. All I could come up with was Ian on his forklift truck and Carol and the girls in Preserves, none of whom were known for being dinner-partygoers. 'Aunty Pam,' I said suddenly.

'Your Aunty Pam?' Daisy stared. 'She's a bit old, isn't she?'

'Bit ageist, that, isn't it?'

'Actually, sorry, I love your Aunty Pam. Invite her. She's great fun. Is she going out with anyone? She's usually got someone on the go, hasn't she? So, how many's that?' Daisy counted on her fingers, licking off the remains of lemon curd as she did so.

'About ten, which is a good number,' I said, beginning to feel a stirring of excitement, not for the actual company as such, but because I was looking forward, suddenly, to getting stuck into the food planning and preparation. 'Mind you, if Pam doesn't bring someone, we're going to be a bit female-heavy.'

'Luca. Ask Luca. You know I've always had a bit of a thing for your brother.'

'I can't think why,' I sniffed. 'He's always been horrible to me.'

'That's because he's your brother.' Daisy grinned. 'This would be a great opportunity for you to build a few bridges now that you're back home. Get to know him all over again.'

'I see him at work. In fact, Daisy, this is beginning to turn into a Piccione works' outing. Mind you, I've been wanting to meet Verity, Luca's new woman.'

'Oh, we don't want any more *women* here. Especially attractive ones which, knowing your brother, she probably is. Forget Luca.'

'No, no, now you've said it, I'd like him to see how well I can give a dinner party.' Why did I always feel the need to prove my worth to Luca?

Daisy suddenly laughed. 'You do realise, if this Verity and Luca remain as a pair, they'll come to be known as *Verruca*? So,' she went on, not waiting for my response, 'I'd better rustle up a couple of spare men… There's always Ian,' she added thoughtfully.

'You make it sound like you're rustling up a couple of ham sandwiches after a session at the pub.'

'Hmm, there's a point: the pub. Lots of lovely local men down at The Jolly Sailor. I'll have a think, don't worry.'

'You do know, not everyone's going to be free at such short notice.'

'Well, that's why I'm going to have a reserve list. Just in case. Right, shall we say a week tonight and work down the list until we have a good enough crowd?'

I knew I needed to pop round next door to Charlie's cottage to welcome Cameron Mancini, but it seemed a bit strange talking to my boss on a personal, as opposed to the professional level we shared at the works. He'd said nothing to me about moving in next door but then, I'd only ever spoken to him about lemon curd and honey, spreadsheets, costs and development. He probably had no idea where I lived. I quickly texted Aunty Pam and Luca, inviting them both to the cottage the next Saturday evening, not thinking for one minute my brother would be free from what I gathered, from my mother, to be a very hectic – and fulfilling – social life.

I cleared up the remains of the toast and lemon curd. Daisy and I might not have carried out the tasting experiment adhering to the strictest of scientific guidelines but we'd both, without hesitation, plumped for the same favourite as well as both dissing the one that was quite revolting, worse even than Piccione's.

I assembled free-range eggs – I'd bought a dozen from one of the farms outside the village – huge, sun-filled Sicilian unwaxed lemons and golden caster sugar, playing around and experimenting with making lemon curd to Aunt Rosina's recipe. Once it was cooling in the fridge, I set to and made two Victoria sponges – one for us and one to take round to Cameron as a moving-in present, sandwiching each with the fresh home-made lemon curd, a sprinkling of lemon zest and a veritable feather pillow of thick whipped cream. Aunty Pam had taught me well, always using a supreme sponge flour and replacing the electric beater with a metal spoon to fold the sifted flour slowly into the batter. The result, though I say it myself, was a cake to die for.

I'd only ever seen Cameron in dark suit, shirt and tie so it seemed exceptionally weird when he opened the door wearing jeans, a rugby shirt and with bare feet. Why those bare feet should make me feel embarrassed, I don't really know; but toes, male toes in particular, are terribly personal bits of one's anatomy, I've always felt.

'Well, this is a bit of a surprise.' I smiled, full of forced jollity. I didn't really, when it came down to it, want my working life mixing with my social life. Not that I had a social life at the moment unless it included going to Angel's birthday party last Sunday and cheering on a truculent Matteo at football. I'd made Angel's birthday cake myself and bought a pack of flat-pack cake boxes to take the pink fondant-iced ballet shoe creation over to Dad's, staying on to celebrate the event with fifteen little designer-clad princesses from her school. The remaining cake box now housed my lemon-curd Victoria sponge.

'A cup of sugar?' Cameron asked, indicating the box in my hand as he let me through the front door of Charlie Maddison's cottage.

'Something of the sort.' I smiled. 'Although I don't know if you eat cake?' As I said it, I realised I knew nothing really about Cameron Mancini apart from him being my boss at Piccione's.

'I can always eat cake.' He smiled back, taking the proffered box and peeking inside. 'Where d'you buy this one? Down in the village?'

Was he being deliberately sycophantic?

'Yes, something like that.' I grinned. 'So, did you know I was living next door to you?'

'Not until yesterday evening; you'd already left and I was telling your dad where I was moving into. A month living at the Holiday Inn down in Midhope had just about finished me off. That's when he told me you'd beaten me to it and were already out here.'

'Only for six months.'

'Oh?' Cameron frowned. 'How come?'

'Daisy has a place at Edinburgh university. She wants to be a vet.'

Cameron did that thing I'd got used to at work: he'd ask a question; I'd answer it and then there would be silence on his part. So then, to fill the yawning gap, I'd end up rambling on, coming out with stuff I hadn't meant to. Typical tactic from interviewers and reporters and the police, most likely learned, in Cameron Mancini's case, from business school at Harvard or Yale or wherever he'd been ensconced back in the States. Sometimes, when he and I had a meeting, I'd see just how long the silence could go on, but it was usually my nerve that broke first and I'd have to fill the void.

As I did now. 'Daisy and I were best friends at primary school.' I smiled. 'And then, after university we went travelling before coming back to the UK and living together in Liverpool for over a year. She's now decided she wants to be a vet like her dad so, once she goes, she'll be able to rent out her cottage for a hugely more exorbitant rate than I'm paying now. You know, to pay for her studies.'

'But after working for Flying High, you started to train as a nurse?' Blimey, he must have been reading my CV or been chatting to Human Resources; I'd never told Cameron Mancini this.

'Yep.'

'And then you went off to the Far East and Sicily?'

'Hmm.' I folded my arms.

'And now you want to come up with a winning recipe for Piccione's Lemon Curd?'

Was Cameron Mancini laughing at me? 'Try it,' I said.

'Try what?'

'The cake.'

'I will, I will. I promise.' He folded his arms as he leaned against the beautiful deep-blue Aga that Charlie Maddison had obviously decided was an absolute must in her kitchen, before glancing at his wristwatch. A rather understated one I noted. 'I'm just waiting for a whole load of deliveries, otherwise I'll be sleeping on the floor tonight.'

'Right.'

'Right.'

There didn't seem much more to say after that.

*

4pm: Frankie, thank you so much for the cake. Finally sat down to a piece. You need to find out the source of their lemon curd. Totally out of this world.

24

Pam

Then

This wasn't the life she'd anticipated.

Pamela had always thought that by the time she'd been out of school for a couple of years, she'd have moved up the career ladder and be at least a junior secretary whether at Piccione's or somewhere else in the town. She'd never actually thought she'd be anywhere but in her own home town of Midhope, never dreamed of moving to the big bright headily dangerous lights of London but, now that she never *would* be part of the capital, she yearned to be down there. Anywhere but here, stuck in the coach house at the bottom of the garden of the Picciones' home, High Royd.

She couldn't quite work out where this fantasy, this ridiculous dream had originated – she'd only ever twice been down to London: once on a day trip from school to see the Tutankhamun Exhibition at the British Museum a couple of years earlier and once on a weekend break with her parents when she was a little girl. She'd enjoyed both visits – loved seeing Buckingham Palace and walking in Hyde Park as well as staying in a hotel in Russell Square where they were each given individual little packs of Lurpak butter and their own jars of raspberry jam which Pamela thought so wonderful, she'd saved hers, keeping it as a sort of souvenir on a shelf in her bedroom until her mother had thrown it in the bin saying it was a dust collector. But it had never really occurred to her that she might leave Yorkshire and move down to the metropolis.

Pamela supposed it'd got into her head when she'd found out Rob was heading down there this autumn to study at UCL. She knew this because Jane was quite friendly with the new girlfriend he'd met at tech – Jane's cousin knew the girl's brother or something. Anyway, according to Jane he'd passed all his A levels and was heading south.

And while she pegged out the baby's little white nightgowns and pink outfits, she thought constantly of Rob. Bending down to the wash basket: Rob dancing to Marvin Gaye; pegging on the line a little vest: Rob inviting her to try the runny Brie; lifting the clothes prop to the washing line: Rob's face when she told him she wouldn't be seeing him anymore because she was pregnant and getting married.

Thank goodness for Pampers. Her mother wasn't impressed that she was using the disposable nappies that had only recently come on the market ('*Pampered Pamela*: I had to set to and boil and bleach and peg out for all you three girls'), but Marco was a modern man and more than happy to shell out for the huge packs of nappies that she carried up to the coach house from the little supermarket in the village on the pram.

Pam would wipe down the light blue Formica units in the dark little kitchen ('I'm going to come down, one day,' her dad promised, 'and, whether they like it or not, chop all those damned trees down and let in some light') hoover the claustrophobic little sitting room with its red-flocked wallpaper, and all the time imagine she was really in a trendy little flat down the Kings Road, waiting for Rob to come home from a day spent studying. She, herself, was PA to some director in a tall glass and concrete skyscraper in Mayfair. She was a bit hazy as to whether there actually were any large office buildings in the Mayfair and Park Lane she knew only from playing Monopoly, but she was sure there must be. She'd be in the apartment – or was that a bit too American? – alright, she'd be in the *flat*, smooching along to The Four Tops as she prepared wonderful little salads with olive oil, garlic and organic green leaves and eating Brie that was just about to run off the table with long sticks of crusty French bread. And there wouldn't be a jar of Heinz salad cream to be seen and…

And then Carla's plaintive cries would bring her back to the reality of her situation and she would sigh, go to pick her up, jiggle her around and berate herself for reading too many novels and *Cosmopolitan*, which whisked her away to another world when she should just be accepting she was a married woman with a new baby.

But she didn't feel like Pamela Piccione, (PeePee for heaven's sake), mum to this squealing little thing with whom she didn't feel much in common and who cried even more ferociously, it seemed, every time she picked her up. She was always annoyed, and yet at the same time intensely grateful when Mrs Piccione – she couldn't think of her as Consettia and certainly not *Mamma*, as Angelo suggested she call his wife – appeared in the little house without knocking and, without a smile, nodded in Pam's direction saying, 'I take baby, yes?' before spiriting Carla away somewhere into the depths of gloomy High Royd.

Pam had never been sure how Angelo had persuaded Father O'Leary, the very young priest over at St Augustine's, to allow her – a non-Catholic, who hadn't seen the inside of any church for years – to be married there without taking some sort of confirmation beforehand. She didn't think Sunday school at the chapel down the road, where Mary Brown had shooed all three girls in turn every Sunday morning (not from any affiliation to John the Baptist himself, but from a need to get them out from under her feet while she beat and martyred herself to the Yorkshire puddings, beef, treacle sponge pudding and Bird's Custard) gave her any points towards membership of the Catholic brethren. Pam wouldn't have been surprised if money hadn't passed hands somewhere along the line, but, by the time the autumn leaves had finally given up the ghost and fallen, she was standing at the altar in a dress made by her mother to accommodate her growing bump, and she didn't much care.

So, here she was, a week before her seventeenth birthday, pulling yet more washing from the brand-new twin tub (which had caused her mother to cry out in delight and then strong-arm her father to head off to Currys) and, let's face it, she didn't think much of this motherhood lark at all.

It was strange actually living with a man. Of course, she'd lived with her dad, the whole family sharing the one bathroom, but that was her dad, she was used to *his* bathroom smells and his forever leaving up the loo seat despite her mother's constant shouting of *latrine* every two minutes. But this was different. So much more personal and intimate, picking out her new husband's pubic hair from the bath and seeing the meticulous way Marco squeezed the toothpaste from the bottom, rolling the tube over and over as he used it up until it was the width of her thumb. Pam sometimes felt she'd been manipulated and squeezed just the same way, but then accepted that marriage to her hadn't been high on Marco's list of things to do before he was twenty-one any more than it was on hers and, more than likely, he was feeling exactly the same way.

Their relationship was probably, she thought, one of polite indifference. After the wedding reception at High Royd, Angelo had driven the pair of them to Midhope train station where, dressed in her going away outfit of the little grey suit her mother had bought for her, and which Pam herself hated, they'd taken the train up to Scotland to spend a few days in Edinburgh. At four months pregnant and with a neat little bump to prove it, she was well over the little morning sickness she'd suffered and was feeling well and strong physically.

If not mentally.

On her wedding night, shy and embarrassed at her nakedness as well as at her changing shape, she'd divested herself of clothes in the privacy of the locked en-suite bathroom and stepped into the cream nightdress Jane had bought as a present for her. Pam had recently been reading a lot of Jean Plaidy historical novels and the daft thought came to her that she was acting like some foreign princess, forced to marry the future King of England, sacrificing herself for the good of the nation.

Or, in her case, for the good of Piccione's Pickles and Preserves, which had made her laugh at her reflection in the bathroom mirror. And which had then suddenly turned into a sob as she so wished it were Rob waiting in the huge double bed in the Waverley Hotel bedroom on Princes Street.

But homesick and missing Rob as she was, a part of her was curious to have another go at the whole sex malarkey. There had been little opportunity in the past couple of weeks before the wedding to re-enact their coming together in the car, which had led her to where she was now. Along with the present of the cream nightgown, a giggling Jane had thrust another parcel into her hands.

'Now, you might be needing this as well.' She'd laughed.

'What is it?'

'Well, your future husband has such a reputation with women, he's obviously highly experienced in… you know… in the bed department.'

'You're making him sound like a double-divan salesman.' Pam had rolled her eyes.

'You know exactly what I mean. So, he'll expect someone with a bit of know-how themselves.'

'Know-how?'

'Hmm. Here. Hot off the press. Just don't let your mum see it.'

'*The Joy of Sex?*' Pamela took out the thick paperback from its wrapping.

'Yes. I've had a jolly good look through it. Blimey, what people get up to. Learn a couple of these tricks and you'll soon be able to stop Marco wandering off down to the girls in Preserves.'

'Is that what you've heard?' Pam was shocked. 'Come on, Jane, tell me.'

'Oh no, honestly, don't worry. Just a rumour about him in Lemon Curd...'

'What? He uses lemon curd...?' Was this a way to get out of the wedding tomorrow? By telling her dad that his future son-in-law dipped his thingy in lemon curd? Her dad wouldn't be impressed with that, surely? They'd let her stay at home and have the baby and have it adopted and then she could go and find Rob and...

'No, you daft thing.' Jane was really laughing now and Pam was worried her mum might come up to see what the hilarity was all about and see the book. 'You know, in that little stock- room just off the Lemon Curd production line? Only a rumour. And started by Maureen, so I wouldn't take it as gospel.'

'Are you still friendly with her?'

'Well...' Jane couldn't quite meet Pam's eye. 'I went down to Moonlight with her last week. I need someone to go out with now that you're... you know.'

'And...?'

'And was Rob there? Yes, he was. And no, he wasn't with anyone despite Maureen trying her hardest to get in there. He was just dancing and dancing. Bloody hell, he's a good dancer. I think you've broken his heart, Pam.'

And she'd cried then, really sobbed, until Jane, frightened at the unexpected outburst of emotion, had shoved the sex manual under the quilted eiderdown and gone to fetch Pam's mum.

Despite there being radiators in the hotel bedroom, a wet and foggy late November evening in Edinburgh was not, and never could be, the tropical idyll one might hope for in a honeymoon and, shivering, Pam slipped between the cold starched cotton sheets alongside a naked Marco. He said nothing but collected her in his arms, warming her hands and feet, which were quite numb – whether from cold or nerves she couldn't quite work out – with his own before turning out the bedside light.

With little foreplay, Marco entered her and the whole thing was over in minutes, leaving Pam confused at the difference in the intense sexual feeling generated on that warm August evening the first time she'd done it compared with this, and the thought that she really must remember to tell Jane she'd wasted her money buying that book.

25

Frankie

'Daisy, we're up to *eleven* now. *And* it's an odd number.'

'Well done. Do you know your prime numbers and square numbers as well?'

'Don't prevaricate,' I tutted.

'Well, does it really *matter*? It's not bad luck or anything, is it? We're only *pretending* we're grown up. We don't want it to be too formal.'

'Well it matters if we don't have eleven lots of plates and cutlery.'

'I can always nip down to Aldi and get a stack of paper plates and cups.' Daisy was hunting in the fridge. 'Have you made any more of that lemon curd? I've become a bit addicted.'

'I noticed.'

'Fabulous stirred into full-fat Greek yoghurt like you suggested.'

'It is, isn't it?' I was momentarily distracted from the

problem of how we were actually going to eat the food I was preparing by Daisy's enthusiasm for my lemon curd. 'Daisy, I've not been sweating away all day making this food to then serve it on paper plates.'

'I'll nip over to Mum's and borrow what we need. You know she hates cooking and entertaining. She's got a pile of stuff we can have.'

'So, eleven?'

'Twelve actually.' Daisy didn't quite meet my eye.

'*Twelve* now? Hell, you're going to have to go back to Sainsbury's, Daisy. How's it got to twelve suddenly?'

'I'm as surprised as you, everyone accepting. Do people really have nothing better to do on a Saturday night than come round here to eat?'

That made me laugh. 'How's it got to twelve?' I asked again.

'Well we *were* an odd number. One man down as it were and knowing you'd not be happy about that, I asked Jamie from Dad's cricket team to come.'

My heart missed a beat, which it always did whenever the village cricket team was mentioned, knowing that Daler used to be a big part of it all.

'Right, good.' I took a deep breath, pushing all images of Daler in cricket whites down on the village pitch out of my head. 'Well at least we're even numbers. Six of each.'

'Actually no.'

'Oh, Daisy! What? You've not invited thirteen? You can't. People will be spooked; it's just not done to have thirteen at a table: The Last Supper and all that.'

'Oh, no one cares; they're an irreligious lot round these parts. Just ask Ben Carey, the vicar. He was crying into his pint down at The Jolly Sailor only the other night about not having a full house every Sunday.'

'Sounds like a game of bingo.'

'Anyway, Jamie couldn't come. Got some hot date lined up from Tinder.'

'So, we're back to eleven then?'

'No, Ruby Morton was there…'

'Ruby Morton? I know that name.'

'In Year 6 with us? At junior school?'

'Gosh, whatever happened to her?' I screwed up my face trying to picture her. She'd been a real little mouse of a thing, in round pink glasses and with sandy hair. Don't think I ever heard her say a word all the time she was with us in Mrs Moriarty's class. I'd *loved* Mrs Moriarty: she'd been there for me, as had Kate and Graham Maddison, Daisy's parents, once Mum upped and left with Paul Stockwell. 'So,' I snapped, hearing myself still angry with my mother, 'now we're *seven* women and only *five* men?'

'I *know*,' Daisy said gloomily. 'Not good. In fact, there's only one single man now between three single women. You can't count Aunty Pam. I know *she's* single, always been single after her divorce from your Uncle Marco, but I can't see the man next door fancying your Aunty Pam. No disrespect to your relatives or anything, but he looks to me to be a bit of a goer…'

'I thought you always reckoned my Aunty Pam was a bit of a goer as well?'

'Well yes, but only with blokes of her own age, surely? Or maybe not? Oh hell, one single man and four single women? Great stuff. Shall I see if I can grab three more men for you three?'

'Us three? What about *you*?' I glared at Daisy.

'*I'm* already booked with the lovely American next door.'

'You're welcome to him,' I said. 'So, going back to Ruby Morton, Daisy. How did that come about?'

'Well, she was in the pub when Jamie turned me down. Asked if *she* could come along instead. Have to say I thought it was a bit presumptuous, particularly knowing your need for order and symmetry: you know a nice neat ratio of men to women.'

'*Ruby Morton* knew that?' I *was* a bit over the top with balance and order – you only had to look at the way I'd sorted my things into the fabulous walk-in wardrobe upstairs to realise that. Maybe because my life hadn't been overly ordered up until now. Still wasn't really, but I was giving it a jolly good go.

'No, *I* know that. Why would *Ruby Morton* know that when she's not seen you since we were eleven? Keep up, will you? She's changed a bit. That's all I'm saying.'

I loved cooking. The lemon curd, the old bone shaker of a bike and following Aunt Rosina's recipes in Sicily had got me through the bad times when I just wanted to come home and throw myself, prostrate, at Daler's feet. Aunty Pam had created a love of baking in me when I was a little girl, but it was Aunt Rosina who had got me into cooking: stirring, simmering, adding a pinch of this herb, and a handful of that, instilling patience into me as she instructed me: '*chi va piano, va sano e va lontano*' – she who goes slowly and carefully, wins the day.

I'd trailed round Sainsbury's sourcing the ingredients I needed, and then spent the previous evening, as well as the whole of Saturday, preparing and cooking the dishes I'd learned at Aunt Rosina's side. Daisy had come up trumps and instead of throwing cutlery and paper plates into the middle of the kitchen table as I'd feared (a huge one, donated from Daisy's Granny Nancy who, allegedly, discarded furniture in search of the more up to date as often as, and in the manner of, her many men friends) she had called in at her Great-Granny Madge's for starched linen, cutlery and (admittedly a mismatch of) plates and serving dishes.

'Oh gosh, Daisy, the table looks fabulous. Who are you trying to impress?'

Daisy was in the process of arranging her mother's beautifully decorated pots with sweet-smelling herbs as table decoration, eschewing spring flowers – apart from the tiny little yellow narcissi she'd found sheltering at one side of the garden – but concentrating on sprigs of early sage, rosemary and thyme.

'Who am I trying to impress?' Daisy asked, frowning at a recalcitrant sprig of rosemary. 'I think it must be Simon and Garfunkel by the look of this lot.' She grinned across at me. 'Well, *obviously* I want Mr Mancini next door to have a vision of me as a little homemaker. He won't know I've not done any of the cooking until he's fallen totally in love with me over my table-decoration artistry and it's too late to refer to (she affected a Southern drawl) *must be able to make a decent pecan pie just like my dear old mom back home* on his list of future wifely attributes.'

'Wrong accent.' I laughed. 'Cameron's from New Hampshire.'

'And also,' Daisy went on, ignoring me, 'obviously I want Gatis Miniauskiene to report back to his brother, Matis, not only how beautiful I looked, but also how I'm now a domestic goddess... God, I hate that term. Hasn't anyone come up with anything better, yet...?'

'Does it still hurt with Matis?' I asked.

'Just a little. You know?'

I did.

'Now, sweetheart, this is Alan Barker.' Aunty Pam pushed a bespectacled and sandy-haired, diminutive chap in my direction and, as she mouthed, 'Sorry, all a bit last-minute – all I could come up with,' over Alan's head, I wanted to laugh, both at Pam's comical face and the immediate thought that her guest would match exactly my recollection of the eleven-year-old Ruby Morton.

'Lovely to meet you, Alan.' I smiled. 'Really good of you to come along at such short notice.'

'Good of me? *Au contraire*.' He rubbed his hands. 'I've been looking forward to this all week.'

'He doesn't get out much.' Pam smiled, patting Alan's balding, gingery pate. 'Which is an out-and-out lie,' she amended. 'He's always out.'

'Oh?'

'Alan is big into Northern soul,' Pam said, almost proudly. 'Biggest collection I've ever seen.'

'Stamps?' Daisy asked, as she retrieved bottles of Fever Tree from the fridge. 'Pokémon Cards? Happy Meal toys? Nazi memorabilia…?'

'No, 45s.' Pam smiled. 'Some really rare stuff…'

'Yep,' Alan said proudly, 'I've just acquired Jack Hammer's "What Greater Love" and King Wesley's "Road Runner".'

'Blimey,' Daisy said, pouring too-big gins and handing one to Alan, 'not *King Wesley…*?'

'You know him?' Alan's eyes were saucers.

'No.' Daisy laughed, as I glared at her. 'But I think I'm about to.'

I found a tall, willowy blonde stood talking to Cameron Mancini in the sitting room once I felt able to abandon the chains of domesticity and leave the cooking to itself. Gosh, she really was gorgeous and Cameron appeared to think so too, so engrossed in conversation he didn't notice my entry into the room.

So, this could be one of two: either the – according to Daisy – very gorgeous Libby Westmoreland, partner of Seb Henderson who together had commissioned Charlie and Daisy to project-manage the whole of the Holly Close Farm site. Alternatively, it could be Verity, my brother Luca's new girlfriend, who Mum was constantly holding up as the Holy Grail for all womanhood.

'Francesca, you've not changed a bit.' The girl left Cameron's side briefly, and I found myself enveloped in a cloud of Chanel's *Coco Mademoiselle*. I recognised the perfume's rose and jasmine undertones instantly, not because I revered or wore the scent myself, but because Mum had sprayed it lavishly ever since Paul Stockwell had first bought it for her when she was sneaking off to meet him when she was still with Dad and still (for what it was worth) at home. I hated it then and I hated it now. This must be Verity then, her wearing of the same perfume as Mum another reason for Mum's constantly singing her praises.

But why was she hugging me? And *not changed a bit*? I'd never met Verity until this moment.

'It's *Ruby*.' She giggled.

'Is it?' I stared. Where was the red hair, the little round pink spectacles, the girl who never said a word? 'Goodness, I'd never have known you.'

'Told you she'd changed,' Daisy said, topping up glasses with white wine before attempting to monopolise Cameron in conversation.

'I only spent a year in Westenbury before Dad's work had us on the move again,' Ruby said. 'And that *was* almost twenty years ago.'

'So, what are you doing back here?' I kept sneaking little looks at her, trying to marry the picture of the colourless, shy little girl I remembered, with the vibrant, brightly hued creature in front of me now.

'Although Mum and Dad only spent a year here in Westenbury, they always loved the village and said, once they retired, they'd aim to come back here. They've just bought a fabulous cottage out by Norman's Meadow. I was made redundant a couple of weeks ago, so decided to pack up my things in Birmingham and move in with them for a while until I decide where I want to be or what I want to do. Mind you...' she turned away from Cameron and lowered her voice '...the view from where I'm standing is looking *very* promising, if you get my drift.' She gave a high-pitched giggle and I certainly did. Get her drift, that is.

'Hello, neighbour, you must be Frankie...'

'Hi, I'm *Ruby*.' Ruby had somehow elbowed me out of the way as her *view* changed with something equally, if not more *promising*, and she was now hugging this new man with gusto. The man managed to release himself from Ruby's clutches long enough to thrust out a hand in my direction. 'Hi, Seb Henderson. We're up at the farm...'

'Oh, my goodness, aren't you gorgeous.' Ruby giggled, (her constant *oh my goodness* as well as her giggling like a drain were both really beginning to grate) licking her lips provocatively and flinging back her long hair, catching Alan Barker on his – rather long – nose. He was skulking on the periphery waiting for a way in.

'Lovely to meet you, Seb.' I smiled. 'Alan...' I grabbed his arm '...do come and meet Ruby, a friend of mine from junior school.' I gave Ruby a determined *Stay!* look, which had always worked with the dogs on Aunt Rosina's farm and steered Seb Henderson towards my brother, Luca, who had just walked into the room with two very attractive women.

'That's it, party's over,' Daisy hissed in my ear as she walked past to get more wine. 'Where've all the *ugly* girls gone, for heaven's sake? We can't compete with this lot.'

'*You* invited them all,' I hissed back, wanting to laugh at Daisy's murderous face as Ruby managed to extricate herself from Alan and his non-stop recitation of all the Northern soul 45s he owned, *had* owned, as well as those he was desperate *to* own, and corner Cameron once again.

'Hi.' Luca kissed my cheek briefly. 'Great place down here. Fabulous.' Praise, indeed, from Luca. But then, it wasn't *my* place he was admiring. He turned to the petite, dark-haired girl who was deep in conversation with Libby Westmoreland and briefly touched her arm. 'Verity, this is my sister, Francesca. Francesca appears to think she has come up with the answer to Piccione's little lemon curd problem.' He laughed, a scornful little chuckle, his raised eyebrow emphasising his derision. 'If there was ever a problem in the first place...'

'Frankie.' I smiled through gritted teeth, ignoring my brother and holding out my hand; I knew I shouldn't have invited the sarcastic sod. Gosh, this girl was tiny – gamine I supposed you'd call it. Even though I'm basically a short-arse like my dad, having inherited his Sicilian stature and height, I felt myself to be a bit of a carthorse compared to this show pony. I don't think she was even five foot tall, but she was beautifully proportioned. And didn't seem at all interested in me or my lemon curd.

Hell, I'd forgotten the nibbles. Food wouldn't be ready for at least another hour and guests were already knocking back the gin and wine as though it were going out of fashion. I did hope Daisy and I had bought enough and although I was hugely relieved to see a veritable vineyard of both red and white accumulating in the kitchen, I had to set to and shift the bottles from where they'd been dumped on the island in the middle of my food preparations. Why do guests always do that at dinner parties? Abandon bags and wine and flowers and chocolates and jackets right where they're not needed?

I cleared the detritus away from the hob – Verity's tiny little pink leather clutch was in danger of going up in flames – and set to, steaming a pile of salted edamame beans, decanting olives in chilli oil into dishes and relieving the little canapes I'd assembled earlier from their plastic wrap in the fridge. I was just about to whistle for Pam or Daisy to come and deliver the goods when Cameron arrived at my side.

'Can I help?' he asked.

'Would you mind? Thank you. It's supposed to be Daisy's job.'

He grinned. 'She's entertaining the troops.'

I grinned back, slightly disarmed by his friendliness. This wasn't the Cameron Mancini I knew from work. Here, then, was my chance to promote Daisy: 'She's brilliant, isn't she? I love her to bits: she's clever, funny, generous – get her to tell you her broccoli joke…' I started to laugh as I drained the podded beans and sprinkled sea salt and sesame seeds, remembering Daisy's original telling of this little joke a couple of years ago in the cockpit of an Airbus A320. 'If you wouldn't mind going round with the wine, I'll follow with the beans.'

Cameron nodded and helped himself to one of the pods, pulling the soft beans from the fibrous pod with even white teeth before looking round for somewhere to abandon it.

'You Americans have such fabulous teeth.' I smiled and then felt a bit silly commenting on my boss's gnashers.

'And you Italians don't?' He smiled back, holding my eye for what seemed for ever and then picked up two bottles of wine from where I'd moved them and, without another word, set off for the sitting room.

Blimey, what was all that about? I must be in need of a man's attention if one slightly smouldering look from Cameron Mancini was making me want to cross my legs. I downed my remaining gin and set off with my nibbles.

26

Frankie

Now

'Ah Francesca, food. I was just wondering when some little *aperitif* might be on its way. We Northern soulers need to keep up our strength. You know?'

I didn't.

Alan rubbed his hands together greedily and I wouldn't have been surprised at the appearance of a long cartoon-like tongue circling his lips in appreciation. 'I love a mangetout,' he said helping himself to a fistful of the edamame pods but, instead of pulling out the soft bean inside, put two entire pods into his mouth and chewed. And chewed.

I watched in fascination as his Adam's apple bobbed hypnotically in his very white neck while he masticated the hairy husks. Eventually he swallowed somewhat painfully and said in a low voice, 'I like to think of myself as a bit of a cook, Francesca – I'm waiting to go on *Come Dine With Me* on TV – so I hope you won't be too offended at a little suggestion that these mangetout may have been picked just a *little* past their sell-by date, *peut être*? Or...' Alan attempted to extract a string of green from between his front incisors '...maybe a little more time cooking?' He patted my arm sympathetically before helping himself to two of the other canapes. 'Now these *are* delicious, Francesca. Remind me to give you my recipe for mashed pilchards and salad cream on TUC biscuits before I leave. Fool-proof and go down an absolute treat.'

The piece of green vegetation still waggled accusingly at me as he waxed lyrical both about his Stax record collection and the starters, mains and desserts – oh, a seemingly *endless* dessert repertoire – for which he'd been lauded over the years. I looked round for escape, or at least help from Daisy and Pam, but Daisy was intent on herding an equally determined-not-to-be-moved Ruby away from Cameron. Pam had found the most attractive man in the room – Seb Henderson – and was deep in conversation, equally determined not to be rounded up and brought back to heel to deal with the quite awful guest she'd brought with her and now happily abandoned.

Luca caught my arm as the doorbell sounded. 'Frankie, you do know Verity is vegetarian?'

'Vegan, actually, Francesca.' Verity gave me an almost accusatory look. 'Everything I eat has to be clean.'

'Oh, don't worry, Verity, I've washed my hands and Daisy has given her granny's plates a good scrub.' I glared at Luca. Why hadn't he thought to tell me his girlfriend was vegan? But why hadn't I, as hostess, ascertained this possibility beforehand? So many people were vegan these days: I'd promised *myself* a look into it once I'd finished that last pack of bacon and eaten up the cheese and eggs in the fridge. Quite possibly, statistically, a quarter of the room wouldn't be able to eat what I'd prepared. 'Let me top up your gin, Verity.' Perhaps if I got her legless, she might not realise the osso bucco was actually meat.

'No alcohol, thank you, Francesca.' Verity quickly slapped a tiny hand over her glass. 'It's incredibly full of calories and been proven to be a big pointer towards cancer in women.'

I was beginning to feel a bit depressed. Hell, what was I going to give Verity – and any other non-meat eaters – instead of the osso bucco? It was one of the meatiest dishes around. I glanced across at Cameron Mancini who caught my eye and smiled: I'd bet anything Cameron was also a clean eater. I'd never actually seen him eat at Piccione's – he either worked through his lunch break or went out for an hour's run, so I had absolutely no idea if what he ate was meat-free or actually even vegan. Weren't all Americans against meat, cigarettes and alcohol? Or was that just Californians? Or was I being *Californiaist*? New Hampshire was surely on the other coast? With a mountain of things I *should* have been doing the other day at work, I'd actually googled a map of the USA to find out just where my boss was from but was distracted, nay shocked, to find Washington had actually moved to the West Coast. I'd always thought the President lived just outside New York on the opposite coast, so had to assume either I'd got it wrong all these years or Trump had taken his bat home for whatever reason and moved himself and his state to the other side of the country and the map. Daisy, laughing, had eventually put me right about there being a Washington state as well as Washington DC, the capital.

Cursing myself for my lack of geographical know-how as well as not considering the vegans and vegetarians who had now, in my fevered imagination, morphed into at least fifty per cent of the guests, I went to answer the doorbell that everyone else appeared to be ignoring. A tiny girl (what was it with these beautifully petite women? I thought we bred them big and tough up here in Yorkshire?) with a mass of dark curls stood on the doorstep.

'Hi, you must be Daisy's mates? I's Deimante Miniauskiene and sis my mans Gatis. Sank you so much for invite. I's brought you pudding: *Skruzdelynas* from Lithuania...' Deimante paused, frowning at her own words. '*Sis* one not brought from Lithuania of course. I makes this one myself at home... *my* home, this afternoon... not come all way from Lithuania and outs of dates... *Daisy*...!' She thrust the towering pudding in her husband's direction – he'd not said a word up to this point – while she and Daisy hollered and whooped and hugged and I began to realise just how much I'd been out of the loop back here in Yorkshire as life went on without me.

Gatis and I grinned somewhat inanely at each other until Deimante turned back to me. 'So, Frankies, you'd runs away? All betters now? You look lovelies. You tells that mans that leaves you for womans who gets herself with baby just to nails him, to eff offs. You far too lovelies to leave. Anyways, plenty more fishes and all that. And *I* needs you... *I* wants you very much indeed...'

I was torn between wanting to laugh at this delightfully open girl, irritation with Daisy who'd obviously told her everything about me and Daler, as well as wondering if Deimante was into kinky sex.

'I don't think Deimante is suggesting anything untoward.' Daisy was laughing. 'Although, to be honest, knowing Deimante, it's a distinct possibility.'

'Footballs,' Deimante tutted in Daisy's direction. 'We need to talks female footballs, Frankies.'

'Brilliant.' My eyes widened at the thought of playing again. 'Let's have a really good chat later.' I took the pudding from Gatis and turned back to Daisy who was talking non-stop to Deimante. 'Daisy,' I hissed, 'Verity is vegan.'

'Is she? Why?'

'I don't know *why*,' I said crossly. 'She just *is*, as are probably seventy-five per cent of the people here. If we'd only thought to ask.'

'There's some rocket, tomatoes and a big piece of cheese in the fridge,' Daisy offered.

'*Vegan*, Daisy…'

'Right OK. Well, there's rocket and tomatoes in the fridge.' Spying Ruby, now almost stuck to Cameron Mancini like Velcro, she set off in their direction to get in between them. 'Ask your Aunty Pam,' she suggested over her shoulder. 'She'll know what to do.'

'Well can you at least, *subtly*, find out who else might have any dietary requirements, Daisy?'

'Right, listen up, you lot,' Daisy yelled above the chatter and Motown music Pam had found on Sonos. 'Any *veggies* here apart from Verity? Speak now or for ever hold a lamb chop on your fork this evening… No? Any coeliacs? Any peanut allergies? Sesame? No? You're OK, Frankie. It's just Verity,' Daisy yelled in my direction. 'The rest of us are rampant carnivores.'

'I can totally understand where vegans and vegetarians

are coming from,' I admitted to Pam as we looked in the fridge and freezer for something to feed Verity. 'I mean, I look down the valley in front of the cottage and see the baby lambs gambolling...'

'Bit young for the betting shops, aren't they?' Pam grinned as she assembled various items on the kitchen work surface.

'...on the daisy-strewn fields...'

'You need to get that girl off the gin if she ends up laid out in the fields.' Pam laughed. 'Right OK: courgettes, olive oil, lemon...' Pam turned to the dining table at the far end of the kitchen '...aha, mint...' She quickly and deftly sabotaged one of Daisy's table decorations. 'OK – Verity's starter is *Minty Grilled Courgettes* and...' Pam's nose was back in the fridge and the larder '...tahini paste, coconut cream, maple syrup, aubergine... any parsley... yes? Right then, you get on with what you have to do – people are getting hungry, sweetheart – and I'll concoct an *Aubergine Tabbouleh* for her main course.'

'I bet your mum didn't teach you how to make either of those.' I laughed, recalling Pam's stories of how her mother had thought garlic was for slaying vampires and rice only for pudding topped with jam.

'My mother went to her deathbed having never tasted hummus or olives.' Pam smiled almost sadly. 'Different era. Oh, I'm sorry about Alan, Frankie,' she went on as she washed and sliced courgettes. 'Why the hell did I bring him?'

'Why *did* you bring him? Batting above his weight with you, isn't he? I mean, he's not exactly Brad Pitt, is he?'

'Oh, Alan's been around for ever.' Pam lowered her voice. 'I had been seeing this rather lovely man,' Pam sighed. 'We had so much in common, loved dancing, loved walking and good food.' She patted her slim waist ruefully. 'Real foodies, the pair of us.'

'But?'

'There's always a *but* dating at my age...'

'Hey, don't think you have the monopoly on dating *buts*.' I laughed. 'At least you *have* dates.'

'Oh, I have plenty of those. I really like men, you know? Really enjoy their company. I need to be hugged and touched and appreciated.'

'Don't we all?'

'I don't see you doing much hugging and touching lately?' She glanced up at me from whisking a dressing of oil and lemon juice.

'Give me a chance,' I protested. 'I've only been back two minutes.'

'Exactly.'

'Anyway, we were talking about you, not me.' I surveyed the set table just as Daisy popped her head round the kitchen door.

'Think we might have a mutiny on our hands if we don't eat soon,' she said, pulling a face. 'Or at least they'll be sending out to the chippy.'

'Tell people to come and eat. We're just about ready.' I turned back to Aunty Pam. 'So, what was the *but* this time?'

'While I was away in Lanzarote with Bev, his ex-wife decided she wanted him back. Have to say, he put up a bit of a fight, but ex-wives usually win, don't they? I'd have brought him here otherwise. He was really lovely: bright, articulate, jolly good in the...'

'OK, OK, too much information. You're my aunt not my mate.'

'You'll always be my mate and my second daughter.' Pam gave me a big soppy kiss. 'OK, bring on the hordes.'

Despite their hunger, it seemed to take for ever to get people settled around the table which, being Daisy's Granny Nancy's abandoned, oversized one, only just fitted into the dining space at the far end of the kitchen. Half the guests decided they needed the loo before they ate, and by the time they arrived at the table the other half, who had seated themselves, had to edge themselves out in order to let the others file back in. Those now standing then decided *they'd* take the opportunity to nip to the loo too in order not to disturb their neighbour twenty minutes down the line. It was a bit like being back on a Flying High economy flight to Torremolinos, or at the theatre when latecomers arrive just as the curtain is going up and everyone has to stand as the newcomers obliterate the play's opening lines with their '*sorry,*' '*sorry, was that your toe?*' '*I do apologise...*' A game of musical chairs, even, but without the necessary one missing chair. Oh, I tell a lie. We'd either gained another guest (nothing would surprise me on that score), or we'd counted out one chair too little. We'd utilised every chair and stool going (including the wobbly one in Daisy's en suite) but Cameron saved the day by dashing back next door and reappearing with a rather lovely, very modern chair, which he gave to Ruby, much to Daisy's chagrin who had placed *herself* next to Cameron, with Ruby far away down the other end of the table next to Alan.

'I'm fine *here*, really, Daisy,' Ruby was saying sweetly as she patted the seat for Cameron to sit beside her. 'Please don't worry about *me*, Daisy. You have enough to think about.' As Daisy had spent most of the afternoon while I'd been cooking arranging her seating plan with military precision in order to have Cameron at one side of her and both Gatis (she wanted him to report back to Matis that life for Daisy was fine without her ex-lover) and Seb Henderson within flirting distance, Ruby's insistence on sitting in Daisy's own allotted place was seriously undermining the whole thing.

With both Daisy and Aunty Pam helping to serve, and appreciative murmurs as my ravioli stuffed with artichokes and pancetta was consumed, I began to relax. Seb Henderson poured me a large glass of a very good Cabernet Sauvignon that Luca had brought in anticipation of our eating Italian and, for once, my brother was being pleasant, even smiling in my direction as we ate.

'Now, Frankies, football. Se village team meet every week on se playing field.'

'OK.'

'I's surprised you not been asked before?' Deimante frowned. 'Daisy say you good player? I very very good player; was just abouts to join *Lietuvos nacionaline moteru futbola komanda*.'

'I'm sorry?' I wasn't quite sure what Deimante was telling me.

'Lithuanian National Women's footballs team,' Deimante said, shrugging her shoulders nonchalantly. 'As goalie. I's good goalie, but Gatis – my mans – say we must leave my homes and come to Englands. So now, I's goalie for Westenbury village team as well as Midhope Town Ladies. Your village want you, Frankies. Your town need you.' Deimante was beginning to sound like that bloke on the World War I poster, but I began to feel a stirring of excitement, a stirring of real happiness I'd not felt for a long, long time.

I looked down the table at our guests eating and laughing and enjoying themselves. What lovely neighbours we had. I was really enjoying Seb Henderson's company and was looking forward to getting to know Libby, his wife, with whom I'd only exchanged a few words of welcome. She was a few years younger than me, I reckoned, but she looked to be up for a few drinks out with Daisy, Deimante and myself. How lovely: a little gang of four friends when, only last week I'd felt bereft of any friends except the girls in Preserves, and Daisy. Maybe I should be including Ruby in this new little friendship group I was planning, although I feared there was only *one* friendship she was intent on at the moment: if she got herself any closer to Cameron, she'd be in his starter.

I decided to help Daisy out. 'Ruby, would you mind awfully helping me out with these dishes? I think you can get yourself out from the table easier than Daisy.' I put my hand firmly on Daisy's shoulder, indicating she should stay where she was and she gave me a grateful look.

'Gosh, what's that?' Ruby asked as I mixed the prepared chopped parsley, lemon zest and garlic. 'Isn't it a bit green?'

'*Gremolata.*' I laughed. 'It's meant to be green.'

'Where do you put it?'

'Put it?' I laughed again. 'It's not a face cream. It goes on the osso bucco which...' I reached into the oven and removed two full trays... 'is right here. OK, if you and Pam could distribute these on the warm plates over there and I'll follow with the risotto...'

'It's a bit yellow, isn't it?' Ruby frowned. 'I thought risotto was white?'

'*Risotto alla milanese*.' I smiled. 'Flavoured and coloured with saffron.'

'My mum's bitch is called Saffron.' Ruby nodded sagely but did nothing towards helping with the food. 'You're a colourful lot, you Italians, aren't you?'

'Sicilian, actually,' I said, thrusting laden plates in her and Pam's direction. 'Thank you. Off you go.'

Anyone who's ever been in charge of a dinner party will tell you that once the main course is served, the cook can relax and enjoy themselves as well. The meat on the osso bucco was cooked to perfection and, as it literally fell off the bone, I sent up a silent little prayer of thanks to Aunt Rosina who'd taken me through the recipe several times back in Agrigento. Verity had looked with some suspicion at Pam's aubergine tabbouleh, giving it a bit of a poke and asking if Pam knew its carb content. 'No carbs in it as far as I know,' Pam had said airily and Verity had tucked in with some degree of enthusiasm.

Daisy had orchestrated place changes in our absence and Ruby was now down the other end of the table where Daisy had originally wanted her, next to Alan and my brother. They seemed to be getting on really well – Luca was going up more and more in my estimation as the evening went on – and this too was making me happy. Maybe we'd both grown up a bit; maybe Luca had also suffered as a result of Mum and Dad's divorce and being sent away to school. I'd always assumed he'd sailed through it all, being the one chosen by my mother to live with her. Maybe it was time to suggest the pair of us get together over a pint down at The

Jolly Sailor and actually talk, something we'd never really done before.

I spent a lovely half-hour getting to know Libby Westmoreland. She'd given up her place at Oxford when she realised she was pregnant with her little boy Lysander, who was now three or four, but had taken up her studies again, this time over at Leeds and wasn't always finding it easy being a mum while training to be a doctor.

'My mum helps out and so does Seb's dad, but they have their own lives.'

'Well, if you ever want a babysitter, just ask.'

'Really?' Libby's eyes lit up.

Hell, I'd obviously had too much wine: I knew nothing about little kids except what I'd learned being with Angel and Matteo. I'd wanted Daler's children so badly that for a while I'd distanced myself from any bouncing babies and toddlers, especially dark-haired, dark-eyed ones. There were very few children where I'd stayed in Sicily, the farms being run mainly by those left behind once children and grandchildren had moved to the industrial areas of the island in search of work.

As Pam and I cleared plates in the kitchen, she put up a hand to her head. 'Sweetheart, I'm going to have to leave. I'm so sorry.'

'Oh no. Migraine again?' I'd seen Pam suffer so many times over the years, I knew the signs. 'How about lying down upstairs?'

She shook her head. 'I thought I was getting away with it. I so didn't want to miss out on your first dinner party, so when I got a few flashing lights about an hour ago, I took the usual stuff. Sometimes it works, sometimes it doesn't.

The flashing lights are really going for it now.' Pam squinted in my direction, rubbing at her head. 'I don't want to start throwing up here and spoiling your lovely do – I'm far better at home in my own bed and sleeping it off.'

'I'll ring for a taxi.'

'Already done. It's here, outside.'

'Oh, Pam…'

'It's fine, sweetheart, all under control. I'm going to have to leave Alan with you, I'm afraid – I don't think I'd be able to drag him away…' she grinned and then winced '…even if I wanted to. I'm just going to slip off while no one is watching.'

I hugged her and walked with her down the tiny hall and outside where an Uber was already waiting to take her home. 'Now,' she said, 'try not to let Alan get too much up your nose and…'

'And?'

'…I want a full progress report tomorrow on any developments with Cameron Mancini.'

Pam winked and then winced again at the effort of doing so before walking down the path to the Uber.

I was particularly pleased with how my puddings had turned out. I'd made *bonet*, the Italian cousin of a crème caramel, but made much more luscious with the addition of amaretti, chocolate and rum; *sbrisolona*, which had turned out a bit crumbly but still very edible and, just for Daisy who couldn't get enough of it, whipped my *crema al limone* lemon curd into Greek yoghurt and double cream and shoved it into the freezer to make a sort of ice cream. With

Deimante's pudding as well, the dining table was beginning to resemble an Italian *pasticceria* and, despite groans of protest that they were too stuffed to even contemplate pudding, plates were eagerly held out for '*just a small slice*' and '*I don't know which to have – I'm going to have to try just a teeny little bit of each one.*'

Verity shook her head and put up a hand – rather like an Italian cop on traffic duty in Naples – and then watched, in the manner of one of Pavlov's slavering dogs, every mouthful that everyone else devoured.

'Deimante, this pudding of yours is wonderful.' It really was. I took another mouthful of the *skruzdelynas*, savouring the honey that ran out of the fried dough.

'Insect mountain.' Deimante smiled through her own mouthful of *bonet*.

'Sorry?' I stopped chewing.

'Ant hill,' Gatis explained, grinning. 'We call sis pudding an ant hill back home.'

'Right.'

'Don't worries, Frankies. No real ants. Sis pudding really good to make here because of fabulous honey.'

It was fabulous. 'Where do you get this honey, Deimante? From Lithuania?'

'No, no, no. From over se hills...' She wafted her arm vaguely in the direction of Piccione's.

'From *Piccione's*? Is this *our* honey?' If it was, I'd better be giving the bees their P45s back again. Both Cameron and Luca were listening intently.

'No, no, no,' Deimante scoffed. 'Sorry, but your honey pretty disgusting. Sorry, sorry...'

'Where from then?'

Deimante waved her arm again. 'Over sere...' She turned to her husband. 'Gatis, where we get honey?'

'Sere's a man.'

'A man?' Cameron and Luca leaned forwards like they were being given state secrets.

'Karam...?' Deimante turned once more to Gatis.

'Karam Yassim. He refugee. Doctor actually. He live out over sere...' Gatis employed the same vague arm-indicating technique as his wife.

'Dr Karam Yassim?' Libby leaned across the table. 'Keeps bees and produces the most heavenly honey? He also has manuka honey. It helped Lysander with his hay fever. He lives out towards the moors; you know, near Upper Clawson?'

Cameron, Luca and myself were just about to ask for more detail when the front door burst open and a voice called, 'Daisy? Are we too late? Is there any food left?'

Everyone turned to peer at the newcomers as Daisy jumped up. 'Oh, Jamie. Come in. Loads of food left. 'What happened to your hot date?'

'It wasn't.' Jamie laughed. He'd obviously been drinking and was slurring his words. 'Sorry to barge in like this.' He grinned round at the rest of us at the table before grabbing Daisy around the waist and giving her a big kiss on the cheek.

Ruby was flinging her long blonde hair back and licking her lips in anticipation of someone new. Strange, I thought she'd already met Jamie down at The Jolly Sailor last week when Daisy invited him over and Ruby had then invited herself. And then I realised she was looking beyond Jamie at a tall, blond-haired, dark-eyed man who was looking exceptionally embarrassed at gate-crashing our dinner party.

'Oh, sorry, sorry, hope you don't mind.' Jamie laughed. 'My friend from uni. We were at Nottingham together...' Jamie turned and actually pulled the man into the kitchen where he stood, totally embarrassed, almost scowling. 'This is Jude – human rights lawyer and, as from a month ago, now prospective parmilentary... larmipentary...' He broke off, giggling.

'Parliamentary?' Seb laughed.

'That's the one. Thanks, mate. Parmimentary candidate to beat that bastard Paul Stockwell... Sorry, no offence, if you voted for him in the past... at his own game. Come on, Jude, Daisy's happy to have us here.' Jamie pulled at the blond-haired man's arm. 'Jude Mansell, everyone.'

27

Frankie

Now

'You OK?' Daisy, dressed in her panda onesie, stood at the side of my bed the next morning, a mug of tea in each hand. She handed one to me as I sat up and automatically held out both hands, one for the mug and the other for the two paracetamol that had always accompanied the tea after a good night out in Liverpool.

'There's not enough liquid here to rehydrate *this* mouth and head,' I said, sipping at the hot tea and knocking back the painkillers.

'Bloody good do though, don't you think? Shove up and let's have a post-mortem.' Daisy climbed in beside me as I moved to one side of the bed and we sat there like an old married couple, rubbing sleep and mascara from our eyes and drinking our tea in silence for a good minute before Daisy launched. 'Honestly, Frankie, your food was fabulous.'

'So were your table decorations and getting everyone

up and dancing.' We'd rolled up the rug, pushed back the sofa and couple of chairs Daisy had inherited from her Granny Nancy and allowed Alan Barker full throttle on the Sonos. What he lacked in social skills he certainly made up for as DJ, as he went through a whole repertoire of soul from early Sam and Dave and Aretha Franklin to Wilson Pickett and Otis Redding and then came a bit more up to date with D'Angelo and Tyrese Gibson. But we all yelled for the old stuff and finished the night with Diana Ross and The Four Tops and more Isley Brothers.

'Of course, this isn't technically Northern soul,' Alan had tried to argue, but no one was really listening to him and we were dancing until around three in the morning to the music we really wanted to hear.

'I actually think Cameron Mancini is rather lovely,' Daisy said, burying her face in her mug.

'I know, you said.'

'Ruby Morton thought so too.'

'She certainly did.'

'But I think he's only interested in you, Frankie.'

'In me?'

'Don't play the innocent with me.' Daisy sighed. 'Come on, admit it, you suddenly found him really attractive too.'

I did.

'I didn't,' I lied. 'You saw him first.'

'Hardly. He's your boss; you saw him over a month ago.'

'Yes, but I certainly didn't see him, you know, *like that.*'

'Like someone you wanted to rush into bed?'

'Yes.'

'Yes what?'

'I mean *no.*'

Daisy dug me in the ribs. 'No, you hadn't seen him like that or no you don't want to rush him into bed?'

'This is a bit like hard work, Daisy,' I said, closing my eyes. 'Look, yes, I saw Cameron in a bit of a different light last night. And yes, I could, I think, if circumstances were different, really go for him.'

'What circumstances?'

I sighed again. 'One: He's my boss; two: You saw him first and three: I'm not sure I want to get involved with anyone again – you know, after Daler.'

'It's been over two years, Frankie,' Daisy said gently. 'You've got to let it go. Get rid of your lifejacket and jump in at the deep end.'

'And *drown*?'

'And get on with your life.'

'I know, I know. I'm just thankful Daler lives in London and I don't have to worry about bumping into him. You know, in the pub or in the library or anywhere else.'

'The daft thing is, you could have carried on with your nursing. You didn't need to give it all up and run away. I mean, he *could* have told you he was going to be moving to London and that you wouldn't be bumping into him on one of his rounds or over the removal of someone's gall bladder.'

'He *did* tell me, Daisy. He begged me not to give up nursing. It was me: I just couldn't do it anymore, couldn't concentrate, kept crying in the sluice room and literally sobbing when anyone didn't make it on the ward – you know, when someone died. I became a bit of an embarrassment, sobbing uncontrollably over someone's ancient granny when the family were really probably glad to see the back of them and already rubbing their hands in anticipation of the will.'

Daisy laughed at that.

'And then, when I was off the ward and back at uni, I was behind with everything: I had essays to get in, end-of-term exams to sit. I remember just sitting in Dad's flat looking at a textbook about the circulatory system – the heart and blood and veins and arteries. And the page just swam in front of my eyes and I had a test the next day and I couldn't tell you where an artery was coming from or where a vein was going…'

'Arteries Always Away from the heart – you know, the three A's?' Daisy patted my arm sympathetically. 'Why didn't you ring me about it?'

I smiled and patted her arm in return. 'What, for a lesson on the workings of the heart?'

'Well I do have a degree in biology. But, no, just so I could calm you down. Get you to take a deep breath, tell you to go for a walk and come back to it once you'd cleared your mind a bit.'

'I did ring you. Several times. But you were obviously totally excited about doing up this place; I didn't want to rain on your parade. Anyway, it wouldn't have worked, I don't think. It was Dad who came into the flat, found me sobbing over the damned page on the heart and lungs and took it away from me. He made me go and stay next door with him and Tammy for a few days. The thing is, he'd seen me just like this when Mum left me…'

'Frankie, she left your dad, not *you*.'

'She left *me* as well, Daisy. She took Luca with her and left *me*.'

'But did you want to leave your dad? You've always been so close to him.'

'I wasn't given the choice. To be honest, if she'd sat me down and asked me where I wanted to live, I'd have probably have said I *did* want to stay at home with Dad. I certainly didn't want to live with Paul Stockwell. Mum was so into him; *I* just didn't seem relevant. She chose him and took Luca and left me.'

'I think you need some counselling, Frankie.'

'No, I *don't*,' I said cheerfully. 'Going away to school, and my football and Aunty Pam got me over my mum. I have a sort of relationship with her now, but I don't think we'll ever be close again now. I've always seen Aunty Pam as my substitute mother.'

'She's brilliant, isn't she? She looked so fabulous in those black leather trousers and heels. Shame she got a migraine and had to leave.'

'Hmm, she knows, when she gets them, the only thing to do is to go home and put herself to bed. She's had them as long as I've known her.'

'I'm amazed she never married again, you know, after her divorce. I thought she'd have been snapped up. She's so vibrant and attractive.'

'Well,' I said, 'as far as I know it wasn't for the lack of opportunity. She's always had relationships, and with some really lovely men, especially after my cousin, Carla, went to university and then to live in Canada. But at the end of the day, as far as I can see, two things stopped her getting involved.'

'Oh?'

'Apparently she felt such a commitment to me after Mum

left, she didn't feel getting married again would be fair on me.'

'Really?' Daisy frowned. 'She was only your aunt. And then by marriage, not a blood relation, surely?'

'Yes, I think she likes to use me as an excuse when she didn't really want to give up her independence and her very full life as a single woman.'

Daisy and I simultaneously drained our mugs of tea, both mulling this over.

'So, you said there were two things?' Daisy leaned over to put her mug down on the floor.

'Two things? Oh, yes, she never got over a boy she met when she was just sixteen.'

'Oh, was he Carla's real father then?'

'No, no, you only have to look at Carla to see she's a total Piccione. Pam had to give up this bloke – Rob I think she said he was called – when she found she was pregnant to Uncle Marco.'

'Blimey, they were a rampant lot in the Seventies by the sound of it.'

'Long story. Ask Pam about it one day. She doesn't mind talking about it. Well, some of it, anyway.'

'Some of it?' Daisy's eyes lit up. 'Sounds a bit of a mystery.'

'Yes, there is something, but I don't know what it is. Anyway, she never got over this Rob bloke and not going to live in London with him which, as far as I can gather, is what he wanted. Before he knew she was pregnant with another man's child, that is.'

'Don't think I'd ever get over having to live next to your Nonna Consettia and being employed in Pickles all my working life – no disrespect to your family.'

'None taken.' I laughed.

'So, we're getting off the point here,' Daisy said, folding her arms and snuggling down into the pillow.

'What point?'

'Cameron Mancini.'

'What about him?'

'Look, I could see his eyes following you all evening.'

'Really?' I asked, pleased.

'Really. And all I'm saying is you mustn't feel guilty about me seeing him first.'

'Even though you actually *didn't*,' I teased.

'A mere technicality. So, I don't want to fall out about this. You know, over Cameron Mancini? I don't want to have to send you to Coventry or ask you to leave just because he fancies you rather than me.'

'I really don't think there could ever be anything between the pair of us. He's a bit too smooth for me, a bit grey pinstriped suit.'

'Hey, that woman in *Fifty Shades* didn't object to a grey, smooth, pinstriped American. I bet under that cool exterior he's a real goer...' Daisy paused and wriggled a bit. 'Hell, why am I giving him to you?'

'Not really my type,' I said, thinking of Daler's long dark curls, jeans and beanie hat.

'Well, I'm handing him over,' Daisy said kindly. 'It's very good of me, I know... No, you don't have to thank me. Finishing off clearing up downstairs will suffice.'

I sat up and stared down at her. She opened one eye and began to laugh.

'The human rights lawyer?' I laughed. 'You ended up

with *him* when I was in the kitchen starting to wash up,
didn't you?'

'I most certainly did not,' Daisy said indignantly, and
then started to laugh. 'But I'm working on it. Going out for
a drink with him tonight.'

'Your phone keeps ringing,' Daisy shouted up the stairs as
I was getting out of the shower. It had taken us a good two
hours to clear up, wash up and make the place exactly as it
was before. Both of us were very conscious – Daisy because
it was her own, first-time-lived-in home and me because I
was the guest – that the beautiful cottage needed looking
after and shouldn't be left to its own devices as we'd so
often left the flat we'd shared in Liverpool.

'Who is it?'

'I don't know.'

'Well, look.'

'It's your mum. Three missed calls.'

Hell. I pulled on jeans and a sweater and ran down to
Daisy who was standing at the bottom of the stairs by the
open front door. The wind that had been blowing down
the valley the last couple of days had retreated back into its
cave and the sunshine was high in a cloudless duck-egg-blue
sky. I could feel the warmth on my face and I wanted to be
out there, on my bike.

I rang Mum back and she answered immediately.

'Francesca, have you forgotten?'

'Forgotten?' Surely, I wasn't meant to be round there for
lunch? Mum rarely did a Sunday lunch unless she was trying

to impress people and I didn't think for one minute there was anything she wanted to impress on me. Besides, I was still full from all the food I'd eaten the previous evening.

'You promised you'd go out canvassing with Paul this afternoon.' Mum sounded most indignant.

'Did I? When?'

'I can't quite remember when, but I distinctly remember you agreeing to it.'

'I was going out for a bike ride.'

'Francesca, I think your father's parliamentary career's rather more important than a random bike ride, don't you?'

I didn't. And since when had Paul Stockwell become my father, for heaven's sake? Stepfather was bad enough. 'Dad's going into politics now?'

'Your *father*'s going into politics?' I heard her sharp intake of breath.

'You just said so.'

'*I* did? I did not.'

The last of the daffodils were enjoying the late April sunshine and the lambs down in the field below were jumping with the pure joy of being alive. I needed to be out there with them. 'Look, Mum, I certainly didn't promise I'd go out with Paul this afternoon.'

'I rather think you did, Francesca.' There was no arguing with Mum when she was determined to get her own way.

'Why don't *you* go out with him knocking on doors?'

'The thing is, Francesca,' she said persuasively, 'the candidate Paul's up against is very young. Very handsome as well, from what I can see on his leaflets. Paul and I both feel a little youth on Paul's side wouldn't go amiss when he's out meeting the public.'

I was very tempted to retort, 'To counteract my stepfather's broken-veined ageing nose brought about by drinking too much whisky at the golf club?' but instead I said, 'Oh, I've met him.'

'Met who?' Another sharp intake of breath.

'Jude Mansell, the main guy up against Paul.'

'Ridiculous name, Jude: it's a girl's name, short for Judith, surely? My friend Judith Parsons at school was always known as Jude. Where did you meet *him*?'

'He came to a dinner party we had last night at Daisy's.'

'You had him round for *dinner*? The very man who is trying to keep your father... stepfather... from his rightful place in The House? Where's your sense of loyalty, Francesca? Well, for heaven's sake don't tell Paul about this.'

'So, I think, not a good idea for me to go out knocking on doors with Paul then?' I asked hopefully. 'You know, when I've been fraternising with the enemy?'

'Well as long as you're not *sleeping* with the enemy, Francesca – I *did* enjoy that film with Julia Roberts – I'm sure Paul won't mind a little fraternisation. But no more, please, if you don't mind. And do tell Paul anything you found out about this Jude character. You know, how he feels his campaign is going?'

I'd said very little to Jude Mansell the previous evening, and all I really knew was that he was probably in his early thirties, had been at university in Nottingham – where he'd met Jamie – before returning to his home town of Manchester to practise law. He was just over from Manchester for the weekend, staying at Jamie's place, while he got to know the area he'd hopefully be representing, a little better. He'd been aiming to get into politics for several years, he said and, with Barry Truelove unexpectedly shuffling off this mortal coil, had seen the coming by-election as a good place to get a foot in the door, as had his party's selection committee. Although Jude was tall, young, and quite lovely to look at, I knew my stepfather's almost fifteen years in politics would give him a big advantage over Jude, a total novice. When I'd finally let it be known that he would be standing against my stepfather, the initial friendliness he'd shown towards me was withdrawn somewhat and he'd wandered off to find Jamie and a drink.

And obviously Daisy.

I was really pleased something might be brewing between the pair of them. Although Daisy would never really admit it, I know Matis Miniauskiene's going back to Lithuania and marrying someone else had hit her really hard, especially when, in hindsight, she knew she'd made a mistake in turning him down because of her fear of commitment.

Going out canvassing with Paul Stockwell was the very last thing I wanted to do on this Sunday afternoon but I decided to go with the flow and actually bike over to Mum's place.

'Going far?' Cameron Mancini was in the garden of the adjoining cottage, taking out from its cardboard packaging, and arranging, a set of newly delivered garden furniture.

'Nice.' I smiled, indicating the rather upmarket-looking table and chairs.

'I know it's only April, but I'm hoping for a good summer this year.' He smiled back. 'I know your British summers can be a washout.' In an old pair of Levi's and a rugby shirt that had seen better days, I really was seeing my boss in a different light. 'Going far?' he repeated.

'Just over to my mother's. I've been roped in to help my stepfather with his canvassing.'

'Do you fancy christening this new furniture when you come back? It's going to be a beautiful day?'

Christen his furniture? I had an awful vision of me stretched across his new wicker table in the afternoon sunshine as he bent over me, Pimm's brimming with fruit and mint (from Daisy's garden) to hand. Actually, it was a rather lovely vision and, as I nodded that yes, that would be lovely and mounted my bike, I finally admitted to myself I'd been acting out various little scenarios like these in my head ever since Cameron Mancini had sat across from us all in the boardroom on my first day as full-time employee at Piccione's.

'We can discuss the lemon curd and honey issues,' Cameron called after me. 'Think about the best way forward.'

Right.

'Are you going knocking on doors like that?' Mum came out to the gate to meet me, looking me up and down the way only Mum could.

'Like what?'

'You know, in your cycle shorts and helmet. You don't want people to think Paul is some sort of health nut. Although, maybe, that wouldn't be a bad thing. Everyone's so bloody fit and healthy and… and *vegan* these days.'

'I can't really see that, Mum.' I glanced towards the door where Paul's straining gut was heading out before him. 'Don't worry, I've got my jeans with me.'

'Jeans?'

'Mum I'm not putting my work suit on if that's what you're thinking.' I don't know why I didn't just cycle off and up onto the moors.

'Well go and get yourself ready, Paul's waiting.' My mother took in my sweating face and mussed hair as I took off my helmet. 'There's a hairbrush and a lipstick in my bathroom if you've not brought your own: you need to show yourself and Paul in a good light if he's going to keep hold of his seat.'

28

Frankie

'Right, Francesca, at this stage of the game we're just doing what's called a *soft canvass*. We knock on the door, introduce ourselves and ask about any local issues that may be concerning them.' Paul pulled over near the recreation ground at the other side of Westenbury where a kids' Sunday afternoon football team was obviously fighting a losing battle against a team from the next village. 'Don't mention what our policies are at this stage. Just let *them* talk.'

'Sorry?' I wanted to be down on the rec with the kids, showing them where they were going wrong. They were using up too much energy, running around like headless chickens but too frightened to get in there and tackle the opposition to get the ball.

'We need to be friendly, cheerful, impenetrable...'

'Go for it, go for goal...' I yelled.

'Well yes, that *is* our aim, but maybe tone it down a bit?'

Paul gave me one of his looks. 'OK, we'll do a few doors together and you can see how it's done and then maybe I'll take one side of the road and you the other?' He looked at his watch. 'Don't want to spend too long on all this; got a game of golf in an hour or so... but don't tell your mother.' He nudged me in the ribs and gave a nervous bray of laughter.

Yes, and I've got a christening in next door's garden, I nearly said, but didn't, grateful that at least Paul and I were singing from the same hymn sheet – party leaflet – with regards how much time we were giving over to this farce.

The first door opened and a tiny, elderly woman in pink slippers eyed us suspiciously. Before Paul could even speak, she shut it firmly on us, her retreating back seen plainly through the coloured lozenges of glass in the green-painted door.

The second household seemed much more promising. A very pleasant-looking man opened the door, looked over my shoulder and yelled, 'Shoot.' This gave Paul the opportunity to do just that, even though his own advice had been, I recalled, to not say much at this juncture. Five minutes later, the man took the proffered leaflet, said, 'Sorry, mate, wrong party,' and wandered across the road to watch the football match.

'You're all two-faced, you lot,' was the opening gambit of the next householder.

'If I were two-faced would I really be wearing *this one*?' Paul came straight back at the guy, grabbing hold of his chubby cheeks and making a sort of duck face, which made me not only laugh out loud, crossing my legs and wishing

I'd gone to the loo before I left home, but also see Paul in a rather different light.

No Political Parties or Religious Cults was plainly emblazoned above *No Traders, Hawkers or Junk Mail* but Paul went blindly in, rapping smartly on the next door and my newly found (slight, let's be honest) admiration for my stepfather went back into free fall.

'Do you think we should…?' I was interrupted by the door opening on a very scholarly type standing arms folded and obviously looking for a good argument. 'Which bit of the above notice do you not understand?' he asked calmly.

Paul thrust out a hand. 'Paul Stockwell. I do hope I can rely on your vote in the upcoming…'

'Why do you feel you can spam my doorstep?'

Paul thrust out a hand once more and repeated, with a little less confidence, 'Paul St…'

'If you can tell me why you think it permissible to enter *my* personal space to spout *your* political agenda then I'll consider voting for you. No? You can't? OK, fair enough…' And yet another door was closed in our face.

'Do you not think people are having a bit of a post-Sunday-lunch snooze?' I ventured when, half an hour later we'd still not been able to ascertain any local viewpoints, gripes or requests (apart from a cocky ten-year-old demanding an open-air swimming pool on the rec) that were worth writing down on my virgin white, unsullied notepad. 'You know, watching a catch up of *EastEnders*? Washing up the fat-encrusted roasting tins? I think you're probably just getting up people's noses. And that's the last thing you want to do, a month before an election.'

'I'm just a bit out of practice,' Paul admitted as we walked down the next street, neither of us, it seemed, with a huge deal of enthusiasm for knocking on any more doors. 'It's been three years since Barry Truelove trounced me at the polls. Not really done a huge deal, politically, since then. Anyway, your mother is determined... *I'm* determined to get back in there. Shouldn't be too big a job with this young pretender to the throne in opposition. Bit of a leftie human rights lawyer, I gather?' He turned to me with a questioning frown. 'I hear you met him? What's he like?'

'See for yourself.' Walking towards us, deep in discussion were three men: Jude Mansell, Jamie and a tall, older man in jeans and navy sweater.

'Frankie!' Jamie bounded up like a Labrador on speed and drew me into a bear hug. 'Great do last night. Don't quite know if I'm on this earth or... you know, the other one?' He rubbed at his eyes and grinned down at me. 'What are you doing in this part of the village?'

'I told you,' Jude intervened. 'She's on the *other side*.'

'Well I don't know about that,' I said, embarrassed as all three of them stood and stared. 'I'm just helping out a family member. And then I'm going out on my bike.' (As if jumping on my bike and heading for the moors somehow counteracted my canvassing for the enemy.) I suddenly really didn't want to be associated with Paul Stockwell. It felt a bit like playing rounders at junior school and, finding myself not on Daisy's side. I'd spend all my time trying to see who they'd got on *their* team and longing to be over there with them instead of being sent off to deep field miles away by bossy captain Andrea Taylor. I'd be standing there with no one to talk to while Daisy was discussing team tactics with the popular girls as well as with David Alliott who we were all secretly planning to marry when we were eighteen. I really didn't want to be on Paul's team.

'Ah, the opposition.' Paul thrust a meaty paw in Jude Mansell's direction. 'All's fair in love and war and all that.' He gave one of his donkey brays of laughter and I shrivelled slightly as the other three shook his hand somewhat unconvincingly.

'Right, we need to get on,' Jude said before turning back to me and asking, 'Is Daisy at home later on?'

'Absolutely.' I smiled and Jude returned the smile – the first one since we'd all met up – and I could see totally what Daisy saw in him. 'Do call over later. There's pudding to finish up.'

Jude raised an eye at the other two, rustled his papers and they were just about to move off when the older man stopped and turned back to me.

'Frankie *Piccione*?' He smiled down at me.

'Er, yes, that's right.'

'So, is your father Marco Piccione?'

'No, he's my uncle.' What a lovely-looking man, I thought. What kind, intelligent eyes. 'Although I've never actually met him.'

'Oh?'

'He went to live abroad before I was born.'

'Oh.' The man raised an eyebrow. 'He married Pamela Brown?'

'My Aunty Pam? Do you know her?'

'I did, a long time ago.'

'Come on, Dad, we need to get on.' Jude Mansell was obviously champing at the bit, determined to get knocking on the left-hand side of the street before Paul got his foot in any more doors, literal or metaphorical.

'Oh, you're Jude's *dad*?' Everything suddenly fell into place. 'Rob? Rob Mansell?'

The older man stared, totally taken aback. 'Did Jude tell you my name?'

'No, Aunty Pam did.' I laughed. 'Many times.'

'Francesca, I think we should be getting on…'

'Come on, Dad…'

The others began to wander off in opposite directions but Rob Mansell and I stood, grinning at each other somewhat inanely.

'You went to live in London?' My glance went automatically to Rob's left hand as he stood there, smiling while pulling a hand through his still-thick blond hair. A broad band of gold was in place on his third finger.

'My wife and I were there for about ten years. We were both heavily involved in politics during and after university, and then we moved up to Manchester.'

'Oh, of course. Jude said he was from Manchester.'

'I'm back here now though.'

'Here?'

'Back in Midhope. My mother's still here but she's getting on a bit now. Still fighting fit and laying down the law, even though she's over ninety. Thought it best, three months ago, to move back here. I missed the place. Totally fortuitous that Jude's hoping to represent the area. I'm not sure how easy he's going to find it; you know, against your *family member*?'

'Paul's my stepfather.'

'Right.' Rob looked down the road where Jude and Jamie

were already in the process of knocking on a red-painted door several yards away. 'I'd better go: I'm supposed to be helping, not standing here chatting to the opposition.' He grinned and made to move off but stopped and turned. 'Say hello to your Aunty Pam. Tell her Rob was asking after her.'

'I will. So, er, where are you and your wife living now?'

'Out towards Norman's Meadow, near my mother.' He paused, looking me fully in the eye. 'My wife died three years ago; I'm a widower.' He raised a hand in farewell and sprinted down the road after Jude and Jamie.

Half an hour later, I'd had enough. I was bursting to get on my bike and cycle out to Pam's place and tell her just who I'd bumped into. Tell her that Rob was back and living not far from Westenbury village itself. And that he *didn't have a wife*. I slowed down a bit at that. Losing one's wife after – I did a quick calculation as we knocked on the last door – over forty years of marriage most certainly doesn't mean one is necessarily in the market for, or on the hunt for, another: the poor man must still be grieving.

'Ah.' The large Afro-Caribbean woman beamed at Paul and me as she flung open her door before we'd even knocked. 'I see you coming up the path. Now, what can I do for you? You can't persuade me to follow Jesus, 'cos I *already* follow the Lord.' I wouldn't have been surprised if she'd finished with *Halleluiah*. 'Down, Esau,' she suddenly snapped and Paul and I both stared. Had she mistaken my stepfather for Isaac's elder son and was wanting him to kneel in the glory of the Lord?

Paul glanced nervously in my direction and I shrugged.

'Get down, Esau,' she said again, swiping behind her large rear at a little Jack Russell jumping up at her legs.

'Paul Stockwell,' Paul offered, the obvious relief at not having to prostrate himself at the woman's feet in order to gain her vote making him unctuous in the extreme. 'Standing at the by-election in the area, and at your service night or day.' Smarmy or what? 'I'm hoping I can rely on your vote?' Paul, now that freedom in the form of the golf course was within sight, was on a bit of a roll.

'Oh absolutely. Though I already told the other chap he could have my vote. Now, can I persuade you in for a cup of tea and a little Bible reading in praise of the good Lord above?'

Paul turned, glanced at his watch and then thrust a leaflet towards the woman at the same time as Esau thrust himself toward my stepfather, lifted his leg and urinated on Paul's trousered one with a self-satisfied expression on his greying muzzle.

Giggling at Paul's dismayed face, I walked ahead of him down the path and back towards the car.

'Bloody dog,' Paul snapped, shaking his trouser leg as he walked, his unposted leaflets flailing into the breeze behind him. 'Come on, I've had enough.'

'Me too.'

'That Mansell chappie seems on the ball,' Paul said gloomily.

'I think you're right,' I agreed.

'Oh, come on, just one more.' Paul indicated with a nod of his head towards a stunning cottage ahead of us, its mellow stone walls fighting for dominance behind a beautiful wisteria. Tiny purple flowers were just appearing

– the display would be fabulous in a month or so. A large white removal van – *Movers not Shakers* – was parked on the road, its back doors open to the elements.

'Oh, no more, Paul. Really, no more. The last thing people want when they're in the middle of moving is party political spamming on their doorstep.'

'Catch them when they're new to the area and don't know any better,' Paul said sagely. Any better? Did Paul not believe his own rhetoric?

'Just this last one,' he went on. 'This place is so wonderful, I'm sure they'll be the sort of people to want me to represent them.'

The ego of the man never failed to amaze me.

With a disgruntled sigh, I walked behind him up the path whereupon Paul shook at his trouser leg once more before giving a ridiculous 'Halloo there!' round the wide-open door.

A tiny little tot of about two came running towards us down the hallway, tripping over her – presumably mother's – high heels as she reached the open door.

'Upsidaisy.' I laughed as she lay there for a split second before pulling herself up and grinning widely in our direction. She was beautiful: dark-haired and dark-eyed, and wearing – I recognised from Angel's dressing-up box – an Elsa of Arendelle outfit over her jeans and sweat shirt with aplomb.

''Lo,' she said, solemnly. 'I'm *Frozen*.'

'It *is* a bit chilly today, isn't it?' Paul simpered, ignoring the unseasonable warmth of the late April sunshine that had accompanied us on this seemingly never-ending trail of Westenbury's electorate. Paul had never learned how to converse with anyone less than thirty or without a glass of whisky and golf club to hand, and looked across at me for help as the little girl gazed at the pair of us, head to one side as she stood, weighing us up.

'Is Mummy in?' I finally asked.

'Ah, welcome, welcome,' Paul said at his oiliest yet, as a young woman headed down the hall towards us. 'Welcome to our village.'

I'd have known her anywhere. Even without the beautifully cut green sari, but dressed, instead, in jeans and what looked suspiciously like a Loro Piana cashmere sweater, was Sienna Dosanjh.

With a racing pulse, I hurriedly looked at the electoral list I held in my hand: Mayfield Cottage – Mrs Edna Bradshaw. But of course, new arrivals to the village wouldn't be on the list as yet. Sienna Dosanjh glanced towards me, totally without any recognition. But then, why would she?

'I'm sorry,' she said, somewhat shortly, taking hold of the little girl's hand. 'I'm just trying to sort out these removal people with our things. I'll get my husband.'

That was my cue to go. I turned, head spinning, and ran and ran, realised I was heading in the wrong direction, turned again and, keeping my head down, ran towards the recreation ground and Paul's parked Range Rover.

29

Frankie

'Sweetheart, what on earth's the matter?' Pam was tying back bunches of exhausted and dying daffodils with a rubber band. I wondered if she had one for me: I was dying inside.

'He's come back.'

'Daler?' Such was my utter misery over Daler's leaving me to marry Sienna and go to London more than two years previously, Pam knew immediately who 'he' was.

I nodded, wiping at my face with my black cycling gloves.

'Come on in. Tea and a piece of shortbread. Works wonders.'

'Pam, I couldn't eat a thing. I feel sick.'

'I know, I know,' she soothed.

'*Did* you know?'

'That he'd come back? No, why would I? Is he back living with his parents in Dosanjh Towers? Have you been canvassing out there?'

'No.' I took off my cycle helmet and laid my face on the kitchen table. 'He's bought the most heavenly cottage out at the other end of the village. Mayfield Cottage? Quite near the rec?'

'Edna Bradshaw's place?' Pam looked up from filling the kettle. She was the font of all knowledge with regards to what was going on in the village since she'd left her little coach house at the bottom of Nonno's garden and bought this house at the far end of the village for herself and Carla, when Carla was small. And where she'd lived ever since. 'She only died six months ago. Absolutely fabulous place, but it'll need a lot of work. Mind you, huge garden at the back. Plenty of scope to extend. I can just see it now – a massive orangery on the back to extend the kitchen... Oh sorry, darling, not what you want to hear. That was so thoughtless of me.'

'I'm going to have to go away again. I can't stay here. I can't live here knowing I'm going to bump into him all the time... I can't do it, Aunty Pam...' I felt hysteria rising and fought to control myself. 'I don't think you realise, understand just *how much* I loved Daler.'

'Sweetie, I understand perfectly.'

'I know we were only together three months or so, but I spent every minute of that three months loving him.'

'Three years, three months, three weeks, three days...' Pam shrugged and pushed a large mug of tea across the kitchen table in my direction. 'When you know, you know.' She looked wistful for a second.

'Oh, Pam, bloody hell, I've not told you.' I rubbed at my eyes and tried to smile. It was a bit of a lopsided smile admittedly but this was such an amazing thing to tell her that I had determined to bike straight over to impart the news. Before I'd fled the scene, knowing Pam was the only one I'd ever gone to – apart from Dad and Tammy – when the chips were down.

'Told me what? What did he say?'

'Who?'

'Daler.' She looked at me strangely.

'No, no, I didn't see him, thank goodness. I just legged it down the garden path when I recognised Sienna, his wife, giving instructions to the movers when Paul and I were canvassing.' My eyes filled with tears again as I recalled Daler's beautiful little girl. And his equally beautiful wife. 'No! Pam, I saw *Rob*.'

Pam went quite pale. 'Rob who?'

'*Your* Rob. Rob Mansell.'

'What do you mean? How did you know who he was?'

'Well, if you hadn't gone home with your migraine last night, you'd have met his son.'

'Rob's *son*?' I could see Pam mentally bringing to mind the men who'd gathered in the sitting room the previous evening as she'd helped me in the kitchen. 'Not that Sebastian? Your neighbour?'

'No, that's David Henderson's son.'

'Is it? Blimey, you do move in exalted circles.' David Henderson lived in the manor house in the village, very near to the church and Clementine's internationally acclaimed restaurant. 'So, which one then? How do you know…?'

'After you'd gone, Jamie – Daisy's friend – arrived with this other bloke who he introduced as Jude Mansell.'

Pam stared. 'Jude? But that's my absolutely favourite name for a boy. Rob and I were both reading *Jude The*

Obscure and I remember saying... Blimey...' Pam was lost for words. 'If Carla had been a boy, she'd have been called Jude. I'd have had a fight on my hands with Angelo of course, but I'd have stuck to my guns. He called his son Jude? And he came round to your house last night?' Pam was like a little girl wanting the whole story from the start to the finish.

'I'd no idea who he was – he fancies Daisy by the way.'

'Not you?' Pam looked stricken as her mind worked overtime.

'No, no. He soon pushed off when he heard I was batting for the other side...'

'You've become a lesbian?' Pam stared. 'I often wondered if maybe *I*...'

'No! Will you stop interrupting, Pam? It's one of your worst faults – did anyone ever tell you that?'

'Sorry, I'm just all of a dither.'

'As I was saying, Jude was totally unimpressed when he found out I was Paul Stockwell's stepdaughter and then he saw Daisy and he had eyes for no other.'

'And Rob was at the party as well?' Pam was getting confused.

'No. Paul and I bumped into them when Jude and Jamie and Rob were out canvassing on the same street just now.'

'Bit unfortunate that, wasn't it? I hope you and Paul got in there first.'

'Why?'

'No, what am I saying?' Pam tutted. 'I certainly won't be voting for that stepfather of yours, family loyalty or no. I shall,' she said almost theatrically, 'be voting for *Jude*.'

I looked at Pam. 'Even though you've not met him?'

'If he's as morally sound as his dad, he'll do for me.'

'Instead of Paul who, let's face it, is morally bankrupt?'

'So, go on then, did you mention me? Does he remember me?' The look of hope on Aunty Pam's face was such, I wanted to cry even more.

'He knew I was a Piccione. He thought I might be your daughter.'

'You're as good as,' Pam said fiercely. 'You know that.'

'I know.' I patted Pam's hand. 'Pam, he's been widowed these past three years.'

'Jude has?'

I knew exactly what she was doing: not daring to hope that Rob might be free.

'No,' I said gently. 'Rob. His wife died three years ago and he moved back from Manchester a few months ago to be near his mother.'

'Rob's living round here again?' Pam's mouth was one big 'O' of shock. 'And his mother's still alive? Oh, she was *such* a lovely woman.'

'You didn't keep in touch with her?'

'What was the point? I was married to your Uncle Marco with a baby. I didn't want to know what Rob was up to in London. That would have crucified me. Anyway, darling…' Pam stood up and folded her arms determinedly '…all that nonsense is in the past: schoolgirl first crush and all that. It's over forty years ago for heaven's sake. You and Daler are in the present. It's you and Daler we need to be discussing.' She suddenly got angry. 'How dare he come back here? How dare he flaunt his wife and child in your own village. In your face. I'm not having it, Frankie.'

'Nothing you can do about it, Aunty Pam. It's me who's going to have to either put up with it or...'

'Or what?' Pam was still angrily flapping a tea towel around the Aga.

'Or I'm going to have to move on again.'

'Do not even think about it,' Daisy fumed just as angrily once I'd biked back to the Holly Close Farm cottages and found her strimming and sluicing and conditioning and moisturising every bit of herself in preparation for, as well as in anticipation of, her first date with Jude Mansell that evening. 'You're not going *anywhere*, Frankie. You've just got to get over him.'

'I *was* doing,' I protested. 'I was feeling so happy thinking about our new girly mates – you know Libby, Deimante – even Ruby Morton – and you and me together down at the pub.'

'That hasn't changed,' Daisy said in some exasperation. 'Although I'm not sure I'm with you on Ruby: she's as mad as a box of frogs.'

'And Luca and I were getting on so well too. I really felt as if I had a brother for the first time in... well for ever.'

'Yes, it was really good to see you two laughing and dancing together. I can't see him and Vegan Verity lasting much longer, can you?'

I shook my head. 'She'd drive him mad I would have thought.'

'Frankie, there's a lovely, lovely man waiting for you next door.' Daisy indicated with a nod of a head towards Cameron's cottage.

I sniffed and wiped my eyes. 'He asked me to go over and christen his garden table.'

'Ooh er, Missus.' Daisy attempted levity. 'I do hope you said yes?'

I nodded.

'Right, upstairs then: showered, shaved, scent yourself to high heaven and off you go with a bottle of wine. There are several bottles of red left over from last night – why do people always take red to a party and then drink all the white? Take your pick.'

Daisy was absolutely right: I was *not* going back down that escape route once again. It was about time I grew up and counted my blessings: I had a job I was actually really enjoying, earning decent money and living in the most glorious of places. The whole spring, and then summer with its long light evenings, its barbecues and its bike rides all lay ahead of me. I might even take a flight back out to Sicily for a week at some point and show Aunt Rosina just how mended I was. I took a deep breath, looking out of the window down Daisy's back garden where she'd been digging a vegetable patch and sowing early broad beans and carrots. I wondered if she'd let *me* have that little patch right next to the field? It was such a massive garden and, although Daisy was an expert and absolutely loved nothing more than being out planting, sowing and weeding, I bet she wouldn't mind me having a small bit of it for myself.

I had a sudden idea that I wanted to buy her a present for being such a wonderful friend. A greenhouse; she'd love a small greenhouse. Angelo and Dad had been more than generous in what they were paying me and I so wanted to do this for her.

There, I told myself as I took deep breaths. *You can do this. You've managed to think of others rather than yourself for at least a minute.* I'd help Aunty Pam meet up with Rob Mansell again. If they didn't fancy each other any longer, at least they could be friends; that would be good. I'd encourage Daisy's relationship with Jude; that would be good too. I'd see more of Matteo and Angel: take Matteo to football matches – no, it would have to be cricket now it was spring, wouldn't it? – and of course there was always Deimante's football team which, she'd assured me, was so low down in the amateur leagues she'd insisted they were to keep on practising, despite the council taking down the goalposts for the new season.

I could do this. I showered, found the pair of new white jeans I'd bought on my shopping trip to Manchester and had been saving for a special occasion (this *was* a special occasion – this was a new grown-up, selfless Frankie Piccione) and hot-brushed my hair into submission.

'You look good,' Daisy approved. 'Fabulous jeans. Get round next door and give it all you've got.'

'In what sense?'

'Whatever sense you want.'

'Do my eyes still look red from crying?'

'Slightly. Hang on.' Daisy ferreted in the kitchen drawer by the window. 'Here, eye drops. For hay fever.'

'But I haven't got hay fever.'

'Irrelevant. They're soothing and will take away the puffiness. Just go and have a drink with Cameron. It doesn't have to be anything big. Just enjoy it for what it is.'

'I think it might be just lemon curd and honey.'

'Fair enough. If that's what floats his boat, go with the flow...'

'Metaphorically speaking?'

'...and then snog the life out of him.'

Cameron was sitting at his garden table, a beer to hand and the Sunday papers spread out in front of him. He was intent on a piece in *The Observer* and didn't see or hear me as I let myself through the tiny wooden gate Daisy had built into the drystone wall separating her own cottage from her sister's.

'Christening present?' I held up the bottle of Merlot and Cameron started slightly before smiling and moving papers and a sweater from one of the chairs. 'You'll have the environmental police after you if they know you've got one of these,' I added, nodding towards the brand-new patio heater.

'I know, I know, but I'm so used to sitting out of doors back home of an evening and I can't bear to waste this glorious view by sitting indoors. Anyway,' he added, 'I hold up my hands: guilty as charged, but have mitigation that, as it's electric – and not gas – it is the eco-friendliest one on the market. What will you have to drink? There's white wine in the icebox...'

'Thank you, just a small one; I think I drank rather too much last night.'

'I think we all did. Great evening. Where'd you learn to cook like that?'

'Aunty Pam, and Angelo's sister – my Great-Aunt Rosina – in Sicily.'

'Ah, Pamela Piccione? She left the party early?'

'Migraine. Didn't want to make a fuss.'

'I was hoping to have a good chat with her. She did a lot in taking Piccione's forwards, I believe?'

'Probably more than I realise,' I admitted. 'She's always just been my Aunty Pam – my second mum. I do tend to forget she was on the board at Piccione's and a lot of new innovations were things she fought for. I suppose you were brought in mainly to replace her.'

'I guess so.' Cameron removed a tiny thread from the sleeve of his immaculately ironed blue and white striped shirt and leaned forwards. 'Sorry, I'm forgetting my manners.' He offered me a dish.

'Interesting. What are these?' I took one and chewed.

'Orville Redenbacher's kettle corn.' Cameron grinned. 'Can't do without them. Had to get a supply of them shipped out to me here.'

I looked at him curiously. 'Do you miss home?'

Cameron shrugged and the closed-down, inscrutable look I'd seen so often at work was back. He was not, I knew, an easy man to get to know.

'What made you leave New Hampshire and come to Yorkshire?'

'What made you leave Yorkshire and run away to Sicily?'

'Who said I ran away?' I felt my face grow warm.

'Both Luca and your dad mentioned it.'

'Yes, my dad certainly would have done,' I said crossly. 'Always liked a bit of a gossip, has my dad.'

'He wasn't gossiping.' Cameron raised an eyebrow. 'He was looking out for you. Telling me to go easy on you.'

I felt my face redden further and I gulped at my wine. 'I

really don't want to be treated any differently because I'm the boss's daughter and because...'

'Because?'

'Just because.'

'Because you found yourself in a bad romance.' He said it as a matter of fact rather than a question.

'You sound like Lady Gaga,' I said. I really would have a word with my dad when I saw him at work the following day. I was embarrassed: what else did Cameron Mancini know about me?

'Lady Gaga?' Cameron laughed, showing those fabulous white teeth of his. 'Not really my thing.'

'So, why *are* you here?' I might as well go for it. He knew all about me, but I knew absolutely nothing about him apart from the fact that he was my line manager and from New Hampshire. And he was very attractive. *If* you liked that sort of smooth, all-American-boy type. Which – an image of Daler's black curls flashed across my mind's eye – I didn't.

'Here?'

'Here.' I folded my arms and leaned forwards in interrogation stance.

Cameron laughed once more. 'I thought you and I were going to make sure Piccione's Preserves are the best here in the UK?'

'Some of them already are,' I said defensively.

'They are, they are.' He laughed again and held up his hands, equally in defence. 'That's why I'm here. Piccione's Raspberry and Strawberry jelly – sorry jam – is also big in the States you know. And, you've got your Aunt Pamela to thank for that. It was her marketing campaigns in the

Nineties and early Noughties that got folk back home changing their jelly eating habits, and turning to your jams.'

I stared. 'I honestly didn't know that. I mean, I knew she'd spent a lot of time out in the States around the time I was down at school in Somerset. She always seemed to be flying off, and I've got a feeling Angelo suggested she actually move out there at least for a while, but she never did.'

'She didn't want to leave you.'

I stared. This man knew more about me and my family than I did.

'Angelo told me,' Cameron said hurriedly. 'He thinks a great deal of your Aunt Pamela. And obviously of you too? I guess he misses not having Marco around?'

'I've never actually met my Uncle Marco. He got Aunty Pam pregnant when they were both terribly young. As far as I know he was a bit of a womaniser, the marriage didn't last long and he met some American woman and went to live out there with her. He and Pam are on pretty good terms now and, as far as I know, she's even stayed with him out in the States.'

Cameron picked up his bottle of beer and drank deeply from it but said nothing.

'You're left-handed?' I observed.

'I am.' He smiled.

I continued to stare, my eye catching the faint white band on the ring finger of his tanned hand. 'You were married?' I asked.

'You sound surprised.' Cameron gave a little grimace. 'But yes, I was married. Actually, still am.'

'Oh?' I looked round as if at least a half a dozen wives

were about to manifest themselves from the open door of his cottage.

He almost laughed at that. 'My wife – soon to be my ex-wife – is at our home in New Hampshire. So, you see, Frankie, you ran away to Sicily and I ran away to Yorkshire.'

'But now I'm back.' I glanced across at Cameron who was watching me intently.

'But are you mended?'

'I had a bit of a setback today, but I'm getting there.'

Cameron stroked my hand, but whether in sympathy or because he couldn't help himself, I really couldn't tell.

'OK, Honey?'

'I am thanks,' I lied.

Cameron frowned and then laughed. 'Frankie, I'm *talking* honey. Listen, your *crema al limone* is out of this world. I'd be happy to put Piccione's name to it. It's just whether it can be manufactured on an industrial scale economically and whether the preservatives we'd have to add to extend its shelf life would spoil the whole essence of the idea. It's going to take a hell of a lot of R and D, but at least we can start to present the idea to Angelo, Luca and your dad as well as the boffins in the labs. If we get the go-ahead, you and I need to begin work on a marketing campaign in the next few months.

'Really? You really like it?'

'Totally. I said so, when I thought your wonderful cake was from the village bakery. I'm just wondering whether we concentrate on putting all our energies into the lemon curd and then look at the honey much later on, or go for that at the same time.'

'Why don't we go out and have a chat with this Dr Karam Yassim,' I said. 'I'd love to meet him. He sounds fascinating.'

'I've been doing a bit of research this morning after Libby and Deimante were talking about him last night.' Cameron had certainly switched to work mode now.

'Oh?'

'Googled him and already rung him and made an appointment to have a chat with him next week.'

'Really? Can I come with you?' I asked. 'I can show you where he is. As far as I know he's out where I sometimes cycle.'

'Absolutely. I told him there'd be two of us.'

'Lovely. It's a date.' I grinned and then felt foolish using the 'd' word.

'A date it is.' Cameron smiled and clinked his bottle against my glass.

This man was growing on me by the minute.

When I got home, Cameron kissing me goodnight demurely on the cheek, I rang Aunty Pam.

'You alright, sweetheart?' she asked. 'I've been worried about you. I did ring you an hour or so ago...'

'I'd left my phone at home. I've been round next door talking with Cameron.'

'And?'

'And he's told me more about you working at Piccione's than I ever knew. I mean, I obviously knew you started as an office girl and then met Uncle Marco, which I suppose elevated you into the company itself?'

'It most certainly did not,' Pam said indignantly. 'If it had been up to Angelo, I'd have been stuck at home forever having endless Piccione babies, and kept in the background to cook and clean and know my place just like Consettia. Even though it was the Seventies, Angelo and Marco were completely embroiled in, as well as perpetuating, the patriarchal society they themselves had been brought up in.'

'But you went out to America?'

'That was much, much later, darling. I'd established myself on the board by then. Told Angelo and your dad we needed to expand into America as we were doing so well in Europe. I think Angelo was fed up of me going on about it and told me basically to sort it. So I did.'

'I did know that. There were a couple of my football matches you missed.'

'Not many, Frankie. I made sure I was there for you when that mother of yours wouldn't shift herself to drive down to Somerset to see you at school.'

'You've never criticised my mum before?'

'No, and I never would to your face. She was your mother and you adored her. Tell you what, darling, next time you're round, I'll tell you all you want to know.'

30

Pam

Then

After the previous year's incredibly amazing summer of 1976, when people in Westenbury had got used to having their tea out in the garden and sleeping with windows wide open, this summer was a total washout.

'We'll pay for it later,' had been the clarion call from her mother throughout those wonderfully hot sunny months when Carla had learned to toddle in the coach house's tiny garden, or up in the much bigger garden at High Royd, in nothing but Pampers and a sun hat.

And they certainly *were* paying for it this year. With everyone still on a post-summer-1976 high and relishing the return of the previous summer's Mediterranean conditions which had turned them into happier, sunnier people, even aping the French and sitting outside the coffee bars like true Europeans, they'd been in for a disappointment as nothing but grey skies, drizzle and rain had put them in their place, reminding them they were still, in reality, in the cold North of England.

Pam glanced out of the window in the over-optimistic hope she might finally be able to peg out the load of washing lurking like a wet dog in the plastic washing basket by the back door but instead sighed, removed Carla from the yellow pedal bin where she was trying to retrieve a broken plastic toy and pulled down the wooden creel from its resting place on the kitchen ceiling.

Pam wondered if she could take Carla up to Consettia for an hour so she could get on with her course work. She'd just completed the first year of her A-level English which she'd started at Midhope tech the previous autumn, catching the bus into town and walking the five minutes past Greenstreet Park (consciously averting her eyes from the secret little hidey-hole that had led to her downfall and the reason she'd ended up where she was today) every Monday evening while Marco babysat. She'd insisted he stay in at least one night a week in order to look after his daughter, not really caring about the rest of the week when he seemed to be constantly out, coming home smelling of other women's scents and crackling with post-sexual adrenaline.

Pam knew she'd enrolled on the course in the hope of maybe bumping into Rob, which was plain stupid when she knew he'd already been in London for two years, but she gained a buzz from being in the same place, maybe even the same classroom, sitting in the same chair he'd occupied in the past. She hoped it might – again ridiculous idea – somehow get back to him that she was following in his footsteps, doing A levels in order to fill her mind with knowledge. She knew he'd approve.

One day, unable to stand being stuck in the dark little coach house with a colicky baby a minute longer, she'd manoeuvred the oversized Silver Cross Balmoral pram Angelo had insisted on buying for them onto the bus, before walking the rest of the way to Rob's house. She'd just stood, like some sort of sad stalker, until she realised what she was doing and, with tears running down her cheeks, hurried away totally embarrassed and mortified. It was the one place she could still feel a connection, however small and however ridiculous. Just to see it. To remember.

But now, after a year of studying, she was almost obsessed with *King Lear* and the poetry of Thom Gunn and Ted Hughes. She'd even persuaded Marco to drive her up to Heptonstall, the tiny village above Hebden Bridge, just to see Sylvia Plath's grave, empathising and commiserating silently with the woman who'd felt death to be a better option than living alone with two small children, once an allegedly violent Ted Hughes had left her for another woman. Not that Marco was violent: goodness no, he'd never lain a finger on her. She'd have been straight back to her mum and dad if he had. Marco wasn't interested enough in her to even lay a finger on her in comfort, in friendship, or in acceptance that they were in this mess together and needed to make the best of it, never mind, thank goodness, in anger. He wasn't *angry* with her; he was *bored* with her. Marco hadn't really shown much interest in Sylvia Plath either, despite Pam telling him in great detail of the American poet's life and work and, although he'd tried not to show it, she knew he was more disgruntled at having to borrow his father's steady rock of a car, abandoning his own little sporty number in their drive, in order to fit in Carla's baby seat.

So, for three hours every Monday evening, she'd been transported to a different world: a world of prose and poetry, of discussion and literary argument and she savoured every single second, tackling each homework task, as well as so much more extra reading, with a fervour that was almost bordering on the religious. Now that she'd taken the end-of-year exams and college had broken up for the summer, she missed it dreadfully. She hadn't told Marco that she was about to enrol for the coming September, not only for the second year of her English A level but also for sociology and politics. She'd already been down to WH Smith in the town centre and bought, and dived into, *Othello* and *A Winter's Tale*, Pope's *Epistle* and – Pam didn't know whether to laugh or cry at this – Orwell's *Road to Wigan Pier*. The *Road to Wigan Casino*, she secretly called it, always wondering, if that place hadn't existed, would she be in the damned mess she was now in?

Picking up these new subjects would entail going to college for one full day as well as the Monday evening and she hadn't yet thought who would take care of Carla, although she was betting Consettia would jump at the chance to get her hands on the little girl. Her mother-in-law and daughter had totally bonded, delighting in each other's company.

As though the mere thought of her had manifested her mother-in-law in front of her, spiriting her down the garden path from the big house, Consettia pushed open the back door without knocking, shook her rain mate over the kitchen floor (Pam had just washed and dried it) and handed over a dish of ravioli.

'Thanks, Consettia, that's so kind. I'll never be able to make this like you.'

'You Yorkshire, not from Sicily,' Consettia said dismissively. 'What you expect?'

'Well it's really good of you; you make it so well.'

'*Didn't she do well?*' Consettia smirked, quoting her favourite line from *The Generation Game* to which she was glued every Saturday evening. 'Any road, *Pamla* (Pam loved the way she introduced Yorkshire idioms into her speech) it make me right fart.'

'Oh?' Pam did hope her mother-in-law wasn't about to demonstrate. She was rubbing at her stomach as if gearing up for such. (Such vulgarity, Pam could hear her own mother who, three years on from her first meeting with the diminutive woman, wasn't her greatest fan.)

'Really fart,' she said once again, rubbing at her stomach. 'I go that there Weight Watchers, I reckon.'

'Oh fat?' Pam said with some relief, wanting to giggle.

'Yes, I say that: *fart*.' She lowered her voice. 'I think I need *operazione*.'

'I don't think you can have an operation to remove fat.' Pam smiled. She rather liked it when Consettia took her into her confidence.

'No, no, *this fart* not too much tagliatelle.' She lowered her voice once more. 'I think baby place *had it*. Buggered.'

'Baby place?'

'Place to make baby.' She patted her middle once again and tutted. '*Utero*.'

'Right. But you've only just had your gall bladder

removed. And last year your fibroids. And before that...'
Pam paused to think.

'Growing-out toenail.'

'Ingrowing toenail,' Pam corrected.

'*Si*,' Consettia said with almost ghoulish relish, 'it stab
like knife going backwards into toe. See...'

She bent to remove her left shoe and Pam quickly said,
'I've seen it, I've seen it, put it away. If you carry on like this,
Mrs P, there'll be nothing left of you.'

'Then I take to my bed and the *Holroyd Whore* win. That
not happen.'

'The Holroyd Whore?' Pamela looked up from fastening
Carla into her little blue mackintosh. Whore was such an
awful word, and for her mother-in-law to be spitting it out
with such gay abandon was quite shocking.

'You keep eye on Marco,' Consettia suddenly said, taking
Pam's arm. 'Piccione men, pah, can't keep it down.'

'Keep it down?'

'Always *up*, you know...' Consettia did something
overtly sexual with her hands, her meaning clear. 'I tell you
now, *Pamla*, you keep eye on my Marco. He going down
same street as Mr Piccione.'

Of course Pam knew about her father-in-law. From her
first day at Piccione's as office junior, the newly married
Margaret Holroyd had been pointed out to her as Angelo
Piccione's mistress. She'd thought it almost thrilling at
the time, like something out of a TV drama. (She, along
with the rest of the nation, had been hooked on *Bouquet
of Barbed Wire* and Pam had since borrowed every one of
Andrea Newman's books from the local library, a place she
seemed to spend more and more time in.) It hadn't taken

her much longer to realise her own husband was having affairs, just like his father, but while Margaret Holroyd was almost exclusively, but allegedly not completely, Angelo's only dalliance, from the different scents and strands of hair on Marco's clothing he carelessly put to the wash for her to sort, she thought not. She wasn't quite sure if they were actual affairs or just sex (was there a difference? She supposed there was) and to be honest she didn't really care.

'I'm going over to the factory later on,' Pam said, desperate to get off the subject both of Consettia's health and the state of their marriages. 'Don't you want to come over and wave a flag with the rest of us?'

Consettia pulled a face. 'I see Queenie better on TV. No need to stand in crowd in rain. Bloody cold Yorkshire even in summer.'

'Well it's not every day the Queen comes through Midhope and right past the factory.' Pam smiled, knowing Angelo had had the windows cleaned and the main factory door repainted as well as ordering a whole load of bunting and flags for the staff and workers to wave in honour of Queen Elizabeth passing by on her Silver Jubilee tour.

'No, it fine. I look after Carla and you go off and shake flag at Queenie.'

'Are you sure?'

'Yes, sure, sure. Come on Carla, *bedda mia* you come with Nonna.'

Just as Pam had settled at the little table she used for her studies, there was a knock on the door and she sighed with irritation before placing a bookmark in her copy of *Othello*. 'Oh, Jane? How come you're not at work?'

'I've left. Gave my notice in last week.' Jane grinned delightedly at Pam's surprised face and went to lean against the stove where it was warm. 'Hell, it's cold, wet and miserable out there.'

'Have you? Why didn't you tell me?' Pam felt a stab of hurt that her best friend was obviously making decisions without confiding in her.

'A bit difficult when you're the boss's wife. Anyway, totally had enough of bloody pickles.'

'It's not as if you're actually on the production line,' Pam said, still smarting at being kept in the dark.

'If I type one more bloody invoice about sodding pickles or lemon curd I'll go mad. There's a big wide world out there and I'm off.'

Pam felt the stabbing pain more keenly. 'Are you? Where are you going?'

'London.'

'Right.'

'Got a job with the Design Centre down the Haymarket, near Piccadilly Circus.' Jane named the areas of London as if they both knew exactly where she meant, which Pam certainly didn't.

'Right.'

'I'm sharing a flat with my cousin in Bayswater. You know, Portobello Road? Notting Hill?' Jane was now seriously name-dropping.

'Lucky you.' Pam tried really hard to smile and be pleased. 'Maybe I could come down and stay?'

'Course you can. Leave Carla with the old dragon.'

'She's not. I quite like her now.'

'Really? She terrifies me.'

'Yes, I could come and stay. Go to the British Library.'

'I was thinking more of Petticoat Lane and Carnaby Street. And Oxford Street.'

'Oh brilliant. Maybe I could get in touch with…'

'Rob?'

Pam nodded and then felt any hope she'd had drain away like water down the sink as Jane fumbled in her trendy straw shopper and handed over a newspaper, folded at an appropriate page. It was the *Midhope Examiner* weekend wedding page and there, right in the middle of the page, was Rob's marriage to a beautiful blonde girl called Jennifer Blake from Manchester.

The weather outside was just as miserable as Pam felt inside. It was obvious Rob was going to end up with someone else once she'd had to end their relationship. And he had all those intelligent and gorgeously trendy girls from university as well as from the whole of London to choose from. Beautiful, leggy girls who would be able to converse with him on up-to-the-minute political thinking, and who read the *Guardian* before dancing the night away with him in some dark, soulful nightclub.

Jane had tried to snatch the newspaper out of Pam's hands when she realised the reaction the photograph and column inches were having. 'I'm amazed he's got married when he's not yet finished university. And I can't believe you still think about him,' Jane tutted. 'I shouldn't have shown it to you,' she added. 'Stupid of me.'

'No, stupid of *me* to have some hope that he was going to bang on the door and rush me off with him back down to London. Me, a provincial married woman with a two-year-old, who's not moved two minutes away from where she started. Why the hell would he do that? Look at her.' They both peered at the photograph closely.

'She'll have had her hair and make-up done professionally,' Jane soothed. 'Everyone has to look fabulous for their wedding photo. She's probably quite plain really.'

'Yes, but look what she does for a living: Jennifer Blake, a parliamentary aid for some minister in Callaghan's government.'

'Labour Party?' Jane had sniffed. 'She sounds like a bit of a red to me.'

'Better than for Margaret Thatcher and her cronies.'

'Do you think so? I quite like Mrs Thatcher.'

Pam grimaced, wiping away an angry tear. She no longer seemed to have anything in common with the people she loved and had grown up with. As well as the people she now lived with.

'And Rob too.' Pam sighed deeply. 'Look, a politics student at UCL, but on a year's work experience in the House of Commons. How exciting; how... how *gratifying*.'

Jane flashed Pam a pitying look, shook her head at the use of such long words to describe something she obviously considered deadly boring and reached for her mac. 'Must be where they met,' she said kindly. 'All a very different world from this.'

By the time she'd walked the forty minutes journey to

Piccione's, Pam knew she had to get on with the life she'd ended up with and make the best of it. She was probably as much to blame for the stalemate in her marriage after almost three years of living with Marco; she felt like it had been thirty-three. It was up to her to salvage it. She needed to talk to Marco about the other women, sit him down and tell him not only did she know about them but it was about time they began to work at this marriage. She was more than a mother to his child, more than cook, cleaner and bottle washer.

As she turned the corner onto the road taken up almost entirely by the Piccione factory and offices, she was somewhat taken aback by the crowd lining the pavement. Because she'd worked upstairs in the offices, rarely having anything to do with the workers on the shop floor (they had their own entrance, their own starting and finishing times as well as their own separate canteen) she'd never really appreciated just how big a workforce was actually employed by the company.

She smiled at people she knew, waved towards Trevor Pickersgill and ignored Maureen Cooper who, in turn, deliberately turned her head away without acknowledgment.

'Have you seen Marco?' she asked Angelo who, as an ardent royalist, was becoming quite agitated at the late arrival of the royal party passing along his road. He paused the polishing of the huge bronze knocker on the main door with his starched white handkerchief.

'Marco? Still in the office, I think. He making important phone call for new deal with Japan and Lemon Curd.'

The Japanese ate Lemon Curd?

'You tell him come down 'ere this minute.' Angelo

scowled. 'Disrespectful to Her Majesty 'is not being 'ere and ready and waiting.'

Pam ran up the stairs to the top floor, determined to start straight away her plan to mend her marriage. The whole place was deserted. He must have made his way down the back stairs and already joined his father and the crowd outside on the pavement. She retraced her steps but, rather than exit back through Reception and the main door, took the stone steps that led down to the Pickles production line and the workers' exit. She tutted crossly when she realised it was locked and turned to walk back the way she'd come. She wasn't much of a monarchist but now she was here, she didn't want to miss seeing the Queen.

A strange panting and banging sound was coming from the line manager's office up the steep wooden flight of steps to her left. Pam stopped to listen again, wondering if she'd imagined it. There, it came again. What had Jane said about Marco and the women workers from Lemon Curd? Fury overcame her as she tiptoed up the stairs; she knew exactly what that noise meant but, outside the door, she listened again. Nothing. She felt a bit silly, standing, alone, dithering at the top of the stairs that overlooked the whole Pickles production line, totally deserted now Angelo had insisted they all gather together outside on the pavement to pay homage to their Queen.

The monarch was obviously on her way: a loud wave of delighted cheering from the pavement below was drifting through an open window as Pam reached for the greasy handle, the noise building to a climax of clapping, tooting and shouting as she pushed open the door.

Terry Pearson from Pickles, his trousers wrapped almost

comically round his ankles, lay prostrate across the line manager's desk as Marco pumped into him from behind, her husband's dark eyes closed in ecstasy as, without any clapping or tooting of his own, he gave a strangled grunt of pleasure at his own climax at the very moment Her Majesty passed by, unheeded, in the street below.

31

Frankie

A week or so after we'd first been told about him, Cameron and I had an appointment to see Dr Karam Yassim, the Syrian beekeeper who lived out towards Upper Clawson. We'd spent the last couple of days working until seven in the evening on an initial presentation to Angelo, Dad and Luca re Aunt Rosina's lemon curd. I'd carried on experimenting with the ingredients at home – anything not to dwell on the awful news that Daler was back and just twenty minutes' drive away from Daisy's. There was a hell of a long way to go – new products like this take literally years to roll out, but we were both so excited about where we were going with it we needed to include Angelo and the others at an early stage before we'd gone too far and they ended up dismissing our ideas. We needed to get them on our side in order to put time, energy and the workforce in our sights. As well as huge amounts of cash.

'You do know this is only the beginning,' Cameron had warned me as we took a break for more coffee. I was already buzzing and on a high that Cameron was, so far, with me on this. 'Don't expect jars of Aunt Rosina's *crema al limone* to be on the shelves of Harrods by next week. These things literally take years.'

'I know, I know. I do have a business studies degree, you know.' This from the girl who only six weeks previously couldn't quite recall the meaning of R and D.

Ignoring the slight petulance in my voice, Cameron studied the huge sheets of presentation paper in front of us on which were all kinds of drawings and ideas, ready to be transferred to a PowerPoint. 'How about pitching the idea of calling it *Frankie Piccione's*?'

'I'm flattered.'

'Well it is your recipe and we'd get in the Piccione name calling it that.'

'No, it's Aunt Rosina's recipe.'

'You've changed it a bit.'

I had. I'd experimented both in the kitchen at Daisy's as well as donning a white lab coat and working with the development team where they had to rein me back in a bit with mutterings of health and safety, shelf life and, more importantly, costings.

'I really don't care what it costs,' I said crossly. 'This will be so fabulous, customers in Harrods' Food Hall will be queuing up for the stuff like the punters did when Heston Blumenthal worked with Waitrose on his Christmas puddings; they were selling for £250 on eBay at one point.'

Cameron had laughed at that and squeezed my shoulder

(rather pleasantly I'd thought, enjoying his touch) and, again, warned me of getting ahead of myself.

Cameron and I had planned to drive out to see the beekeeper man straight from home around 9am, but just as we were setting off – me in Kermit and Cameron about to follow in his rather upmarket two-seater – he flashed me as I began to head up the lane and I stopped, got out and walked back to him.

'Karam says can we make it an hour later?'

'OK. Is it worth going into the works first? It's totally in the opposite direction.'

'Actually, do you mind if I take the hour to pop in to see if I can get an emergency dental appointment?'

'With *your* fabulous Californian teeth? What's up?'

'Will you stop that?' Cameron grinned from his driving seat as I stood in the lane, flashing said amazing gnashers in my direction. 'Piccione's Cantucci,' he said looking slightly embarrassed as he rubbed at one of his teeth with his thumb. 'I've become a bit addicted to the stuff and broken a tooth. It needs to come with a health warning.'

'It's all good stuff.' I grinned. 'Full of almond pieces. I tell you what,' I went on, 'rather than going into work, you go to the dentist – see if they can fit you in for an emergency appointment – and I'll pop in and see Aunty Pam for a quick coffee. It's on the way out to Upper Clawson. I'll give you the address and you could meet me there and also meet *her* properly.'

'It's a plan, although we don't have that much time. I really need to have this tooth filed down – it's cutting my tongue to ribbons. Just two minutes at your Aunt Pamela's place though and then we need to get on.' He roared off in a plume of exhaust fumes and I waved at Seb Henderson who'd just come out from the farmhouse, and then I jumped into Kermit and set off to Pam's.

'Coffee?'

'Please. Make a big pot: Cameron's meeting me here before we go out to meet Karam, the bee man.'

'Could I come with you? I've heard so much about him and what he does for both refugees and the unemployed round here.'

'I don't see why not.'

'The thing is, I've always fancied being a beekeeper. I wonder if this Karam man would mind if I volunteered to help?'

'I doubt he'd mind. Probably could do with any help going. I'm going to go in Cameron's car when he gets here although, I suppose, we could all go in mine.'

'I'll take my own and then I can stay or leave at my leisure.' Pam looked at me. She knew me so well. 'First of all, how are you this week? You had a hell of a shock the other Sunday when you knew Daler was back.'

'I'm OK. Counting my blessings, like Mother Teresa.'

Pam laughed at that. 'I thought she counted other people's? Look, just try and keep out of Daler's way and when you see the three of them out together, which you *will*, be friendly, pat the little girl on the head and shake the wife's hand. And for heaven's sake don't let Daler see how you feel. So, are you feeling a bit better because of a certain rather attractive American?'

'Might be.'

'Has he, you know…?'

'Has he what?'

'You know…'

'God, Pam, for a mature, intelligent woman you can sound remarkably like a teenager at times.' I frowned at her as she passed me a mug of strong Italian coffee.

'Making up for lost time: my own teenage years were taken away from me.'

'This is what I keep saying, Aunty Pam – there's loads of stuff I don't know. Apart from Marco always being after other women and then running off to the States with one, I know very little. I mean, where did he meet her? I wouldn't have thought there was an excess of American women in a village like Westenbury?'

Pam sat down at the kitchen table and took a sip of the hot coffee she'd just poured, obviously collecting her thoughts before she spoke.

'Your Uncle Marco didn't like women much.'

'Oh? He beat you? He was a wife beater?'

'No! No, no. He never laid a finger on me. Literally. He was gay. He *is* gay. Marco was gay, but had to hide the fact because in the early Seventies, although homosexuality was legal in the UK by then, it had only been legal for ten years.'

I stared. 'That's the *last* thing I thought you were going to say. Goodness. And Angelo never knew?'

'Angelo knew alright.' Pam snorted dismissively. 'He'd caught him once with an older guy who worked in the warehouse. Marco was only seventeen or so at the time and Kenneth Berry groomed him somewhat.'

'Are you saying if he hadn't been "groomed" he wouldn't have been gay?'

'No, of course not. I'm not saying that at all. But I think, quite possibly without Kenneth Berry, he might have married, had children although possibly come out at a later date.'

'But he *did* marry and have Carla with you.'

'Yes, yes, all I'm saying is that when Angelo caught them "at it" – sorry, Frankie, dreadful expression – his one aim in life was to get Marco married off as quick as he could. He told Marco he needed to get a wife and to all intents and purposes be seen as *normal* – again, sorry, dreadful, terribly outmoded thinking but this was the 1970s. If you were gay, you were different. Apparently, after that, Angelo sat him down and said what he got up to in his own time was up to him, as long as he didn't bring shame on his family. But if he wanted to be part of the Piccione family and produce an heir, he needed to get on with it. I can see by your face you're not really understanding all this, Frankie? Being gay in a small Yorkshire community like this, you know, where men are men and drink twelve pints a night and go down t'pit and want their meat and two veg on t'table, as well as Marco coming from a hugely Catholic family – totally irrelevant that Angelo has spent his life being adulterous of course – was most certainly not the norm. And if it *were*, it was hidden, swept under the carpet and men – and I guess women – encouraged to get married, produce children and become "normal".'

'So how did you find out?' I asked, still reeling from something that had been kept from me all these years. 'Did Marco eventually tell you?'

'Goodness me, no. Well, I thought it a bit strange that he didn't want anything sexually to do with me. He was OK for a hug or two but, you know, we had absolutely nothing in common. He'd fulfilled his part of the bargain he'd made with Angelo. He'd got a pretty young girl pregnant and married her without any argument and there was a bambino on the way. The coast was clear for him to be out picking up men.'

'Really?'

'Hmm. I'd absolutely no idea. At the time I think Marco was experimenting with it all. He certainly was very promiscuous. This is the time of men in parks – really quite awful for them. I thought he was out with other *women*. And that didn't bother me much. I was still so in love with Rob Mansell and so desperately unhappy, I really didn't care at all.'

'So how did you find out?' I asked again.

'The Queen's Silver Jubilee visit to Yorkshire, July 1977. It was also the day I found out Rob had married Jennifer Blake.'

'You knew her?'

Pam smiled. 'No, not at all. I saw his photo in the local paper, even though he was married in London. I suppose his mum put it in. It had such an impact on me, I remember her name clearly. Anyway, even though I was feeling pretty awful – you see, Frankie, I'm able to understand *just* how you're feeling about Daler – I went down to the works in order to wave my patriotic Union Jack with the rest of them. Angelo was getting cross because Marco wasn't down on the street with the others and I went inside to find him. And I did. I certainly did.'

'Not with this Kenneth bloke again?'

'No, no, no. Kenneth Berry had long since been given his

marching orders – and probably a payoff from Angelo to keep his mouth shut too. Marco was with a much younger man – Terry Pearson I think he was called.

'And you saw him?'

'Hmm. A huge shock for the naïve girl I was then. And it only occurred to me years later, that Marco was actually breaking the law. While homosexuality, quite rightly, was now legal, it was only legal between consenting adults over the age of twenty-one. While both Marco and Terry were consenting adults, I think Terry was probably only in his late teens. Anyway, I went straight to Angelo's office and waited for Angelo to come back up from the street. I think he was hoping to keep on celebrating with some of his bigwig restaurant and council friends he'd invited round. There were certainly bottles of champagne, glasses and Twiglets laid out...'

'Twiglets?'

'Before your time, Frankie. We were somewhat less sophisticated then, than now. So, instead of an afternoon celebrating with Midhope's finest, Angelo found me waiting like a madwoman.'

'Blimey.' I'd seen Aunty Pam lose her temper only once – my mum had turned up late for my leaving do at school in Somerset – and it wasn't a pretty sight.

'I went for him.' Pam looked slightly embarrassed.

'Physically?'

'Hmm.'

'But how did you know he knew?'

'Oh, it all just made sense somehow. It all fell into place and it hit me I'd been a pawn in the whole thing to whitewash what Angelo couldn't accept from his eldest son. I became quite hysterical – I think finding out about Rob's marriage a couple of hours earlier hadn't helped – and Margaret Holroyd and Miss Bryan from Personnel…'

'Personnel?'

'…HR before it got its fancy new name… They took me down to Matron in sickbay and then the four of them: Angelo, Miss Bryan, Matron and Margaret Holroyd sat me down and talked at me. Not to me, *at* me. I said I was going home to my mum and dad and taking Carla with me which, of course, I was totally within my rights to do. I could have got a divorce, no problem.'

'So why didn't you?'

'I didn't want to be back at home without a job and living with my mum who wouldn't have understood any of it. She'd probably have preferred I shut up and put up and got on with my marriage rather than the shame of telling the neighbours I'd walked out on my husband who was a, you know…' Aunty Pam lowered her voice in parody of her mother '…homo-sex-u-al.'

'Surely not?'

'Believe me, Frankie. Dad would have probably gone round and thumped Marco, which wasn't what I wanted.'

'Wasn't it? He'd got you pregnant, Pam, almost deliberately so he'd be seen as someone who was into girls?'

'I felt very sorry for him. He was as unhappy being married to me as I was to him. Being gay today isn't always as easy as people like to make out, you know, but, forty years ago, it just *wasn't* acceptable, especially round here. We still called gay men quite dreadful names.' Pam shook back her blonde hair in some distress. 'So, once Matron down in sickbay had given me a spoonful of something from a bottle – she kept a cupboard full of the stuff to soothe hormonal girls with period pain and for anyone having a bit of a panic attack or migraine – I made a deal with Angelo.'

'Did you? Just like that?' I knew *I'd* been pretty good at getting my own way with Nonno Angelo over the years, but tales of his in-fights and stand-offs with others in the Sicilian community, as well as the town's businesspeople and the local council were legendary. I couldn't see him going along with Pam's requests without putting up a bit of a fight.

'I told him I was no longer going to share a bed with Marco; I was going to go to college full time to get my A levels and then to either Leeds or Manchester university to do a business or English degree. And eventually, I wanted a place on the board at Piccione's.'

'No!'

'Yes.' Aunty Pam smiled. 'You know, Frankie, when I look back at my twenty-year-old self, I am totally filled with admiration for her. If he and Marco didn't agree to this, I told Angelo, I was going back to my parents immediately; Consettia wouldn't see anything of her grandchild – I knew your grandmother wouldn't allow Angelo to get away with *that* – and I would spill the beans re Marco being a homosexual and being caught with his pants down in the pickles.'

'Goodness.' I didn't quite know what to say. This, after all, when it came down to it, was blackmail. Of my grandfather. 'Good for you,' I eventually said.

'Within a year, Marco had met some American guy who had been sent over on secondment to study textiles – this area, as you know, was at the top of its field with regards textiles – at Goodners' mill up the road. Nine months later, they left to live together in San Francisco where, although homosexuality had only just become legal, it rapidly became a bit of a refuge for gay men, and homosexuality not only accepted, but the norm.'

'But I still can't believe you've never told me all this. Does my dad know?'

Pam nodded. 'But he promised Angelo he would never tell your mum. I know she's your mum, but it would have been something to hold over the family. She would have revelled in it.'

I frowned at that. 'It's not a big deal being gay anymore. You know, people accept you're either gay or straight. If you'd just come out with it, it would have caused a bit of a stir and then that would have been it, surely?'

Pam paused. 'The thing is, Frankie, almost twenty years or so ago, Marco was told he had HIV. His partner had had an affair, and he contracted AIDS and died.'

'Marco died?' My head shot up at that.

'No!' Pam tutted loudly. 'We wouldn't have pretended he was still alive if he'd actually died, you daft thing.' Pam paused, frowning. 'At least, I don't *think* Angelo would have. Anyway, poor Marco nearly did die. He was able to take advantage of the new life-saving drugs that were coming onto the market twenty years ago, or so. Was a bit of a guinea pig, I suppose. Angelo and I flew out to San Francisco under the pretext of meeting people interested in marketing our preserves...'

'When I was down in Somerset?'

'Hmm. Angelo had already found a priest to give Marco his last rites. Anyway, thank goodness he didn't die. He's not a well man, he takes a lot of medication, but has a really super new partner – Johnny – who cares for him and bullies him about taking his supplements and eating the right foods. The pair of them do a lot for AIDS and HIV charities.'

I turned to the window as the throaty growl of a car outside interrupted our narrative as well as our thoughts.

'So, Cameron got it wrong when he said you'd spent a lot of time in America promoting and marketing Piccione's jams?'

'Not at all. Initially I went out to the states to see Marco. You have to remember he is still Carla's father, still Angelo's son, and I always reckoned he'd been as much a victim of Angelo's conniving as I was. Anyway, I realised I really liked California. I adored San Francisco and, with Marco on a highly active antiretroviral therapy to counteract the HIV and prevent full-blown AIDS, he and I became good friends. Daft isn't it? It took a divorce, HIV and twenty-five years living apart to find we actually did have a few things in common.'

'You had Carla in common.'

'Of course. She's known from being a teenager her father is gay; it's just a matter of fact, in the same way that I'm straight. With her settled in Vancouver and Marco in California, it was easy for the three of us to meet up, or for me to fly from one to the other. Marco had never had any interest in expanding Piccione's into the States but, once I was there and looked around a bit, I saw it as a great opportunity to get our foot in the door.'

'You spent a lot of time in San Francisco, didn't you? You were always out there.'

Pam nodded. 'Mainly there, but flying over to meetings in New York as well.'

'Why didn't you move over there – live and work permanently in America?'

'Oh, I'm a Yorkshire lass at heart,' she said vaguely as Cameron rang the doorbell. 'I was able to fly out every couple of months and control operations from this side of the Atlantic.'

'It was because of me, wasn't it?' I held Aunty Pam's eye until she looked away.

'You were going through a lot,' she said eventually. 'You were only ten when your mum left and then you were sent away to school. Your mum and I totally fell out about that; I was cross your dad didn't do more either, but he thought it would give you some stability when everything else was imploding.'

'I was fine. It took a while, but I settled.'

'Well, there was no way I was going to move permanently away from you. I wanted to be in the country if you needed me.'

The doorbell rang again, somewhat impatiently this time and I moved to hug Aunty Pam. This was something else I'd never known: she'd sacrificed settling in California because of me. It was humbling.

I belted myself into Cameron's passenger seat. 'Tooth fixed?' I asked.

'Temporarily.' He smiled, lifting his lip with finger and thumb. 'I had to wait, but they were able to file down the sharpness at least. I've a proper appointment for a couple of weeks' time.' He leaned across me. 'Your seatbelt's not fastened properly,' he said. 'It can be a bit awkward.' He smiled again as he moved back to his own seat and I realised just how much I'd missed the intimacy of a man's touch, even the simple task of helping with a seatbelt. I glanced across at him as he started the engine, his hands tanned and masculine on the steering wheel, and I tried to work out what I felt for Cameron Mancini. He'd certainly grown on me since that first morning in Piccione's boardroom when he'd lectured us all on our shortcomings in business, as well as some of our products. I liked him enormously, I realised, and really enjoyed working with him. For the first time since I was nursing, I loved going into work, knowing I had challenges to juggle, problems to solve, new products to come up with.

Did I want him to kiss me? I think I did. Did he want to kiss me? Again, I think he did, but I really couldn't be certain. Maybe our eyes needed to meet over a jar of pickles and, like in some daft romantic film, we'd know.

With Aunty Pam following on behind, we drove the ten miles or so out to Upper Clawson and the area beyond the river, in front of the Pennines, that had been given over to Karam Yassim and his volunteers for beekeeping.

'Welcome, welcome.' A bearded man in his mid-thirties was waiting as we pulled in through an obviously new five-barred gate. We bumped across the field until we came to a standstill by a railway carriage that had been converted into an office.

'I really not sure I can be of help here.' Dr Yassim smiled, once we'd returned the protective suits, hoods and gloves he'd fitted the three of us out with prior to taking us on a tour of the field, which housed fifty or so hives. Now back in the railway carriage, we tasted and delighted over different samples, raising our eyes at each other as we accepted Karam's honey was vastly superior, on a totally different planet, to the mass-produced stuff we filtered, boiled, pasteurised and bottled on the production line down at the factory.

Karam made coffee, offered custard creams and then went on, 'My honey not for commercial production. It not a money-making project, here to make rich people richer. Instead it bring people together, give the bees and people work, give displaced and unhappy people hope. We make a sense of community. Do you do that with your production line?'

I glanced across at Cameron and wondered if he was feeling, as I was, slightly ashamed that we'd driven up here hoping for some quick-fix notion on how to improve Piccione's Honey. To cash in, literally, on the project that had taken off so well up here, producing the ambrosial, clover-tasting honey we'd been given to sample. I glanced across the myriad hives to where a herd of the black and white Friesians was contentedly chewing the cud in the morning sunshine. A land of milk and honey indeed.

'Thank you so much for sharing your time and expertise with us, Dr Yassim,' Cameron was saying, reaching for the grey pinstriped suit jacket he'd abandoned round a chair an hour earlier.

'It Karam. Please, call me Karam.' His brown eyes were gentle, intelligent and, with a pang, it reminded me of looking into Daler's eyes. 'You help by telling people about this project, raising awareness of refugee from all over world. As well, I know the man who want to be MP round here…'

'You know Jude? Jude Mansell?'

'I do know Jude. Lovely man. He visit here lots of time. Want help everyone who got nothing.' Karam's face clouded somewhat. 'No, what I try say is I know that the *other* man who want become MP want these fields for building new houses for villagers. I understand people need somewhere to live, but terrible if he win…'

'Paul Stockwell?' Pam's face was inscrutable.

'That the one. Let just hope Jude is winner and not Mr Stockwell. You try let everyone know we don't want bees to go for building. He grinned. 'We very happy to accept donation… and, of course, more than happy you come volunteer.'

Aunty Pam, who'd said very little on our tour of the hives except to give little squeaks of delight as she tasted the honey at its different stages, put up her hand like a child wanting to be milk monitor. 'Yes please,' she said with a big grin on her face. 'When can I start?'

Slightly chastened, and with the added realisation we had one hell of a way to go to improve Piccione's Honey, the three of us took our leave and made our way down the makeshift wooden steps of the railway carriage and into the bright May sunshine. A lark was intent on ascending the blue sky ahead of us and I stopped abruptly in delight as I heard the first cuckoo call of the spring coming from the small copse of beech and oaks to our left.

'Pamela?' A tall fair-haired man in jeans and flat cap

was heading our way as I stood, delighting in the different birdsong, and the other two went ahead, making their way back to the cars. 'Pam?' Cameron and Aunty Pam stopped as the man caught them up. 'It *is* you, isn't it?'

'Rob Mansell,' Aunty Pam said, her face drained of colour. 'It's been over forty years.'

32

Pam

Now

Pam thought he must surely be able to hear the pounding of her heart, see the racing of her pulse, be aware of her dry mouth that was rendering her speechless.

'Hello again.' Frankie was speaking to Rob, introducing him to Cameron Mancini, making small talk about the beekeeping project. And then, leaving Cameron to chat some more, Frankie had stepped back in her direction. 'We're off, Aunty Pam, we need to get back to work. See you soon...' And Frankie had hugged her goodbye and whispered in her ear, 'He's so lovely, Pam. And so are you: thank you for not leaving me, to live in America. Love you lots.'

And then she and Cameron were gone, leaving her wondering if there was anything between Frankie and her new boss and thinking surely it would be a good thing if there was? Anything to concentrate on bringing the world back the right way up and to the present day, instead of feeling she was in the grip of a centrifugal force intent on taking her back over forty years to when she'd told Rob she was getting married. To someone else.

'Pam?' Rob was standing next to her, looking down at her. She'd never forgotten how tall he was, had never forgotten how strange it had felt standing next to a so-much-smaller Marco in the huge Catholic church as the priest, glancing in some disdain at her barely disguised little bump, had declared them man and wife and she'd felt the coffin lid descend and heard the nails banging in, one by one.

'Hello, Rob. Frankie said she'd seen you and you were living back round here again.' Pam thought, if he continued to look at her, taking in every aspect of her, she might just drown in those chocolate eyes of his.

'Hang on, give me a couple of minutes. Karam is expecting me; let me tell him I'll be with him in five.' He ran back to the railway carriage and, as she waited, Pam moved off the path as several others began to arrive, presumably offering their services as volunteers.

'Come on.' Rob smiled when he arrived back at her side. 'There's a sheltered bit of grass over there. Let's go and sit down and catch up.'

Pam followed him over to the patch he'd indicated and he took out a waterproof from his backpack and laid it on the grass for them both to sit on. 'You've not changed a bit, Pam.'

She laughed at that. 'I hope I've become wiser and more tolerant. There have been times when I've felt bereft of both qualities in my lifetime.'

'Well, you're still pretty damned gorgeous. I can't believe we're both in our sixties, can you?' Rob actually put his head back at that and laughed.

'Nope. But sixty is the new forty I keep telling myself.' Pam paused. 'Frankie told me you'd lost your wife. I'm sorry.'

'She'd been very poorly for a long time.'

'But you have Jude?' Pam felt herself redden slightly. 'The name we…'

'…always said we'd call any sons we'd ever have…?' Rob hesitated, embarrassed. 'We never said *together*.'

'We *didn't*.' Pam smiled, trying to put him at his ease. 'You were allowed to call *any* son of yours *Jude*. I'd have done the same if I'd had one. Does Jude have brothers or sisters?'

Rob shook his head. 'Jenny was already several years older than me and we'd been married over ten years and had almost given up hope of having kids before Jude came along. I'm a bit concerned that I'm living my own life through him somewhat at the moment. I so want him to win this by-election – not just because he's my son, but because he has a big heart, he's pretty sound and I think he'd be bloody good for the area.'

'I've still to meet him but I know both Frankie and Daisy – who Frankie lives with – are impressed with him. Particularly Daisy.' Pam laughed at that.

'And what about you? How many children do you and your husband have?'

'I have one daughter, Carla, from my marriage, and the reason why I had to *get* married. The marriage lasted three years; my ex-husband lives in San Francisco and my daughter lives in Vancouver. My other daughter, Frankie, lives here in the village.'

Rob frowned. 'I thought she was your niece?'

'I adopted her many years ago.' Pam smiled at Rob's confusion. 'Oh, not formally: Frankie still belongs to her real parents, particularly her dad, Marco's younger brother, but I love her as my own daughter. I've always been there for her when sometimes her real mother hasn't...'

'Paul Stockwell's wife?'

'Hmm. Bit of a pair, both of them. And,' Pam said, suddenly remembering, 'Karam was telling us Paul is electioneering on the mandate of building houses out here?'

'Apparently. Problem is it's not really classed as greenbelt: common land rather; moorland almost. We're on the very edge of the Pennines, miles from anywhere. I'm not convinced people would actually want to live out here. It's a long way from either Midhope or Manchester.' Rob turned to look at her. 'And you never remarried?'

'I had my moments.'

'I'm not surprised.' Rob smiled down at her and she had to look away. 'Did you carry on working at Piccione's?'

'You were my point of reference,' Pam admitted. 'I went to do A levels at the technical college like you had and then, as soon as Carla was in school, I did a business and marketing degree at what was still Midhope Poly before it became the university. I did my Executive MBA part time at Leeds after that, and was on the board of Piccione's until earlier this year.'

Rob stared. 'Goodness. How did you have time to do anything else?'

'I didn't really. I brought up my two girls, got into baking and cooking, spent a lot of time in America during the last fifteen years or so...' Pam grinned '...and, lest you think I was living as some sort of nun, I can assure you I've swiped left and right quite a bit in and amongst all that.' Pam felt herself flush. For God's sake, what was the matter with her? Why on earth had she said that? He'd think she was some sort of man-eater.

Rob looked at his watch. 'I've come here to help Karam; I'd better get on.' He stood up and started to pack away his waterproof. 'It's been lovely to see you again and catch up, Pam.'

'Hasn't it?' she returned brightly, burying her head in her bag so he wouldn't see the naked need in her eyes. She'd obviously totally frightened him off with that damned stupid remark about being on Tinder.

Ask for my number, ask me out for a drink, ask me to marry you...

'See you, Pam.' Rob turned and waved at Karam who was beckoning him over. He patted her arm and set off towards the beekeeper.

Pam found her keys, shrugged her bag onto her shoulder and set off in the opposite direction towards her car, such a feeling of loss and grief descending on her, she almost couldn't work out where she was going.

'Pam?'

She turned. Rob had run back to her side. 'You wouldn't like to come round for a picnic at the allotment one evening, would you?'

33

Frankie

Now
May 2021

'**Y**our Aunt Pamela looked as though she'd seen a ghost.' Cameron glanced across at me as we bumped across the hillocky field towards the gate.

'Gosh, this is like a roller coaster,' I said as the car wheel hit a particularly pernicious mound and my right arm connected with Cameron's. It was rather nice and I did little to remove it. 'Aunty Pam? I think she thought she *had* seen a ghost. That was the man she fell in love with when she was just sixteen, but had to leave when she found she was pregnant to my Uncle Marco. She'd not seen him since.'

'And that's how she ended up becoming such a big part of Piccione's? Getting pregnant to, and marrying the boss's son?'

'Well, yes, but it wasn't like that to begin with. If Angelo had had his way, he'd have kept all women out of the management side of things – would have had them stuck at home doing the housework and having little Piccione bambinos to add to his dynasty, like Consettia was happy to do.'

'How do you know she was?'

'What?'

'Happy to stay at home and bring up the kids and have nothing to do with Angelo's growing empire?'

I had to think about that one. 'Well, it's what women in the Fifties and Sixties did, isn't it? Particularly when they couldn't speak the language too well and their family were far away.'

'*My* grandmother certainly didn't.' Cameron smiled. 'She started a mail-order business in the late Fifties selling leather purses and belts from her kitchen while my grandfather was out working at the bank.'

'Really?'

'Hmm.' Cameron pulled out into the main road and accelerated, and I realised there was no longer any need to be so close to him. I sat back in my seat.

'Go on then, how did she do it?'

'Granny Mancini sourced the purses locally and started with one ad in a woman's magazine. Five years later she produced her first mail-order catalogue, concentrating on personalising the items she was selling. You know, personalised brooches, cufflinks, buttons as well as the purses and belts. Eventually, my grandfather, realising what a potential goldmine this was, quit his own job and went in with her.'

'I hope he didn't take over?'

'Not at all. At a time when white, middle-class women tended to stay at home and live the American dream with their new washing machines and TV sets, Granny Mancini was grafting from the minute she got up until she went to bed. She remained company director, with my grandfather on the board, but she certainly didn't let him take over. Mail order was the forerunner of buying online, I guess. You could sit in the comfort of your own home and choose items without having the bother of going shopping.'

I nodded as I recalled the huge, exciting catalogues that would arrive in their cardboard containers up at Nonna's house. 'Consettia was totally addicted to them.' I smiled. 'She never learned to drive, never took the train over to Leeds or Manchester, but would sit with her catalogues: Kays, Grattan, Littlewoods and endless cups of tea, trawling through the polyester skirts and blouses to get her fix. All sorts of strange things would be delivered for the kitchen and bathroom, as well as the new clothes she wore every Sunday for church. Angelo eventually got really cross with her when she ended up with a treadmill...'

Cameron laughed at that.

'Was it ever used?'

'No, course not. Ended up with all the other stuff – the foot spa, the matching set of luggage, the orange squeezer, the breathable corset she couldn't actually breathe in – up in the loft. I suppose her sending off for these unnecessary things helped to compensate for Angelo's affairs, his leaving her at home while he was constantly out with his business associates. *I* loved the catalogues too. There was something quite thrilling, sitting in a corner of that huge, old, wood-panelled sitting room by myself, a heavy catalogue on my knee, looking at women in their bras and knickers.'

Cameron laughed out loud at that. 'I thought it was just teenaged boys like me who did that.'

'It was almost soft porn. I knew Consettia would find it strange, a ten-year-old getting her kicks from looking at bras and corsets. She caught me once. "You no shoulda be looking at big-bosomed ladies in their pants," she said, snatching it out of my hands.' I laughed at the memory. 'My mum, of course, when I begged her to send off for catalogues of our own, thought it was all terribly beneath her – terribly infra dig – unless it was a Harrods or upmarket garden furniture catalogue….' I paused. 'I don't know why I'm telling you all this.'

Cameron took his hand from the steering wheel and stroked my arm. I didn't pull it away. 'I think we all need to talk about our childhoods,' he said as he pulled into Pam's drive and I scrabbled for my car keys in my bag. 'See you back at the works. I'll put the coffee on and we can talk honey.'

'What do you reckon, Francesca?' Cameron folded his arms and leaned back in his chair.

'About Karam's honey?'

'Hmm.'

'Divine stuff, isn't it?'

'But?'

'But nothing to do with us, I wouldn't have thought?' I glanced over at Cameron to gauge his reaction.

'Why not?' He was frowning at me, not understanding.

'Why not? Well, for a start, it's *his* project: *his* bees, *his* way of making honey non-commercially. I don't see where Piccione's could come into this. It really has nothing to do with us. I mean, what's your vision with all this, Cameron?

Having thousands of Karam's beehives in the car park here?' I looked out onto the tarmac and concrete where a bevy of forklift trucks was bustling to and fro like a colony of yellow, antlered stag beetles. Not a great deal of clover or spring flowers – apart from several baskets hanging somewhat morosely from hooks on the main door, still to come into bloom – to delight and encourage bees into making honey as fabulous as Karam's.

'No, of course not,' Cameron said. 'We'd look into buying and extending the area up on the moorland around Karam's field.'

'You've only seen the sheltered field at the opening to the moors.' I shook my head. 'You need to be up there when it's November, when it's blowing a gale off the Pennines and it's nothing but rain and low cloud. That would really piss the bees off, I can tell you now.'

'They'd be fast asleep and hibernating by then,' Cameron argued.

'Don't blame them. I hate November myself.'

'Well, we could send them off to Tenerife for a month's winter break.' Cameron laughed. 'You know, like Angelo does.'

'Actually,' I said, 'as far as I know, the colony eventually leaves the nest and mates, while the young queens gorge on nectar and pollen to build up fat in their bodies over the winter.' I'd always thought it sounded rather cosy. Fancy being able to hide away and gorge yourself with the sole purpose of getting fat without anyone (your mother) telling you you were putting on weight. 'But don't you see?' I went on. 'If Piccione's got involved it would all become too commercial; too much about money-making?'

'Well, yes, that's what I'm here for – to help Piccione's make money.'

'But surely not at the cost of taking over a fabulous project to help refugees and those out of work in the area.'

'There'd be loads of jobs for the unemployed once we had thousands of beehives up there. It would be a whole new industry.'

I wasn't convinced. It all seemed a bit mean, a bit like barging our way in uninvited and taking over because we had the means to do it. I looked across at Cameron who was still totally animated both with what he'd seen – and tasted – that morning as well as a vision for the future of Piccione's Honey.

Cameron brought the legs of his chair upright once more and in doing so leaned across the table. 'I've a meeting with a supplier in ten minutes. How do you fancy having dinner with me tonight? We could carry on this conversation then. I've been wanting to try out this place in Westenbury village ever since I arrived.'

'Clementine's? By the church?'

Cameron nodded.

'You'll never get a table, just like that. The place is booked up for months ahead.'

'Not on a Monday.' Cameron waved his phone in my direction with some degree of triumph. 'Already booked for two. It'll mean an earlyish table, I'm afraid, but a table nevertheless.'

I took a long look at this man in front of me, trying to weigh him up. Did he always get what he wanted? Cameron Mancini was obviously a chip off his grandmother Mancini's old block.

'We can go straight from work,' Cameron said, standing and reaching for his suit jacket. As he turned, pulling on the grey, pinstriped jacket, I took a sneaky look at his physique: at his broad shoulders moving slightly as he adjusted the collar and straightened his maroon silk tie in the crisp white shirt. He ran his fingers unselfconsciously through his cropped light brown hair and I tried to imagine putting my arms around him. Dismissing an image of Daler's wild black curls escaping from beneath his beanie hat that was trying to encroach on my imagination, I reckoned putting my arms around Cameron Mancini, standing and smiling down at me, would be very nice.

Very nice indeed.

'Oh, you're off on a date with the man next door? How brilliant is that?' Daisy, already loved up just ten days or so after meeting Jude Mansell, was more than happy to encourage blossoming relationships for anyone else.

'It's not a date,' I said almost crossly. 'He's my boss and we're going to discuss honey.'

'Oh, is that what they call it these days? And he's taking you to Clementine's? Make sure you choose the bouillabaisse with crab and poached lobster. Ooh, and the rose-petal panna cotta with lavender shortbread, if they still do it.'

'Seriously, Daisy, we're simply extending the working day. I just popped home to change. Don't want to be wearing a business suit for my first visit to Clementine's.'

'Is Cameron picking you up?'

'No, he's going straight from work, so I'm driving down.

He has a couple of meetings late this afternoon and into the evening. The man's a total workaholic.'

'Shame, that means you can't drink too much.' She frowned. 'Come on, I'll drop you down there and then you *can* have a drink. You could do with loosening up for when he kisses you.'

'Loosening up? I'll loosen *you* up, you baggage. And kisses me?'

'I rest my case.' Daisy grinned. 'Stop the frown, you'll get wrinkles. Just relax; go with the flow because yes, you can be a bit uptight you know.'

'No, I *don't* know.'

'You shouldn't drink *too* much though…'

'OK, you can drop me off if you've got your mum's car, but I never drink too much.'

'You knocked back quite a bit at our do the other Saturday night.' Daisy pulled a distinctly schoolmarmish face at me. 'And you need to be thinking about getting into training.'

'Training?'

'Deimante's football? You're the new centre forward and I'm sub and manager.'

'Sub? You've never played football in your life, have you?'

'Certainly have,' Daisy replied sagely. 'With Dad only having two daughters instead of the sons he won't admit to wanting but never having, he used to have me and Charlie in the back garden most weekends. Whichever dog we had at the time was always in goal. Admittedly, I'm better at rounders and cricket, so I do hope no one breaks a leg and I have to actually run around. I'm far better standing on the sidelines with a pint sneaked out from The Jolly Sailor in my water bottle, exhorting you all on, as trainer/manager.'

I laughed at that. I knew Daisy wasn't kidding.

'So, what are you up to this evening?' I asked.

'I'm meeting Jude and Rob up at Karam's beehives.'

'Oh?'

'There's a bit of a meeting on with Jude and those trying to keep – sorry, Frankie – your stepfather out, as well as his plans for housing up there.'

'Oh, don't be sorry. I certainly don't intend voting for him. It'll cause even more of a rift between us if I don't help Mum to get Paul back into Westminster... and out of her hair... but seeing him in action when he was canvassing, as well as visiting Karam's place for myself this morning, I know I only want to help with the project up there.'

'What about Piccione's plans to encroach on Karam's project.'

'How did you know that?'

'Pretty obvious when you and Cameron were up there this morning.' Daisy raised an eyebrow. 'The last thing the project needs is being taken over for commercial gain, you know. I'm serious, Frankie.'

'So am I, Daisy.'

'Good. OK, that's alright then. Right, let's see what you're wearing under that coat?'

I unbuttoned the long, camel trench coat Daler had bought for me when he still loved me. I'd lusted after it in the upmarket dress shop in the village; Daler had seen me looking and, without a word said, had presented it to me a week later. It was our three-month anniversary he'd said and he wanted to wrap it round me, button me up in it and never let me go. That had been a week before the wedding in Leeds. I'd hidden the coat at the back of the wardrobe once Daler had left, refusing to get it out and wear it but unable, as Tammy had suggested, to take it down to the hospice shop or put it on eBay. The early spring evening had turned chilly and, feeling much stronger and braver than I'd done for months, I'd taken it out of its polythene cover and slipped it over the black dress I'd chosen to wear for a meal at a posh restaurant.

'Good choice,' Daisy said, admiring the Reiss bodycon dress. 'Not too over the top to frighten him off, but subtle enough to make him want to know what's underneath it.' She paused. 'What *is* underneath it? I do hope you've abandoned those ancient greying bras and pants you've had the audacity to peg out in my garden to public view recently?'

'Mind your own business.' I grinned, tying the belt of the coat, pulling up the collar and sticking my hands in the deep pockets of the soft wool and cashmere before making for the door.

Cameron was already sitting at a table in the orangery of the restaurant as I was shown in by one of the young waiters dressed in the black jeans and orange-logoed T-shirt in which all Clementine's waiting staff were attired.

Daler had wanted to bring me here, but we'd had to cancel when his shift on A and E had turned into a real emergency when two young children were rushed to Midhope General after a house fire. The little boy hadn't made it, despite Daler administering every treatment going and, he'd said, would I mind awfully cancelling – he didn't feel like eating out after that. I didn't mind at all. Instead, I'd cradled Daler's head in my lap, and tried to take away the hurt and the awful images imprinted on his brain, even when he was asleep. He'd had several nights of nightmares and he began to wonder whether he was actually cut out to be a doctor after all. Everyone else on his shift seemed to have just got on with their lives, although, I assured him, they probably hadn't. At least now that Daler had left medicine and – presumably – had been moved back to the Dosanjh sandal factory in Leeds, he wouldn't be subject to tragedies such as that anymore. And Sienna wouldn't have to cradle his head and comfort him as I once had done.

'Hi, Francesca.' Cameron stood up and waited while I handed my coat to the waiter and sat down myself before retaking his seat. 'You look very lovely. What will you have to drink?'

'Just a Perrier, I think.'

'Join the club.' Cameron held up his glass. 'This *is* a business meeting, after all.' His smile gave every indication he thought the evening was anything but that. 'This really is a fabulous menu,' he went on. 'As good as any in London or San Francisco.'

'San Francisco?'

'One of the best foody places in the world.'

'My Uncle Marco – Aunty Pam's ex-husband – lives there. Has lived there ever since he and Aunty Pam split up.'

'I know.'

'Oh? Did Angelo tell you?'

'Well, he did, but I already knew. I've actually met your Uncle Marco Piccione.'

I stared. 'I think I will have a glass of wine.' Cameron poured us both a small glass and then I launched. 'Well, that's more than *I* have. And you never said?' I waited for him to carry on but, instead, he dipped bread meticulously into a bowl of chilli oil and offered it across the table. I continued to stare as I chewed. Was this Cameron's way of telling me he was himself gay?

'My wife's cousin lives in the North Beach area,' he said finally. 'He's involved in the same Help for Aids charity your Uncle Marco and his partner, Johnny, spend their time working for.'

'Bit of a coincidence that, isn't it?'

'Not really. I'd heard of Piccione's of course, in the same way everyone has heard of Heinz or Oreos. I was really interested hearing Marco talk about his family business back home. I think he has quite a bit of regret he no longer has any part in it, and, because of his health issues, wasn't able to work with your Aunt Pamela on helping to set up Piccione USA out in the States when she offered him the chance.'

'Aunty Pam offered him the chance?' I frowned. 'Do you know, I sometimes think I know nothing about this family of mine. I mean, I didn't even know Marco was gay until this morning.'

'This morning? Really?' ~~Marco~~ Cameron looked slightly relieved. 'When you spoke about Marco going off with an American woman, I realised you didn't know. And obviously not my place to tell you.'

I nodded. 'Yes, how ridiculous is that?' And then I started to laugh. 'Fancy, Aunty Pam offering one of the Piccione's – her ex-husband – an actual job. You couldn't make it up, could you?' I nibbled on a breadstick. 'So, not really a coincidence then?' I asked.

'My wife and I had gone over to San Francisco for a break from work with the intention of trying to mend our marriage. We'd been going through a bad patch for over a year: I wanted children; she didn't. I didn't want a life without children, Frankie.'

'I can understand that.'

'A life just working and doing more deals. Anyway, despite visiting some wonderful restaurants and meeting some fabulous people, the week away was a disaster. I think I probably spent more time with Marco and Johnny than my wife who was constantly on her phone, working.'

'What does she do?'

'Rebecca? Finance. Ends up flying over to Wall Street several times a month.'

'From New Hampshire?'

'She has a flat there. It was getting so that I was only seeing her at weekends. She's determined to push through that glass ceiling.'

'And you didn't encourage her?'

'Of course I did. I wanted for her everything she wanted for herself. I even offered to become a house husband.'

'Really?'

Cameron nodded. 'But she was having none of it. Said she didn't have the time – or inclination – to be throwing up and getting fat, as well as the months she'd have to take away from her work.'

'It's strange, isn't it?' I mused. 'We probably wouldn't bat an eyelid at a bloke saying that – you know that he didn't have the time to have children, that his career is far too important to give it up to have children. And yet, when a woman is honest about the way she feels: that she's not ready for children, that her love of her work comes first, we see her as being somehow unnatural. Going against nature and the reason she's on this planet.'

'Age-old story.' Cameron smiled slightly. 'Anyway, I ran away, like you.'

'Not really like me, you know. You had a choice to stay with her and accept her for what she was. I mean, you must have talked about all this when you got together? If she'd told you then that kids weren't on the agenda, I suppose it's being quite arrogant to assume she'd eventually come round to your way of thinking.'

'Arrogant?' Cameron raised an eyebrow. 'A bit harsh, that.'

'I'm sorry, you're right, that was a bit uncalled for.' I drained my glass of wine and Cameron reached to refill it. 'All I'm saying is, if you knew the score at the beginning of your relationship, you can't blame your wife for not changing the goalposts.'

'OK, the reason for my running away wasn't quite as dramatic as…?'

'As?'

'Your guy?'

'Daler.' I still found it hard to say his name out loud, particularly to someone who didn't know him.

'Daler telling you he was getting married to someone else.'

'Dad been gossiping again?'

'Luca actually.'

'Luca?'

'Hmm. You know, the way you talk about him sometimes

I think maybe you give the guy a bit of a raw deal. He was looking out for you.'

'Well he never has before,' I said indignantly.

'Maybe you've never let him?'

'Rubbish.'

'Just saying.' Cameron broke off, concentrating on his food. 'Wow, this is fantastic.'

'You don't know Luca like I do.' I wasn't letting this go.

'Well, I've been working pretty closely with him these past couple of months. He seems pretty decent to me.'

'He went off with Mum. Went to live with her. I lost both of them.'

'Not his fault, surely?'

'He was twelve at the time. He was big enough to decide where he wanted to live,' I said, remembering. 'He could have chosen to stay at home with Dad and me. Stay in our family home.'

'Twelve's a bit of a strange age for a boy. Neither man nor boy. Not supposed to cry. Supposed to man up and all that. He was delighted when you invited him round for dinner last week?'

'Was he?' This didn't sound like the Luca I knew.

'Yes, although surprised. He said he didn't think you'd invited him to anything before.'

'I suppose that's because I never imagined he'd accept.' I was feeling really quite put out now.

'He showed me all your football stuff.'

'*Showed* you?' I put down my fork and stared. 'Showed you what?'

'Cuttings from the sports pages when you were playing for the England Schoolgirls' team.'

'Luca has kept cuttings from when I played football?' I was totally taken aback. 'I played quite a few games for England Schoolgirls when I was down at school in Somerset.' I suppose football was my absolute life at the time. 'Probably why my A-level results weren't wonderful,' I added gloomily.

'And did you ever suggest that Luca should come and watch you?'

'Oh, he was far too busy getting all A stars at A level and then a first at Warwick to bother with me.'

'But did you ever ask him?'

I shook my head. 'But then I broke my ankle badly – really badly – and it put me out of trials for the England Women's team. I went up to university in Newcastle – Northumbria, not the elite Newcastle – and, while I did play for the university women's team there, I also discovered men and alcohol.'

'Men and alcohol?' Cameron looked slightly worried, as if I'd said I'd discovered axe-murdering.

'I'd been so into my football training and fitness regimes at school, alcohol was definitely off the menu. Recovering from a broken ankle and being in a strange city, I suppose I embraced the whole freshers thing – they know how to party up there – and had a whale of a time. Fell in love several times a week, drank too many shots, and discovered men fancied me…' I laughed at the memory of my nineteen-year-old self.

'Why wouldn't they?'

'Oh, I suppose Mum had always said I wasn't feminine enough – you know, playing a man's game as it were.'

Cameron took my hand. 'Do you think the reason you

reacted so badly to Daler leaving you was because you felt rejected once more?'

I smiled. 'Don't try to psychoanalyse me, Cameron. The reason I reacted so badly to Daler leaving me was because I loved him. He was the missing part of me. I seemed to find myself when I found him.' Gosh this was all getting a bit heavy, a bit profound. 'When I lost him, through no fault of my own, I lost part of myself again.'

'And are you finding yourself again?' Cameron looked hopeful.

'I think so,' I said.

'Anyway,' Cameron went on, 'Marco and Johnny and I sat and chatted for hours over good food and drink while I was with them in San Francisco.'

'Where was Rebecca?'

'In the hotel room, working. She was trying to conclude a big deal that had been unexpectedly brought forwards.'

'You can't blame her for doing that. I suppose she could have flown back to New York? You'd have done the same if, for example, acquiring that land up by Karam's place was dependent on you being on the phone.'

'I did blame her. Here we were, trying to mend our marriage, trying to find a way forwards and she couldn't get off the damned phone or out of the hotel room to eat with me. Marco told me your Aunt Pamela was on the point of retiring from Piccione's and that someone would be needed to take her place at Piccione's USA and I said I was interested. Marco had a long chat with Luca on the phone – he knew talking to Angelo or Joe probably wouldn't have got him anywhere...'

'Oh?'

'Much as I like the guys, they're not overly forward-thinking.'

'I know, I know.' Working with them both, I'd come to the same conclusion. Angelo did very little these days apart from put in an appearance at the works when it suited him, and I'm not sure Dad, much as I adored him, had ever been a go-getting businessman. He was too much of a home bird, was too fond of his home comforts to be at the cutting edge of taking Piccione's forwards. 'So, it was Marco who suggested you come to the UK?'

'No, it was me. I had long-distance chats with Luca and we both agreed, with Pamela stepping down here, that it wouldn't be a bad idea for me to see what was going on in this country. I know Luca had a bit of an argument on his hands persuading Angelo and your dad.'

'You don't come cheap?'

Cameron laughed at that. 'I don't come cheap. It seemed a good opportunity to put space between myself and my wife. Once I got the idea into my head of coming over here, I just went for it.'

'You were punishing her? Holding it over her like the sword of Damocles?'

'I think I was feeling a bit like that. I'm not proud of myself.'

'You regret coming?'

'At first. Not now.' Cameron smiled and held my eye. His mobile rang and with a 'sorry' he reached for his suit jacket to turn it off, giving me the opportunity to take in the light-coloured cropped hair, the immaculate linen shirt, the loosened silk tie. And the chance to try and sort out just what I felt about this man. I'd worked with him every day for the past six weeks or so and grown to like and respect him enormously. The way he was looking at me now, things were, I reckoned, about to get complicated. If only he wasn't my boss, if he wasn't living next door... if I could totally eradicate Daler from my head.

'Shall we go?' Cameron caught the young waiter's eye and he bounded over, still full of energy after a six-hour shift.

'You don't want coffee?' the kid asked.

'Oh sorry.' Cameron, ever the gentleman, held up a hand to the waiter and turned back to me. 'Do you, Francesca?'

'I don't actually.'

'Any tea, fruit tea... liqueurs? Port? Petits fours?' I'd bet anything the kid had been practising the latter, his French accent heavily laced with Yorkshire.

'No really, fine.'

'We can have all of those back at the cottage.' Cameron looked at me steadily.

Even the petits fours?

'Lovely,' I squeaked. I was feeling nervous: a girl knows when a man is interested. When he wants to take things a step further. We'd done the eye catching and holding thing, the lingering looks over the desk at work where I'd felt safe. Now, there was just me and Cameron, a ride home together in his car; both getting out at the same place. I was so out of practice with what might come next, I found myself twittering: just off to the loo, won't be a tick and checking my teeth for specks of spinach; adding lipstick, sniffing my armpits, spraying a shot of perfume. And then wetting a paper towel and attempting to remove what I'd just sprayed on in an attempt to not appear too keen. I was looking alright, if a little flushed from the couple of glasses of wine.

What if I couldn't remember what to do? Oh hell, where did I put my hands when he kissed me? I had a quick practice in the mirror, lifting one leg slightly from the tiled floor like they always used to do in old black and white films (but not necessarily on a tiled ladies' loo floor) closing my eyes, lifting my arms, trying to imagine running my hands through short hair instead of Daler's long black curls.

'Are you alright, dear?' An elderly woman in twinset and – yes – the mandatory pearls stood at my side, concern etched on her face.

'Fine, fine. Thank you. Just practising a particular tricky yoga position. Helps with, erm, digestion…'

'Really?' She looked at me doubtfully. 'I'll have to give it a go; my acid reflux is the absolute devil after a meal too late at night like this one.'

Late at night? I looked at my watch; it wasn't yet 9pm. I smiled sympathetically in the woman's direction, took a deep breath and set off.

Cameron was waiting outside for me and we walked together to his car, our arms brushing occasionally. At one point I thought he was going to take my hand, but then we were at the car, he was opening the door for me and the moment was gone. The evening was chilly and I pulled my collar up and slipped my hands into my coat pockets before releasing them to do up the seatbelt and then, not quite sure where to put them or what to do with them, laced them together at chest level and, realising I must look as if I were deep in prayer, let them fall to my lap.

Goodness, what was the matter with me? The anticipation,

I supposed, of what might come next. I glanced at Cameron and he smiled across at me, but we drove almost in silence the ten minutes home, the air in the car crackling with something: whether it was anticipation, lust or nerves, I couldn't be sure.

Cameron cut the engine. We sat in the shared drive to the cottages, both of us, I think, unsure what to do next. And then he leaned over and took my face in both his hands and kissed me. It was a very lovely kiss: cool, non-invasive, questioning. The ball was in my court, I knew: I could do this, I wanted this.

My hands made their way up to his hair and, while the sensation of short springy hair at my fingertips was a bit of a shock, it most certainly wasn't unpleasant. Rather nice, in fact. Encouraged, Cameron went in for a second kiss. 'Coffee?' he eventually smiled down at me.

I nodded.

We unbuckled and exited our respective doors, banged them shut and simultaneously turned towards the darkness of Cameron's cottage to the left of us.

'Frankie!' Daisy's front door was open and she stood on the doorstep, illuminated only by the overhead lamp, another figure in a silhouette behind her. 'Frankie,' she hissed again, more urgently this time. Whoever it was standing behind Daisy now moved in front of her and I saw a flash of blue jeans, white trainers and black curls escaping from underneath a hat, as the figure ran towards me down the poorly lit path.

Daler?

Beside me, Cameron stood stock still and then set off at a run himself towards the figure as I stared, unable to move or utter a word. Surely Cameron wasn't going to land him one?

'Cameron, darling.' The woman was in his arms. 'I'm sorry, I'm so sorry…'

34

Frankie

Now

'Thank goodness she didn't catch you at it,' Daisy breathed, handing me a mug of Horlicks. I'd have preferred wine, but Daisy said she needed the Horlicks – as well as the large slab of walnut and coffee cake Tammy had sent over via Dad at work – to soothe her frazzled nerves from looking after Cameron's wife while I was out on the razz with him. 'I've been waiting like a cat on the proverbial whatsit waiting for you both to come back,' she said through a mouthful of cake. 'Had to leave the front door slightly open so I'd hear Cameron's car.'

'Sorry, Daisy.' I frowned, placing the mug on the kitchen island and hunting for the bottle of wine I knew was in the fridge. 'I loathe Horlicks. The losing football team at school had to drink a pint of cold Horlicks.'

'Sounds like utter bliss.'

'Tasted like cold sick.'

Daisy took another mouthful of cake, not put off by my

description of the disgustingly lumpy cold Horlicks and eyed me speculatively. 'You alright? I'm sorry.'

'Sorry?'

'You *know*. You were getting on so well with Cameron. I had high hopes of being fitted for a bridesmaid dress. Mind you, you'd have had to let me choose my own colour: just so you know, teal, turquoise or mauve do absolutely nothing for me.'

'It's fine. Really.'

'Really?'

'We had one kiss, two kisses actually. Daisy, it wasn't right. He didn't smell right.'

'He *smelt*?' Daisy looked shocked.

'No, no. He smelt lovely. Just not, you know, *right*. Not right for *me*. I didn't want to bury my nose in his armpit.'

'Well, I reckon that's what Rebecca Mancini will be doing right now. He obviously smells just right for her.'

'What's she like?'

'His wife?'

I nodded.

'She's lovely, Frankie. Sorry, I really liked her. She arrived in a taxi over an hour ago – I did try and ring you as well as text you…'

'I turned it off after Cameron told me his wife was always on the phone when they were out for dinner and it was the cause of most of their arguments.'

'Ah, trying to make a good impression, were you?'

'Yes.'

'So you're upset?'

'No, I'm not. I'm actually just so thankful you appeared

at the door. I think I probably was going to go with Cameron next door even though I knew, after the second kiss…'

'He didn't smell right?'

I nodded. 'I don't think we'd have actually ended up in bed together. If we had it would have been horribly embarrassing at work. We'd have had it hanging over us. You know, were we going to be just friends or, as we'd done it once, did that mean we had to keep on doing it? Do it again even though one of us – or even both of us – didn't want to? Were we going to end up making out over his desk…?'

'Making out?' Daisy was scornful. 'You spend one evening with the man and you're talking American.'

'I've been working with him six weeks.' I smiled.

'Yes, well, I have noticed a couple of Americanisms creeping in. You actually said you were going to take the *garbage* out yesterday. You'll be striding out on the *sidewalk* tomorrow.'

I laughed at that. 'I'm fine, I really am.' I hesitated. 'The thing is, Daisy, when I saw his wife running down the path – you really need to get some better lighting out there, you know…'

'No, no, it'd disturb the badgers and the owls.'

'When I saw his wife running down the path,' I repeated, 'I thought it was Daler.'

'Did you? Why?' Daisy looked mystified. 'Rebecca Mancini looks nothing like Daler apart from hair about the same length.'

'Don't know really,' I answered, feeling a bit foolish. 'Jeans, long dark hair, hat…' I trailed off. 'I wanted it to be Daler so much. I thought he'd come round to find me.'

'You've got to forget him,' Daisy said, patting my arm.

'Do you know,' I said, suddenly thinking on my feet, 'I might just ask to have a stint at Piccione's Distribution in New York at some point. I feel *so* much more confident in what I can offer to Piccione's now, and both Aunty Pam and Cameron have talked so much about it recently, I can feel it beckoning.'

'New York? Frankie, you are *not* running away again. Anyway, you've only been in this job six weeks.'

'No, no, I wouldn't be running away. It's something I know I could now do.' And I really felt I could.

'Goodness,' Daisy said, staring at me, 'these past six weeks have been the making of you, haven't they? You've gone from being a miserable runaway to believing you can manage the Piccione Empire single-handed overnight.'

I laughed at that. 'I'm standing my ground *here* at the moment. It might hurt like hell, Daisy – and it bloody well does – but I'm *not* going to let Daler's coming back to Westenbury have me running off again. Just something to think about for the future.' I smiled. 'I bet it would be great.'

'Well, as long as you don't leave me down here alone before I leave for Edinburgh: those badgers and owls can be a bit scary when you're here by yourself. Once I've gone, you can get yourself off to America, I suppose.'

'How did it go with Jude this evening?'

'Oh, Frankie, he's absolutely lovely.' Daisy was animated and I was pleased for her, if not a little envious. 'I don't want to rush this one; I want to savour every little bit of him. You know...'

'Not dragging him off to bed then?' I laughed at Daisy's serious face.

'Absolutely not. This one's for keeps, if I have anything to do with it. He was here earlier and we had a drink and just chatted. If his dad is anything like Jude, I can totally understand why your Aunty Pam never got over him. Jude is so... so *honourable*. And I don't think I've ever had that in a boyfriend before.' She smiled at the thought and I went over, poured her a glass of wine and hugged her.

Cameron didn't come into work the next day.

'Where is he?' Luca demanded accusingly, coming into my office as I struggled to understand some statistics on my computer. 'I hear you had dinner with him last night.'

Did Luca think I'd *eaten* him?

'His wife turned up at the cottage,' I said simply.

'His *wife*?' Luca stared, folded his arms and then did something totally unexpected: he came over and gave me a hug. A bit of an embarrassed, loose hug, followed by a clearing of the throat, but a hug all the same. 'I'm sorry, Frankie. You and he were getting on so well. I thought maybe, you know...?'

'I thought that myself, Luca.'

'I'm sorry. After all you've been through... with Daler.'

Goodness, this was a first. Luca had never alluded to, let alone shown sympathy for, the disastrous ending to my relationship with Daler.

'It's fine, Luca, really. Honestly.' And I meant it. It really was fine. A relief really. I'd dipped in my toe and realised I wasn't ready to dive in to that big scary ocean of relationships. Was this how Aunty Pam had felt all these years? Knowing that the one she really wanted had got away? I had a sudden revelation that, like Aunty Pam, I wanted to work my way all the way up to the top in my family business. *My* family business. I felt almost overcome with a fierce pride in Piccione's in a way I never had before.

'Oh, hell,' Luca suddenly said. 'This doesn't mean we're going to lose him, does it? He's not going back to America?'

'I've no idea.' I smiled. 'But, while we're on the subject of America, I'd like to be first in the queue for anything that comes up in New York.'

'No way,' Luca almost snapped. 'You're not leaving me here with these old codgers. Now we've finally got some more young blood in the place, we're keeping you here. Especially if Cameron is off.'

'I'm serious, Luca.'

'So am I,' Luca said. 'Listen, Frankie, spend three months or so in the States, maybe in a couple of years' time, but you and I are going to be running this place soon. We need you here. *I* need you here.'

'Right.' I stared at Luca. Was he on something?

He looked distinctly embarrassed, fiddled with a couple of files on my desk and cleared his throat again. 'Look, I think you're doing a really impressive job here with the lemon curd.' He paused. More throat clearing. 'And, I know you and I haven't always seen eye to eye...'

He could say that again.

'But I suppose I've always been a bit, you know, jealous of you.' Luca's face reddened and he continued to fiddle with things on my desk.

I stared. 'Have you? Why?'

'Well,' he said, almost crossly, 'you got to stay with Dad

at home. While I had to go and live with Mum and bloody Paul Stockwell.'

'You did *not* have to.' I frowned. 'You were twelve. You could have made the decision to stay with us.'

'Mum said the law was that when parents divorced everything, including the kids, had to be shared equally.'

'Like the CDs and the dinner service?' I asked, remembering the bitter arguments over those, as well as just about everything else Mum demanded she had a right to take with her.

'Hmm. Mum said Dad had chosen you.'

'You didn't believe that, did you? You were twelve years old, for heaven's sake.'

'Oh, only for a while. And then I was shipped off to boarding school and I just got into being there and none of it seemed to matter anymore. Mum used to get cross when I wanted to come and stay with Dad and Tammy and you and the little kids during the holidays. And then I was expected to take over here as soon as I left university. No swanning off or travelling with a pack on my back for me. *You* were well sorted.'

'Now you're being ridiculous,' I scoffed. 'You could have done what I did and gone travelling.'

'There was always pressure on me as the only son... And yes, I *was* envious that you were off and away from this place.' Luca had the grace to look a little shamefaced.

'And that's it?' I shook my head in disbelief.

'No.' Luca grinned. 'You were a bloody good footballer when I couldn't even kick a ball straight.'

*

The somewhat strange revelation that my brother Luca quite liked me after all, and certainly didn't want me rushing off anywhere soon, together with the new pride in Piccione's I suddenly seemed to have acquired (Piccione's: *my* company) had me leaving my office and walking round the production lines and distribution warehouses as if seeing them for the first time. It took me a good couple of hours, but I took in every single corner and aspect of Piccione's: from the loading bays where the raw materials for the pickles and preserves were delivered and stored, on to the production lines, up into the laboratories and through the offices and even down to the canteen kitchens where the cooks were throwing metal containers around in the usual flurry of steam and stress that dishes wouldn't be ready when the lunchtime buzzer sounded to summon the workers to down tools at twelve. I crossed the yard, dodging a couple of vans and fork trucks as well as three young girls from HR, embarrassed to be caught on a sneaky fag break, enjoying the May sunshine on my face after being inside.

'Y'alright, love?' greeted me everywhere I went, the workers more than happy to stop and tell me what they were involved in, any problems they were having and any gripes they might be feeling with regards to working conditions or machinery that wasn't up to par.

I spent the longest amount of time in Preserves – which was obviously my domain – chatting not only about jam and honey but also being shown photographs of Carol and Deb's new great-grandchildren. These women were great-grandmas? Well, I supposed, having your first child at sixteen meant, by the time you were in your late fifties, that was more than feasible.

'What *you* doing down here?' Dad smiled as I walked back through Pickles where, jacket removed, he'd been deep in conversation with two blue-overalled service engineers who were now hitting at an overhead metal pipe with a couple of hammers. 'That's it, Joe,' one of them shouted down at us, giving Dad a thumbs up. Dad wiped his forehead with the back of his head and returned the gesture.

'Just getting to know my factory a bit more.' I grinned, slightly embarrassed at what I actually *was* doing. I'd only been back two months and I was surveying my pickle kingdom as though I were its queen.

'*My* factory?' Dad raised an eyebrow and laughed at the possessive pronoun. 'Good for you.' He reached for his jacket hanging on a metal tap and took my arm. 'Everything OK, Frankie? You settling in here and down at Daisy's? Cameron Mancini not giving you too much hassle?'

'No, Dad, really, everything's fine.'

'Only, I don't know if you know, and I don't want you getting upset, but I've just heard Daler Dosanjh is back.' Dad was looking really worried.

My heart missed a beat as it always did at Daler's name, but I managed a smile. 'I know, Dad, I know. It's OK, don't worry, I'm not about to get the next plane out of here. I'm here now and I'm staying. Right, can we have a quick chat about where we've got to with the new lemon curd...?'

The morning's impromptu tour of the works was followed by a similarly makeshift board meeting called by Angelo who made an appearance after lunch wanting an update as to what was going on. Where was Mancini? Why had he and I been out looking at that Syrian fellow's beehives? What were we up to? Margaret Holroyd had obviously been in there dishing the dirt and stirring it as usual. I gave her a knowing look as I determinedly closed the heavy boardroom door on her hovering. Blimey, I was getting carried away with my status if I was trying to bar Angelo's mistress from taking the minutes I was convinced were just an excuse to nosy her way into family business.

'Why you shut Margaret out?' Angelo started crossly.

'Never mind Margaret, Nonno,' Luca said irritably. 'We weren't expecting any meeting. We're all busy. Come on, what's up?'

Angelo glared across at Luca, raised a questioning eye towards Dad and then pointed a finger at me. 'I hear Sandals Man back in village.'

'So I believe.' I raised my own eye back. 'And?' I added calmly.

'I not have you running off again. Off drinking dodgy cocktails in moonlight in Thailand. Off back to Rosina. You keep out his way, you hear?'

'I've no intention of going anywhere near Daler, Nonno. He is a married man with a child.'

'Hmm.' Nonno narrowed his eyes. 'And you been out with Mancini? He married man too. What is it with you and married men? Plenty *single* fish out there. I don't want you upset when Mancini go back to States and you run off again, drinking dodgy...'

'OK, OK, Dad. We get the picture.' Dad shook his head crossly.

'For your information, Nonno,' I snapped heatedly, 'Daler was thoroughly *single* when I was with him. Cameron is my

boss, a friend and more than married to Rebecca who is
with him at the cottage at the moment. After all the long
hours he's put in recently, I think he deserves some time off
to welcome her here, don't you?'

'You not upset the wife here?' Angelo looked at me
suspiciously for any signs of distress on my part.

'No, of course not. Anything else?'

'You planning to put thousands beehives in my car park?
In my loading bay?'

I actually laughed at that. 'Cameron and I are just looking
at the feasibility of making our own honey.' I smiled.
'Pointless putting them anywhere near the factory where
there are very few flowers.'

'Hmm.' Angelo narrowed his eyes once more. 'You
getting ahead of yourself. You concentrate on lemon curd
and leave my car park to cars not bees. Talking of lemon
curd—' I swear Angelo's eyes became slightly misty '—I just
been in lab upstairs with George. I taste Rosina's *crema al
limone* you insisting on. Take me back to when I little boy.
Good girl. You doing alright.'

35

Pam

Now

'Come on, Pam, let's look in your wardrobe and decide what you're going to wear. This is so exciting. So, so romantic.' Daisy was pouring wine for the three of them although Pam's pulse was racing to such an extent, she felt any alcohol would send her totally over the top.

'Steady on.' Pam pulled a face. 'When I asked for a bit of advice re what to wear in order not to look too keen, I wasn't expecting the pair of you to turn up as ladies-in-waiting and insisting on putting me through my paces.'

'Now don't be ungrateful, Pamela and don't eschew our generosity in coming over in order to have you looking the very best you possibly can. This is such a fabulous, momentous occasion; we want to be in on it as well. We're not going to let you keep it all to yourself... No,' Daisy tutted as Pam brought out a pair of black, straight-legged trousers and a horribly beige shirt, 'you look like you're off to the office rather than meeting up with the only man you've ever loved.'

Pam shook her head in Daisy's direction. 'You're making me more nervous, Daisy. Will you stop it and just bugger off back home?'

'So,' Daisy said, rifling through Pam's closet, 'what did you wear on that very first real date with Rob? You know, when you both realised this was what you wanted? At the picnic on his mother's allotment?'

Pam's head shot up from the drawer where she was trying to make a decision re bra and pants. Black? Red? White? 'How do *you* know about that, Daisy?' She stared across at Daisy who was now holding up a white silk shirt while pairing it with a soft grey woollen pencil skirt.

'White, absolutely.' Frankie smiled in Pam's direction before turning to Daisy. 'Yes, how *do* you know that, Daisy? *I've* never told you.'

'Rob told Jude and Jude told me.' Daisy fished out a pair of flat leather grey boots and cast a critical eye over their shade. 'Hmm, it might be May but you don't want to be tottering about in summer sandals – not on an allotment.' She gave them a quick rub with the sleeve of her sweatshirt and then added, 'He thinks it's all wonderfully romantic.'

'Really?' Pam felt her pulse rev once more. 'Jude doesn't, you know, mind?'

'Mind?' Daisy frowned. 'Why should he mind?'

'Well, some people don't like the idea of their parent getting on with their life once their other parent has died.'

'Not Jude, I can assure you.' Daisy spoke with all the confidence of having known Rob's son for ever rather than the reality of all of ten days or so. 'Rob, apparently, has not had an easy time these past few years. He nursed and cared for Jude's mum for a long time, you know. Just when they thought she was in remission, it seemed she wasn't. I get the impression she wasn't the easiest of patients. Became very demanding, bitter even.'

'I think I'd have been *more* than bitter.' Pam gave a little sad smile. 'Knowing I wasn't going to get any better and was going to have to leave Rob. For ever.'

'I know, I know.' Daisy placed the skirt, shirt and boots on Pam's bed. 'Really awful for all those involved seeing someone suffer like that. But that doesn't mean, Pam, that you can't go out on a date with Rob, you know. Life goes on. And,' she added, 'at the end of the day, you *did* see him first.'

She could, she knew, have made her way there, blindfolded. Over forty years on and yet it seemed like yesterday. Pam tutted at herself for coming out with such a cliché, albeit unspoken with no one else party to the thoughts tumbling through her head. She pulled up outside his mother's cottage, parking alongside a shiny new black *Evoque*.

'My only nod to materialism.' Rob grinned as Pam, heart thumping wildly, made her way to the green-painted door where he stood, barefoot, waiting for her. 'It's got a brilliant sound system. Hang on, I'll just get some shoes on.'

He disappeared and Pam looked around her, taking in the tubs of fading daffodils, the scent of new-mown grass, the pungent tang from the farms further up the lane and the first swifts swooping maniacally to reclaimed nests in the eaves. It had been the beginning of autumn the first time she'd been here with Rob but, apart from the change in the season, a newly cobbled driveway and a brand-new fence around the actual garden, nothing seemed much different from how she remembered it.

Rob reappeared with a huge picnic basket. 'Come on, I'll show you the way.'

You don't have to, Pam thought as she followed him: *I've made my way from the house, up through the yard and climbed this stile and into the allotments every single night in my dreams*. 'Thank you,' she said to his back.

'We can actually sit outside if you'd prefer.' Rob hesitated as they stood outside the garden shed. 'It's a lovely evening… up to you… bit chilly…' He trailed off, seemingly unsure of himself.

He's nervous, Pam thought. *He's actually nervous*. 'How about we sit outside for a drink and take in the remains of this gorgeous spring evening?' Pam pulled a scarlet pashmina from her bag. 'We can always move inside to eat.'

Rob opened the shed door and went inside, placing the wicker basket on the floor, and Pam saw that the table inside was already laid with a white damask cloth and starched napkins and she knew, from a recognised sensation both in her nose and in her chest, she was in great danger of crying. When was the last time she'd cried? Not for years and years. Maybe if she'd let it all out instead of bottling it all up and just getting on with it, she wouldn't have suffered all those years of migraines? Oh hell. What the *hell* was the matter with her? Pam dashed an angry hand across her cheek but the traitorous tears kept on coming and she sat down on the bench, fumbling in her bag for a tissue.

'Pam?' Rob was by her side, handing her a glass of

something fizzy. She took it, downed half the glass and, through a combination of bubbles and forced-back tears, offered up a ridiculously inane smile.

'Hay fever,' she sniffed, rubbing at her nose. 'Always gets to me in May.'

Rob put down his glass carefully on the bench and took Pam's hand in his own. 'Me too.' He smiled. 'Although, over the years, whenever I've thought of you – and believe me, Pam, you've *never* been far from my thoughts – I appear to have suffered from hay fever whatever the season.'

Pam reached a hand to his face and Rob leaned in, kissing her open mouth. He tasted of champagne and peppermint. Of hope and new beginnings. 'Come on,' he said eventually, 'I think I promised you a picnic.'

36

Frankie

I'd just lowered myself into the corner bath in my tiny en suite and closed my eyes against the long day I'd arrived home from only ten minutes earlier – I was planning on a glass of wine (it *was* very nearly the weekend) beans on toast in front of the TV and an early night – when Daisy shouted round the door.

'Can you give me a lift, Frankie? I've not got Mum's car at the moment.'

'Take Kermit. You're insured.'

'OK, thanks.' She was gone before I'd even asked her where she was going, but back just as I was settling into the bubbles and considering a snooze.

'Won't start, Frankie.' Daisy sounded cross.

'What have you done to it? It was fine when I drove home.'

'Well, it's not now. Come and look at it, will you?'

'Daisy...!'

'Please, Frankie. I need to get out to Karam Yassim's place. Jude's just rung me to say he's worried a meeting they're having up there might turn a bit nasty.'

'You should be keeping out of it then. What can *you* do about it?'

'Very little probably, but I'd like to support Jude. Come with me? Show everyone you might have been canvassing for your stepfather, but you won't be voting for him?'

'OK, OK, give me a second.' I turned regretfully to the tub, pulled the plug on the hot water and, after a quick rub-down with a towel, grabbed jeans and sweater and pulled my damp hair up into a ponytail.

'Come on,' Daisy urged me, halfway down the garden path.

'Nope,' I said, shaking my head a minute later. 'I think you've flooded the carburettor. Leave it ten minutes and we'll try it again.'

'I don't want to wait... Cameron!' Daisy had spotted Cameron doing something manly with his garden heater and she called across to him. 'Could you possibly give us a lift up to Karam Yassim's place? Jude's a bit worried...'

'Don't drag Cameron up there,' I hissed. Cameron had not turned up for work the past two days – it was pretty obvious he and Rebecca had battened down for the duration and were making up for lost time and I was feeling highly embarrassed at my near miss of being caught by Rebecca in her husband's arms. 'If Jude's worried there's going to be trouble,' I went on, 'he shouldn't have asked you to go there.'

'He didn't. He told me to stay away.'

'There you go then.' I was already regretting pulling the plug on my bath and agreeing to go with her.

'Come on,' Cameron shouted back. 'I'll give you a lift. I was thinking we might go out to grab something to eat at the Coach and Horses up at Upper Clawson later on. It's on the way, I believe.' Cameron didn't quite meet my eye as he said *we*. Rebecca Mancini appeared at the door, obviously wondering what was going on. 'Grab your jacket, Rebecca, we're just giving our neighbours a lift.'

Rebecca Mancini was dark-haired and olive-skinned and for a split second I understood why I'd mistaken her for Daler the other evening. She was still in jeans – but this evening they were white – and snow-white trainers with a vibrantly pink oversized sweater on top. 'Do I need to change my outfit?' she asked. 'What's the protocol in your diners round here?'

'I shouldn't worry,' Daisy shouted back, trying not to appear impatient. 'You look lovely. Grab a jacket – it can get cold up near the moors – but, honestly, come as you are. We don't stand on ceremony too much round these parts. Come on, Frankie, if you're coming.'

Once in the front seat and belted in, Rebecca Mancini turned to me in the back and held out a hand. 'Hi. You must be Francesca? Cameron's told me so much about you.'

Not that he kissed me – twice – three evenings ago, I bet. She was jolly and vibrant and talked non-stop about everything from how much she loved *'this crazy little country of yours'* to regret that *'my life/work balance was all out of kilter and as a result I almost lost the love of my life.'* She stroked Cameron's arm possessively and, while he looked slightly embarrassed, I did wonder if this wasn't perhaps a warning shot across my bow that she knew what had been going on with Cameron and for me to back off. Daisy, sitting next to me on the back seat, obviously thought so too and she dug me in the ribs to let me know exactly that.

We headed for the same spot Cameron and I had parked several days earlier, but this time there were so many cars already in situ we had to drive back down the lane and then walk up and through the gate to where a crowd was gathered in a nearby field. It was still light, a large blood-red sun hanging on tenaciously to the glorious May evening. There must have been a hundred or more people gathered round Jude Mansell who was standing on a box of some sort, clapping and encouraging him as he spoke of his plans and ideas for the area if they would only give him their vote at the local by-election. The majority of those gathered were, it appeared, there to hear Jude speak as he encouraged them to vote for him and, in doing so, putting their vote against the idea of building an estate on these fields that was home to Karam's bee project.

Jude was speaking calmly, his father to the left of him and Karam Yassim and a couple of people from the council, involved in deploying both refugees and the unemployed towards the project, on his right. I felt uneasy after the phone call Jude had made to Daisy earlier and Daisy, clutching at my hand, obviously felt the same.

Without warning, a beer bottle flew from the back of the crowd towards Karam, falling short of its intended target and landing with a thud on the grass behind him. Jude stopped talking, one hand held up in defence mode as several car doors slammed in unison and a group of around eight men moved towards the back of the crowd, silent but ominous in their approach.

'BFTB,' Daisy whispered.

'Sorry?'

'Britain For The British,' Daisy said in disgust. 'Troublemakers, all of them.'

'I'm not sure we should be here.' I frowned. 'Perhaps we should move back to the car?'

Cameron was obviously thinking along the same lines and was trying to persuade Rebecca back to where we had parked. But by the gleam in her eye and her determined stance, I could see both she and Daisy were in for the duration.

'The BFTB are against the idea of giving work to refugees,' Daisy was saying in a low voice. 'Giving *anything* to refugees – or *anyone* not born in this country – whether it be shelter or work or anything. They'll absolutely hate the idea that Karam has set up this project to help those people they despise, especially when your stepfather is egging them on to believe that local housing could be built here instead.'

'It's almost moorland, for heaven's sake,' I tutted. 'There's no real infrastructure; people wouldn't live out here…'

'Britain For The British!' came the rallying cry from the back as a plethora of bottles went up – and came back down – in almost perfect synchronicity.

'Hell, they've obviously practised that,' Daisy squeaked as a bottle hit her on the arm. 'They must think they're Robin Hood and his merry bloody men, but with bottles instead of arrows.'

'Wrong side,' I said grimly. 'He was with the good guys.'

'Please go back to your cars,' Jude shouted as calmly as possible to those gathered around him. 'Please don't retaliate.' The newcomers appeared to retreat at that, turning and walking away from where Jude was standing, but were then joined by five or six others from the crowd, pulling out baseball bats and sticks and making their way to the beehives in the next field.

'No way!' Daisy shouted in fury, racing off after them, Rebecca Mancini, despite Cameron's attempts to stop her, following hot on her heels.

'Come on,' I shouted back at Cameron. We ran after the other two who were almost at the hives.

Daisy, who was there first, shouted, 'Don't you fucking dare!' and draped herself around the nearest hive. 'You'll have to hit me first and then you'll be up for manslaughter. Murder, probably. How does thirty years in Wakefield Top Security grab you, you great fucking oaf? Hmm? Hmm?'

Rebecca did exactly the same and Jude, Cameron and myself along with ten or so others who'd raced up with us, followed suit. Then came a bit of a stand-off as the troublemakers, seeing three women in front of them, looked to their leader, a small sandy-haired bloke, for instructions as to their next move. With a nod of his head towards the unguarded hives at the far end of the field, the guy turned and the others made to follow just as two cop cars and one large van, blue lights flashing, had the troublemakers dispersing and running – literally – for the hills, a sea of blue racing after them. At least three of the hives were completely destroyed, smashed to smithereens by hate, the only reparation being the retaliation of several hundreds of bees going after two of the men in a merciless revenge.

An ambulance was already bouncing its way – more blue lights – across potholes and imploding molehills towards Karam's office.

'That was quick,' Daisy said angrily. 'Personally, I'd have

let the bastards be stung to death. Jesus, I've been stung too. She stood away from the hive, her legs trembling, her face and hands already inflamed with red.

'I don't think they're here for bee stings,' I said, sucking at two painful stings of my own on my left hand. 'Someone's hurt down there.'

The four of us made our way back down the hill to where Karam and a few others were doggedly picking up bottles and bits of glass, two paramedics moving quickly towards Karam's office.

'Frankie, I think it's your Aunty Pam.' Daisy, ahead of us and trying to follow Jude, was able to see the patch of grass at one side of the office where a blonde-haired woman lay underneath a man's jacket. She set off at a run and I followed.

My Aunty Pam lay on the ground, her face, hair and white T-shirt covered in blood, a large shard of glass sticking out at an ugly angle from a gash in her neck.

'She was hit twice,' a white-faced Rob Mansell was explaining to the paramedics. 'A wine bottle caught her fully on the forehead and floored her and then she was showered with the debris from two more as they crashed into the wall behind her.'

'Pam? Aunty Pam?' I knelt at her side, not realising I was cutting myself on the shards and slivers of glass that surrounded her. 'Is she OK? Is she going to be alright?'

'I'm fine, don't fuss,' she said weakly, patting my hand and trying to sit up.

'Don't let her sit up,' a voice said. 'The paramedics have got the equipment she needs, but I'll go in the ambulance to Midhope General with her.'

So distraught was I at seeing Aunty Pam lying bleeding on the grass, being attended to by the paramedics, it didn't immediately register who was standing washing their hands at the sink just inside the open office door.

'This Dr Daler Dosanjh,' Karam said, helping me to my feet and tutting at the pinpricks of blood appearing through my jeans and on my hands. 'Good job he here and know what to do.'

37

Frankie

Now

'**B**ack where we started,' Daler said, not smiling as he handed me the Styrofoam cup of coffee in A and E. It was just as disgusting now as it was then. How long ago had it been, Daler leaning over me, black curls escaping from his beanie hat, as he helped slot coins into the dilapidated coffee machine under the stone stairs? 'Two years, eight months and ten days,' he added without any help from me who knew, verbatim, to the very day, how long had passed since that early morning dash to this very waiting room where Daler and I now sat once again.

'Really?' I said coldly. 'You have an excellent memory.'

He shrugged, unable to look me in the eye. 'How are you, Frankie? I hear you're back working for your grandfather and father?'

I nodded. 'Look, you really don't need to stay here with us, Daler. Thank you for your help, but I'll be fine. I'm sure they'll be wondering where you are back at home,' I added pointedly. 'I'm just going to wait until the doctor comes back and tells us what's happening...' I stopped speaking as Rob Mansell appeared at our side.

'I wanted to know what was happening,' Rob said. 'I drove over.'

'You look like you've been in a fight,' I said, eyeing his cream-coloured polo shirt and black jacket, which still carried blood, whether his own or Pam's I wasn't sure.

'We were,' Rob said angrily. 'I thought there might be a few hecklers out there but never expected that lot. How is she?'

'We're just waiting...' I broke off as the doctor we'd seen earlier approached us.

'A lot of blood, but not as bad as it could have been.' He smiled. 'The glass punctured the tissue and nicked the artery – hence the amount of blood – but luckily there was no movement laterally in any direction from the point of entry.'

'Sorry, what does that mean?' I asked.

'It means she'll be fine. We're going to keep her in overnight and check her in the morning for any damage to nerves and blood vessels but as far as I can see, you did the right thing immediately, which helped. She has a huge bump and nasty bruising on her forehead as well as some concussion where the bottle hit her – it must have been going with some speed and force. And incredibly unlucky that another bottle broke behind her and a shard stuck in her neck; never seen anything like that before, to be honest. She'll be fine. She's sleeping now; don't disturb her. We'll give you a ring when you can pick her up in the morning.'

'Is your car still up at Karam's place, Daler?' Rob asked.

Daler nodded.

'Come on, I'll drop you off at home, Francesca, and then drive you back out there, Daler. Jude and Daisy and a load of others are helping clear up while Karam tries to salvage the bees.'

'Will they have just flown off, I wonder?' I edged nearer to Rob, not wanting to look at, or have any more contact with Daler. I needed to get out of there, needed to get home to sob myself senseless. 'I've been doing a lot of research on honey bees and how they work together in the hives, Rob,' I went on, moving up close to him while talking ridiculously quickly and portentously in an effort to get Daler out of my peripheral vision, as well as my head. 'I think, if there's a living queen and enough worker bees to create a new home, you know, in a hollow tree or something, sometimes the remaining part of the colony will try to do that.'

'I've spent a lot of time up there with Karam lately.' Rob was looking at me strangely as I successfully managed to elbow Daler from the conversation. 'Fascinating creatures, bees. I think, if the queen is dead, but there is part of the old hive remaining and a sufficient number of worker bees, it's possible the caretaker bees will quickly move to create an emergency queen cell. If they're successful, the new queen, caretaker and forager workers and some drones for mating may stick around long enough to rebuild the colony at least temporarily nearby...' Rob was warming to his theme, and I desperately tried to listen, to smile, to take it all in, but I couldn't give a fuck about fucking bees at this moment in my life. Sorry, bees.

Daler was adding nothing to the bee conversation but appeared edgy, anxious. 'You go on,' he said, suddenly. 'I won't be a minute.' He stopped as Rob and I made our way towards the entrance doors and as I turned, desperate to keep him with me – if only for a few more minutes – but equally as desperate to get away from him, I saw he was making a phone call and then speaking quietly and rapidly to whoever he was calling. Sienna, I supposed, and felt physically sick with misery. It was no good. I couldn't do this: couldn't survive with Daler living so near to me once more. I was going to cry whenever I saw him, unable to be with him, to have him love me like he used to.

'It's too far out of your way,' I suddenly said to Rob, thinking on my feet. I just couldn't sit in a car with Daler for the next twenty minutes and not grab hold of him and cry and bury my nose in his armpit and hold him until I had to be scraped off him. 'Daisy's place is in the opposite direction. Honestly, really,' I added as Rob protested. 'Taxi... look... over there... I'm fine... I'm off. Thank you for coming to the hospital...' And with that, I scarpered, jumped into the waiting taxi and cried all the way home.

'What the hell was Daler Dosanjh doing up at Karam's place?' Daisy asked crossly. She ran fingers through her mussed-up hair and pulled at her sweater as I popped my head round the sitting room door. Mood music, playing quietly in the background, had obviously been getting her and Jude into exactly that, and I retreated to the kitchen, slightly embarrassed as well as trying not to be horribly envious. Jude was really special, I could see, and Daisy deserved to find happiness with this lovely man, but their cosying up with a bottle of wine on the sitting room floor was doing absolutely nothing to lift me out of my unhappy state.

'Rob seemed to think he's up there a lot,' I said. 'Actually, you know, if I remember rightly, that very first evening Daler took me down to help at the Langar meal at the Gurdwara, he mentioned something about Karam then. I think he's known him a long time.'

'You OK?' Daisy asked.

'Yes,' I said, brightly, 'absolutely fine.'

'Well, if you're sure. You know, I would say, get another glass and join us but…'

'Get back in there, Daisy.' I smiled. 'I'm off to bed.'

'Yes, you need your sleep.'

I wasn't convinced I was going to get much sleep that night, whether I needed it or not.

'For football practice tomorrow, Frankie. You'll probably need to go straight from work, so take your kit with you.'

'Oh, Daisy, I'm not sure.'

'No arguments. If *I'm* getting my shorts on and airing my white knees to the world, so are you. If I'm not down for breakfast…' She grinned and nodded somewhat lasciviously behind her in Jude's direction and, despite myself, I smiled. '…I'll see you on the playing field behind the Jolly Sailor at seven.'

38

Frankie

Now

'I'm sorry,' Cameron said, handing me a take-out coffee. 'Peace offering?'

'What are you sorry for?' I asked, knowing perfectly well what he was trying to say.

'You and me? The other evening... I'm sorry.'

I smiled, put my coffee down and walked over to him. He took a slight step backwards, frowning nervously at my approach. I stood in front of him, went up on my tiptoes and reached behind him in an attempt to take his hair in my hands. 'Nope,' I said, laughing.

'No? No, what?'

'It would never have worked. I can't feel your hair in my hands.' I smiled again. 'Honestly, Cameron, I'm really happy for you. You know – that Rebecca and you seem to be working things out.'

'Really?'

'Really.'

'The thing is, if my wife hadn't reappeared at such an untimely moment, I was, I know, more than happy to whisk you off to my side of the cottages.' He frowned again. 'I'm not sure what that says about me or my marriage? I know what it says about my fancying you though...' Cameron trailed off, seemingly unable to look me in the eye.

'And I would have been happy to be whisked.' I smiled, knowing it was a lie. I had an awful feeling I'd have run scared at the last minute, and then had to face the awkward situation of working with Cameron, knowing I'd turned him down.

It had all worked out for the best.

'She's lovely, Cameron,' I said, meaning it. 'Rebecca is really lovely.'

'She is, isn't she?' His face softened and we grinned at each other, daft grins that meant we understood each other, we were still friends and whatever *might* have happened a couple of nights ago wouldn't be spoken of again.

'How long is she going to stay?'

'Probably for the duration,' he said, hopefully. 'Until I'm done here, anyhow. I've no plans to rush back to the States just yet. I think Rebecca is seeing this as a sort of gap year. She's put her job on hold, which I think is immensely brave of her. Whether she'll go back to the same job or look for something else, who knows? I didn't realise just how stressed she'd become. Anyway, she's always wanted to come to the UK, so we'll do a lot of sightseeing, go over to Europe; do the usual touristy things. And, you know... take it from there?'

I did know.

*

'Right, ladies, give me ten.'

'Ten what, Deimante?' An exceptionally pretty girl kitted out totally in designer sports gear, her face fully made up, stood in the evening sunshine, hands on hips, trainer-shod feet in third ballet position.

'Don'ts you be give me sat, Scarlett,' Deimante Miniauskiene shouted. 'Ten burpees. You knows how we starts.'

Scarlett grinned and proceeded to execute the most graceful burpees I'd ever seen. She reached for the sky, then hit the grass, legs perfectly co-ordinated behind her before reaching upwards once more. She did at least fifteen without stopping and without breaking a sweat as the rest of the twenty or so women watched on in awe. Deimante shouted at the rest of us to 'gets down and dirties, you lots. All of yous,' before jumping up herself.

'Me as well?' Daisy looked horrified. 'I'm assistant manager and first aider.' She held up the green plastic case with its white cross she'd filched from the vet practice earlier that day. 'Don't let me forget this, Frankie,' she hissed a minute later from her position on the ground. 'Dad'll go ape if he knows I've borrowed it. I *was* going to bring the mini fire extinguisher as well, but I couldn't get it off the wall.'

'Why?' I laughed, jumping skywards. 'Don't put me off... three... four...'

'Health and safety and all that... eight... nine... I take my position very seriously...'

'You're cheating... five... six...'

'Didn't get much sleep last night... twelve... thirteen.'

'Too much information... seven... eight...'

'I'm in love, Frankie... eighty... eighty-one... a hundred and six...'

'I know.' I sat on the dandelion-strewn grass, trying to get my breath back. I'd thought I was pretty fit after all the bike riding I'd been doing lately. Obviously not. 'Jude's lovely,' I added. 'I totally get what you see in him.'

'He is, isn't he?' she said dreamily, lying back on the grass.

'OK, OK, no sittings on arses,' Deimante shouted. 'We has just four months' trainings before new season starts at end of August. We has two new players here: Frankie, who was professional for England Football team, and Daisy – who wasn't.'

'Schoolgirls,' I muttered in some embarrassment as all the other girls and women turned to stare. 'England *Schoolgirls*. And very, *very* lapsed.'

'We see.' Deimante grinned. 'We see just what you do. I myself in goal. Very good goalie in Lithuania.'

I felt a challenge had been laid down. 'Right, come on then.' I laughed, running for the ball. 'Let's get going.'

'Shouldn't we be doing a bit more warming up?' Scarlett pouted. 'We don't want to pull anything.'

'Not what you were saying in that dive in Leeds on Saturday night, Scarlett.' Her mate grinned. She was a hefty girl, a glorious bust straining at her white Nike top, and probably better in a rugby team than football, but I wanted her on my side.

Scarlett pouted a bit more, insisted we all do ten minutes more – fairly gentle – stretching and then we were off.

It was like riding a bike – it never leaves you. I was back, playing for England Schoolgirls, racing up and down the field, Aunty Pam and Dad and Tam cheering me on as I wove through the opposition scoring goal after goal after goal.

'Yous good.' Deimante grinned as we sat, breathless during the break. 'Best I seen since coming to this godforsaken place.'

'Godforsaken?' I laughed. 'I thought you liked it here in England. In Westenbury?'

'Oh, I do, I do. *Godforsaken* is wrong words? I loves this country. I happy here. Just no good footballers for team. Until now. We going do great things together, Frankies, you and me. We rules the world.'

I laughed out loud at that. It did feel so good to be back playing again. I realised I'd not even thought of Daler for the last hour or so. 'Well, the village teams maybe.'

'OK, we changes sides a bit now. I want yous, Georgia—' she pointed at the large girl all in white who'd previously been working with me '—defending Frankie now. Don't let her gets away with anything. Not a dick bird.'

'*Dicky* bird,' Daisy shouted from the sidelines, where she was examining a plant closely. 'Got a bit of a stitch. Carry on without me. Now Ruby and Libby have joined us, you can do without me for the next few minutes. I'm watching to see who's any good and making notes.' Daisy held up the pad and pencil she'd brought from the vet surgery, the face of a large cartoon dog grinning out across the field at us.

Georgia certainly knew what she was doing. While I was still convinced she'd be better suited for a game of rugby and that at any moment she was about to tackle me to the ground, her defending was spot on and for a big girl she was jolly speedy, approaching like an express train, thundering down the field and then, with some very nimble footwork, retrieving the ball for her team.

Westenbury Village Cricket team had now arrived and were in full practice on the ground adjoining our playing field and, at one point, now that my team was facing that direction, I lost control of the ball several times, imagining Daler in his cricket whites just a few feet away from me. I was convinced I'd seen someone with black curls racing down the highly mowed and tended pitch.

'What matters wis you?' Deimante demanded crossly from between her goal posts (two kit bags, the actual goalposts having been taken down for the summer by the council). 'Keep your eye on bloody ball or I get sub on.' Deimante glanced across at Daisy who appeared to be making a daisy chain ring for her left hand.

Daisy glanced nervously towards the buxom Georgia who was revving up once more and reiterated, 'Keep your eye on bloody ball, Frankie. For heaven's sake!'

Incensed, I started running and running with the ball towards Deimante in goal. Georgia was behind me, catching up. I could hear her breathing, saw a glimpse of white top and then she was on me, tackling me to the ground.

'What the eff you sink yous doing to my best player?' Deimante shouted furiously, her chance of saving a goal made void in one fell tackle.

'I need to talk to you, Frankie. This appears to be the only way I can pin you down without you running off.' Daler had his arms firmly round me, refusing to let me up off the grass.

'Get off me, Daler,' I snapped. 'What the hell do you think you're doing?'

'Is sis attempt rape?' Deimante loomed above us. 'ABH? GBH? Assault? You wants me call the fuzz? Daisy,' she yelled across to our manager who was now in the process of fashioning the wedding ring to go with the engagement ring sitting on her third finger, 'gets the fuzz!'

'Please, Frankie.' Daler's huge brown eyes never left my own.

'Can you nots wait until practice over?' Deimante snapped.

'Daler, there's nothing to talk about,' I said, tears rolling down my face. I brushed them away crossly.

'Please, Frankie.'

'You waits over there,' Deimante said crossly to Daler as though she were talking to one of the children at Little Acorns village school where she was lollipop lady and teaching assistant. 'You sits nicely over sere and waits until we finish.'

Every time I glanced towards Daler who'd now been joined by Daisy on the wooden bench at the very far end of the playing field, they appeared to be deep in conversation. My heart soared as hope filled every part of me and then plummeted into my football boots as I saw a beautifully dressed dark-haired and coffee-skinned woman with a little girl – Daler's little girl – approach the bench. The woman held the little girl out to be kissed and then walked off with her towards the cricket field car park.

'Frankie, bloody concentrates,' Deimante kept yelling at me down the pitch, but I couldn't.

'Own goal, you pillock,' Ruby shouted in glee as I shot the ball past our own goalkeeper, and she dived the wrong way in an effort to save it.

'OK, OK, enough,' Deimante shouted. 'Go sorts out your lof life, Frankies, before I put yous on transfer list.'

Daler and I walked in complete silence across to The Jolly Sailor. I needed a pint of lemonade and then several gins.

'OK,' I said, past caring that I was hot and sweaty, that any make-up I'd started with had now totally slid off my face. I downed the lemonade. 'What is it?'

'I'm not married anymore,' Daler said, simply.

'Really?' I snapped. 'How come I saw your wife a couple of weeks ago then?'

'Did you?' Daler seemed surprised. 'Where?'

'I was canvassing with my stepfather. It was a huge shock when Edna Bradshaw on my constituency list turned out to be you. Or rather your wife.'

'You came out to the house? You knew I was back from London?'

'I wasn't there *intentionally*. I wasn't casing the joint or looking for *you* if that's what you were thinking. The last place I wanted to be was *your* doorstep. And, I just saw your wife again with your daughter back on the field half an hour ago? I assume it *was* your daughter?'

Daler nodded.

'So, how does it work? You're no longer married, but you still share your daughter?'

Daler shook his head. 'That was my sister on the field. Didn't you recognise her? Juneeta's been helping to look after Anya until I find a decent nanny.'

'It was Juneeta?' I'd just assumed it was Daler's wife.

'Yes.'

'Oh.' I glanced across at Daler. 'So, your little girl is called Anya? It's a very lovely name. I saw her at your doorstep. She's very beautiful.'

'I think so.'

'So where is your wife?'

'We're divorced.'

'After just two years?'

'We should never have married.'

'Where is she?'

'She lives back in London but spends much of the time in Dubai.'

'And she's left her little girl?' I frowned. How could any woman do that?

'Yes. The last thing she wanted to be was married to a GP living in a Yorkshire village.'

'A GP?' I stared.

'Hmm. I was desperate to get back to medicine, but knew I couldn't do hospital work while I was caring for Anya. I'm filling in as locum for six months at the surgery in Heath Green. I knew I didn't want to stay in the sandal business – it's just not me, Frankie – I didn't want to stay in London and I didn't want to be with Sienna. I'd done the necessary GP training while I was still down in Coventry, just before I met you.' Daler held up his hands, almost in despair. 'I *hated* running Dosanjhs in London. I didn't want to be there in the huge gated house we were living in, in Surrey, but Sienna wanted to be near Gatwick so she could fly off to her friends in Dubai whenever she wanted.'

'So, you've crawled back up here, thinking I'm just going to fall back into your arms and take over from where we left off?'

'I've not crawled anywhere, Frankie. If it wasn't for you, I would have tried so much harder to make my marriage work. I'm very ashamed that I was unable to make a go of it.'

'And that you've left your little girl without a mother?'

'As I said, I'm not proud of myself in all this. I just couldn't do it any longer. I missed you so much. Needed you so much.'

'So what was your wife doing at your house the other day? She called you her husband.'

Daler shrugged. 'We're actually divorced. It came through while we were still in Surrey. I'd moved back up that weekend and she'd come up with me and Anya to say goodbye. She's gone off to Dubai now for six months. She has another man there. He certainly doesn't want to be saddled with a little girl.'

'Saddled with? *You* don't feel that about Anya, do you?'

'Oh my God, no. She's my life. I adore her.'

I didn't say anything for a while as I digested this bit of information. 'Does it hurt that your wife is with another man?'

'No!' Daler shook his head with some vehemence. 'No, not at all.'

'Do you not worry that she's going to be back, demanding to have custody of Anya?'

'All the time. I couldn't lose Anya. I've been back several weeks now, but I didn't dare come and find you: Anya has to come first, you see.'

There was silence between us. I would never be first in Daler's life again, even though he was free, even though he was no longer married.

Eventually Daler took my hand. 'I had to lay my cards on the table, Frankie. I love you, love you more than any woman I've ever known. I still want you, but I don't know if you are with anyone yourself – don't know if you are willing to accept me as I am: slightly battered, slightly less wealthy than I was, and with another female in my life.'

'Daler, you once said that I was the other half of you.' I felt tears threaten once more. 'You broke my heart totally when you went, but two halves are no good apart. You are *my* other half.' I stared at him. 'You are enough, a thousand times enough.'

Daler took my hand, brought it up to his face and, with his own tears threatening, simply nodded before taking my face in both his beautiful strong hands.

Six months later…

'Frankie, this is so different from last time.' Aunty Pam stared at my reflection in her dressing table mirror and then turned to actually face me.

'Hang on, turn round.' I frowned. 'I almost had it then.'

Pam turned back with some impatience as I struggled once more to attach the fiddly little headdress into her blonde hair. 'There, that looks fabulous.' I hugged her. 'Of course it's different from last time. You didn't actually want to *be there* last time as I recall.' I hesitated and caught her eye once more in the mirror. 'You do want this, Aunty Pam, don't you?'

'More than anything in the world. I've waited over forty years for Rob, Frankie.'

'Well then, there you go.'

'It's just…'

'What?'

'You don't think it's all a bit *quick*?' Pam pursed her lips in the mirror, looking anxious.

'Quick?'

'It's only been seven months since Rob came back into my life.'

'Hey, at your age you need to get on with it, Pamela. You've no time to be messing about.' Daisy, struggling with the wire cage on a bottle of champagne, started to laugh.

'Thank you for those few kind words, Daisy.' Pamela stood up and smoothed away an imagined crease on the beautiful cream woollen dress she'd chosen for her special day.

'Not at all,' Daisy said cheerfully, pouring champagne into four waiting glasses on the bedside table. 'I need to address my future mother-in-law with nothing *but* kind words if I'm going to persuade her to babysit for all the offspring Jude and I will be producing.'

Pam and I turned as one to stare at Daisy. 'Have you something to tell us?' Pam asked, eyebrows raised.

'No,' Daisy tutted, handing Pam a glass before downing her own in one. 'Right,' she added, once she'd replaced her glass and repainted her lips in the mirror, 'that's put me in the mood for a good knees-up. And no, of course I've nothing to tell you in *that* department. I've another three years at university to get through before Jude and I can even *consider* babies.' She looked wistful for a moment but then smiled. 'If you can wait over forty years, Pam I'm sure I can wait four.'

'It's so good you were able to get on the veterinary course

at Liverpool instead of Edinburgh, Daisy, even if it does mean you dashing down the M62 every day.' Pam reached for her own glass and took a sip, closing her eyes slightly against the bubbles.

'It really isn't too bad a journey from Jude's house in Manchester,' Daisy said. 'I can get there in under an hour, or take the train. And when Jude isn't in London, we're always back at Holly Close Farm for the weekend so he can be here for his constituents. As well as for me.' She laughed at that.

'Yes, it's all worked out beautifully for you both, hasn't it?' Pam frowned, taking in the champagne on the side. 'Why *four* glasses?'

'Actually,' I said, moving to the bedroom window as a car pulled up outside, 'I think we need five.'

'You said to pour *four*, Frankie...' Daisy looked slightly put out. 'I can't see anyone,' she added, peering round the rose-coloured curtains.

'Hang on,' I said, heading for the bedroom door. 'Won't be a sec...'

'It's not Jude, is it?' I could hear Aunty Pam's worried voice. 'With Rob? Bad luck and all that to see the bride before the ceremony...?'

I ran down the stairs to let in the two people standing somewhat hesitantly on the doorstep. 'Carla, I'm so glad you were able to make it, after all. How is he?'

'Broken leg,' she said shortly. 'I've been telling that husband of mine for years he'd come a cropper one day on that motorbike of his. He thinks he's still sixteen rather than pushing fifty.' Carla shook her head. 'But he insisted I leave him at the hospital and catch the plane without him.'

'Your mum still thinks you're not coming, you know,

Carla. And she certainly won't be expecting *you*, Uncle Marco. It's really good you were able to take Steve's seat on the flight. Gosh, you look so much like Angelo.' I turned to face the uncle I'd never met until that moment.

'Heaven forbid.' Marco Piccione smiled before kissing me on both cheeks, Sicilian style. 'Francesca: the niece I've never met.' He held me at arm's length and gazed into my face. 'You've definitely got the Piccione genes, *bedda mia*. Come on, let's surprise the bride-to-be.'

Daisy and Jude made their way, hand in hand, and so very obviously in love, down the aisle until, halfway down, Jude kissed Daisy's cheek and led her to her seat next to my dad and Tammy and the rest of the Picciones before continuing on to where Rob waited at the front of the church. Lynne, Pam's elder sister, turned to whisper something to Janet, the youngest of the three Brown sisters who had never married, but who had made something of a name for herself in international relations, often appearing on TV and speaking on the radio. They both turned in anticipation as the organ sent up the first notes to herald the arrival of the bride.

'Are you ready?' I asked as Pam arrived at the church door on Angelo's arm and the church filled with the strains of Stevie Wonder. She nodded, seemingly unable to speak, and Carla and I stepped into our places behind her. As we walked slowly down the aisle, nodding and smiling at family and friends, my eyes searched for those only of one other.

'I love you,' Daler mouthed as we passed the end of the pew where he sat with Anya on his knee.

'Whoa,' Carla whispered out of the corner of her mouth. 'That is one hell of a gorgeous man you ended up marrying.'

'I know,' I said, tears threatening as I blew a kiss towards my husband and my beautiful stepdaughter. 'I really, *really* know.'

Acknowledgements

I have absolutely adored writing *A Family Affair* because I've been able to indulge myself in a bit of my own family history. My grandmother was born Madelena Scaramuzza, her father being Antonio who was an immigrant from Possili near Naples, and I've loved growing up not only knowing of my Italian ancestry but also, in later years, doing a huge amount of research to discover more of why and how Antonio had to leave Naples to settle and work in the industrial mills of the old West Riding of Yorkshire.

A big thank you to Joe and Luanda Longo, lovely friends who sat with me, on the eve of the first lockdown back in March, and gave me so much information about being brought up in a Sicilian family as well as advising me of the endearment bedda mia which Joe's mum still uses daily. Thanks also to all the other Italian and Sicilian-descended friends who, at social gatherings, despite my not speaking a word of Italian, have laughingly accepted me as one of their own. An honour indeed!

As a teacher, I've always loved teaching RE and been fascinated by the Sikh idea of sharing food to all those who need it at the daily Langar meal. As such, it was great to be able to include a chapter where Frankie makes her first visit to a Sikh Gurdwara and ends up helping out. Huge thanks to Abbie Chahal who not only took me through the protocol both of serving and receiving the Langar meal, but also advised me on the arrangements for, and again the protocol at, a typical fabulous Sikh wedding reception. I long to be invited to one!

I loosely based the character of Karam, the Syrian beekeeper, on one Dr Ryad Alsous who several years ago set up a beekeeping project in Marsden, a few miles from here. The project, managed by Sanctuary Kirklees with help from the Trust, among others, aims to help refugees and the long-term unemployed to find a sense of purpose through beekeeping. Although I have never met Dr Alsous, his work must be acknowledged here, as well as the hope that the current lockdown hasn't interfered too harshly with his bees and this brilliant project.

Thanks, as always, to my lovely agent, Anne Williams at KHLA Literary Agency, and to the fabulous Hannah Smith, my brilliant editor at Aria, Head of Zeus as well as the superbly efficient Helena Newton, copy editor and proofreader who, together with Vicky and the rest of the team, have helped to make *A Family Affair* the best it can possibly be.

And finally, to all you wonderful readers who read my books and write such lovely things about them, a huge, heartfelt thank you.

About the Author

J ULIE HOUSTON lives in Huddersfield, West Yorkshire where her novels are set, and her only claims to fame are that she teaches part-time at *Bridget Jones* author Helen Fielding's old junior school and her neighbour is *Chocolat* author, Joanne Harris.

After university, where she studied Education and English Literature, she taught for many years as a junior school teacher. As a newly qualified teacher, broke and paying off her first mortgage, she would spend every long summer holiday working on different Kibbutzim in Israel. After teaching for a few years she decided to go to New Zealand and taught in Auckland for a year before coming back to Britain.

Julie now only teaches when the phone rings asking her to go in for supply work, but still loves the buzz of teaching junior-aged children. She has been a magistrate for the past twenty years, and, when not distracted by eBay, Twitter and Ancestry, spends much of her time writing. Julie is married, with two adult children and a ridiculous cockapoo called Lincoln. She runs and swims because she's been told it's good for her, but would really prefer a glass of wine, a sun lounger and a jolly good book – preferably with Dev Patel in attendance.

You can contact Julie via the contact page, on Twitter or on Facebook.

Hello from Aria

We hope you enjoyed this book! If you did, let us know, we'd love to hear from you.

We are Aria, a dynamic fiction imprint from award-winning publishers Head of Zeus. At heart, we're committed to publishing fantastic commercial fiction – from romance to sagas to historical fiction.

Visit us online and discover a community of like-minded fiction fans.

You can find us at:

www.ariafiction.com

🐦 @Aria_fiction

📘 @Ariafiction